ACCLAIM FOR *SOUL'S GATE*

"Truly a story about freedom from things that we hold on to, this tale will captivate readers and encourage a more active, dynamic spiritual life."
—*RT Book Reviews*, TOP PICK

"[A] spiritual-warfare thriller that brilliantly takes four perfectly normal people . . . on a journey that begins with skepticism and ends up in places they could never have imagined or predicted."
—*CBA Retailers + Resources*

"Readers with high blood pressure or heart conditions be warned: this is a seriously heart-thumping and satisfying read that goes to the edge, jumps off, and 'builds wings on the way down.'"
—*Publishers Weekly*

"Powerful storytelling. Rubart writes with a depth of understanding about a realm most of us never investigate, let alone delve into. A deep and mystical journey that will leave you thinking long after you finish the book."
—Ted Dekker, *New York Times* best-selling author of *The Circle Series* and *Forbidden* (with Tosca Lee)

"Tight, boiled-down writing and an intriguing premise that will make you reconsider what you think you know about the spiritual realm."
—Steven James, national best-selling author of *Placebo* and *Opening Moves*

SPIRIT
BRIDGE

ALSO BY JAMES L. RUBART

The Well Spring Series
Soul's Gate
Memory's Door

Rooms
Book of Days
The Chair

SPIRIT BRIDGE

A WELL SPRING NOVEL, BOOK 3

JAMES L. RUBART

THOMAS NELSON
Since 1798

NASHVILLE   DALLAS   MEXICO CITY   RIO DE JANEIRO

Published in Nashville, Tennessee, by Thomas Nelson. Thomas Nelson is a registered trademark of HarperCollins Christian Publishing, Inc.

The author is represented by the literary agency of Alive Communications, Inc., 7680 Goddard Street, Suite 200, Colorado Springs, CO 80920. www.alivecommunications.com.

Thomas Nelson, Inc., titles may be purchased in bulk for educational, business, fund-raising, or sales promotional use. For information, please e-mail SpecialMarkets@ThomasNelson.com.

Publisher's Note: This novel is a work of fiction. Names, characters, places, and incidents are either products of the author's imagination or used fictitiously. All characters are fictional, and any similarity to people living or dead is purely coincidental.

THE NEW KING JAMES VERSION. © 1982 by Thomas Nelson, Inc. Used by permission. All rights reserved.
Scriptures from THE HOLY BIBLE, NEW INTERNATIONAL VERSION®, NIV® Copyright © 1973, 1978, 1984, 2011 by Biblica, Inc.® Used by permission. All rights reserved worldwide. NEW AMERICAN STANDARD BIBLE®, © The Lockman Foundation 1960, 1962, 1963, 1968, 1971, 1972, 1973, 1975, 1977, 1995. Used by permission. Holman Christian Standard Bible®, Copyright © 1999, 2000, 2002, 2003, 2009 by Holman Bible Publishers. Used by permission. Holy Bible, New Living Translation. © 1996, 2004, 2007 by Tyndale House Foundation. Used by permission of Tyndale House Publishers, Inc., Carol Stream, Illinois 60188. All rights reserved.

Library of Congress Cataloging-in-Publication Data

Rubart, James L.
 Spirit bridge / James L. Rubart.
  pages cm. -- (A Well Spring novel ; 3)
 ISBN 978-1-4016-8609-3 (pbk.)
 1. Paranormal fiction. 2. Magic--Fiction. I. Title.
 PS3618.U2326S65 2014
 813'.6--dc23

                    2013047137

Printed in the United States of America

14 15 16 17 18 19 RRD 6 5 4 3 2 1

FOR MOM, WHO TAUGHT ME TO
DREAM AND SHOWED ME WHO I AM.

"*Your real, new self . . . will not come as long as you are looking for it. It will come when you are looking for Him. Give up yourself, and you will find your real self. Lose your life and you will save it. Submit to death, death of your ambitions and favorite wishes every day and death of your whole body in the end: submit with every fiber of your being, and you will find eternal life.*"

C.S. Lewis, Mere Christianity

⊙NE

THE WELL-MANICURED FINGERS CURLED INTO A FIST AND slammed onto the stone table hard enough to rattle the glasses filled with a pale-blond liquid. It also served to focus the attention of the sixteen who sat around the table.

"You let him slip through your fingers like dust." Caustin uncurled his fingers and then clenched them together again as if kneading the hilt of the sword that hung on his hip. "If it were my choice, you would already be flayed and hanging above the pit."

Caustin pulled rapid breaths in and out as his gaze lasered in on Zennon.

"Calm." Caustin's master, who sat to the right, stretched out his fingers on the cool stone, but that was his only movement. "We will hear a response from the accused before you speak again."

"He is incorrect, my lord." Zennon gave a slight bow of his head, looked up again, shifted his gaze to Caustin, and refused to drop his stare even though the eyes of his superior held death in them. *Give in to intimidation? Never.*

"I'm wrong?" Caustin leaned forward and his body quivered as if he was about to lunge across the round table and attack. "You have failed to destroy the Warriors Riding. Am I incorrect about that fact?"

"Yes. You are badly mistaken." Zennon bowed and kept his

head down longer this time. *Play the game. Give the false respect this imbecile requires. Bide the time because it won't last forever.*

In truth, the time to strike was almost here. If one more member of the council would turn, the moment would be seized and Caustin's head would be separated from his body for eternity. Then Zennon would stand next to the Master in his place. "He is a fool, my lord."

Caustin flicked his finger to the right and then the left. Instantly Zennon was yanked from his chair and his arms were pulled tight across his back. The soldiers in Zennon's command who sat to his right and left didn't move to help. He didn't expect them to.

Caustin pulled back slightly but still rested most of his weight on his knuckles, pressed hard on the stone table. "Normally I would slice your throat open for your expression of insubordination, but since the Master is willing to hear an explanation for your failure, I will allow you to speak."

They released Zennon and he returned to his chair. For that insult alone he would kill Caustin. Zennon seethed with rage, but he couldn't allow it to be seen. Not in front of the other warlords. Control was power. The slaying would come later. In private. Where he could savor Caustin's cries for mercy and watch him die slowly and in excruciating pain.

The Master still didn't move. "Review his actions." As the three words leached from his dark maw, they seemed to soak up the light in the room.

Caustin pointed at Zennon with a thin finger. "He was given dominion over Reece Roth, Dana Raine, Brandon Scott, and Marcus Amber. His assignment was simple. Take them out. Destroy their mission. Instead, they have thrived and continue to grow in influence around the globe. Yes, he destroyed Reece's eyes, but he now sees again, with a sight far more powerful than what he had before. Yes, he took out Brandon Scott's singing voice, but it is a minor victory."

Caustin pulled back from the table and paced behind the Master and the four warlords to his right and left. "Under his watch, the angel Tristan Barrow formed an alliance with the Warriors. Zennon knew Barrow before the leaving—he knew Barrow's power and what he was capable of—and yet Zennon was not able to take the precautions to stop it."

Zennon ground his teeth and forced restraint on himself.

"He infiltrated the life of Marcus Amber as a high school student but was discovered before any real damage was done. Then he tried to lure Marcus into an alternate reality and again was unsuccessful."

Caustin's voice rose. "Then a legion of underlings was obliterated when he tried to destroy Reece, Dana, and Brandon. The Wolf was destroyed instead. The talk-show host Carson Tanner has turned back to the narrow path and now is broadcasting a new message across the American continent. Poison seeping into ears of millions of followers of the Nazarene."

Caustin once again pointed at Zennon. "Finally, he allowed the magician to escape, which could decimate a crushing amount of what we have accomplished over the past hundred years if he remembers who he truly is."

The Master turned his malevolent gaze to Zennon. He blinked but refused to drop his eyes. "That Simon the magician no longer resides in the alternate realities is true, Master," Zennon said.

Caustin strode back to the table and slammed his fist down again. "I call for destruction of the accused."

Zennon shifted back in his chair, pulled his gold coin out of his pocket, and spun it on the table. The light from the candles seemed to soak into its surface, making it thicker, and the sound of the coin rang off the table with greater volume. "You see only inches into the lake, Caustin, while I see with great depth. This war is far from over."

Spittle formed in the corners of Caustin's mouth as he leaned forward. "Far from over? Again and again you have—"

"Enough, Caustin." Their Master's voice rumbled through the small council room. "You have spoken." He turned to Zennon and nodded.

"Fellow warriors." Zennon met the gaze of every council member at the table, then pointed to Caustin. "You've heard the words of this fool. You've feasted on his accusations—I see it in your eyes. You salivate for my demise. But it will not come. I have not lost. These minor setbacks will only serve to pave the road of my ultimate victory."

For the first time, a shard of doubt passed over Caustin's face and hesitation wavered in his voice. "What do you feel you've—?"

"Feel! This is not about feelings, is it? It's about facts." Zennon raised his fist and slammed it onto the table in the exact manner Caustin had at the start of the council. Again the glasses rattled, but this time the one in front of Caustin tipped over and spilled its yellow liquid over the edge of the table.

"See?" Zennon smiled. "I can be as childish as you."

The demon didn't move as the liquid spilled onto his lap. "I will kill you."

Zennon's show of defiance riveted every eye in the room on him. Now to finish strong. "The Warriors Riding have attained certain victories, but when is an enemy most vulnerable? When they are tipping back the elixir of conquest and are drunk on the wine of their inflated belief in the loss their opponent has suffered. While they have been focusing on the chess piece right in front of them, I have been planning my moves far into the future."

Zennon turned and spoke to the Master. "I caused Simon the magician to leave the alternate reality. And now, because of what he did for Marcus Amber and the other Warriors, they will fully inculcate him into their inner circle. They will trust him. Embrace him." Zennon flipped the coin into the air, let it land on his palm, and slid it back into his front pocket. "I foresee him being invited to Well Spring where he will change everything in my favor."

"Explain." The Master's voice grew louder, and Zennon knew he must not waste words.

"As I just said, the magician did not escape. I let him go. And while the first phase of my plan with him and the Warriors was thwarted and certain casualties occurred, the second phase is now in place, which will bring about a triumphant conclusion to this war."

Zennon stood and leaned forward on the table, his palms spread wide. "If we are to achieve a resounding victory, it is not enough to destroy Reece and the other members of his band. Their message has spread too far. Killing him would only serve to make him a martyr and rally the millions around the world who look to him for sustenance. They follow Reece. He is their guide. They listen to him. Hundreds of thousands now drink from his stream."

"Continue," the Master said.

"We must change Reece Roth at his core. Blind him spiritually. Help him forget his identity as I did to the magician. Cause what resides inside Simon to spread to all of the Warriors and beyond them."

"Simon has been infiltrated." The faintest hint of a smile appeared in the Master's eyes.

"Yes. He carries the warfare inside. But he has no idea. No one does." Zennon bowed, smiled, and once more forced himself to hold his Master's gaze. "But Reece and his fellow Warriors are about to feel its effects when it is unleashed on them."

The Master ground his knuckles into the table. "And that will happen?"

"Very soon."

TWO

"WHEN WERE YOU GIVEN THIS?" REECE SAT IN HIS upstairs den on Thursday and gripped the armrest of the chair he sat in. So much for any kind of reprieve for the Warriors after the battle against the religious spirit seven days back. He took another drink of his late-morning tea. It was lukewarm but he didn't care.

"I received it yesterday afternoon," Doug Lundeen said.

"Interesting that it was sent to you just days before our first gathering after getting back from Well Spring."

"I agree. It is the Spirit's leading."

"If the words are true."

Doug didn't respond.

Reece shifted in his leather chair and breathed the mid-July air coming in through the open window that overlooked his lush Pacific Northwest backyard. "What if they're not ready to hear this?"

"I don't believe we have a choice."

"They've just been through an emotional Ironman triathlon." Reece rubbed the scar tissue where his eyes used to be with his thumb and forefinger.

"You've been through an emotional one as well, and my deep wish is that there was time to refresh and rest, but apparently there isn't."

"Read it again." Reece needed to hear it once more. Let the words soak in. Try to figure out what exactly each part of this new prophecy meant and how it would impact the Warriors Riding.

The rustle of paper filled Reece's ears and Doug cleared his throat.

WHEN it is time, you will join them,
    THE FOUR: THE TEMPLE, THE LEADER, THE TEACHER,
AND THE SONG,
    THEY WILL NEED YOUR STRENGTH FOR THEIR LAST
BATTLE TOGETHER,
    FOR THEIR GREAT ENEMY IS MOUNTING A FINAL
STRIKE AGAINST THEM AND WILL HOLD NOTHING BACK,
    AND YOU WILL STEP BOLDLY BEFORE THE TEMPLE
AND HE WILL RECEIVE YOU,
    AND YOU MUST TAKE THE LEADER INTO THE GATE-
WAY OF DEATH,
    AND IN THE GATEWAY ONE WILL REMAIN, WHICH
WILL BRING SORROW BUT SET IN MOTION THAT WHICH
MUST BE,
    AND YOU WILL EMBRACE THE TEACHER FOR HE IS
THE FRIEND OF THE RESTORER,
    AND ONE YOU WILL TRAIN WHEN THEY ASK IT OF
YOU—AND ONLY THAT ONE WILL YOU TRAIN,
    YOU ARE A WARRIOR OF WARRIORS, LIVE IN THE
TRUTH OF WHO YOU ARE,
    AND RIDE WITH THE WIND.

It made little more sense than the first two times Doug had read this new prophecy. Someone else join the Warriors? Why? When? For what purpose? "Who is the one the prophecy was given to?"

Doug sighed. "I already told you, they requested I not say."

"This is me, old friend."

A second later Doug patted Reece on the back. "Yes, yes, and you know I would tell you if I could. But this person was told by the one who gave the prophecy not to reveal any identities. It wasn't an option."

"You trust this person, the one the prophecy was spoken over?"

"As much as I trust you, Reece."

A small list of names raced through Reece's mind. Doug's closest allies. The ones he'd told Reece about and the ones Reece had met. But none of those men made sense to his mind or his heart. But since when did God's thinking mesh completely with man's?

"And you believe the prophecy is true," Reece said.

"Reportedly this person has sought wisdom and revelation from the Spirit as to the truth of these words for the past year, and they told me they are true. And I believe them."

Reece blew out a slow breath. "It doesn't take a genius to figure out the prophecy is talking about Zennon attacking us."

"Of course."

"The Leader in the gateway." Reece gripped the arm of his chair harder. "I will not allow Dana to die."

"No. We will not."

"And who is this 'restorer'? Brandon?"

"That is not clear, is it?" Doug sighed. "What do you see as our next steps?"

"We send out an e-mail to the Warriors about tomorrow night. Tell them we have an announcement, to be praying about it, and leave it at that."

"Agreed."

Reece let his head ease down till it rested on the back of the chair. They weren't ready to hear about another battle, let alone engage in one where Zennon came after them with everything left in his arsenal. What they were ready for—what they'd most certainly earned—was rest. Refreshment from each other's company. But it seemed a dead-end sign had been placed at the end of that road, and the one the Spirit was taking them down instead was peppered with land mines.

THREE

"ANY GUESS AS TO WHAT THE ANNOUNCEMENT IS REECE and Doug have in store for us?" Dana brushed back her light-brown hair and looked at Marcus as she took a sip of her iced tea. They sat in overstuffed chairs in the great room of Reece's log cabin-style home on the outskirts of Seattle. She loved his home almost as much as she loved Reece's private ranch in Colorado: Well Spring.

Marcus sat straighter and pushed up his glasses. "My fervent hope is he announces that our battles together for the kingdom have reached their conclusion. That it's time to retire Warriors Riding, he has commenced construction on a private luxury compound on the north side of Fiji with all the money he acquired selling his photography business, and he's sending Kat and Abbie and Jayla and me there to live in paradise for the rest of our lives."

Dana crossed her legs and smiled at the professor's humor. "I think there's a greater chance that a wormhole will open up in Reece's kitchen over there and we'll all take a trip to the far side of the universe."

"All things are possible with a Creator such as ours, and there is a substantial amount of evidence that wormholes could be around every corner." Doug ambled into the living room from the kitchen. He carried a glass of ice water in one hand and a notepad in the other.

"You have to know what he's going to tell us, Doug," Dana said.

"Yes, I do." Doug settled into the leather couch across from Marcus and her.

Marcus pointed at Doug's notepad. "Would you like to give us a preview before Reece comes down and Brandon arrives?"

"Yes, I would." Doug smiled. "But I'm not going to. You all need to hear this at the same time."

"Okay." Dana clapped her hands together. "Then at least answer a question I've been dying to know the answer to ever since Reece first trained us."

Doug cocked his head.

"Reece trained the Warriors. You trained Reece. Who trained you?"

"Did you know Reece has asked me the same question a number of times?" Doug rubbed his knuckles. "I'm afraid I can't tell you, just as I have never told Reece. Not yet anyway. But things have transpired recently that make me think I will soon be able to. That a long missing piece of the puzzle will finally be restored to its rightful place. And when it is, I will be released to tell the story of the man who discipled me in ways he cannot imagine."

Dana studied Marcus's face. He looked tired, older than last time she'd seen him, and why wouldn't he? He was probably thinking the same thing about her. Their recent battle against the religious spirit had been triumphant, but also exhausting. Probably one reason Reece hadn't gathered the five of them together till now. She appreciated the break. It gave her the chance to get caught up on her work down at the radio station as well as take a few evenings around Puget Sound to exercise her love of photography.

At the same time, she'd missed being with the other Warriors the past eight days. And she wanted to see Brandon. She was worried about him. He'd gone hermit on them since they got back from Well Spring. No contributions to the group e-mail they were all part of. No every-other-day witty text messages to the group either.

Now they were together again as planned, but an ominous tone had been cast over the gathering because of Reece's cryptic e-mail: *When we meet, Doug and I must speak to you about what is coming next for us. It won't be easy to hear, but the Lord is our shield, always.*

"In some ways it seems like years since we were at Well Spring together. In others it feels like we were there yesterday," Dana said.

"Time tends to accelerate as we grow older." Marcus drew a small circle in the air with his silver mechanical pencil.

"Do you mean time accelerates literally or figuratively?" Doug patted his slightly oversized stomach and gazed at Marcus.

"My reference was to the physiological sensation of time increasing its velocity as we accumulate more years."

"I love you, Marcus." Dana laughed. "Since Brandon isn't here to translate, allow me the honor. Do you mean we feel like time goes faster as we age?"

Marcus brushed back his thinning brown hair and smiled. "Certainly that would be one alternative way to my thought."

"I can relate, Dana." Doug sipped his ice water. "Since I'm pushing seventy-three now, days seem to fly by like months instead. By the time I reach 173 years of age, the days will seem like seconds."

"You're going to live that long?" Dana smiled at his sense of humor.

"Why not? People used to live far longer. Or maybe I won't die and will simply be carried to heaven as Enoch was."

"There is always the possibility you are Enoch." Marcus pushed up his glasses again.

"Yes, I suppose that is possible. But in this case not true." Doug leaned to the side and tapped Marcus on his kneecap. "Sometime we should chat about the literal acceleration of time. And its literal deceleration." Doug winked. "It's almost time for that lesson, I believe. So many more lessons to teach all of you before my time on earth is finished. Even many lessons for Reece."

Marcus stood and meandered over to the river-rock fireplace that dominated Reece's great room. He placed his hands behind his back and tapped his foot on the hardwood floor. "I'm quite familiar with the physics behind theoretical time travel, time compression, and acceleration."

"Oh, I know you are, Professor. But as you might have surmised, I'm not talking about theory."

Marcus smiled, stopped tapping his foot, and leaned forward. "Your next statement will likely be that we have the ability to do time manipulation ourselves."

"No, not us. But through the one who holds the universe in his palm, the one who is far beyond the reaches of time because he created it, to that I speak a resounding yes."

A voice sounded from above them. "There are things I don't know, old friend? Lessons I still need to learn?"

Reece stood at the top of the stairs looking down on them, as much as it was possible for a man to look whose eyes had been destroyed—not seeing as most did, but still seeing. The prophecy fulfilled. *"And for one, their vision will grow clear."* A vision that allowed Reece to see into the spiritual realm, an ability to see outlines and shapes in the physical world.

"I trust you've all made yourselves comfortable?" Reece shifted on his six-foot-five-inch frame.

"Will Brandon be engaged with us this evening?" Marcus glanced at his watch.

Reece clomped down the stairs. "He said he would be."

Dana looked up. "Really? You spoke to him?"

"Only via e-mail." Reece eased toward Dana. "Come here, friend."

She rose and a smile broke out as Reece opened his arms. She loped over to him and buried herself in his massive arms. "Hi, Reece."

"It's good to see you, dear one. I know I said this back at Well Spring, but I have to say it again. You stood strong against Zennon and the spirit of religion when we were inside the spiritual realm. You were a light for Brandon and me as darkness closed in. You are truly the Leader. No father could be more proud of his daughter than I am of you."

Dana closed her eyes and pressed her head against Reece's chest. "Does that mean I can adopt you as my dad?"

"What? I thought the paperwork already went through." Reece released her and smiled. She squeezed his hands and sat back in her chair.

"When will my hug be bestowed?" Marcus asked.

"The moment I start thinking about you like a daughter." Reece grinned and then cleared his throat. "Now, has anyone else heard from the Song?"

"I have not," Marcus said with a grim look. "I left him three messages over the past eight days that have not been answered. And I stopped by his house but he wasn't home."

"I left him five." Dana sighed. "No response."

"I fear our friend is not doing well." Doug shook his head. "Reece and I tried to drop in on him too, and either he wasn't there or wasn't answering the door."

"Why do you say he's not doing well?" Dana asked.

"I've sensed it. I've heard the Spirit tell me that." Doug glanced at Marcus and her. "Haven't you?"

She nodded. He hadn't responded to her messages, but she attributed it to the inevitable struggle Brandon must be feeling after losing his voice during the battle with the demons and needing to work through it alone. But alone was rarely good.

Reece strolled into the kitchen, then returned a few minutes later with a tray of cheeses and crackers. For the next ten minutes the four of them caught up on how Marcus's physics classes were going at the University of Washington, Dana's latest highs and lows at the radio station, Reece's increased ability to see into the spiritual realm, and how Doug had put his home in Colorado Springs on the market.

"You're moving out here full-time?"

"For what's coming, I will need to be more accessible to all of you, I believe. I'm looking at houses in Woodinville, Bothell, and north Redmond. I'll be back and forth between here and the Springs every four or five days till I find a house, but yes, the Pacific Northwest will soon be my new home."

"Speaking of what's headed our direction, do we want to call Brandon—see if he's on his way?" Dana said.

Reece lifted the glass lid of his watch and touched the face. "Twenty minutes late. Usually it's only ten. Unlike you, Dana, who has probably never been late for anything in your life." Reece closed the lid of his watch and tapped it. "I'm going to assume he's not coming. So let's get started."

As his words faded, a light rap on the front door filled the great room. It had to be Brandon, even though Reece had told all of them many times that knocking was never required. That whenever they came over they should come right in. A second later the door opened and Brandon stepped through, then wiped his feet on the tan mat just inside the foyer. His face was dark. He wore jeans more torn than usual, and the T-shirt under his Windbreaker looked like its wrinkles had wrinkles.

He took off his coat and tossed it onto the coatrack next to the stairs. He ran his hands through his long dirty-blond hair and sighed.

If Marcus looked like he'd aged a year in the past month, Brandon seemed like he'd aged ten. His thick hair was matted and circles had grown under his eyes. Looked like he hadn't showered in at least three days. Even if he had, no razor had touched his face in at least six—the last time he shaved might have been at Well Spring. Dana didn't need spiritual discernment to know Brandon was tanking.

"Did I miss the party?" Brandon opened his hands and bobbed his head from side to side.

"No." Reece's face was hard. "We were just about to get out the hats."

"Fab. Let's get down tonight. Do a little dance and all that. My thirty-seventh birthday is gonna be here before you know it, so maybe we can wrap that into tonight's celebration as well."

"Are you sure you want to be here?" Reece's voice was low and devoid of emotion.

"Are you asking me to leave?" Brandon rasped out. His voice had improved, but not a great deal. It still sounded like he'd gargled gravel to start the day. "Why would I not want to be here?"

"You don't look so well."

"Really." Brandon narrowed his eyes. "And tell me, how would you know that, blind man?"

All sound was sucked out of the room. But if Brandon had hoped Reece would take the bait, he was disappointed.

"Because in the way I still can see, there is an evident sadness around you. And resignation. Among other things, such as your giving footholds to spirits that are not of the Light."

"Then you need glasses, Reece-O. I'm doing great. Faannnntastic. Couldn't be better. In fact, just knowing I'm a member of the illustrious Warriors Riding makes it a wonderful day. I mean, wow, if it weren't for you, I wouldn't be where I'm at right now."

Again Reece didn't respond to Brandon's jab.

"Why don't you take a seat, friend, and we'll get started."

Brandon stared at Reece, and Dana guessed what Reece saw in the spiritual realm was a spirit of bitterness swirling all around the singer. When she glanced at Marcus, he offered a raised eyebrow but nothing more. Doug held his palms up as if to say, "Peace."

Reece waited till Brandon settled into the overstuffed chair to the right of the fireplace. Then he stood, his legs slightly wider than shoulder width, and prayed for their time together. When he finished he spoke just above a whisper.

"Thank you all for coming on such short notice. My hope is that the past eight days have been a time of refreshment for you." He turned toward Brandon for a moment. "If they haven't been, then I pray tonight will be. We need each other, and I'm afraid in the coming days and weeks, we will need each other more than we ever have. We will need to rise up like we've never done before."

Brandon tapped his feet and clenched and unclenched his hands. He sucked in and puffed out shallow breaths. His gaze darted around the room as if looking for some type of rescue, but none was in sight. If Dana didn't know him as well as she did, she'd say he was having a panic attack.

"Yesterday Doug was sent a prophecy he read to me, and we have been praying over it ever since then. At this point, we both believe it is real. We've been listening to the Spirit, trying to understand precisely what is coming our direction. We must prepare—"

"I've had enough come at me for three lifetimes." Brandon snorted. "I'm done with having things come at me. It's time for a long sabbatical. I need some easy."

"I understand that feeling. I suspect we are all feeling that way to some degree. But in this war there is no neutral zone. No quarter. No time-outs, and this is not a game where we can leave the field. And this prophecy speaks of—"

"Oh my." Brandon wagged his head back and forth. "That's so poetic, Reece. I think I'll put it in a song and sing it for you out at the fire pit on a sunny Seattle evening. It's simply beautiful." Brandon mock slapped his forehead. "Oh, wait. Silly me. I won't be able to do that ever again."

Dana glared at Brandon. It had been a long time since she'd seen him like this. Unless someone at least appeared to take his side, the meeting would head over a cliff in seconds.

She fixed her gaze on him as she spoke. "I understand where Brandon is coming from. Even soldiers in war get to rest. They get furlough. They get to sleep and regroup. We've been through enough for this century and the next. We need a chance to get our strength back."

"I agree." Reece paced in front of the wicker chair in back of him. "We do need that. As I already said, it's what I hoped this past eight days would be for us. But I can see it has only served to exacerbate our fretfulness and give the enemy a chance to offer us lies we might be tempted to agree with that would undermine the ministry."

Reece was astute enough not to single out Brandon as the one displaying the greatest example of that stress.

"Can we get to the specifics of what precisely this prophecy says?" Marcus opened his journal and smoothed the page. "Because I believe the Spirit has told me some things about the coming days as well."

Reece and Doug turned to each other, and Dana had little doubt Reece was using his spiritual eyes to see some kind of answer from Doug. The big man turned after a few seconds and rubbed his hands together before speaking. "That we will face Zennon once more. That we will have to sacrifice—"

"That's it!" Brandon sprang to his feet and shot his fist into the air. "You're a winner because you've just said the secret magic word, Reece Roth! *Sacrifice!*" He spun toward Marcus. "Nicely done. Professor, I'm guessing you've heard the same thing as Reece and Snugly Dougly so you're also going to take home fabulous prizes that will make your life complete. Well, *sacrifice* is the word that makes Brandon Scott say buh-bye, so glad I could be on the program, thanks for all the wonderful parting gifts, looking forward to the reunion show in about a trillion years."

Brandon strode to Reece's front door and yanked it open. "I'll send you a postcard and a jar of sand from the beach I'm headed to, along with my Warriors Riding membership card. In other words, I'm not coming on your trip to Well Spring in a couple of weeks, so you can give my space to someone else. I'm sure hundreds are pounding on the door in order to take my place and get their lives shoved into a shredder. And, Reece? Thanks for inviting me to this group in the first place and destroying me." He gave a salute and stepped through the door. "Have a great life, all of you. I'll be in touch in twenty years."

The front door slammed hard enough to shake the walls at the front of Reece's house, and after the sound faded, silence fell on the room like they were in a morgue.

After a minute, Doug turned to Reece. "Did you see that coming?"

"No. You?"

"It isn't a complete shock."

The big man turned to Marcus and Dana. "Were either of you surprised?"

Marcus shook his head. "As I indicated earlier, he has been unresponsive to my e-mails and phone calls, which caused a certain amount of trepidation inside me, but no, I didn't expect this."

"Dana? Any idea what's going on with him?"

"Isn't it obvious? Didn't you listen to what he said?" She stared at them and stopped herself just short of letting out an exasperated sigh. Men. Sometimes the thick matter between their temples resembled brains only in the most literal sense. "You don't understand the artist mentality, do you?"

She stared at Doug and Reece, and then focused her gaze on Marcus. "At least *you* have to know poets and authors and musicians and painters and the like have a seventy percent greater chance of struggling with depression, right?"

She drew a breath through her teeth. "The highs are sky high and the lows are the deepest valleys for many, many artists. For them to be able to tap into the emotional depth you see in their novels, songs, and paintings, they have to be able to experience great sorrow along with great triumphs."

If her words had any impact on them, it wasn't evident from the blank looks on each of their faces. "Is this making any sense?"

"Go on," Reece said, and the others nodded.

"Here is Brandon Scott, one of the most successful Christian artists ever, who has sold millions and millions of albums and played in front of hundreds of thousands of people all over the world. Then *boom*, his record label basically drops him and his manager and ex–best friend effectively slides into his spot in the world of music. But there's more. He's been told he's the Song, one of four members of a thirty-year-old prophecy, but then he sacrifices himself for me and his throat is almost destroyed, and odds are he'll never sing again.

"It would be wonderful if we were all able to get our entire worth and identity from being a child of the King, but it doesn't always work that way.

"Yes, Brandon was healed of a great deal of his feelings of worthlessness when he was given the name Maximus by the Spirit. But do you see the problem with that? He's been forced to throw down his sword entirely. What is he doing of worth in his mind right now? Last month during the battle, his singing was instrumental—no pun intended—in our victories over Zennon."

She turned to Marcus. "You're the one who broke the hold of the spirit of religion in the physical realm, which broke the hold in the spiritual. I'm the one who held out against the deception and led us away from the lie and into the truth that the Jesus-rider was really Zennon.

"You acted as the Teacher, Marcus, and will continue to. I acted as the Leader, and I pray I can serve well in that role. Reece, you can't help but be the Temple. The health and well-being of the Warriors rests greatly on you as we go on. But how will Brandon be the Song going forward?"

"Maybe he can sing in the spiritual realm in a way he can't in the physical," Marcus said.

"Maybe? What if he goes in and tries and it doesn't happen? What then? If he can't, it would be extremely easy for him to take on the mantle and name of Worthless once again."

Her words seemed to sober the men, and they stayed silent for a long time. When that silence was broken, it was Reece who did it.

"He must be the Song going forward. Do you remember me saying before the battle with Zennon and the religious spirit and their army of demons that the Spirit told me without Marcus we would be lost?" Reece paused. "That's why it was crucial we find him?"

"Yes," Dana said.

"The Spirit told me the same thing about the coming war, but this time the critical member of the team is Brandon. He must be the Song in ways none of us have imagined." Reece tapped a foot against his dark hardwood floor.

"That might be somewhat difficult with him in his current frame of mind," Marcus said.

"Clearly." Doug nodded.

"The difference is, I had no doubt Marcus would respond to the call once we rescued him from the cliff where Zennon tried to bury him in the alternate realities. With Brandon, I'm not so sure what he'll do. He obviously doesn't want to be rescued, let alone respond."

"So what do we do?" Dana said.

"He needs a one-on-one conversation." Reece stopped tapping his foot and tilted his head toward her. "With the one who has had Brandon inside their soul. The one who trusted Brandon more fully than any of us is the one he will most likely let inside, whatever is going on. The one he is still in love with."

Dana sighed and slumped back on the couch. Of course it needed to be her. Who else? "I'll call him in the morning. But don't say he's in love with me. And don't say, 'But it's true.'"

She wasn't ready to deal with that. Yes, Well Spring had stirred her heart again toward him. Yes, major sections of the wall between them had come down, but there were still so many bricks and rubble at the base of the wall that might never be cleared away. And most days she had little desire to crawl over them. But other days she did. Why did her emotions have to be so schizophrenic? Because something about Brandon still felt . . . off. And until it didn't, she would guard her heart like it was the gold inside Fort Knox. But it didn't mean she couldn't try to offer him hope.

"What do you want me to do?" Dana leaned forward and clapped her hands on her knees. "Are you thinking soul travel?"

Reece shook his head. "Not anything that extreme yet. I was thinking a cup of coffee—just the two of you—might be a good start."

She jerked her head up. "Did you know I promised him that?"

Reece nodded. "We all know. Brandon was pretty pumped about it back at Well Spring. You know guys never can stop talking to each other about stuff like this." He smiled.

"That's funny."

"That he would even speak of it to us should tell you how much he's wanted to do it. And it might be the thing to snap him out of whatever grizzly bear trap he's caught himself in."

"Great." Dana sighed. "The problem with that is, sometimes the hunter shows up when you're springing someone from the trap."

FOUR

SIMON PACED ACROSS HIS POSTAGE STAMP–SIZED APARTMENT late Friday night, blinking and clenching and unclenching his fists like he was squeezing two stress balls.

He had to find a way to stop the low humming sound that had filled most of his waking moments for the past nine weeks. Had to. Couldn't, shouldn't, wouldn't be able to take it much longer. But how would he make that happen? When he'd come back or broke out or escaped or whatever you want to call it from the . . . uh . . . other side, or alternate world, or parallel life, or other universe, or whatever it was Zennon trapped him in, his mind had been quiet. But ever since he'd talked to Marcus about his choices, the humming had pounded away at Simon with only infrequent breaks.

Not knowing where the sound came from was a serious detriment to his finding what was producing the humming and stopping it. But he did know where the sound came from. Sort of. The sound didn't come from a clock or watch or time bomb or a metronome telling him how to keep plunking the keys on a piano with the right timing. No, it came from inside his head or his bed, and it was red, full of dread—

Stop it!

He pinched his thick salt-and-pepper goatee and clacked his teeth together as if he could distract himself with the noise and tactile sensation. Hardly. *Something else, find something else.*

Simon snatched a deck of Bicycle playing cards off his kitchen counter and pulled out fifty-two of his best friends. All of his other friends were gone now. Long ago. Except for the professor. They were friends, weren't they?

But magic was his only true friend. The one who had never let him down. His escape from everything from the time he was seven. It always took him away from the pain when it started to rain and there was no ground to gain.

He brushed back his graying dark hair, stumbled into his living room, and slumped onto his dark-blue couch. Simon lifted a card off the top of the deck, placed a corner of the pasteboard in between the tips of his first and second finger, and flicked his wrist just like *Genii* magazine had taught him all those decades back.

The card sliced through the air for thirty feet, then slowed and fluttered a few feet higher, and settled back down into a cardboard box he'd set up in front of the fireplace. The penalty for missing was an incinerated card. The penalty for leaving the alternate reality Zennon had locked him in for so many, many years was . . . Simon didn't know.

He didn't believe the demon would let him go this easily, even with his mind as muddled and muddy and oh so ruddy. He couldn't be pleased with what Simon had told the professor. No, Zennon wouldn't like that at all. Simon tried to focus on the cards, but he couldn't with the swirling thoughts of gloom pushing him toward his doom and filling every room.

"Stop it, please!" He pressed his hands to the sides of his head as if that could keep him from rhyming.

He should go find Marcus Amber and see how that whole thing turned out. Get the details. Had he made it? Did Marcus stop himself from slipping down the rabbit hole inside the rabbit hole inside the rabbit hole like a mole without a soul? Yes, yes, of course the professor had made it. Simon had snuck into Marcus's class on the U-Dub campus and watched him teach one of his summer classes just a few days ago.

He tossed another card. Another landed in the box. He threw one more, one more, one more, don't make me snore. Five for five. The touch was still there. Back in the day, he'd been one of the best card throwers in the country. Almost as good as Ricky Jay was in these times, who could embed an ordinary playing card into the side of a watermelon and ended up starring in a James Bond movie. Non sequitur. He smacked the side of his head but the humming continued.

Simon squeezed his temples again till they hurt. He shouldn't be thinking like this; this rambling, jabbering kaleidoscope of thoughts that always made his brain feel like mush. Shouldn't? Sure, right, easy to say. *Think straight. Come on now, brown cow, who is always calm with never a row. Rau? Row?*

Simon moaned. Some days he controlled the humming. Or didn't let it get to him. But there were bad days like today when the noise seeped through his brain and seemed to scatter like head lice when he tried to stop the sound. He fumbled for his music player, snatched it up, and stuffed his earbuds into his ears. *Come on, Bing, bring it, bing it, let's all sing it.* Mr. Crosby would drown out the humming and drumming that was always thrumming in his mind.

"Sunday, Monday, or Always" filled his senses and Simon sighed. It would be okay, they would, they should, and it would be so good, like alabaster wood. Simon smiled. Alabaster wood. That would be a sight.

He thought again of Professor Amber and his big friend Royce, or was it Rice? What did the professor call him? Reece? Yes. Simon was sure of it. Reece would be listening to sixties and seventies rock and roll. And he should. It was the music he'd grown up on. Which was why Simon was listening to Bing. That was his era. But no one knew that. They thought his age to be in his midfifties. Yes, his body was that age. Or at least it was in the condition of most fifty-year-olds. But not his mind. Not his spirit. Not his soul. No, the big three had lived much longer than his body. They'd lived so long. So many years. Too many years.

He scratched himself but the itch was inside as if some sickness had taken root inside him and was trying to get out. He should call the professor. Marcus Amber, a good man. And Simon had helped that good man with a critical choice. A choice of a lifetime. And the professor must have chosen well. Simon sighed again and pulled out his silver coin. If only, if only, if only he had chosen as well as Marcus.

But Simon's chance was gone. The chance to do the right thing for the kingdom that lasts forever, the chance to do something in this life that would echo into eternity and never fade from notice. But he'd made choices that kept him on the other side for too long. Break on through to the other side.

Simon *had* broken through to hundreds of other sides with help from his pal Zennon, and Simon wished he could warn people that there was nothing worth seeing. Because Zennon was not a pal. Not a friend, no, he was one who tried to bend and then to end. End what? His life, so full of strife, and now the memories cut like knives.

But now, he'd wound up back in this reality, the real reality, and the One had set him free, and he would never go back. Never. But he wasn't free. Wouldn't ever be free. Not here in this life.

Simon set down the rest of the cards and padded over to the three-pegged coat stand next to his door. He snatched a worn leather coat, pulled open his front door, and walked out. Lock the door? Nah. There wasn't a thing inside his apartment worth stealing.

Simon strode east toward campus. He needed to see Marcus. Tell him why he needed to be careful. What to look out for. And why Simon believed Zennon would be coming for the professor and the rest of his friends in a way far worse than anything Marcus could imagine.

FIVE

On Saturday morning, Brandon shifted on his couch and peered at the door that led into his home studio. It was open a crack. Hadn't he closed it? If he hadn't, he should have. Should have welded it shut. Should have poured gasoline all over the room, lit a match, and torched the place. But he loved music. How could he kill the desire inside?

He turned back to his big-screen TV and stared at some old movie from the eighties. But he couldn't focus on the film. All he saw was himself standing onstage with thousands of people with their arms raised singing along with him and the band, and then everyone vanishing, leaving him alone onstage with nothing surrounding him but silence.

Brandon grabbed the bag of sunflower seeds next to him, ripped it open, and popped half a handful into his mouth. They'd never let him down. Wow. How pathetic when the most reliable friend in his life was a bag of seeds.

He snatched the remote off the couch, turned off the TV, and tossed the remote onto the floor. Maybe Zennon was right when he'd said Brandon was all about Brandon. The demon's words sliced across his mind: *Your singing career has been about you. Always about you trying to fill the hole left vacant from your childhood.*

Brandon glanced at the oversized book on his coffee table:

Treehouses of the World. How many years had he dreamed of building a tree house? Since he was twelve, at least. But back then his stepmom had squashed the idea moments after it slipped from his mouth. Now he had the land and time to burn.

He flipped through the book and stared at tree houses with two stories and decks and lights and winding staircases. Yeah, right. As if he had any idea how to start a project like that. And at the moment he wasn't in the mood and doubted if he'd be in the mood to do much of anything ever again.

He turned the TV back on and surfed through the channels till he found a different movie full of explosions and gunfights. But it didn't make the hole in his mind or heart or spirit or soul grow any smaller. After five minutes he gave up trying to bury the flickering desire deep inside, stood, and strode toward the door of his studio.

Brandon stepped into the room that held his guitars and a small recording setup. His Taylor guitar sat in the corner exactly as he'd left it three weeks ago. Part of him longed to pick it up and feel the weight of it on his right leg, feel the steel strings under his fingers, feel the body of the guitar against him. Hear the sound of his favorite chords filling his soul.

But to what end? All that would accomplish would be to remind him of what had been ripped from his hands when he saved Dana. What had been stolen. The thief came to kill, steal, destroy. Goal accomplished. But what about the rest of the verse? Jesus came to give life abundant, right? Really? Where? When would he get that life? He shuffled to his right and slumped against the wall. He had nothing left.

Now that everything was stripped away, the hole was gaping—which proved Zennon's words to be true. Easy to say you'd give it all up before you had to. A lot easier to lay down your life for a friend when you didn't realize what the aftermath would be.

Had he thrown himself between Dana and the demon who was about to kill her because he'd get some reward for doing so? No. He did it because he loved her. But he wouldn't be honest if he didn't admit he expected some kind of positive result to come out of it. Like Dana and him finally back together again. Wasn't that the way it was supposed to work?

✚ ✚ ✚

Dana woke on Saturday morning knowing what she needed to do, with a bigger part of her wanting to do it than the part that dreaded the idea. It surprised her. She'd expected to wake up seriously queasy about the task of calling Brandon, but now that she'd had three cups of strong black coffee and spent an hour soaking in a waterfall of her favorite movie sound track, the idea felt okay.

She eased into her den and picked up her cell phone, ambled through her living room, through her front door, and sat on the wicker chair on her front porch. A pair of midmorning joggers ran past and waved. A man and woman. Smiles on their faces—probably nothing to worry about except keeping their heart rate at 155 beats per minute. Would that ever be her? Thirty-seven years on earth. She couldn't be that old, could she? Were kids even possible at this point? She pushed the thought to the side and dialed Brandon's number.

"I might be sorry I missed you. I don't know. Only one way to find out. Leave whatever you want to say and see if I call you back. Brandon out."

She shook her head. He'd changed the message. She'd always seen hints of his cynical side. But this, combined with his meltdown last night, meant something was seriously wrong in Brandon land. Dana didn't leave a message.

✚ ✚ ✚

Brandon's cell phone buzzed. He pulled it from his pocket and glanced at the screen. Dana. Forget it. He wasn't taking that call. Probably calling to talk to him about last night and talk him into . . . whatever. It didn't matter because he wouldn't even listen to her

28

voice mail if she bothered to leave a message. He didn't need saving. Reece must have put her up to it.

He looked around his studio before he backed out and shut the door hard behind him. Music and he were over. He was the Song. Was. Past tense.

✠ ✠ ✠

Should she try Brandon's landline? Why not? Dana stared at her cell phone and smiled to herself. It had been almost four years since she'd called Brandon at home. The last time she'd done it they'd been engaged. Before he'd broken her heart into a trillion pieces.

But things had changed when he'd gone into her soul and brought healing. Things changed again last month when he risked his life and destroyed his voice in order to save her. She'd forgiven him and even opened her heart to the idea of friendship. And in the quiet moments at night before sleep took her, the faint, barely visible light of love. That was only the flicker of a thought, but for the first time since they'd returned from Well Spring, she admitted there was a faint light burning on that hillside a million light-years away.

She started to dial and two thoughts struck her. First, she didn't remember his home phone number, and second, somehow her fingers did remember. Muscle memory? Her fingers crisscrossed across her phone's keypad, then she held the phone up to her ear. Why was her heart beating a little faster? Ridiculous. It never felt weird dialing his cell phone. Of course that hadn't been exactly commonplace for the past four years either.

As Brandon's home phone rang for the fifth time, Dana prepared herself to leave a message. She didn't want to. She wanted to talk to him. Get a clue why he'd stormed out of the Warriors Riding meeting. Get a clue as to whether she should press the issue or just let it go. It wasn't like him. He was having more than an off couple of days.

"Hey."

His voice startled her.

"Hi, um, wow . . . I didn't think you were going to answer."

"Sorry to disappoint you. I can hang up."

"No, I'm glad you picked up. I was trying to figure out what kind of message I was going to leave." The tone of his voice sounded better than it had last night. Maybe a good sign.

"What kind? There are different kinds? Like different flavors of ice cream? Just leave a stupid message."

She'd wanted to get a sense of where he was—if last night was an anomaly or his new standard behavior—and now she had it. The message was back off. But that didn't work for her. It was time to point out the elephant in the center of the room and make Brandon admit it was bright pink.

"What's going on with you? Why are you acting like a moron?"

"You're saying I shouldn't have left last night? Or that I shouldn't have done my impression of Game Show Bob? I practice that one all the time. I think it's really good."

"You didn't just leave. You jumped into the china shop with your bull costume on and didn't leave one plate standing."

Brandon didn't answer, and for a moment she had the sense the next sound she'd hear would be a dial tone. "Are you there?"

"Yeah."

"So are you going to tell me?"

"You want to know the truth?"

"Yes."

The phone went silent for more than twenty seconds. "I lost it in a big way last night, didn't I?"

Dana didn't answer. There was more to come and she didn't want to dam up the flow.

"I took a firecracker and somehow turned it into a colossal stick of dynamite that none of you deserved to watch explode."

"I think there's more to tell."

"Okay." Brandon paused again. "I've built an impressive cave of self-pity and I'm spending the majority of my time hanging out in there. You should see the wallpaper. It's extensive. It has a collection of all my faces that are ticked off at life, ticked off at Reece, and ticked off at God."

"Do you want to tell me why?"

"You've always been a bright woman, Dana. Just think about it for a moment. I'm sure you'll figure it out."

"I can guess, but I'd rather you tell me."

Again Brandon didn't respond.

"I called because I care about you, and I'm worried about you."

"That's touching."

A quote from a speaker Dana heard when she was in her late teens popped into her head. *People treat you the way they feel about themselves.* Time for a different tact. "Remember our talk just before we came back from Well Spring?"

"Why would I have forgotten it? Hello? My voice is gone, not my brain."

Dana bit her tongue. Brandon was rarely if ever this acerbic. But it didn't mean she was going to back down. "Humor me. What was the last thing you said to me as we sat above the river and that I agreed to do with you?"

The answer didn't come right away. "Coffee. Just you and me."

"Yes." Dana pressed her lips together for a second. "Don't you think it's time we did that?"

For the third time Brandon went silent, but this time it lasted far shorter and his tone of voice did a 180. "Yeah, maybe it is." He paused and it seemed as if his breathing calmed. "I'd like that."

Dana shifted the phone to her other ear. "What are you doing tomorrow afternoon?"

"Having my nails done."

This was good. His sense of humor was returning without the acid coating. "Do you think you might have some time after the pink polish dries?"

"Would I have to come out of my cave?"

"Yes, you would."

"What about taking a shower?"

"Not necessary, but I would greatly appreciate it."

"Done. Maybe I'll even wash my hair."

"I don't want you to push it just because it's me."

Dana hung up the phone and sighed. She wasn't ready to be his doctor on this one, but there was little doubt this surgery needed the touch of a woman.

SIX

COFFEE TIME. BRANDON SMILED. THIS WAS GOOD. HE'D tried to push down the idea of Dana and him together again ever since they'd joined Reece's team fourteen months ago, but he'd never succeeded. Now he knew why. Yes, his voice had been stolen, but it seemed highly likely he was about to be given something even better in return. He grinned and shook his head. Amazing how one little change in circumstances could instantly take his attitude to the side of the street the sun shined on.

Brandon stepped into the flower store on Sunday afternoon, and the fragrance of the place took him back to the last time he'd bought flowers for Dana. Over four years ago. But time hadn't erased his memory of her favorite kind. Bluebells. Simple. Delicate. The same flower he'd brought her every month on the day of their first date. Her smile flashed through his memory. He was about to see it once again.

Ten minutes later he walked out of the flower store with a spectacular arrangement of bluebells, but not cut like he'd always brought them to her before. This time they were growing in soil almost black in its richness. Too obvious symbolically of where he wanted their relationship to go? No way. He wanted Dana to get a very clear message of his heart for her and his dreams for them.

He glanced at the card he had made her that sat on his car's passenger seat. If you could call it a card. He'd found a fallen tree branch in his backyard yesterday evening and spent last night and most of the morning sanding it till it was smooth as satin. Then he'd written: *"A branch of forgiveness and new beginnings"* on the limb and finished the project by shellacking it multiple times.

As he pulled up to the curb in front of her house, his pulse spiked. Stupid. It felt like a first date. But it was just coffee. No, it was much more. He felt it. She had to be feeling it too. This was the start, a new chance for them, and it was going to be powerful. A rebirth, a restoration of what was lost.

He spoke a quick prayer and stepped out of his car. Maybe one thing in his life wasn't going down in flames. And this was the one that meant the most to him. He rang the bell, and a few seconds later the faint sound of Dana clopping across the hardwood floor of her entryway seeped through her front door.

She opened it, her green eyes bright, a smile on her lips. A shy smile? A smile of anticipation? Maybe it was only his imagination.

"Hi, Brandon."

"Hey." His return smile wasn't shy; it was an ear-to-ear grin.

He pulled the flower arrangement out from behind his back, and her gaze fell to the bowl of flowers in his hand. "What's that?" When she looked back up, her smile had weakened.

"Flowers. For you. And this too." He held out the flowers and the branch. She hesitated before taking them. When she did, her smile couldn't even be classified as weak. It was comatose.

"Um, okay." She continued to stare at the flowers and the branch. "Thanks."

"Don't tell me you've turned your back on bluebells." Brandon smiled again in defiance of the sliver of angst growing in his stomach.

"No, never. It's great. They're great. The stick is great. Really. Thank you for . . . bringing them." Her voice went flat. She glanced furtively back and forth between the arrangement and him. "Come in, I'll set them down and we can go."

Brandon stepped through her door and the witticisms that always so naturally popped down into his brain vanished. Dana strode over to the counter, plopped down the flowers and his branch, and wiped her hands. The flowers slid to the edge of the counter and the bowl came to rest with an inch hanging over the edge, but if Dana noticed she didn't say anything.

"Careful."

"Okay." She gave a muted smile. "Sorry."

"The guy at the store said it's been watered and you don't have to worry about watering again for a couple of days. And that you can either let it grow in here, or plant it outside if you want. But it'll need to be in a shady spot."

"Ready to go?" Dana grabbed her coat off the back of a kitchen chair and glanced at him.

Why was bringing her something a crime? Did her last boyfriend, Porky or Pearly or Perry, whatever his name was, bring her the same exact thing and it surfaced a bad memory? This wasn't exactly how he saw her reacting.

"You have a thing against flowers and well-sanded sticks these days?"

"I told you they're great. They are, really. Thanks again." She stood with her hand on her front door knob, her gaze out toward his car. "Can we go?"

"Sure."

Wow. He made a mental note. Flowers bad. Sanded stick bad. No idea why and probably not the moment to ask. When they arrived at his car, he reached out to open the passenger door for her but she skipped ahead of him and opened it for herself. "Thanks, but I've got it." She got in and yanked the car door shut before he could close it for her.

Flowers and sticks *very* bad. They pulled away and he glanced at Dana. She gazed straight ahead. A few minutes later she reached toward his CD player. "Mind if I get some music going?"

"Yes." He gripped his steering wheel hard. He didn't want to fill the silence with music. He wanted to figure out what was going on inside her head. "Things okay at the station?"

"Fine."

Strike one. "How's Marcus doing?"

"Good. He and Kat and their girls took a long weekend and went to Lake Chelan together. Sounds like they had fun."

Not a base hit, but a walk at least. He might as well try one more swing. "I've been looking forward to this."

"This what?"

"Time together."

Dana turned and looked out the passenger window, then pulled her arms across her chest.

He didn't follow up with another question. Whatever he'd done had thrown liquid nitrogen all over their date, and at this point pressing for more conversation wouldn't help. He waited for Dana to break the silence and when she did, it didn't thaw the ice cloud in the air between them.

"Have you been playing at all?"

Great. The most off-limit subject possible. Let's dig into the wound and see how high the pain meter is pegging. "Playing?"

"You know what I mean."

"No. I haven't been." He massaged the steering wheel.

"Not at all?"

"Didn't I just say no?" He gripped the wheel harder. "I can't touch that yet."

"Can't touch your guitar or can't touch the subject?"

"Both." He glared at her. "Did Reece put you up to this? Getting together with me? Or did you want to all on your own?"

This time the silence lasted longer.

"Do you want to talk about the other night?" Dana said.

"Not really."

"You should." She rubbed her forehead.

"I think we should start this whole conversation over." Brandon took a right-hand turn and pulled up to the curb half a block later, directly in front of the coffee shop. "How are you? I'm fine."

"Me too." The hint of a smile played on Dana's face.

They sat in the back of the shop and for ten minutes talked about nothing of consequence, but their meandering conversation seemed to thaw the ice curtain Dana had thrown up the second she saw the flowers. By the time Brandon was halfway done with his caramel macchiato, the usual warmth had started to come back into her eyes and Dana seemed back to being Dana.

The small talk continued but that was okay. Being with her, just the two of them—not because they were at Well Spring or with the other Warriors—was enough. Five minutes later, Dana's laughter and now-relaxed shoulders gave him the courage to toss out an idea he'd thought about daily since their talk back at Well Spring.

"I'm thinking it might be fun to take a little day trip together."

"Where?" She frowned.

"Up to Larrabee State Park." He reached across the table and gave her hand a quick squeeze. "You know, where we—"

"I know what we did there." She pulled both hands off the table and set them in her lap. "Why do you want to go back?"

"Why wouldn't we? It would be the perfect place to rekindle—"

"Brandon." Dana pushed her chair back a few inches. "I'm sorry if I gave you the wrong impression, but we need to back up a bit."

"Back what up?" He gripped the edge of the table with both hands. "What are you trying to do?"

"What do you mean? I—"

"I said I'd have coffee with you." She crossed her legs. "That's all."

"So is this where you explain the ice-queen routine?"

She tilted her head back, then turned it to stare out the window at the cold Seattle rain.

"Did I miss something back at Well Spring? Wasn't that you sitting with me and we talked about us and you said there was, 'one person you've thought of from time to time lately'?" Brandon opened his arms wide. "That wasn't me?"

"Yes, you did miss something or . . . okay, you didn't miss it, but you've added to whatever went on there or what you thought went on there. I have thought of us from time to time—what the future might be—but . . ." She sighed. "If you think I was saying we should start dating again, you misread me.

"I do want a friendship with you." Dana pulled her light-brown hair back behind her ears. "Maybe . . . maybe even a close friendship. But I don't have any idea what that looks like."

She clasped her hands tight. "Brandon, with what it seems like we're about to go through with Warriors Riding and what you're going through and what I'm still working through, I'm not ready for anything more than that. And neither are you, okay?"

Brandon's body felt like he'd taken a bath in Novocain. This was not the Dana he'd talked to back at the ranch after the battle where he laid down his life for her. The one who seemed—not seemed—*was* open and tender and thinking about them in a way far more than friendship. "What's going on with you? What do you have to work through?"

"Don't start in on me."

"Start in on you how?"

"Just don't."

Brandon crumpled his coffee cup and tossed it into a garbage can five feet to his right. "I didn't make up our conversation at Well Spring. I don't care how deep down they are, I know you still have very real feelings for me. For us."

"You didn't imagine it." Dana rubbed her face and sighed. "But since getting back I've given it a lot of thought. We were both caught up in an emotional moment. And yes, I have had flickering feelings for you. But I think they're remnants of something we once had. The emotions you might have if you bumped into a girlfriend from high school or college and spent time together. I've wanted to tell you this, but you haven't exactly been accessible. Plus, I didn't want to hurt you because I thought you were feeling exactly how you *are* feeling. I'm sorry, Brandon. You and I aren't going any further than friends."

"No chance?"

"I'm sorry." She shook her head.

He stared at her as his gut filled with a slew of cannonballs. Just being friends wasn't good enough. Even close friends. She didn't have feelings for him? He didn't believe her. For some reason she was pushing down whatever she truly felt inside. But it didn't matter. She believed it. Her wall had gone back up, and he had no idea how to bring it down.

SEVEN

A KNOCK ON BRANDON'S FRONT DOOR MONDAY AFTER-
noon yanked his mind away from an absolutely riveting match of
online, beginner-level chess. He logged out and pushed away from
his computer with a bored sigh. No wonder he'd never bothered to
learn the game.

Whoever was at the door knocked again. He wasn't expecting
anyone. And who dropped by unannounced these days? Brandon
blew out another sigh. Might as well. He shuffled to the door and
opened it to find Doug standing on his porch. "Might I come in?"

"How are you, Brandon?" Doug asked after they had settled
onto the couch and love seat in the family room and gone through a
smattering of small talk.

Brandon gazed at Doug with respect. *How are you?* Such a
simple phrase, uttered millions of times across the country every
day with an appalling lack of sincerity. But not from Doug. The way
he said it, leaning forward slightly, his brows furrowed, his tone
with its soft intensity, Brandon knew the older man meant it with
everything inside. And not only meant it, but expected a reaction
equally sincere. "I'm fine" wouldn't cut it.

But Brandon wasn't going to deliver the honest response. Not
because he disliked Doug. On the contrary, he thought the universe
of the man. But Doug was too tied into Reece—Doug was the fifth

Beatle of Warriors Riding, for crying out extremely loud—that made him guilty by association. Brandon didn't want whatever he said to be repeated and analyzed by anyone. No more Warriors. No more Dana. No more music. So now he was going to indulge that dream he'd had since he was a kid and build a tree house. That was his new mission.

"I'm fantastic."

Doug nodded, his piercing gray eyes boring into Brandon's till he had to turn away.

"Really, I'm doing okay." Brandon took a drink of his Gatorade. "I know the meltdown on Friday night says otherwise, but I just needed to get that off my chest, and it helped, and now I'm working through it and I'm going to be fine."

Doug didn't answer till Brandon looked into his eyes, which said Doug didn't even start to believe him.

"Someone very close to me gave me the prophecy Reece and I spoke of the other night, and as you know, it indicates Zennon will—"

"Oh boy, how exciting. I want to learn more. Do I lose my arms this time?"

"It indicates Zennon is mounting a charge against us that will be far greater than what we've experienced so far."

"Is that supposed to inspire me?"

"Reece and I have prayed extensively over the prophecy." Doug bowed his head and clasped his hands. "I believe we've heard from the Spirit that without you, the casualties will be substantial. That without you, much will be lost. You are the key, and just as Marcus made a choice, you will have a choice to make that will shift forces in heaven and on earth."

"I don't suppose you want to let me in on what that choice will be."

"The answer to that has not been given to me."

"Nothing like a little pressure of having to make the right choice to save the world to jump-start my day." Brandon shook his head and slumped back on his love seat. "Sorry, Doug. I'm done with the

Warriors. Maybe not forever, but for right now, it's over. I want to feel normal again. At least try."

"You are more than needed, Brandon. You will be at the fore-front of this war and are the one who can release God's power in ways beyond our comprehension."

"Sorry, wish I could help, but I did my hero bit during our last little skirmish against the Wolf." Brandon pointed to his throat. "So I'm all tapped out on the battle front. And I did my part of the prophecy, you know? Death before the appointed time and all that? So I figure the Warriors can now ride without me."

"It's not something you can stop. You will take your place whether you want to or not. It is your destiny. Give in to hope. Restoration is coming. Life will come out of death for death cannot hold life in its clutches."

"Tell that to my voice."

"He has not forsaken you, Brandon. You will sing again."

"Oh really? With this voice?"

"No. With a voice you can't imagine."

"When? Is this where you tell me I'll sing like I used to when we all rendezvous on the new earth?"

Doug smiled. "It will be far sooner than that, I believe."

"Uh-huh."

"You can't stop his relentless pursuit of you. Love is patient. Kind. Endures all things. Believes all things. It protects and perse-veres. Love never fails. Love cannot be stopped. And he is Love."

EIGHT

On Wednesday after the sun broke through the late-morning fog, Brandon headed for the Edmonds waterfront on Puget Sound just to get a change of scenery. He was the key to whatever this battle was? Sorry, there weren't going to be any locks in his future. God and Reece and the others could find someone else.

He sat for an hour and watched the ferryboats chug in and out of the Edmonds slip. Straight in front of him was the Edmonds Underwater Park where scuba divers descended to explore old boats, a sunken dry dock, tires full of sea anemones, and search for crabs that skittered across the ocean floor. Little buoys with red dive flags and diagonal white stripes across the flags signaled divers below.

Slightly to his left, in between the dive park and the ferry, families and couples and elderly men sauntered along the small stretch of beach, poking at rocks and strolling out on the short jetty that jutted into the blue-green waters of Puget Sound. The briny smell of the ocean tickled his senses and for a few seconds he forgot about everything except this moment.

A car stopped in back of him and its tires scraping against the curb yanked him from his moment of peace. A young couple pulled out a blanket and a picnic basket. After they settled in, they poured two glasses of what appeared to be white wine and spread out crackers and what looked like brie cheese.

They toasted each other, but the woman's eyes seemed dead. Somehow Brandon knew whatever the toast was—it sounded like an anniversary from the snatches of conversation he overheard—she was only going through the motions.

As he turned back to watch the divers slog in and out of the water, a melody filled the air—so crisp and clean Brandon knew immediately it was sung live. No words, just notes from a . . . He laughed at himself. He couldn't tell what instrument played the song. Some musician he was.

As the song grew, Brandon almost gasped. It soared through his mind into his heart and made him want to shout with joy and a moment later took him to a place of profound sadness. A song hadn't affected him this deeply in years. Maybe ever. But where was this one coming from? The music seemed to come from all around him.

He spun slowly in a full circle—pushing himself around on the grass with his heels—looking for the source but saw no one. He glanced at the couple to his left and then at a teenager with a skateboard and a German shepherd ten yards to his right. Neither seemed to have the least interest in the song. How could they not have some sort of reaction? Then the words started. It was a song about longing and regret and trying to hope when hope refused to come.

When it was over, Brandon sat with his arms around his knees, and a chill raced over his body. Stunning. He glanced around once more, but it seemed he was the only one along the strip of grass who had been moved by the piece or even heard it.

A few seconds later, he began to sing the song, but too soft for anyone to hear. His voice sounded rough, of course, but he didn't care—couldn't care. The song refused to let him think about anything but itself, and he couldn't hold back. He let his raspy voice grow louder.

When he finished, the sound of muffled crying floated over to him from his left. It was the woman who had sat down earlier. After a few minutes of tears, she dug her fingers into the man's coat, pulled him toward her, whispered in his ear, and pointed in Brandon's direction. Within seconds the man began to sob as well.

Brandon turned away but couldn't stop from watching with his peripheral vision. They held each other for a few minutes, then pulled away and talked with animated gestures and held each other again. Laughter. More crying. Then a silence that seemed louder than their passionate whispers to each other. Finally they gathered up their blanket and food and drink and walked to their car.

After their trunk slammed shut, she held up a finger. "Wait," she said and shuffled over to Brandon. Her eyes were still wet from tears. She squatted next to him and closed her eyes a moment before opening them and staring into his with a quiet intensity. "How did you know?"

"I don't—"

"How could you know about what I've been going through? Where did you learn that song? How did you know those words"— she blinked back tears—"were exactly what I needed to hear? It's like you wrote that song for me. For us."

The woman wanted to know where the song came from? So did he. "I didn't write it. I heard it for the first time while we were sitting here."

"Heard it where?"

"It was all around us. You guys had to have heard it too."

The woman furrowed her brow. "There wasn't any song till you started singing."

"You didn't hear anything before I—?" Brandon stopped himself. Why ask her again? He didn't think she was lying. But if she couldn't hear it, how could he?

"Thank you with everything inside me. And that's from both of us. I don't know who you are or how you did that, but for the first time in three years, I have hope." She glanced at her man. "We both do. For the first time in five years I know I'm going to make it."

She covered her face with her hand as fresh tears came and she wiped them away. "Thank you, thank you, thank you. I wish I had better words, but just thank you, okay?" She reached out and squeezed Brandon's hand, then scampered back to the man who stood holding the passenger-side door open.

She leaned into him and pressed her head against his chest. The man looked over her shoulder at Brandon, nodded, and then mouthed the words *thank you.*

Brandon stared at the car as it pulled away. What just happened? How did they even understand the words with his burnt-out, raspy voice singing?

A few seconds later the teen with the skateboard shuffled over to him. "Amazing song, brohan. Is it yours?"

Brandon shook his head and smiled at the kid's shirt that had a picture of a diamond on it and said "Don't judge me yet, I'm still in the rough" underneath it.

"No."

"Whose is it?"

Brandon didn't think before answering. "God's."

"Cool. God could totally chart out with that one if he recorded it."

"Chart out?" Brandon knew what he meant, but his mind was only half engaged in the conversation. He was still trying to figure out what the Spirit had just done.

"Number one in the sun, man."

"God in the Top 40." Brandon laughed. "That would be interesting."

"He should let you record it. Rockin' song, even more rockin' voice. You should be a singer."

"My voice?" Brandon cocked his head. "Yeah, right. Maybe I could sing once upon a long ago and far away."

"Sorry." The kid frowned. "Not on your track, jack."

"What?"

The kid smiled. "What I mean is, I'm not tracking with you. You don't like your voice?" He shook his head. "Crazy."

"Not cool making fun of someone older than you." Brandon stood and pulled his car keys out of his pocket.

"Dude, your voice is unlike anything I've ever heard. Straight up." The kid held up both palms. "I'd pay serious coin for one of your albums, so keep rockin' it."

Doug's words floated back to him. *Restoration. It's on its way.*

Was it possible? Brandon massaged his throat as he thanked the kid and turned to go. Was it healed or was the kid delusional? His voice had sounded raspy when he'd sung the song, and it was highly likely the teen's definition of "rockin' voice" might be far different from Brandon's.

He turned to the kid. "You like gritty voices?"

"Nah, not really. I don't look it, but Bublé is more my style. Josh Groban too, you know?" The teen smiled. "And your voice crushes on both of 'em."

Brandon jogged back to his car, jumped inside, and fired it up. He took a few minutes to let what had happened soak in, but as soon as he reached I-5, he dialed Doug's number.

"You're not going to believe this," Brandon said.

"You've had a revelation."

"I think I might have been healed." Brandon swerved around a minivan going sixty as he headed toward home.

"Tell me why you think that."

"I don't think it, I know it. My voice has been restored."

"When?"

"Just now. Ten minutes ago down in Edmonds." Brandon told Doug what had happened and the older man listened without comment. "I'm back, Doug. I almost don't believe it myself, but I'm back. I'm the Song again. You were so right."

Doug didn't respond.

"Are you there?"

"Yes, Brandon. I am. Be careful, son."

"What does that mean?"

"I'm not sure, but this isn't what I sensed the Spirit saying when he told me you'd be restored."

"What else could it be? Are you saying the couple and the kid weren't hearing straight?"

"Again, I don't know, but I do have a strong sense you should be careful."

"Careful of what?"

"Of letting your soul be deceived as to what really happened down on the Sound."

"Our wavelengths are missing each other. Not with you at all here."

"I'm sorry. I wish there was more I could say and that I was clearer in my own mind about what is going on here."

"Me too." Brandon jammed on the gas. "I gotta go."

What was wrong with Doug? He comes over and spouts all that verbiage about being restored, and then when it happens he wants to toss ice water on it? It didn't matter. The instant he got home, Brandon was going to prove the restoration was real.

NINE

BRANDON BOLTED THROUGH HIS FRONT DOOR AND TOSSED his keys onto his kitchen counter. They slid across the surface and smacked into his stainless-steel toaster as he jogged toward his studio. What was wrong with Doug? Brandon didn't need doubters; he needed someone to celebrate with him. *Fine, Doug. Be a downer. Doesn't matter.*

Unbelievable. *Boom!* Just like that his voice was restored. *So cool, Lord.* The doctors had said maybe—a less than ten percent chance maybe—his voice would get close to what it was before. But they hadn't factored God into the equation. Close to what it was? Way beyond close if the kid was right.

Brandon had always had a good voice, maybe great, but not in the same league as Bublé or Groban. If the couple and the kid down in Edmonds were right about how his voice sounded, God had restored his voice in a way only he could do it—even better than it was before.

"Freedom!" he shouted as he fired up his computer and set up his mics. He'd record the song he just sang down in Edmonds. Yes, it was God's song as he'd told the kid, but that didn't mean he couldn't get it down on tape as a tribute to what God had done in the couple, and in him.

He closed his eyes and waited for the words of the song and the melody to fill his mind as it had an hour earlier. But nothing came. It was like a dream where the images were staggeringly vivid but faded within moments of waking.

Despair sloshed through Brandon's mind, but then he laughed. Of course. It was her song. Their song. For them alone. For them to carry in their memories and no one else. Brandon was the instrument, but that was all and why the song was gone. Exactly how it should be.

So he would lay down a different song. Which one? He snapped his fingers. The choice was obvious. One of the first songs he'd ever written: "Chain Break." Perfect because of what God had just broken loose in him.

Brandon hit Record, opened his mouth, and sang the first line with his old confidence. But what fed back through his headphones sounded hideous. Why were his headphones distorting the sound of his voice? Brandon tried it again. Same result.

His legs shuddered and he slumped to his knees. It couldn't be. He tried it a third time and sang till the chorus, then played it back. Atrocious. His voice was as trashed as ever, back to where it had been weeks ago, maybe worse.

His guitar slipped out of his hand, crashed to the floor, and sent out a discordant sound. Brandon turned and walked out of his studio and slammed the door behind him. He snatched his cell phone from his pocket and called Doug again.

"You knew, didn't you?"

Doug didn't answer for a moment. "No. Not entirely. But I suspected something like this might happen."

"What is going on?"

"Come to Well Spring with us next week."

"What is going on, Doug?"

"Can you believe God is in this?"

"I don't know."

"Come to Well Spring."

"Sorry, Doug, it ain't gonna happen."

TEN

THE UNSETTLING SENSATION WASHED OVER MARCUS FOR the third time—the feeling of someone staring at him. There was no scientific evidence to back up the impression, but there was no scientific evidence for teleportation or invisibility or the power of prayer or traveling inside someone else's soul either. Yet those things certainly were not only possible but had become facts—and almost normal—in his life and the lives of the other Warriors.

He turned back to his book, *Separating Soul and Spirit: A Quantum Understanding.*

The warm summer sun was almost too hot for Marcus as he sat on a bench in the University of Washington's Red Square. He'd come hoping to see Simon, but so far there had been no sign of the magician.

His cell phone rang. It was Kat. "Hello, wife of my youth."

"Sorry, you just missed her. This is the wife of your middle age."

"Forty-four is not middle-aged."

"I'm glad to hear you're going to live past your eighty-eighth birthday. I want you around." Kat paused. "I was praying just now and have a feeling you need to find Simon. He's going to play a significant role in what the Warriors will be facing soon."

"That's excellent confirmation of what I've been feeling as well. Which is why I'm sitting in Red Square right now hoping he'll appear. I want to speak with him. I need to speak with him."

"He'll show. Maybe not today, but he will."

After their standard "I love yous," Marcus ended the call and turned back to his book. The moment he picked it up, his cell phone buzzed again. He didn't recognize the number, but the area code indicated the call was generated from somewhere in the Los Angeles area.

"Marcus Amber here."

"You saved my life, Professor." A low, animated voice poured out of Marcus's phone.

"Carson Tanner?"

"In body, soul, and spirit. How are you, Marcus?"

He smiled. It was good to hear the radio talk-show host's voice. "All systems are firing with adequate strength at the moment, and you? Nice to hear from you."

"I meant to call you before now, but I've been working sixteen hours a day since you paid me that in-studio visit."

"I see."

"So do I. Now. And you're the one who handed me the glasses that allowed me to get my vision back to where it should be. Wow, what a ride I've been on. All good. All freedom. Big changes, you know?"

A deep sense of relief settled on Marcus. He'd feared the radical change in Carson during his encounter with the radio-show host had been more out of the emotion of the moment than a true revolution. Every day since his showdown in Carson's studio almost two weeks ago, Marcus had interceded for the man.

"Have any quantifiable results come out of your long hours?"

"Without question. Radical shift on the level of a 9.7 quake." Marcus heard a smile in Carson's voice. "You haven't been listening to my show? C'mon, Professor."

Marcus mentally flicked himself on the forehead. Of course. Why hadn't he tuned in to the show to see if Carson had made any programming alterations that would reflect the shift in his heart?

"I have to confess I haven't. That likely would have answered a considerable amount of my questions."

"Like if my rebirth was real." Carson chuckled.

"Since you raise the question, yes, precisely."

"It's real, baby. We've revamped the entire show. I've sat down in person with six of our seven major sponsors and did a video call with the seventh. I met with each of my staff one-on-one and asked for their forgiveness. I've started a gathering once a week for any of my team who wants to come, and we've been pushing into freedom."

"It's exhilarating to hear that."

"And the e-mails from listeners are mind-blowing. We're changing lives, Marcus. The themes we talk about now are spreading like gas-soaked wildfire."

"How are your ratings?"

Carson laughed. "That's pretty funny. Just this morning someone asked me that and I had to answer, 'I have no clue.' I had to ask Sooz what they were. Up until our encounter, I could quote enough statistics to impress even you, Professor. But since our meeting I've lost all interest."

"Why is that?"

"I've learned a simple lesson that you and the other Warriors probably already know. Ratings aren't success. The world cares about them, but God doesn't. Based on 'ratings' and followers who stuck around, Jesus was one of the biggest failures in history."

"Agreed. But you still have sponsors and advertisers who will want to know if their money is well spent."

"Sooz told me the show is trending twelve percent higher than we've ever been."

"Congratulations."

Carson laughed. "Hey, you know I could do your ministry a lot of good. Get you a lot of exposure. Since I slammed the Warriors so hard in the past, I'd like to make up by running some free ads and promotions. Pump you up big-time. I've talked a little about what you've done for me, but I'd like to make it official. Whaddya think?"

Marcus smiled at the kindness but shook his head. "I'm thinking not."

"Really?" Carson's voice was incredulous.

"You said you're not about the numbers. Reece isn't either. None of us are. We've had offers from major players to do a reality TV show based on what's going on with our ministry. We've had men and women with deep pockets want to help us build a huge staff with satellite offices in other parts of the world, as well as a dozen other similar offers, but we've clearly heard the Spirit say over and over again, 'Stay small.'"

"You're not small. You're worldwide. How many people are on your e-mail subscriber list?"

"Two hundred and eighty thousand and growing."

Carson whistled. "Those're serious numbers for such a short time you guys have been around. And without pushing the ministry at all."

"I suppose it is. But the power isn't our number of followers. The true power of Warriors Riding will always be the people who have taken the message back to their cities and countries. We'll always be a nuclear-filled iceberg."

"That's an interesting image. Care to elaborate?"

"Warriors Riding has a great deal of influence, but most of it is below the surface where no one can see."

"So you fuel the people who fuel the people who fuel the people."

"Precisely." Marcus leaned back on the bench. "As Reece says, we're not out to form a mega ministry because the day we start getting big is the day we die."

"Okay. I respect that. But just know if you ever change your mind, I'm here for you." Carson blew out a quick breath. "Listen, gotta run. Can we touch base again in a few weeks?"

"I'd like that."

As soon as Marcus hung up, the sensation hit him again, a feeling of certainty he was being watched. He looked up and turned his gaze to U-Dub's Odegaard Library and made a slow sweep from left to right. No one stared in his direction. He started to turn back to his book but spun back a second later. Movement near the base of the library snagged his attention. A head peering around the corner, then pulling back.

Marcus waited and the head came around the edge of the building again and stayed there. Was it him? Marcus smiled as Simon rose from behind the brick wall and strolled toward him.

Finally. He'd been anxious to speak with the magician ever since the Warriors had returned from Well Spring nearly two weeks ago. But if Simon didn't want to be found, he wouldn't be. Marcus could have gone to Simon's apartment, but the magician had forbade him from doing that for reasons he wouldn't explain. And leaving messages on his cell phone held less than a twenty percent chance of being answered. Probably because most of the time Simon didn't know if he had a cell phone or not. But now, finally, he would have the opportunity to speak to the man who had saved him, saved all of the Warriors.

The magician, taking time to notice every blade of grass and smell every flower laid out before him, ambled toward Marcus like he was in the middle of the University of Washington arboretum. While he was still twenty yards away, Simon opened his arms and wiggled his fingers as if to beckon Marcus to come his way.

Marcus stood and strolled toward Simon. His friend looked well overall. The magician's goatee was flecked with a spot more gray than the last time he'd seen him, and his clothes hung a mite looser. But other than that he looked the same.

"Simon, my remarkable friend."

"In the end, I was indeed a true friend, and by the sound of your voice, I'm guessing you made the right choice." The magician wiggled his slightly oversized ears.

"Yes, I did. If I hadn't, I don't think I'd be here."

"True, *mon frère*." Simon nodded and folded his arms as a smile played on his face.

"That is something I've been longing to talk to you about."

Marcus motioned back toward the bench on which his book and briefcase sat. "Care to join me in accumulating a splash of vitamin D from the star above us?"

Simon squinted into the sun. "We Seattleites can't overdose on it, can we?"

"Not likely."

As they walked and then sat down, neither man spoke. Marcus wasn't sure where to begin but finally said, "You were aware of the choices I was going to face on the cliff and in front of the door of my memories, weren't you?"

"I did indeed know, like falling summer snow, which comes when unexpected, but can form a kind of nexus."

"That isn't a perfect rhyme, friend." Marcus grinned.

"No. 'Tis not. It's a slant rhyme or oblique rhyme, but I don't think I need to explain such mundane definitions to a man of your cranial prowess."

"It's good to see you, Simon." It wasn't in Marcus's nature to hug the man, but seeing the magician again almost made him do it. Instead, he squeezed his friend's shoulder.

"You as well, Professor." Simon leaned forward on the bench in a mock bow. "I'd like very much to hear how you escaped from Zennon's hell."

"I almost didn't. I came very close to making a choice that would have left me there. Without you, I'm afraid, I would have chosen poorly. Words aren't adequate to thank you for what you showed me down by the fountain back in June."

"It was my great pleasure."

"And you did it through a card trick."

Simon pulled out a deck of cards and opened the case. "Visual and tactile lessons tend to sink into the brain with much greater intensity than simply saying the words, don't you think?"

"Yes."

"Then why don't you apply them more often in your classes?"

"I probably should." Marcus smiled and pointed at the cards. "Perhaps you should teach me a few tricks."

"Are you quite serious or a touch delirious?"

"Maybe both."

"Lessons are of course free for you."

"I might take you up on that."

"Anytime." Simon bowed again.

Marcus studied the magician. The man fidgeted as he always did, shifting his weight back and forth from hip to hip, his eyes always moving. Most people would describe Simon as being slightly off. Marcus would describe him as being slightly tormented. More than slightly. Simon needed relief and restoration, but Marcus had no idea where to begin. "I want you to meet the others."

"Others?"

"The other members of the Warriors Riding."

Simon shook his head. "I'm good at a distance. Good with a crowd. Not so good close up and personal."

"You're good with me."

"I make it with you most of the time, yes. But it's not always easy, makes my head feel breezy. And I came to you because I saw myself all over you. I sensed it. I saw what Zennon was doing to you. I couldn't let what happened to me happen to someone else."

"What happened to you, Simon?"

"No, no, no, that would be a blow." He waved his hand as if to push away a memory. "Not back there, only here, elude the fear."

Marcus leaned in. "Come meet my friends. They want to thank you. It was not just my life you saved. Freeing me from my past allowed me to go to battle in a way that brought great victory to my closest allies. That's why I want you to meet them. Why they want to meet you. But also, I believe they can bring you healing."

"I can't. Not now brown cow." Simon shuffled the deck, then sprang them into a card fountain. "You and they are involved in strange things on the fringe of God. I need to stay as far away from them as possible."

"You mean soul travel. Sending our spirits into the souls of others to fight for their freedom and healing. Traveling into other spiritual realms. Fighting spirits not of God."

Simon stuck his fingers in his ears and shouted, "La, la, la, la, la. I can't hear you." A thin sheen of sweat appeared on his forehead.

"Because you spent such a great deal of time in another reality."

"Never again, if you are my friend, speak of that path." Simon stood, spun in a full circle, jerked two steps away, spun again, and staggered back. "Never. I'm done traveling anywhere spiritual or delving into spiritual matters that dance on the razor's edge, till I shed this body for good."

"My apologies."

"It's okay." Simon winked. "But let's let the subject drop."

"But I have to speak of one more item." Marcus leaned in. "There's a third reason I want you to meet the other Warriors. I believe we need you."

"Why?"

"Because a war is coming far bigger than any we've faced before. And we believe Zennon is behind it."

"And since I know him—"

"Yes." Marcus spread his hands. "We need to know everything he's capable of."

"It's more than you can imagine."

"We need to know his tactics."

"Layer upon layer of deception. You cannot defeat his mind. He's far smarter than any of you could dream of being. Even you, Professor."

"What else?"

"Don't underestimate him. He's cunning. Vicious. You might think you know his plans, but you don't. He's nine steps ahead of you and then the lies will start to spew. Plus, he has the angel of light dance down to perfection. He'll fool you just like he did when he pretended to be your daughter's boyfriend."

"Come and teach us about him."

"I don't know." Simon held up his silver coin. "So you liked my trick that showed you the path to make the right choice?"

Ask him again.

The voice of the Spirit was so clear, Marcus didn't hesitate. "What happened to you when you didn't make the right choice, Simon?"

Simon's slate gray eyes went cold. "I told you, even in my mind I can't go back. Vicious attack." He stared at his cards and cut them with one hand, but his other hand shook. "Because I still can't tell if it's more than in my mind, which isn't kind . . . brings emotions of serious decline."

"My impression is you need to speak of it. With someone who has faced the same choices and can walk through it with you. Healing can come for you as it did for me."

"No. Too late, he's shut the gate." Simon turned to the left and continued to execute various one-handed cuts.

"If you ever have desire to speak of it, I would like to hear your story."

"Maybe. A very large maybe." Simon shook his head and the brightness in his eyes faltered. Then the magician's face went pale and his eyes locked shut. "Don't make me go back there, Professor, please."

But if the look on his face was any indication, Simon was already gone.

ELEVEN

As the words escaped Simon's mouth, a memory buried under decades of time bubbled to the surface. He sat in the bedroom he grew up in, his hands over his ears, but it didn't help much.

The screaming above continued and seeped down through the ceiling, settled on Simon's ten-year-old shoulders as he sat in the center of his room, and soaked into his soul. He blinked back tears and opened his book, *Tarbell's Course of Magic Volume 1*, a gift from his uncle the previous Christmas. He crawled over to the door of his closet, pulled it open, and snuggled up against the back wall where he'd laid out a blanket for his frequent visits. There he buried himself in the pages that would teach him how to instantly switch places with a volunteer from the audience, and make a ring crawl up a rubber band, defying the laws of gravity, and how to amaze anyone with a pack of playing cards.

He took the four aces out of his Bicycle deck and whispered the things he was supposed to say as he made them change into the four kings and then the four queens and then the four jacks with faster and faster flicks of his wrist. He smiled as the yelling from his parents faded and the imaginings of standing on a stage in Chicago or Los Angeles or the big one—New York—filled his mind.

Plus, the party was almost here! The one where he would

perform for those little kids and show them a world of astonishment and wonder. A world where people would love him and cheer for him and made him feel like he mattered. He would put on a show they would always remember.

The scene in his bedroom vanished, and Simon breathed a sigh as he stole a glance at Marcus. But then another memory sliced into his mind—one much worse—the day all the gears of his life's final destruction started turning.

He stood in front of a small audience of men—seven or eight if he remembered right. Simon's father sat in the back row with his arms folded, a smirk on his face. It wasn't easy getting this audience to come. But in the end Simon, convinced his dad to invite some of his buddies to come over and see the show. This would be the one that would make his dad proud.

His father hadn't ever shown interest in Simon's magic, but it didn't matter. Today he would prove to his dad that his magic was mesmerizing and worthy of his dad's praise. And maybe, just maybe, they could start to learn magic tricks together. Study books and go to shows and even perform together someday. That would be true magic!

He performed all of his most powerful tricks for the men: making small billiard balls multiply and disappear, tearing up a chosen card, then making it vanish and reappear fully restored inside an orange, and pulling a rope right through one of the men's arms. But he saved his best trick for the finale.

Twelve-year-old Simon pulled out four silks—one blue, one green, one yellow, and one red—and waved them through the air. "As you can see, each of these silks is a different color and they are completely separate from each other."

Again he showed the men each silk one at a time. Then he rolled the four silks into a tight ball. "Now watch closely because in the blink of an eye, you're going to see a miracle!"

Simon tossed the silks in the air, and a moment later a flash of fire exploded above him. When the smoke cleared, the silks fluttered down into his waiting hands. But now the silks were melded together in a swirling pattern of colors.

The men gave him polite applause, except for Simon's father, who turned to the man next to him and laughed. "Can you believe it? Silks? Playing with silks. Can I get him interested in football? No. Baseball? No. Basketball? Doesn't interest the kid. Can't even get him to fire a BB gun. But magic grabs his little pea brain, and it hasn't turned him into a rabbit; it's turned him into a sissy boy."

His dad laughed along with most of the other men, and in that instant, Simon was the assistant and his dad had just sawed him in half.

The next day after school, Simon sat alone in a park near his home practicing a coin roll across his fingers and pretending he could run away from home. He had no brother. No sister. No friends he could talk to. And his mom . . . she wouldn't stand up to his dad anyway, so what was the point in trying to tell her about what had happened?

"Hey."

Simon looked up from his picnic table to find a guy who looked like he was in college standing nine or ten yards away, hands shoved in the front of his slacks. A gray velvet bag hung from his wrist and his dark hair flopped down on his forehead.

"Who are you?"

The young man took out a pack of cards and made a perfect fan with one hand. "My name is Aaron. And yours is Simon, right?"

"How do you know my name?"

"My dad is a friend of your dad's. He came to your show yesterday and told me about it. That you're a magician just like me." Aaron grinned but his smile quickly faded. "And he told me what your dad said. Sorry about that. That wasn't right. I bet he doesn't really feel that way. Just trying to be funny, you know?"

"It's okay."

"Mind if I sit?" Aaron pointed at the table.

"Sure. I mean, no."

For the next two hours, Aaron showed Simon amazing moves with cards and coins and sponge balls and matches and pencils and rings till Simon's mind spun with the excitement of it all.

"You're amazing!" Simon grinned.

"Ah, thanks, but I've just been practicing a lot longer than you." Aaron shoved his cards and coins and his other props into a small bag and stood. "Listen, I have to go now, but if you like, you can start coming to a magic club I'm part of. We get together once a month and show each other tricks and stuff."

"That'd be great."

"Okay. So if it's all right with your dad, I'll pick you up next Monday night around seven." Aaron scribbled on a small sheet of paper. "That's my phone number. Ring me if you can't come. If I don't hear from you, we'll learn some more cool stuff together."

"My dad won't care if I go." Simon scratched his fingernail along the wood of the picnic table.

"Hey." Aaron's gaze seemed to pierce Simon. "It's going to be all right. Most dads are like that. You'll make it, okay?"

Simon squeezed his lips together and nodded.

Aaron took a step away, then turned back. "You have a big brother?"

"Nah, it's just me."

"Well, you do now." Aaron grinned and loped off and Simon smiled.

For the next ten years, Simon didn't miss a night at the magic club. Neither did Aaron. By the time Simon moved away from Seattle after graduating from college, the hook was set so deep inside his soul it was part of him.

⊹ ⊹ ⊹

"Simon?" Marcus said for the third time. From the look on the magician's face, wherever he'd slipped off to was a place of darkness. "Are you okay?"

Simon blinked as if waking from drug-induced sleep and peered at Marcus. "He won't let you rest. Never. He's out to destroy you. All of you."

"Zennon."

"Yes, Zennon, of course. To bring devastation across many nations." Simon stood and started to walk away.

"Simon, stop."

The magician turned.

"I can't help but say this again. I believe you're part of defeating him more than you can conceive."

"If I am, I don't want to know about it. I've done enough and enough has been done to me." Simon shook his head, sighed, and called out over his shoulder as he trudged away, "Don't contact me anymore, Professor. Our time together has come to an end."

TWELVE

BRANDON SAT ON HIS DECK TWENTY MILES EAST OF Seattle on Saturday afternoon and watched a stiff breeze buffet the Douglas fir trees in his backyard. The sun cast thick, black shadows across his well-manicured lawn and his wind chimes chattered at him. The only other sound was the clink of ice against his glass of Mike's Black Cherry Lemonade as he downed the last of the beverage.

In the old days he would have had music blasting from the outdoor speakers, but those days were over. Music was the last thing he needed. Then again, maybe it was the first. He didn't care. He didn't want to hear it. He shifted in his Adirondack chair, trying to think of nothing, but not having a great deal of success.

The thought of playing again—singing again—was like a boomerang he tossed away, but it kept returning no matter how far away he flung the idea. Something miraculous had happened down in Edmonds and he couldn't ingnore that fact. Doug said God was in it. Sure he was.

Intellectually he knew his soul was starving without music, but he couldn't convince his heart of that truth. Too painful to be reminded his dream was dead forever. He was the Song? Right. What role did he have in Warriors Riding now? He felt like one of those old-school actors who wasn't relevant anymore but was still invited to the award ceremonies for sentimental reasons. His cell phone vibrated and he looked at the caller ID. Reece. Great. Doug's tag-team partner.

"Yeah?"

"You need to hear the truth. And accept it." Reece's voice was monotone.

"What is this? First Doug and now you? Can't you just leave me alone?"

"No." Reece paused. "You're not on this journey alone, Song."

"Don't call me that. I'm not the Song. Not anymore." Brandon kicked at a green leaf on his deck. "That died. I will never be that person again."

Reece didn't respond.

"It's over for me. Forever. Done. Finished. Gone. Sign the papers and turn over the deed."

"If you're so convinced of that, then why do you still seek it?" Reece said.

"I'm not."

"Hmm."

"I just want to have some kind of purpose again."

"So this is all about Brandon Scott?"

He didn't answer.

"I've learned a few things during my sixty-four years. One of them is this life is not about you. Not even a little about you or me. We no longer live a life in the flesh, but a life in the Spirit. A life where we have given up what we want. And we pursue what he wants. And you're being the Song is part of what I believe the Spirit wants."

"For some strange reason I don't want anything to do with music anymore. Any insight as to why I might feel that way?"

"As I just said, you are still the Song. You can't run from that."

"Sure I can, Reece. I just bought a pair of stellar track shoes and I'm sprinting faster than the Flash." Brandon scowled. "You got your sight back, at least in a way. I have nothing. I had this wild, insane idea that Dana and I might have something, at least the hope of a future together, but even that has crashed and burned like a kamikaze fighter."

"You have everything."

"Really? I must have misplaced my everything because I can't seem to find it." Brandon patted his front and back pockets and then his chest. "Dad gum it all to tarrrrrnation, where da heck did my everything go now, y'all?"

"That's quite humorous."

"It doesn't sound like you're smiling."

"Blind people rarely smile."

"Is *that* supposed to be funny?"

"Mildly," Reece said. "You have the Spirit inside you. That is everything."

"Is that how you felt when you first lost your eyes? Completely content? We both know it isn't."

"True."

"And now you've got this superpowered spiritual laser-beam eyesight where you can see into the spiritual realms all around us." Brandon stood and paced on his deck. "And somehow see shapes and outlines of people and whatever else as well. Funny how your attitude has improved since that happened."

"It improved long before I got a new kind of sight."

"That's because you had hope. You believed the prophecy would come true and you would see again."

"What do you believe, Brandon?"

"Nothing left in that candy store, Willy. The kids have cleaned out the chocolate bars and the Wing Dings, and there aren't going to be any candy canes this Christmas."

"At least you still have your sarcasm." Reece gave a soft chuckle. "Don't give up on hope, son."

"I don't even get why you and Doug are pushing for something more. The Warriors are done, aren't they? The prophecy is fulfilled, Reece. I don't see why we can't disband this thing."

Brandon shuffled through a stack of papers on his end table

and pulled out a copy of the prophecy. "Listen to your prophecy carefully, Reece:

When the time comes, the Spirit will reveal each of them to you. You will teach them the wonders of my power they can't yet imagine. And instruct these warriors how to go far inside the soul and marrow.

They will rise up and fight for the hearts of others. They will demolish strongholds in the heavens and grind their enemies to dust. Their victories will spread across the nations. You will pour out your life for them and lead them to freedom, and they will turn and bring healing to the broken and set the hearts of others free.

And when the Wolf rises, the four must war against him and bring about his destruction,

Only they have hope of victory.

And for one, their vision will grow clear.

And for one, the darkness of choice will rain on them,

And for one, the other world will become more real than this one,

And for one, death will come before the appointed time.

"See? It's over. You taught us your skills. We took out the Wolf. Marcus did the choice thing. Our message is certainly spreading across the nations, one little gathering of believers at a time. Have you been reading about the number of groups—?" Of course he hadn't. "Sorry."

"You don't have to be."

"Warriors Riding groups are forming in the UK, Australia, South Africa, Wales, Korea, I kid you not."

"Yes, I know."

"So why can't we let it continue to spread on its own at this point? They don't need us anymore." Brandon stepped off his deck onto the grass. "The death of my career certainly came before the appointed time, so that part of the prophecy is done. Your turbo-charged vision is certainly the answer to the clear-vision part, and with that, the spiritual world is much more real to you than this one. Finished."

"But there is another prophecy now."

"Yeah, Doug told me about that. I'm supposed to believe it's real, right?"

"Yes."

"And when were you going to tell me about it?"

"It's what we wanted to tell you at the gathering on Friday night where you—"

"Came off the rails and slammed into the other trains on the neighboring tracks. I know. Bad behavior. Sorry."

"Come to Well Spring with us, Brandon."

"My answer hasn't changed since talking to Doug." Brandon stepped back onto his deck and slumped back into his chair. "I gotta go."

"Pray about it, Brandon. Not a rub-a-dub-dub, thanks-for-the-grub, yay-God prayer. A real one. Which means listening more than speaking."

"I'll think about it." Brandon tossed his cell phone onto the small, round wooden table to his left. He sat up and tried to believe Reece's words and tried to listen for the Spirit's voice but gave up after a few minutes. He was about to go inside when he saw something move from the corner of his eye.

He turned to his right and stared at the thick row of fir trees along his property line. There. High up, maybe eighteen or twenty feet above the ground, something was moving. He rose from his chair, walked the fifteen feet to the end of his deck, and eased down the stairs leading onto his thick jade grass. What *was* that?

A blurred picture of a woman the size of a small movie screen shimmered against the trees. The tone of her skin and her dark hair made her appear to be African-American, but Brandon couldn't tell for sure. The image was transparent, but he could make out her walking through a building made of glass. Businesspeople moved past her from in front and behind. Was she wearing a dark sweat suit? It seemed out of place. She smiled and shook hands with someone who had his back to Brandon.

As he stared at her, she became more solid but still too blurry to completely make out her features. Then her surroundings changed. He could make out a field with trees forming a half circle around it. As more of the vision came into focus, Brandon saw a swing set and merry-go-round with a few children playing on it.

The woman pulled a granola bar out of her pocket, turned it over, and stuffed it back into her sweat suit. She stared at the children, looked up at the sky, then down at her upturned hands in her lap, and began to cry.

That's when the music started. A song of such joy it created an instant discord between the woman's racking sobs and the tune that swirled around Brandon's head. Even before the words started, he knew the song was about her deepest fear. This time the lyrics leaped out at him immediately.

> *Push your body, push your talent, take it to extremes,*
> *Will they love you, when it's shaken, no longer their great dream?*
> *Can you leave it, lay it down, when the race comes to an end,*
> *When the cheers have vanished, and the spikes are tarnished, will*
> *they still call you friend?*

The rest of the lyrics flowed into his mind like a river, but the words weren't what set Brandon's heart pounding. It was the music. A melody that pierced him like a rapier where one edge of the blade was cast from the fires of joy and one from the fires of pain.

Brandon fell back into his chair and the vision faded along

with the song. For a few seconds he begged for it to come back, then turned and staggered across his deck and into his house till he reached his studio. He picked up his guitar. He had to get this down on tape. The guitar felt strange in his hands, but he threw off the feeling and punched Record. He wouldn't lose this song like he'd done last time.

Maybe this was the way he would be the Song again. No, he couldn't sing like he used to, but he could write the songs, record them, produce them, reach the world through the voices of others. Maybe Doug and Reece were right. Maybe God was in this.

A giddiness washed over him that he hadn't felt since he recorded his first album. This was it, the key to his return. The Spirit had given him a song of such power, there was no question in his mind it would be a major hit. He'd done some producing—three albums and a couple of singles. He'd always said he'd get more into that side of the business someday. Someday was here.

He laid down the melody on tape—he didn't care that his voice sounded like metal on concrete—scribbled down the lyrics, and then tried a variety of chord progressions, searching for ones that would fit the melody. Once he found them, he toyed with making the song up-tempo or keeping it slow as he'd heard it out back. In the end he decided on keeping it slower. In twenty minutes he was ready. He hit Record and began to sing.

Stop.

The voice of the Spirit was not still and it was not small. It thundered inside him and Brandon blinked. "Lord?"

This is not your song; it is not for you. It is her song, for her alone.

"What does that mean?"

The song will remain with you till the time.

The time? "What time, Lord?"

You will know.

Brandon set his guitar back onto its stand and stared at the strings as if he'd never seen them before. Why had his life become such a kaleidoscope of confusion? Why couldn't God just give him his voice back? Give him a relationship with Dana? What was God doing?

Something in his gut said answers would come soon—but not the ones he wanted.

THIRTEEN

Two days later, the god of awkward meetings paid Brandon a visit. He was in Seattle strolling through Pike Place Market looking for original photos of old guitars. He looked up right after he paid for a shot of a Gibson Les Paul from the forties and saw Dana walking toward him. Great. His heart rate picked up. What was she doing down here on a Monday afternoon? Shouldn't she be at the radio station? Next to her walked a woman who looked vaguely familiar.

God was in all things? Then why force him to bump into her? If Dana was done with him, why couldn't he be done with her? Whatever. He'd get through it. This was inevitable, wasn't it? No, it wasn't. If he was finished with the Warriors, there would be no reason to see her ever again. Yeah, right. As if it could be that easy. She and her dive-into-your-soul emerald eyes were in his life forever and ever amen. *Accept it. Deal with it. A little hello, small talk, how are you, how are the Warriors—have you seen any of them lately? How are things at the station? And get out of there. Not a big deal.*

He gave a halfhearted wave as the two women clipped toward him. If Dana was uncomfortable seeing him, it didn't show. "Hey," she called out from twenty feet away.

"Hey."

When Dana reached him, she gestured to the woman next to

her. "Brandon, I'd like you to meet a recent acquaintance of mine. This is Sandra. Sandra, this is my friend, Brandon." She turned to Brandon. "Sandra is part of a national radio campaign and is in town visiting our station as part of the promotional push. She'll cut some liners for the client and maybe even some liners for my station and a few of the other stations in our group. I'm showing her a few of the sights around Seattle."

Brandon stared at the woman. Tall. At least five foot nine. And he knew her. He'd at least seen her face before. Without question, but from where escaped him. One of his concerts maybe? No. Something caught in his spirit. It wasn't at a concert, it was somewhere else, but he had no recollection of a conversation.

"Have we met, Sandra?"

"I don't think so, but I know who you are even without Dana making the introductions." She smiled and extended her long arm.

"You do?"

"Aren't you Brandon Scott? The singer?"

"I used to be."

"I thought so. My sister has all your music. Forces me to listen to it all the time."

Brandon laughed.

Sandra looked at him with her head tilted. "You say you used to be. Care to explain how you changed into someone else?"

"It took a great deal of work and a decision to trust God to ruin my life."

"I see." She nodded, her brown eyes narrowed, and in that instant Brandon knew who she was.

"Oh, wow. You're Sandra Aspen. From the Olympics."

"Not true. I didn't come from the Olympics. I came from Maine." She smiled. "But I did compete in the 2000 and 2004 games."

"Wow. This is wild. You won a gold and two silvers in Athens. Silver in the 100 and 200 meters and gold in the four by one hundred."

"I'm impressed. You're obviously into track and field."

"Actually I'm not. Only once every four years. For some reason

I can't stay away from the Olympics. You knocked me out that year. It is a true pleasure to meet you."

"Thank you. It's good to meet you as well."

"What have you been doing with your life since the games? Those Olympics were your last competition, right?"

"Yes, I retired after Athens." A darkness passed over Sandra's eyes. "I've been dabbling in various things since."

She looked down and Brandon's mind locked on to the image and froze it in his brain. Yes, he knew her from her track-and-field days. But he'd seen her much more recently. It was her in his backyard. In the vision. Along with a song that ripped his soul apart with its power and beauty.

"Are you okay, Brandon?" Dana touched his shoulder.

"I'm fine."

"You don't look fine. You look as white as that cloud over our heads all of a sudden and like you're about to faint."

"Yeah, I do feel a bit strange. Probably bad sushi for lunch."

A compulsion rose up in him to sing the song for her. Not a good plan. With his raw and raspy voice? No thanks. Wouldn't make Dana look good. Him either. But the feeling only intensified. He couldn't. Impossible. Not even in private, let alone here in the middle of Pike Place Market. And to a complete stranger? Huh-uh.

You can. You are the Song.

I can't. My voice is gone. Plus, I don't remember the song. I don't remember the words. I don't have my guitar . . .

Remember what I told you?

Brandon pressed the heel of his hand into his temple as if he could force the idea from his mind. But the impulse continued to grow at an exponential rate.

Okay, let's make a fool of myself.

"I need to ask you a question, Sandra."

"All right." She folded her arms and gave him a curious look.

"I'll warn you, this might sound very strange."

"Don't worry. You wouldn't believe some of the questions I've had over the years."

"This one might be the winner."

"Really." Sandra glanced at Dana and then back to Brandon. "Lay it on me. I'll let you know if it is."

"Recently were you by yourself in a park with two swing sets and a merry-go-round? Next to a lake with a long, old, piling-style dock jutting about fifty feet out into the water? And a green rowboat was tied up to it?"

Sandra's eyes went wide.

"You pulled out a granola bar or PowerBar or something, then stuffed it back in your pocket without eating it. Right beside this little bed of yellow and blue flowers."

Sandra tried to smile but it died a second later, and her eyes narrowed and her voice grew soft. "How do you know all that?"

"I know, I know." Brandon took a step back and held up his hands. "Kinda creepy, but I swear we've never met before. And I have no clue how to be a stalker. You can ask Dana."

"Then how—?"

"Are you . . . ?" Brandon hesitated. "I take it if you've listened to my music you believe in God?"

"Sure. I'm no churchgoer, if that's what you mean, but I'm a spiritual person and I believe there is a God, yes."

Brandon dropped his head as if it could make the compulsion go away. He had no wish to put Dana in an awkward position and even less desire to make a fool out of himself. "Sorry, I shouldn't have told you—"

"I repeat, how did you know about the merry-go-round, and lake, and green rowboat?"

"Here we go." Brandon gave Sandra and Dana a weak smile.

Dana tilted her head and frowned at him with a please-go-away-now look. "What do you think you're doing?"

"The Wild Goose is leading and I'm going to follow."

"Wild Goose?" Sandra pointed at Brandon and turned to Dana. "This guy is your friend?"

Brandon glanced around. No one was close enough to overhear their conversation, but if he sang they would.

"I had a vi— I had a dream and you were in it. You sat on that bench in that park, and from what I saw you weren't having the greatest of days. And while I watched . . . while the scene played out, I heard a song." He hesitated and opened his palms. "And I'd like to sing it for you."

Sandra folded her arms. "Did you say it was a dream or a vision?"

"A vision."

"Brandon Scott had a vision about me." She put her hand on her hip and cocked her head. "I know you're hyperspiritual from listening to your music, but you're starting to get a little freaky."

"As you might be able to tell, my voice is pretty scratchy these days." Brandon cleared his throat. "That's what I meant by 'used to.' I can't sing anymore. Or I should say I can barely sing. I was . . . injured . . . in the throat and it destroyed my voice. But I feel like I'm supposed to sing this song for you."

"Right now?" Sandra glanced around at the shops and the people strolling up and down the street. "You're one of those freakout, charismatic, squirm-on-the-floor types, aren't you?"

"No. I'm not, but I feel like the Spirit—"

"You feel like the *Spirit* is telling you to sing. Like the Spirit of God? The Holy Ghost and all that? What, are you going to start dancing around and speaking in tongues?" Sandra held up her hands. "You're right about the weird question thing. You definitely win the gold."

Sandra took three slow steps backward. "I'll talk to you later, Dana. I'm headed back to the hotel. I'll talk to you never, Brandon." She continued to walk slowly backward, apprehension on her face.

Sing.

Now?

Yes.

Why not? He didn't have much of a life left anyway. He would play the fool, not care what anyone thought. Brandon opened up his mouth, and as he did it felt like his pride spilled out and dropped onto the concrete at his feet.

But it didn't matter what his voice sounded like. This wasn't about him; it was about this lady, Sandra, and what the Spirit had given to him to give to her. He didn't remember the words or the melody—didn't have a clue where to start—but again, it didn't matter. He glanced at the people milling through the market on either side of Dana and him and pushed from his mind any concern about what they would think about his ragged voice. He breathed deeply and sang.

As the first words hit the air, astonishment spun through him. This couldn't be. His voice sounded strong and clear and stunning. The tone was deeper and richer than he'd ever experienced. His heart raced. This shouldn't be possible. But just as it had been up in Edmonds, it was happening.

"Push your body, push your talent, take it to extremes." When he finished the first line of the song, he stopped.

Sandra stared at him in awe. Her face grew a shade lighter. "Wow."

Brandon stared at her as she eased back toward him.

"Why'd you stop?" Sandra came alongside Dana. "And I'm not getting the voice-is-gone thing at all, honey. I've listened to a lot of your tunes, and you never sounded that good. Ever."

Heat rushed through Brandon's body. He wasn't imagining it. She'd heard it too. This new voice God had given him.

"Don't just stand there with your mouth hanging open like a junkyard dog. Let's hear the rest of it." Sandra beckoned with her fingers.

Brandon started over, this time closing his eyes and singing it as if he and the Olympian were the only ones in the world.

"Push your body, push your talent, take it to extremes,

"Will they love you, when it's shaken, no longer their great dream?"

As he finished the second line, he heard Sandra pull in a quick breath.

"Can you leave it, lay it down, when the race comes to an end,

"When the cheers have vanished, and the spikes are tarnished, will they still call you friend?

"There is one who longs to love you fully, and draw you deeper still."

When he finished the fifth line, he opened his eyes. She was two feet away with tears in her eyes, staring at him. He couldn't tell if her face held anger or deep longing. A few more seconds revealed it as the latter.

"Hope reborn and dreams uncovered, destiny fulfilled.

"Take his hand and run the distance, the path is lined with gold,

"But getting there requires a death, then beauty will unfold."

By the time he finished, she sobbed with her face in her hands. Dana took her by the arm and led her away from the market to Victor Steinbrueck Park overlooking Puget Sound, right off Western Avenue. No one was in it, and once they reached the center of the small grass lawn, Dana took the lead.

"Looks like God might be doing something here," she said gently.

Sandra nodded and took the tissue Dana offered her. "When I stopped running, others started. Away from me. Everyone wants to be famous, you know?" Sandra looked up, her eyes red. "Everyone wants to be loved. And I believed they loved me. I believed he loved me for who I was, not for what I did. And when I came home and found that note . . ." She broke down again. When she raised her face a few minutes later, every shred of toughness had disappeared.

They sat in silence as Sandra leaned into Dana and Dana held her tight.

"If it's okay with you, Brandon and I are going to pray for you."

Sandra nodded again, and for the next five minutes Dana and he prayed and listened to what the Spirit was saying about Sandra and prayed some more.

"I don't understand it. I feel hope for the first time in . . ." Sandra wiped her cheeks.

"Me either," Brandon said. "No, I'm not kidding."

Sandra smiled at him with a mixture of laughter and tears.

By the time they finished, a lightness sparkled in Sandra's eyes and a tangible peace surrounded her.

"Strangest and best question I've ever been asked." She reached out and hugged Brandon and he hugged her back. "Thank you for everything."

As she strolled off, Dana's eyes stayed wide for a long time. "Wow, that was something."

"What part?"

"All of it." Dana turned for a few seconds in the direction Sandra walked, then turned back and stared at him like he'd grown wings.

He grinned at her. In a way he had. He was the Song again. "That look means something."

"I've never heard you sound like that. Ever. I don't know how to describe it." She shook her head. "Your voice . . . never . . . I mean . . . you know I've always loved your voice, so don't take this the wrong way. But compared to what you sounded like before, this is a million times beyond."

"Are you serious?"

"That was the most beautiful voice I've ever heard. You're healed."

"In a way, maybe." Brandon gazed out over Puget Sound. "But not like you're thinking. This is something else."

"What do you mean?"

"I'm not exactly sure. I'm trying to figure it out, but I have a feeling when I sing his songs, I get the voice you heard. When I sing my own, I get the raspy voice you're hearing right now."

"And you have no idea when he's going to give you the next song?"

"Exactly."

He turned to go, but before he could step away, Dana reached out and tugged on his arm. "Hey, can I tell you something?"

Her eyes were almost as soft as they'd been back at Well Spring when they'd talked about a coffee date. Was he getting a glimpse of how he suspected she really felt deep down about him, about them, or just some leftover emotions from the time with Sandra?

"Anything."

She glanced at the ground, out over Puget Sound, and finally back at him. "I want us to be close. I mean . . . at least closer than we are now. I'm just . . . it's just that . . . I think we need to wait and—"

"I think we just need to—"

"No." Dana held up her hand and made a quarter turn. "Stop. Let's just keep it right there for now. Okay?"

No, it wasn't okay. Brandon couldn't shake the feeling they were supposed to be more than close, or closer—whatever that meant. As unyielding as it might sound, for him, their relationship needed to be all or nothing. And he wouldn't apologize for that. They were supposed to be together like they were four years ago. Engaged. On their way toward spending the rest of their lives together. But Dana wasn't ready to get even within a football field of that door. Brandon nodded. "Okay."

"Thank you."

"Um-hmm."

She walked away for two steps, then turned back. "This thing with Sandra? I think it's going to happen to you again. Soon."

FOURTEEN

THE MONTBLANC PEN IN HIS HAND SHOOK. NOT FROM fear the words he'd scrawled on the pages in front of him weren't true. He knew they were from the Spirit. And not from what the words portended for the five of them. His hand shook from the adrenaline that flowed from his head and heart into the palm and fingers of his right hand. From anticipation of what the five would think and feel, and how they might be inspired when they read the letters. How these letters might guide them and bring freedom.

He straightened the six or so pages in front of him and stared into the flame of the oil lamp that sat on the cherrywood desk. How long would his own flame continue to burn? Years? Decades? Months? There was still so much to do. But if his time on earth was only days more, it would be all right. All would be right. In this age or the next. And these letters were only a small part in the grand play where all the world and all the heavens were certainly a stage, and he was simply playing his part. William indeed had it right.

He turned back to the page and stared at the paragraph he'd just written. Had those words come from his hand? He knew they had, of course, but he didn't fully recognize what was written there. He smiled. Good. It confirmed the words weren't coming entirely from him but from the Spirit as well. And they would need these words. If not now, someday soon.

Was he worried the Warriors would interpret what he'd written correctly? Yes. And no. It wasn't his place to fret about how each of their letters would be received. His job was to write them. And pray they would hear the Spirit's voice as they took in the contents and then decided how to act on the information.

He sighed and set the pen down. *Someday soon.* The words circled his mind like a blue heron circling high above a lake, watching, waiting to streak down, strike hard, and snatch a fish from the water. Years of life left in this mortal body? Yes. He felt it. Which made the letters unnecessary. So why did he feel compelled to write them?

He slumped back in his chair and sighed. One more letter to write, and it wouldn't be recorded with pen and paper. He walked outside and vowed to finish it, then put all the letters in the box before dawn crept across his windowsill.

FIFTEEN

On Tuesday morning, Brandon drove east on I-90 toward the little town of Hyak on the top of Snoqualmie Pass. His seven-year-old mountain bike, which had logged maybe seventeen miles on it, sat tied to the top of his Toyota Tundra. He needed to get away. Think. Do something metaphorical and physical at the same time.

Should he go to Well Spring with the others? After yesterday's weird display of God's love down at Pike Place Market, Brandon's definite no had turned into a definite maybe.

He needed to figure it out. Figure himself out. Let Reece and the others know if he was going this week or not. So he was about to head into the darkness to see if there was any light at the end of the tunnel. Literally.

He would take a ride on the John Wayne Trail, the perfect adventure for a mid-July Seattle day. The mountain bike trail was a stretch he could hop onto just west of Hyak. A few minutes' ride would take him to a two-mile train tunnel first carved into the Cascade Mountains back in the early nineteen hundreds. Over two hundred thousand hikers and bikers went through it every year, and Brandon figured since it was only twelve miles from his home, it was about time he partook of an adventure in his own backyard.

He stopped at the entrance and looked at the archway. The

tunnel had closed in January of '09 for eleven months because chunks of concrete had started raining down from the ceiling. But it had been fully repaired. Supposedly. He laughed to himself. If this was the way God wanted him to go—so be it.

He coasted into the tunnel and came to a stop twenty yards inside. The light from behind him still gave a smattering of light here, but twenty yards ahead there was only blackness. Wow. Only two miles long and he was freaking out. He needed to get it together. But it was a perfect analogy for his life. No light. Only darkness ahead. And only a tiny bulb on his head that he hoped wouldn't wink out halfway through. Should he go back to see if he had another flashlight in his trunk?

No.

The voice of the Spirit was soft, but the word was clear. He needed to get going.

As he eased forward it felt like he was entering the Mines of Moria in *The Lord of the Rings.* Should he stop? Should he avoid the trolls while he still could? Ridiculous. He was going through. He flipped on his helmet light and was surprised how little of it penetrated the darkness. Brandon turned and looked back, and the sunshine seemed to invite him to return to the entrance. It felt strangely like a tug-of-war. What was wrong with him?

He pushed off and slowly pedaled deeper into the tunnel. The tunnel curved slightly to his left, and in a few minutes the remaining light from the tunnel entrance was gone. Utter darkness. Apparently he picked the right analogy. Headlamp wasn't nearly bright enough. Should have brought a spotlight.

He'd heard a pinprick of light from the other end of the tunnel could be seen, but either his eyes weren't working like they used to or someone had turned off the sun at the other end. Brandon pedaled on, listening for sounds of other riders or walkers and hearing nothing but the spin of his tires on the asphalt.

How long had he been under the mountain? It felt like days when in reality it had probably only been ten minutes. Brandon guessed he was doing five miles per hour, which meant he should cover the length of the tunnel in another ten or twelve minutes. He should have brought a watch.

Finally. He saw light far in front of him. And whatever was at the far entrance appeared in the opening in the shape of a cross. Amen. He was ready to get back into the light.

He pumped his pedals till his quads burned and the opening grew larger every second. As he exited four minutes later, a palpable weight rose off him. He'd never been afraid of the dark—but then again, he'd never been in a pitch-black tunnel two miles long.

Brandon coasted to a stop and gazed down the trail that ran straight ahead. The clouds he'd seen when he entered the tunnel had left, and the sun was out in full force. He looked back at the tunnel and into the darkness. He'd been inside for probably twenty-five minutes. What would it have been like to work for years inside the mountain?

A lone biker sat on the edge of the trail, his arms around his legs. He looked to be in his early thirties. A dark-green backpack sat next to him, and as Brandon's brakes squealed, the man turned. He stared at Brandon, nodded, then turned back around.

Brandon set his bike down and ambled toward the man. "How're you doing?"

"Me?" The man got to his feet and brushed dirt off his dark-gray biking shorts. "Really good, thanks. If life got any better it'd probably take two of me to handle it."

"Nice line." Brandon glanced behind him. "Did you come through the tunnel, or are you about to go through?"

The man pointed west away from the tunnel, down the gravel road. "I came up the trail, so I'm about to go through. My first time."

"Darker in there than I thought. I'd heard you could see light from the other end, so I figured I wouldn't need that strong a light. Wrong. I almost went back to my car to see if I had an extra flashlight. Only would have taken ten or eleven minutes, but I had this weird feeling I wasn't supposed to. Once I got to the heart of the

tunnel, I wished I would have ignored the feeling and gone back."
Brandon laughed.

"So it was good?"

"It's a rush. But not sure you'd want to turn off your light when
you're in there all alone."

"That'd feel like death, I'm guessing." The man cocked his head
and gazed at Brandon in a way that was ... off.

Brandon stared at the man, and as he did a song began to play in
his head. *Here we go again.* At first there was only music, no words.
Great crashing cymbals and soaring violins filled Brandon's heart,
and then the other instruments slipped away till all that remained
was a piccolo playing a song that could turn a desert into an ocean.

The second movement of the piece started, and as it did Brandon's
mind filled with cascading images of the man sitting next to him. Not
good. If the images were from God, God would have to show up and
do something powerful. Brandon waited for the words of the song to
come, and when they did the images he'd seen all made sense.

Life is stolen, lives are shaken, so deep and to the core,
Pain is spreading, his life is shredding, this is eternal war,
Fear has crushed him, horrors rushed him, illusions, but so real,
He needs awaking, not this taking, with blood about to spill,
Daughters yearning, the future burning, before their sun can shine,
Grant him grace, extend our mercy, a touch of the divine.

A few minutes later the song ended. It didn't take someone with
the professor's brain to figure what this guy was about to do. How
was Brandon supposed to get into this? With Sandra, Dana had been
there to break the ice. Here he was dealing with a total stranger.
"Hey, pal, don't kill yourself, okay?" probably wouldn't be the most
effective intro. Cold sweat broke out on his forehead.

"I don't suppose you heard that?" Brandon asked before he could
stop himself.

"Heard what?"

"Nothing." He held out his hand to the man. "I'm Brandon, by the way."

"Good to meet you. I'm Garen." The man shook Brandon's hand.

"Is this a solo trip? Any wife or kids still coming up the trail?"

"Nope, all by myself today, but I am married. For almost seven years and not even a hint of itching going on." Garen scratched his forearm and grinned.

"Nice." Brandon swallowed hard and tried to smile.

"Plus two of the most gorgeous daughters you'll ever set eyes on. They're just six and four, but I still oil up my shotgun every other Saturday night. I'll be ready for those boys who'll be sure to be coming over when they reach the teen years." He winked. "What do you do?"

"I'm kind of a musician."

"A songwriter?"

"I do write songs."

"I figured you probably weren't on the singing end of things with a voice like that." The man smiled. "Unless the Bob Dylan style is making a comeback."

"Not that I know of. No, I don't sing much anymore." Brandon rubbed his throat. "Hey, Garen, are you a Beatles fan?"

"Kind of. I know some of their songs."

"A friend of mine loves 'em. You know the song 'Yesterday'? It's the most covered song in the history of music. Do you know how McCartney came up with it? Apparently he woke up one morning with the song in his head. The whole melody was there and he had no idea where it came from. He thought he'd heard it somewhere and asked around to see if he'd picked it up unconsciously from someone else. But he didn't. It was his. From a dream. *Boom.* Just appeared in his head as if from nowhere."

"Didn't know that."

Brandon picked up a piece of old wood—probably off the old railroad trestle. "I can relate to that story."

"How's that?"

"Same thing's been happening to me lately."

"Getting songs like that, you mean? In your dreams?"

"Not in my dreams, but yeah, I'm having songs kinda pop into my brain, I guess you could say." Brandon grabbed his knees and squinted down at the river below them. *Keep going. You haven't scared the guy off yet.* "And sometimes it happens at the weirdest times. Like after I've ridden through an old abandoned tunnel on the John Wayne Trail."

"Okaaay." The man drew out the word, but the look on his face said he would humor Brandon at least a little longer. "So what kind of songs do you get?"

"Most of the time they're about specific people."

"I'm not sure why I'm asking this because I think I already know the answer, but why are you telling me this?"

"I think I might have just heard a song about you, and I want to tell you about it, but I don't want the idea to freak you out."

"You don't even know me."

"Yeah, I know. But just like James Paul McCartney had this song pop into his head unannounced, I had a song pop into my head unannounced just now. And like I said, I have this strange feeling it might be about you."

"All right." Garen scooted a few inches to the left and narrowed his eyes.

"And I'm thinking I'd like to try it out on you, you know. Sing a few lines and see what you think."

Garen craned his neck in all directions as if looking for something. "The cameras are trained on me right now, aren't they? Are you like some bizarre magician or mentalist? Undercover weirdo?"

"Look, you say the word and I'll get back on my bike and get out of here right now."

"This is too strange."

"I know. And it's going to get stranger."

"How?"

"I think the reason the song popped into my head is something or someone much bigger than me is behind it." Brandon stared at the man. Were those tears?

Garen dropped his head and mumbled, "Yeah, why not? Sing me your song."

When Brandon finished he turned to Garen. The man's head was in his hands. "Who are you?" Garen looked up and wiped his red eyes.

"A man. A friend maybe. Most of the time I'm not sure anymore."

The man stared at Brandon long past uncomfortable. Tears continued to stream down his face. A few other bikers passed them, but if Garen noticed he didn't give any indication.

"I had one goal when I came up here today." Garen picked up a rock next to him and tossed it over the edge of the bank toward the river. "Only one." He reached inside his pack and lifted out a pistol and held the gun up to his head.

"I was going to end it. Ride five minutes or so into the tunnel, get off my bike, and *boom*. Good-bye." He lowered the gun to the gravel between them but kept his forefinger on the trigger. Brandon could see the safety was off.

"I was counting down from sixty to zero. When I reached three I was going to head for the tunnel and get it over with. Do you know what number I was on when you came pedaling up?"

Brandon shook his head.

"Three." The man wiped his nose. "I'm kinda glad you didn't go back to your car for that extra light. You know?"

Brandon stared at the man and gave a slow nod.

"Please take that." Garen pulled his finger from the trigger, set the gun down between them, and patted it.

Brandon slid his hand over the gun, lifted it, and set it down on his other side.

The man smiled. "You're not a gun guy, are you?"

"Not so much." Brandon chuckled. "Could you tell from the fear in my eyes or the sudden rivers of sweat pouring off my forehead?"

"And the way you picked it up." Garen tilted his head back and closed his eyes. "You know, at first I wasn't going to stop here. But at the last second I decided I would and take a moment to burn the memory of my wife and daughters into my mind." He turned and squinted against the sunshine. "Just in case there really is a heaven. I want to remember them."

"What happened?"

Garen closed his eyes and pressed his lips together so hard his face shook. "I had an affair. I can't tell my wife. It would destroy her."

"And leaving her like this won't?"

Garen opened his eyes and laughed, a sad little laugh that said killing himself was worse. "Yeah, it's more selfish this way, I suppose. This is crazy, but your song did whatever it was designed to do. I'm going to have a conversation I swore I would never have."

"Do you really have a shotgun?"

Garen shook his head and tossed another small stone over the side of the bank.

Brandon watched it splash into the stream. "Probably a good thing."

"I agree."

"Can I pray for you?"

"Pray?" Garen gave Brandon a crooked smile. "I liked the song. But I'm not much of a praying sort."

"You don't have to say a thing. And you don't have to agree with a single word. Just listen."

"Yeah. Okay."

After he finished, Garen wiped his eyes again. "You're a preacher, huh?"

Brandon smiled at the idea. He supposed in some ways he was a preacher. "No, not like you're thinking of it. Like I said, just someone who loves songs. Just someone Jesus knows."

"Do you think he knows me?"

"Without question." Brandon laughed and pulled a scrap of

paper out of his day pack and wrote his number on the old Red Robin receipt. "Anytime day or night, you call me, okay? I'm there."

Brandon got back on his bike and pushed off. Just before he entered the tunnel, Garen called for him to stop.

"Hey, just wondering. You ever thought about being a singer? Your voice is pretty rough when you talk, but when you sing . . . wow."

Brandon shook his head and smiled. "Stay strong, Garen. He sees you out of the corner of his eye, and his eye will be on you the rest of your days."

On the way home Brandon tried to sing, but his voice was as bad as it had ever been. But this time it didn't matter. Before he reached home he'd left a message on Reece's cell phone and on Doug's. Both were the same: "I'm going to Well Spring."

SIXTEEN

"IT'S TIME FOR US ALL TO GO IN TOGETHER."

Doug clasped his hands and leaned his head back as they sat around the fire pit at Well Spring on Friday evening. When he brought his head back down, the look on his face was more intense than Dana had ever seen it. This was a man ready for war. "We need this foray into the spiritual realms if we are to be ready for Zennon and his army when he launches his final assault."

Battle. Army. War. Dana shook her head. That's all Reece and Doug had said to them for the past few weeks. Nothing more. Not any details of where or how or when Zennon would attack or what each of their roles would be in it. They'd said Brandon's part was critical. But wouldn't all their parts be critical? And why hold back the information if they knew more than they'd told? Because they didn't know? Or because they didn't want to tell Marcus, Brandon, and her?

She glanced outside as dusk brought darkness down on the ranch. She tried to shake the feeling that the fading light was only from the day slipping away and not from another kind of darkness come upon them. She should feel hopeful. Something had convinced Brandon to join them here, and he seemed even more settled than when he'd sung the song for Sandra. But Dana didn't feel hope. Only dread that hung on her like a watermelon-sized stone.

"When is this battle coming? And what is it going to look like?

93

I don't understand why you're not telling us. And why haven't you read this new prophecy to us?"

Doug answered by standing and walking over to the couch and sitting next to her. He ran his hand over the top of his gray hair and turned to Reece. "What do you think?"

Reece nodded. Doug nodded back and pulled a folded piece of tan paper from his pocket.

WHEN IT IS TIME, YOU WILL JOIN THEM,
THE FOUR; THE TEMPLE, THE LEADER, THE TEACHER,
AND THE SONG,
THEY WILL NEED YOUR STRENGTH FOR THEIR LAST
BATTLE TOGETHER,
FOR THEIR GREAT ENEMY IS MOUNTING A FINAL
STRIKE AGAINST THEM AND WILL HOLD NOTHING BACK,
AND YOU WILL STEP BOLDLY BEFORE THE TEMPLE
AND HE WILL RECEIVE YOU,
AND YOU MUST TAKE THE LEADER INTO THE GATE-
WAY OF DEATH,
AND IN THE GATEWAY ONE WILL REMAIN, WHICH
WILL BRING GREAT SORROW, BUT SET IN MOTION THAT
WHICH MUST BE,
AND YOU WILL EMBRACE THE TEACHER FOR HE IS
THE FRIEND OF THE RESTORER,
AND ONE YOU WILL TRAIN WHEN THEY ASK IT OF
YOU—AND ONLY THAT ONE WILL YOU TRAIN,
YOU ARE A WARRIOR OF WARRIORS, LIVE IN THE
TRUTH OF WHO YOU ARE,
AND RIDE WITH THE WIND.

No one spoke. Doug leaned back on the couch; Marcus and Brandon stared at him with narrowed eyes as the words of the prophecy settled like weights onto Dana's soul. *"Take the Leader into the gateway of death"?*

Brandon finally broke the silence. "No one is taking Dana through some gateway."

Reece shook his head. "No, they are not."

"But if that thing is true—"

"It isn't clear that the Leader is the one who will stay in the gateway." Reece stood.

"Then who is the one—?"

"We don't know that 'great sorrow' means death."

Brandon stood as well. "It's a pretty good guess, bub!"

"My friends," Doug said.

Marcus opened his palms. "And who is this warrior the prophecy speaks of?"

"Friends," Doug repeated.

"I'd like to get back to this gateway of death someone is supposed to take me through." Dana leaned forward.

"Friends!" Doug stood, and all of them went silent and focused their gaze on him. "It is time to go in. Trust now. He holds us all in the center of his hand."

Doug sat again and patted the back of her hand like a grandfather and it helped. A little. But not enough. Going in? After hearing that? It felt off. More than off, but when Doug offered his hand, she took it, as did Brandon on Doug's other side. As soon as Marcus and Reece joined hands, Well Spring vanished and her vision went dark. But a moment later she streaked toward a wall of stars so thick, she didn't see how they would get through it. The sensation of her spirit accelerating faster than her mind could grasp wrapped itself around her, and her worry melted away. Joy flooded every microscopic part of her being and she wished for the ride to last for hours.

The five of them slalomed through the stars like a galactic skier racing near the speed of light, but too soon they slowed and their trajectory changed. When she felt ground beneath her feet, Dana expected her breathing to come in gasps, but all that came out was laughter.

"I never want to get used to that." Brandon grinned.

Dana looked into his eyes and nodded. His smile was almost back to being the old Brandon's. Almost. Something was missing and she could pretend she didn't know what it was. He missed her. Whenever she looked at him, she saw his—should she call it love?—for her. She saw it right now. It was unsettling and reassuring at the same time. Because he did love her. And how could she deny she wanted to be loved? By him. She *wanted* to be noticed. Fought for, as he'd already proven he was willing to do.

So what was wrong with her? Why wasn't what he'd already shown her enough? Was it time to give in? Maybe. No! It wasn't. She shook the arguments from her mind. This wasn't the time or place to try to untangle the spaghetti-like thoughts twisting through her mind. *Let it go.*

She turned to look at Reece. The big man stared back at her with his brilliant blue eyes once again restored as they always were in the spiritual realms. He wasn't any less in the physical world but here he could see, and she missed being drawn into his eyes like a father draws a daughter.

"It's good to see you, Dana." He smiled and she returned his with one of her own.

They stood in the center of a quaint, open-air town square paved with thick gray cobblestones. A soft wind swirled through the square and brought the smell of burning leaves. There was no sound, and gray clouds that matched the color of the stones at their feet were washed across the sky.

"Where are we?" Brandon asked.

"So it begins." Doug sighed and his eyes took on a sadness so deep, tears rose inside Dana. Something was very, very wrong about being here, and the joy she'd felt during the journey was gone.

"What begins?" Marcus shifted his weight back and forth on his slender frame. Concern was etched into the professor's face, which probably matched her own. Whatever she felt, it was obvious Marcus felt it too. She turned and looked at Reece. Confusion was splayed on his face as he stepped toward Doug.

"We shouldn't be here, friend." Reece grabbed his beat-up dark-tan Stetson and shoved it down farther on his head. "I'm getting an extremely bad vibe about—"

Before Reece could finish, a noise like massive stones smashing into each other shot through the air around them. In the next instant the gray clouds turned darker. A smoky presence filled the edge of the square and moved toward them. Inky blackness swirled around the figure, then melted into a solid body. The demon they knew as Zennon.

His dark hair almost reached his thickly muscled shoulders. He stood fifty feet away from them, a mocking smile on his face. He'd changed. Far larger than the last time they'd seen him. Close to seven feet tall now. His features had grown sharp and even more handsome. But hard. His eyes darker, with an intensity that sent a chill through Dana. Seconds later three more demons—each a head taller than Zennon—appeared on his right and left.

"I didn't think you'd show, old man." The demon paced slowly in front of them.

"You can't win, Zennon." Doug's voice was calm. It was obvious he was somewhat surprised at the appearance of the demons but not entirely.

"Win what?"

"This war."

"The war? *The* war. You mean tossed into hell at the end of the age with all the others who decided to follow Lucifer? We will see, won't we? But that battle is centuries in the future. Right now, all I care about is this war between you and me and your pathetic Warriors Riding. This battle, here and now, which I can most assuredly win. A battle I am winning already." Zennon pulled a long black sword from his belt. "Are you ready to die, Doug?"

"If he wills it." A sword shimmering with blue light appeared in Doug's hands.

"Then let us begin."

Reece stepped in front of Doug and took him by the shoulders. "What are you doing?"

"What I have been called to do. Nothing more."

"This isn't what I expected."

"Nor I."

"He said he didn't think you'd show, like you knew you were coming here."

"He might have known. I did not."

"You didn't know we were coming to face Zennon?"

"Not us. Me." Doug drew a deep breath. "That part is clear to me now. But no, I didn't know this is where the Spirit was going to bring us. Just that I was to follow his lead."

"Great. Lead followed. Now let's get out of here. I have a feeling it would take all of us to defeat these three, and I don't think we're ready for this kind of battle."

"Leave? No. Not yet." Doug placed his hand on Reece's cheek. "It is all right, friend."

"It's not. He's far stronger than we've ever seen him. Can't you sense it? The enemy has given him more authority and power. More skill."

"There is no power greater than the One."

"He's going to kill you, Doug."

"If the Lord wills it."

"You can't die." Reece's face went pale.

"'Every man dies. Not every man really lives.'" Doug smiled. "From *Braveheart*."

Zennon scraped the tip of his sword along the stones at his feet and raised his voice.

"This has been so touching, but enough."

Doug raised his sword and stepped toward the demon, but Reece grabbed his arm. "I can't let you do this."

"You must. Do not intervene. It will be all right, I promise. Trust me."

Pain was evident on Reece's face, but he nodded. Doug covered Reece's hand with his own and eased it away, then strode toward the center of the square to meet Zennon. When they both reached the middle of the cobblestones, they circled each other twice before Zennon's blade flashed toward Doug.

Doug blocked it easily, then stepped back two paces and raised his left hand. A ball of blinding white light was unleashed and streaked across the six feet between them. But before it reached the demon, Zennon raised a hand and the ball exploded in a shower of red light.

"Not bad, Lundeen. I see you're going to make this last longer than I thought you would. Maybe stretch it out to thirty or forty seconds instead of five."

"You won't win, Zennon. This battle or any other. Your destruction is coming and the power of the Christ will overcome you once again."

His face contorted with rage, Zennon leapt toward Doug and swept his sword in a wide arc. "Now!" the demon screamed as the blow slammed into Doug's sword. The impact sent Doug staggering back but he kept on his feet.

Zennon strode toward him to press the moment and unleashed another three strokes of his dark sword: at Doug's head, his legs, his body. Each time, Doug blocked the assault, but each time with less speed.

"Getting weak this quickly, old man?"

Zennon didn't wait for an answer and rained blows down on Doug from above, then the side, then straight ahead. The clash of their swords rang through the square like a twisted symphony of cymbals and both began to breathe heavily.

But suddenly Doug spun to his left with a supernatural speed and sliced at Zennon's right side. The demon blocked the attack but not fully, and the blow tore into the upper part of Zennon's leg. Dark-red blood spilled out and the demon's face turned black.

He roared with fury and attacked Doug again. But his rage made his assault less disciplined, and Doug not only parried the demon's blows, he drew blood twice more. Once on Zennon's right arm and once on his left hip.

Hope rose in Dana, but then she looked at Reece. He sucked in rapid breaths as he clenched and unclenched his hands. Fear radiated from his face and eyes, and in that moment Dana realized Doug couldn't win alone. Even though Reece's mentor had drawn first, second, and even third blood, his strength was waning, and if Doug's strikes had hurt Zennon, there was no visible evidence to back it up. Sweat glistened on Zennon's body and face, but he seemed just as fast and strong as when the battle started.

"Enough." Zennon grinned, wiped blood from his thigh, and licked it from his palm. "Does not taste the way yours will, Lundeen." The demon raised his sword and raced toward Doug.

A battle cry erupted from Reece's mouth and he sprinted toward Zennon, but the two demons with him stepped in front of Zennon and drew their swords in perfect synchronization. Reece didn't slow. Just before reaching them, he spun and whipped his sword around his body like a discus thrower.

The move startled the two demons, and when Reece's blow struck, it knocked the sword out of one of the demon's hands and sent the other one back two steps. Reece didn't hesitate. He drove his sword into the heart of the demon that had dropped his sword, and as if it were one fluid motion he slashed at the throat of the other demon. But Reece's blow was blocked as the two circled each other.

A thick voice came from the demon. "The chance to take down the mighty Reece Roth." The demon grinned and stepped toward Reece, his sword swinging from one side of his body to the other.

"Your last chance." The instant Reece spoke the words, he feinted high with his sword, and the demon took the bait. Reece dropped to a knee and his sword blurred from the speed with which he wielded it. The blade severed half the demon's torso and he collapsed onto the cobblestones.

Reece spun to face Zennon, the Temple's eyes on fire. "C'mon, Zennon, take me down."

"Nice try." Zennon laughed at Reece but kept his eyes fixed on

Doug. "I could so easily, you know. But this is not the time. Now say good-bye to your dearest friend."

Reece leapt toward Zennon, but before he'd covered half the distance, Doug and the demon vanished.

"No!" Reece leapt to the spot where they'd disappeared, bowed his head, and went completely still. A few seconds later he rose back up. "There." He pointed across the square at an eight-foot-tall, thick bronze gate embedded in a stone wall at least forty feet high. "We have to get through."

He started to sprint toward the gate and the rest of them followed, but an instant later a swarm of twenty or thirty demons appeared in their path. Reece turned his head and shouted to Brandon, Marcus, and her. "We have to take them out fast!"

Swords appeared in all their hands and none of them hesitated. In less than two minutes, every demon had been destroyed. Reece tossed his sword to the ground and it clattered on the stones at their feet. He took six massive strides toward the gate and glanced at his hands. Instantly two fireballs appeared. But their intensity went far beyond the ones Brandon or she had ever conjured in the past. Both were white-hot and the heat coming off them stung her face.

The big man hurled both fireballs at the gate at the same time with a speed that stunned Dana. They exploded into the gate, and the structure shuddered like paper in a strong wind and the stones shook under their feet. While the fire still spread across the gate, another two streaked through the air. As two more appeared in Reece's hands, he glanced at Brandon and her as if to say, "What are you waiting for?"

In the next fifteen seconds, twenty-six fireballs detonated against the bronze gate. Although it shuddered violently each time, when the flames and smoke cleared, the gate still stood strong.

Reece closed his eyes. "What do we need, Lord?" After only a few seconds his head snapped up and he riveted his gaze on Brandon. "Song, you must sing. It's the only weapon that will take down the gate in time. Sing!"

Brandon staggered forward as if he knew he couldn't refuse. "But . . . no, I can't—"

"You must." Reece's eyes were ice. "We have to get to him."

"My voice is gone."

"It doesn't matter. Sing anyway."

"I can't," Brandon rasped out. "Don't you understand? I can't sing with my own voice. All I've been able to sing are the songs I've heard from the Spirit, that have been given to—"

Reece grabbed Brandon by the shoulders. "But in here you can. You have to be able to. If you don't, Doug will die."

"My . . ."

"Now!" Reece screamed the word and his face turned red with the effort.

Brandon started to sing, but it wasn't with the stunning voice Dana had heard in downtown Seattle. It wasn't even the voice he had before the demon had put a jagged gash in his throat. It scraped out of his mouth and the sound made her gasp. It was horrible. Ten seconds of mutilated melody eked out of Brandon's mouth.

Brandon stopped and then tried again. Another ten seconds passed, but this time his voice was even worse. He tried once more, but after a few seconds Brandon stopped. Reece's eyes were frantic. He stared at Brandon and was about to speak when a thick voice oozed out from behind the gate.

"If you want in so bad, then join us."

A great creaking sound filled the air and they all spun toward the gate. It quivered for a few seconds and then swung open. They rushed through it. Doug lay alone in the middle of a small, raised wooden stage twenty feet away. His body convulsed and blood covered his clothes. His eyes were closed and a sheen of sweat covered his face. His gray hair was splayed across his forehead. Zennon was gone.

Reece reached him first and clumped to his knees on the rough wood. "Doug!"

The only response was a soft moan.

Reece glanced at them. "Join hands, we have to get him out of here."

They slid back into their bodies at Well Spring, and Reece lurched up from his chair and crumpled to one knee on the stones around the fire pit. He staggered to his feet, stepped around the pit, and took Doug in his arms, glancing wildly at the rest of them.

"Talk to me!" Reece continued to spin his head back and forth. "I can't see how bad it is. Only darkness near his chest. Tell me."

Dana knelt next to Doug and fought back tears. "I think his ribs are crushed. And he's bleeding from a deep wound over his heart and on his head. Reece, I think he's dy—"

"No. Don't speak it. We have to get him to St. Vincent."

"No," Doug's quiet voice sputtered. "That's not needed." Blood bubbles spilled over his lips. "It has arrived, Reece, in all its glory."

"What?" Reece's voice shook.

Doug laughed, a weak laugh that made the blood bubbles pop. "My chariot. The one taking me to heaven."

"No, we'll teleport to the hospital."

Doug gazed at Brandon. "This is not your fault."

Brandon's body heaved with sobs. "I'm sorry, Doug. I'm so sorry. I should have been able to—"

"No, it's a lie." Doug gasped for air. "Don't give in to it. Promise me."

Brandon nodded, but his face said he would have a difficult time keeping the promise.

"When the time comes you must sing with everything inside you. Your whole life will be in that moment and the time is coming soon."

Doug's body was racked with coughs. Then he tilted his head slightly toward Reece. "Don't hold it against him, friend."

And with that, Doug Lundeen was gone.

✠ ✠ ✠

The next morning, Dana woke at first light and slipped into a thick gray sweatshirt and matching sweats. The air bit into her face, but it didn't occupy her thoughts for more than a second. They were consumed with questions about Doug's death. They'd always been stronger than Zennon in the past. Why not this time? It didn't make sense. Doug was stronger than any of them. He should have been able to break free. His death was a dream. A nightmare. In a few seconds she would walk into the main cabin and find Doug sitting in front of the fireplace with a volume of George MacDonald's *Unspoken Sermons* in his hands and a giant cup of tea next to him on the coffee table.

Reece only spoke four sentences the entire day, and all of them were directed at her even though Brandon and Marcus were both in the room when he said them.

"I've talked to Doug's family. The funeral will be in ten days in Colorado Springs. I'm assuming you and Marcus will be there. I don't care what Brandon does."

SEVENTEEN

"Have you seen enough, Master, to set me free from the authority of this cretin?"

Zennon bowed and kept his head down as the rest of the council muttered obscenities. Some directed at Zennon, some at Caustin. All of them felt the issue was not worth taking the time to address in a council meeting. But Zennon had pushed for the audience. Sitting under the imbecilic Caustin for one more moment was like being doused with the Holy One's fire.

"He's done nothing!" Caustin slammed his hand onto the table.

"Doug Lundeen is dead." Zennon rose and faced Caustin. "Reece Roth blames the musician for the death, which will drive a wedge between them and create a rift nearly impossible to breach."

"So what?" Caustin stuck out his thick chest. "So what!" He turned to the Master. "He kills Lundeen and thinks the battle is over?"

"No, fool." Zennon gripped his sword. "It has just started. But everything is moving exactly as I have foreseen and will not stop till they are all destroyed and hundreds of thousands of the Warriors' followers have been turned."

"What of the new prophecy?"

"It is nothing."

"You do not know that. If they—"

"Enough." The low, guttural voice of the Master turned Zennon and Caustin toward the front of the table. "You both waste our time with your petty arguing. There will be restraint between the two of you till this is finished or you will suffer greatly." The Master paused. "Zennon, the destruction of Lundeen is to be commended. Until your next report, leave us."

"Yes, my Master." Zennon left the room, his body shaking. Not the outcome he'd anticipated. He'd done enough to warrant release from the fool's authority. The door of the council chamber shut, and he leaned back against the wall and closed his eyes and tried to quiet the rage that surged through his veins.

An instant later his windpipe was cut off and he whipped open his eyes. Caustin had his hand around Zennon's neck and a thin short blade descended toward his eyes. Zennon blocked the blade and slammed his fist into Caustin's nose and his grip loosened.

Half a second later Zennon held his knife to Caustin's throat and pressed it deep into his skin. "You think yourself a warrior near my skill. You are wrong. The only reason I won't gut you right now is because the Master would want answers as to why I disobeyed him."

Caustin growled. "The council is on my side. The only thing that holds them back from letting me annihilate you is the death of Lundeen. That's nothing. He was old. He wasn't the one of the new prophecy. His death will only rally them—"

Zennon pressed the blade deeper and pulled it a millimeter to the right. A dark line of blood sprang out on Caustin's neck. "Talk less, Caustin. You'll live longer."

"I suggest you make some real progress before you try to speak nonsense to the council again."

Zennon shoved Caustin to the ground. The day was coming when his blood would flow freely. But far from soon enough.

EIGHTEEN

DANA'S MIND COULDN'T GRASP IT. SHE SAT NEXT TO REECE in a church on the outskirts of Colorado Springs and tried to accept the fact Doug was gone. The heat of the early August afternoon was winning the war over the church air-conditioner, and she wiped her forehead.

Dana glanced at Reece on her right. If she was in a daze, he was probably comatose. His mentor and best friend gone. Why? Why would God send them into a place for Doug to be killed? It made no sense.

She looked again at Reece and then pressed into him and wrapped her arms around his shoulders. "Would it be terribly cliché to say Doug is at this moment being flooded in inexpressible joy? That our mourning is not for him but for us?"

"Yes, it would be. Horribly."

"I'm going to say it anyway."

"I'm glad you did." Reece gave a sad smile.

"It seemed like he almost knew it might happen."

"It doesn't lessen the pain." Reece drew in a deep breath. "But you're right. He's dancing now. His body is restored and life has come into every fiber of his being. And we'll be okay."

Reece's words floated down on her like snow, melting away before she could let them sink in. *Would* they be okay? Doug had been so instrumental in everything they'd done. And what about Brandon? He had just started to show flashes of becoming himself again and then this happens? And why couldn't he sing? What happened to him in there? And how much of his despair and inability to act had to do with her rebuff of his attempt to rekindle their romance? No. She wouldn't let herself take even one step down that road.

"Now, one of Doug's friends would like to say a few words."

The pastor's voice snapped Dana out of her contemplation, and she watched a heavy-footed Reece trudge to the podium. He stood for a good twenty seconds before speaking.

"My name is Reece Roth, and I had the great and humbling honor to be able to call Doug Lundeen my friend. Doug did not use that word lightly, nor do I today. For Doug, when he called someone friend, it meant he was willing to lay his life down for you."

Reece's head tipped forward and he paused. "Many of you here today I know. Many I do not. But it is not a cliché to say all of us—known or unknown—are bound together this day by an extraordinary man. I've come to learn that Doug Lundeen had the ability to make everyone he grew close to feel like he was their best friend. If the men here were of the marrying age, my guess is Doug would be the best man at every one of our weddings."

Reece continued his heart-stirring eulogy, but Dana couldn't focus. Where would the Warriors go from here? Until now, she hadn't realized the confidence Doug had given her. Knowing Reece had someone he trusted and could rely on for wisdom with every decision made her feel like she was on a solid bridge as they crossed the canyons of their destiny. Now it felt like they were walking on a rope bridge with most of the slats missing.

The rest of the service was a blur, and soon Reece, Marcus, Brandon, and she followed the other mourners into the church's large reception hall. More precisely, she and Marcus followed. Brandon seemed to drag himself into the hall. And he kept a sizable distance between Reece and him. It was obvious Doug's death tore at Brandon like a saw across his heart. She knew because she knew him. And she knew that while his mind and heart were buried with guilt over what he hadn't been able to do, an equal measure of another emotion stabbed him which was even more brutal. Worthlessness. If he couldn't even be the Song inside spiritual realms, what good was he to the Warriors? She'd tried to talk to him about it outside in the foyer before the service had started, but the conversation was decidedly one sided.

"Stay in the truth. Reece is wrong to blame you for Doug's—"

"Sure."

"It's true. You tried to sing with everything in you. I saw it."

"Okay." Brandon studied the floor.

"Why can't you believe that?"

"Okay."

"Not okay." Dana yanked Brandon's arm and he looked up at her. "Reece is only blaming you because he's trying not to blame himself. He thinks he acted too late. He thinks he should have engaged with Zennon right from the—"

"What am I, Dana? Tell me." She stared at him but didn't respond. "Answer? I'm nothing." Brandon stepped back and looked at the cream-colored ceiling. "Worthless once again. Doug says I'm key to whatever Zennon has in store for us, but I'm not buying it."

"Are you kidding? Think about what you've done for Sandra, and Garen, and those people down in Edmonds."

"So what? Even if I sing a few songs of heaven for people, what happens when that's over? I want more of a life than just that."

Dana squeezed his arm. "You're not worthless. The enemy is trying to resurrect your old wound."

"Feels pretty new right now."

They'd talked more, but the conversation went in circles and nothing was close to resolved by the time they were ushered into the sanctuary.

Dana glanced around the reception hall. Poster-sized photos of Doug covered the walls, and it struck Dana how accomplished the man was—and how she had no idea of the things he had achieved. After the four of them meandered through the room for a while, chatting politely with people each of them knew, they gathered along one of the side walls and gazed out at the friends and family paying Doug last respects.

Dana turned to Reece. "I don't think I've ever asked how you and Doug first met."

Reece stood like stone. If he'd heard her he gave no indication.

"Reece?"

Again he didn't answer. His face turned forty-five degrees to the left as if his gaze was fixed on that side of the room.

"Reece?" She gave his arm a slight squeeze.

He started and turned. "I'm sorry, Dana. Did you say something?"

"Only three times." She rubbed his arm. "Are you okay? What are you . . . um . . . staring at?"

Reece bent down and lowered his voice. "Is there a woman on the far side of the room who is looking this direction? I think she's holding a cup of coffee or tea or punch and is by herself."

Dana scanned the wall in the direction Reece faced, and her gaze stopped on a woman who stood along the wall at the back of the hall. She wore a black gold-embroidered silk kimono, along with a crystal-embellished leather belt. Her white heels with black ankle straps looked like they might be Nicholas Kirkwood. She looked young, early twenties at the most, and Reece was right. She stared directly at them.

"Yes." Dana looked away. "She's Asian, dark hair almost to her shoulders, average height, thin frame. Attractive. And I'd describe her countenance as confident but subdued."

"Marcus?"

"Intelligent would be my first descriptor. And Dana's perception of confidence is accurate, I believe. This young woman stands alone in a gathering that is predicated upon interaction with fellow mourners, yet she shows no indication of being uncomfortable in her solitude."

Reece didn't ask Brandon for his impression.

"Why, pray tell, are we so interested in this female?" The professor pushed up his glasses.

"The aura surrounding her is striking. Bright gold light is radiating off of her like a fountain. But it's also tinged with hints of dark red. It's different from any other I've yet seen and definitely powerful."

"Is the aura a you're-on-our-side-powerful or a we-could-be-in-for-a-battle powerful?" Dana asked.

"I would guess the former."

"Do you believe it would be pertinent to implement an engagement strategy with her here and now?" Marcus said.

"One more time, Professor, for those of us with pea brains." Brandon snorted. "How many translators does Kat have to have to understand your dinner conversations?"

"I was simply asking if we should—"

"No. That was not simple." Brandon held up a finger. "Here's simple: 'Hey, think we should try to meet her?'"

Dana glared at Brandon and he glared back. It wasn't fair for him to take out his pain on Marcus by snarking at him.

"Is she still looking our direction?" Reece asked.

Dana glanced up. "Not only looking at us, she's coming this way."

The woman seemed to glide over the floor, and her shoes made no sound on the hardwood of the reception hall. She stopped a few feet in front of them and nodded at each of them before resting her gaze on Reece.

"Hello, Reece Roth."

Reece tilted his head as if trying to find a spiritual frequency that would show him more about this woman. "Have we met?"

"Yes, we have. But it was long ago. I've heard stories of you since I was a child and have continued to hear them into adulthood."

"From who?"

"A mutual friend."

"Does this friend have a name?"

Her eyes turned sad. "From Doug." She looked down. "I'm deeply sorry for your loss."

"Thank you." Reece extended his arms to either side. "These are my friends: Dana, Marcus, and Brandon."

"It is truly an honor." The woman nodded at each of them.

"Might I ask your name and how you knew Doug?"

"Of course. My name is Miyo." She bowed. "Doug was my—"

"Miyo?" Reece leaned forward. "Is it really you? But you're a little girl."

She smiled and her eyes almost closed. "I was, yes, certainly when we met, but now I've matured to the ripe old age of twenty-three."

"I'm . . . You . . . I remember you well. Has it been that long?" Reece rubbed his jaw. "It was astounding the spiritual maturity you had at that age. What were you when we met? Eleven?"

"Ten."

Reece went stiff. Likely because it was the same age as when his daughter, Willow, was murdered nearly three decades ago. But if he'd lost his composure, he regained it a moment later.

"Doug loved you very much."

"Yes, we were able to spend a good amount of time together as I grew up."

"Did he tell you about my sight? Do you know about—?"

"Yes. He spoke to me often about Warriors Riding and what the Spirit has done and is doing in the world through the four of the prophecy."

There was respect in Miyo's dark-brown eyes, and yet Dana instinctively knew this woman had a strength and self-assurance that was rare for someone her age.

"Did Doug continue to train you as you grew up?" Reece asked.

"Indeed." Miyo bowed again. "My grandfather taught me many astounding things."

The tone of her voice certainly wasn't one of arrogance, but it wasn't humble either. She might have been describing the weather.

"Are you in college?"

"I graduated from college when I was nineteen. Since then I've been working in the publishing industry."

"As?"

"An editor. For my father's small publishing house."

"Did Doug tell you he and I spoke recently about you coming to Well Spring someday?"

"He did tell me that, yes." She glanced at each of them.

Reece shifted his weight, then grew still, his spiritual eyes fixed on Miyo. "Were you aware that for the past six months he's been suggesting you join the ministry?"

"Yes." Miyo again glanced at the rest of them, not with a look that wanted their approval, but one of mere curiosity as to what they might think. "And what was your reaction to that suggestion, Reece?"

"I told him I thought you were too young, but it's something I might be open to, and we should talk about it again in a year or two."

"I see."

"But I believe you would benefit greatly from coming to and going through one of our training weeks at the ranch. There is much you could learn, I believe. After that we could talk again about the idea."

"I see," she said again and hesitated. "I appreciate your invitation to come to Well Spring."

"Will you come?"

+ + +

As the words left Reece's mouth, he was surprised by how much he wanted the answer to be yes. Probably because she was related to Doug. And if Doug had trained her, then they shared more than just a bloodline. There would be pieces of Doug throughout her soul, heart, and spirit.

Miyo was young, probably almost as green as Dana, Marcus, and Brandon had been when they first came to Well Spring. But that didn't matter. If Reece was honest, he would love having her as part of the Warriors. But that was his emotions talking. Wisdom would say get to know her first. See how she responded to a weekend of Well Spring training. And then explore the idea of her joining the others and him for greater things.

"My grandfather gave his heart to you." Miyo took Reece's hands. "Your friendship was one of the great treasures of his life here on earth. Because of this, I have a great love for you as well. I don't believe this is the last we will see of each other, Reece Roth. And I believe that next time will come very soon."

The red and gold glow around Miyo grew brighter, and a sense of joy and laughter seemed to spill off of her and surround him. But as he reached out his hand toward her to say good-bye, the glow around her vanished.

"Wait a minute, hold on, everybody," Brandon said.

Reece turned toward Dana. "Did she just—?"

"Yes, she did. Gone. And I think you know I don't mean she walked away. I'm assuming she used a technique we've all grown familiar with over the past year and a half."

Marcus chuckled. "It's apparent Doug taught Miyo more than just the rudimentary elements of the extraordinary spiritual life in his classroom."

"How much do you really know about her, Reece?" Dana asked.

"Doug said she was the most spiritually attuned person he'd ever met. And that I would benefit from knowing her. I scoffed at the idea at the time."

Marcus cocked his head. "After seeing that demonstration, I would have to conclude you've just entered a no-scoffing zone."

✞ ✞ ✞

An hour later the four gathered outside the church. "Thank you for coming. All of you." Reece didn't look at Brandon when he said it, but it was a start. Dana wanted to squeeze Brandon's hand as if to tell him Reece would come around, but she worried the signal would be crossed and he'd read something into the gesture she didn't mean. Or wasn't ready to mean.

They stood in silence for a minute before Reece turned and faced west. "I want us to stop by Well Spring before we head back to Seattle. There's something I believe we need to do all together. A place we need to go."

"And where would that be?" Marcus said.

"I think you can guess. We need refreshment. Hope. Restoration. A time of healing from the loss of our fellow Warrior. Direction from the Spirit on where we go from here."

Dana took Reece's hand and pretended she could grasp it hard enough to squeeze the sadness out of his voice. "I'm thinking you're thinking of taking us to a place you can't find on a map."

"That would be accurate." A sad but hopeful smile appeared on his face. "Let's go."

NINETEEN

IT WAS PROBABLY BRANDON'S IMAGINATION, BUT THE AIR felt heavy. His soul certainly did.

After a quick late dinner on Saturday, they gathered at Well Spring's fire pit and watched the flames shoot into the sky. The last time they'd sat around this pit they'd gone in with Doug, and his empty chair loomed large in Brandon's mind.

Reece said he was going to take them to a place of refreshment. That they needed it. Understatement of the year, probably the decade. But the way Reece had treated him since Doug's passing made Brandon wonder if coming to Well Spring had been the right decision. If he hadn't come, Doug might have still died, right?

But at least Reece wouldn't blame him for it and launch guilt at him like it was a spear. Doug said it wasn't Brandon's fault. But if not his, then whose? He should have been able to sing. He'd sung for the couple in Edmonds, for Sandra, and for Garen. So why couldn't he do it inside a spiritual realm?

Brandon shook his head. No. No more questions that were impossible to answer. He wasn't going to let the guilt take him. Dana was right about his role in Doug's death. He had done everything he could to sing. But that made it worse because his best effort amounted to nothing. Worthless.

And now they were gearing up for some massive assault from Zennon, and Brandon wouldn't be able to wield his greatest weapon against the demon because it had vanished. Great. Just spectacular.

"It is time." Reece raised his head and held out his hands to Marcus on his right and Dana on his left. Brandon didn't wonder why Reece had set it up this way. There was no way the big man would take Brandon's hand.

Moments later, the four stood on the shore of a small lake Brandon guessed to be a mile and a half long and half a mile wide. Rolling hills on the other side were spotted with tall pine trees and sparse patches of green shrubs and wildflowers. Directly across the lake, a large rocky hill fifteen hundred feet high shot into the sky with two lone pine trees sitting along the top of the ridge. The lake was glass and gave a perfect reflection of the hill and trees.

As he soaked in the view, peace settled on him even though he didn't deserve it.

It's my pleasure to give you my peace, Brandon. Take it in. All of it.

As contradictory as it was, the voice of the Spirit sounded in his mind both soft and loud at the same time. For the first time since Doug's fight with Zennon, Brandon let all thoughts slip away, and he stood and basked in the glory of God's creation. If only he could stay here forever.

To their left, far off in the distance, a series of mountains covered with a dusting of snow sat under a smattering of white clouds. The way the mountain ridges ran, Brandon saw what looked like the form of a lady lying on her back, her hair shooting out from her head, her legs raised slightly.

"Lady of the Lake." Brandon pointed at the ridgeline. "Can you see her?"

"You're right. I see her too." Dana laughed.

Marcus bit his upper lip and nodded. "Yes. I see her." He shifted his gaze from the lady to the rocky hill across from them and turned to Reece. "Over the years when you've encountered others in the spiritual realms, how often are they of the enemy and how often are they of God?"

"That's an intriguing question. I've never considered it." Reece looked down for a few moments, then raised his head. "I would say more often than not when I've met another being inside a soul or spiritual realm, they've been evil. Why do you ask?"

Marcus peered across the lake at the top of the ridge. "Because I think we are about to have one of said encounters with a visitor, and I would like to know if we need to be on guard or not."

Dana moved a few steps away from the others and shielded her eyes from the sunlight, and Brandon did the same. The professor was right. A tiny figure high above them strolled along the ridge to the right of one of the pine trees. From this distance it was impossible to tell if it was male or female.

"So you didn't give out an invitation for someone else to join our party?" Brandon said.

"No."

"I'm guessing this is one of those times where you'd like to be able to see with those spiritual eyes of yours and get a feel for what kind of Beach Boys music she's putting out."

"'Good Vibrations' by Brian Wilson, off *Pet Sounds,* 1966." A hint of a smile appeared on Reece's face as he answered Brandon. It vanished a moment later, but Brandon saw it. It was the first time Reece had given any kind of warmth toward him since Doug had died. It gave him hope. Exactly what Reece said they all needed.

"What are you sensing, Dana?" Reece asked.

"That whoever it is, it's female and not evil."

"Brandon?"

Again, hope stirred inside. The first time he'd asked Brandon's opinion on anything since the death almost two weeks back.

"That she knows us."

"Professor?"

"I would toss my proverbial hat into the same ring as Brandon. And then I'll go a step further and confess I have an educated guess as to her identity." The professor clasped his hands and stared at the figure and went silent.

"Hello?" Brandon smacked Marcus on the shoulder with the back of his hand. "Care to share it with the rest of the class?"

Marcus opened his mouth, but before he could speak, bright-green light flashed across the ridgeline and blocked the person from view. The same light flashed again an instant later, halfway between them and the ridge, and a final time right in front of them. When the light faded and their eyes readjusted, a woman stood in front of them, her face split by a thin smile.

Miyo. She glanced back over the lake to the ridge she'd come from. "Even more beautiful a view from this vantage point."

"What are you . . . How did you . . . get here?" Reece stood with hands on hips, surprise on his face mixed with a scowl.

"Don't look so stunned, Reece. You think you're the only one Doug taught how to travel within the spiritual realms?"

"I know there are others Doug trained and I know he trained you. What I'm surprised about is your ability to—" He stopped as if catching himself from stepping off a cliff.

"To what?"

Reece glanced at the ridge, then back to Miyo. "Seeing you move from there to here in the manner in which you did was . . . entertaining."

"More like a shock given the look on your face."

"Entertaining." Reece grimaced.

"Yes, of course." She grinned at him. "I take it you don't know how to travel like that. Which surprises me." Miyo spun in a half circle and her swirling black-and-sapphire top flowed around her like it was part of her body. Even Brandon knew her clothes were designer made. She glanced at each of them. "Teleporting in the physical world is a lot harder than doing it here."

"It's not something we've delved into at this point," Reece muttered.

"Is that a euphemism for 'I don't know how'?" She laughed, not in a mocking way, but one of playfulness. "I thought my grandfather would have taught you all his secrets."

"Apparently not." Reece stared at her.

"It seems he was holding out on you."

"I hardly think so."

"Then based on the experiential evidence, your thinking might not be completely accurate in this area." She smiled again and walked over to the trees and examined the fruit thoroughly before choosing an apple near the center of the tree. Miyo rubbed the apple on her dark-blue pants and took a bite.

"We can eat them?" Dana stared at Doug's granddaughter.

Miyo turned and smiled. "As you've no doubt heard from Reece or Doug, we are not human beings having a spiritual experience; we are spiritual beings having a human experience. This is our true nature. And yes, one day we will have resurrected bodies to go along with it, but just as wounds we receive here are carried into the physical world, many elements of the physical world and things we can do there are reflected here."

Brandon studied Reece's face. Again their mentor seemed surprised. Was this another new revelation for him?

None of them spoke, and after a few more moments of awkward silence, Miyo said, "Tell you what. I'm going to take a quick walk along the lake. You can talk about me behind my back, and after a short while I'll return and we can get down to business." She turned without waiting for a response and strolled down to the water's edge.

When she was out of earshot, Dana said, "Who is she? I mean, we know she's Doug's granddaughter, but I'm guessing you know more than that. Give us a little background."

"Doug's son married a woman from Japan when he was in the service. Miyo was born there along with a brother whom I've never met. The family moved to the US when Miyo was four or five, if I remember right, and they ended up a few hours from Doug and his wife. Doug took an interest in Miyo—said there was a connection immediately—and he always spoke her name with great tenderness, great affection, and great respect."

"Anything else?" Dana twirled her finger around a lock of her light-brown hair.

"That she was strong in the Spirit from a very young age. That if she stayed on the narrow path, she would be a formidable warrior."

"From what we've seen so far, that seems to be the case," Dana said.

"What do you think of her?" Reece asked Marcus.

"Her abilities seem considerable." The professor gazed in the direction Miyo had walked. "But what I want to know more about is her heart."

"Well spoken," Reece said.

A few minutes later, Miyo strolled back, a smile on her face. "It's so beautiful here." She stopped a few feet from them and set her gaze on Brandon. "So, musician, what's your opinion of my getting involved somehow with the Warriors Riding?"

Brandon jerked his thumb toward Reece. "I'm still agreeing with what Reece said at the wedding. Thinking you're a little young to be stepping into our arena."

"Tim's first letter, chapter four, verse twelve," Miyo said.

Brandon turned to Marcus. "Help us out, Whiz-Brain."

"'Don't let anyone look down on you because you are young.'"

Miyo cocked her head at Marcus. "Impressive. Your reputation precedes you."

"What reputation would that be?"

"My grandfather profiled each of you. And I—"

"Profiled?" Brandon said. "I've been profiled?"

"In all your glory, Brandon Scott." Miyo smiled. "He explained a great deal about each of you, yes, and about the things the Warriors Riding have done. Your stories have inspired me and encouraged me greatly in my own journey." She bowed in the beautiful style of the Japanese.

Reece took a step toward her. "We would be honored if you

would join us tomorrow at Well Spring Ranch for the day. It will give us a chance to get to know you better and you to know us."

"I would like that. And it will give me the chance to make my deliveries. I have something for each of you."

TWENTY

"MIGHT I GIVE YOU YOUR LETTERS NOW?" MIYO LOOKED around the fire pit at each of them late on Sunday afternoon. Marcus had, of course, been curious as to what Doug's granddaughter wanted to deliver, and it seemed that question had now been answered.

"The letters were written by my grandfather, as you might have anticipated. One for each of you." She picked up the flat wooden box she'd kept by her side most of the day. It appeared to be six inches wide by a foot long and made out of myrtlewood. A lacquer finish made the box shine with an almost unearthly light. Appropriate since the box was undoubtedly Doug's.

Miyo lifted the lid and removed what looked like four envelopes. A fifth remained in the box. She handed Brandon his letter first, then Dana, and then one to Marcus.

Marcus judged by the weight of the envelope that the letter was only one page. On the envelope—in what he estimated to be eight-point font in a decorative script—was his name: *Professor Marcus Amber* and underneath it, *My friend.*

"When did he give these to you?" Marcus asked.

"He didn't." Miyo sat back in her chair as a wistful look filled her eyes. "A few days after he died, my father asked me to help him go through Grandpa's things, and we found this box in his study sitting in the center of his desk. We opened it and found six letters. Dated recently. One was addressed to me. I read mine and at the bottom of the note were instructions for me to give each of you your letter as soon as I could."

"Thank you," Dana said.

"You're welcome. My hope is they bring you hope as the one he wrote to me did." A look of consternation passed over Miyo's face. "But I'm afraid they will also bring you trepidation."

"You gotta like this lady, Prof." Brandon kicked Marcus's chair. "She utilizes terminology almost as indecipherable as yours."

"Please tell me you see the irony in that sentence," Marcus said.

Miyo waited till Brandon's chuckles faded, then stared at the musician with a look that shouted, *Get serious.* She certainly knew how to command a room. Twenty-three in age, but far older in experience.

"I suggest each of you open your letter in privacy. Mine said I was free to share what my letter contained with the four of you if I chose, but of course the instructions in your letters might be different. In any event, you might want to keep its information to yourself." She turned to Reece. "If you don't mind, I would like to give you your letter when the two of us are alone."

"Fine." Reece stood and shoved his hands in his pockets. "Let's do it now."

⊹ ⊹ ⊹

Reece and Miyo walked to the big cabin on the north end of the ranch that he'd had built a year ago to accommodate the surging size of the groups that came to Well Spring for training. They sat in the corner of the large room where the sun streamed through the picture windows to warm their faces.

He stared at the glow around Miyo that outlined her body. It shifted from gold to silver to white and back to gold. He'd never seen anything like it on anyone else. Granted, his new spiritual eyes didn't always allow him to see people with this much detail, if at all, but of the people he had seen so far, Miyo was the most fascinating.

He saw her reach toward her chest and pull out a rectangular object that had a faint, thin line of light around it. It had to be his letter. Fire seemed to drip off her finger as she ran it along the edge of the envelope. "Can you see what I have in my hand?"

"I can see the outline of an envelope."

"So your sight allows you to see objects?"

"Sometimes yes, sometimes no. Usually just an outline around the object that allows me to figure out what it is."

"Are you ready?" Miyo leaned forward.

"You're sure Doug wrote it?"

"Why do you ask that question when you already know the answer?"

Reece didn't respond. The honest response would be that he didn't want to read words Doug had penned probably only weeks ago. Plus, he would need Miyo to read them, and he wanted to be alone when he heard them.

Also, Doug's words would undoubtedly stir up the feelings of loss that stung his mind and heart like a series of unending needle pricks. Feelings of anger. Despair. Bitterness. He'd already been through the gamut of emotions over the past ten days and again at the service, and he didn't want to go through them once more.

Miyo leaned farther forward. "I realize this likely will not help, but I faced the same emotions of loss when I read my letter."

Great. She was a mind reader as well. No, not true. Just sensitive to the obvious.

"I'll need you to read it to me." Reece sighed.

"Your message is for your eyes only, just as my message is for mine alone, just as it is for the rest of the Warriors."

"If I had eyes I'm sure that would be true. But since my new-fangled vision doesn't allow me to do things like read, I'll have to rely on your narration. I'm sure Doug would understand."

"I disagree." The sound of ripping filled the small room, and Reece saw Miyo's hands and the faint outline around the envelope twist and then light spill out of its end and rain down like a cluster of Fourth of July sparklers. Whatever was contained in the letter had power. "There's a thin flash drive in here. Doug recorded your letter. I'll plug it into my laptop and hit Play and leave. All right?"

Reece nodded. A few minutes later she had things set up, and then Miyo's footsteps faded across the floor. As the door to the large room clicked shut, Doug's voice came over the computer's speakers. Reece's eyes watered and he allowed himself to sink into the last message from his mentor and friend.

"Reece, my old friend . . ."

Doug stopped to laugh and Reece couldn't decide if he loved the sound or hated it.

"We had some great adventures together, didn't we? Indeed we did, but they are nothing compared to what is to come and what we will do together throughout eternity. Do not forget that—this is only one age of many more to come, and I can't wait till you join me on the other side.

"Please indulge me for a moment. I've always loved it in TV shows and movies when the person on the tape or in the letter says, 'If you're listening to this tape or reading this note, then I am dead.' So now I've said it to you."

Doug laughed again and it made fresh water come to Reece's eyes.

"I'm sorry for your loss because I know you loved me. But cry for you, not ever for me, because you know where I am now. I have run the race, I have finished the course, and I believe I have run well."

Doug paused and Reece heard the sound of a river in the background. Was it the one at Well Spring? Is that where he recorded this? That would be fitting.

"This might be hard to accept at first, but you need to receive Miyo as my replacement in Warriors Riding. She walks in the power of the Spirit like no one I've ever seen, and that includes you, friend. She is young, yes, but only in body and years, not in her soul. I have taught her all I know.

"You were always one for keeping a journal of all the things you've done, all the secrets you've learned, all the experiences of the worlds the Spirit opened up for you. I've kept a journal for the past thirteen years as well. I felt it was time to record the things I've learned. But I didn't use pen and paper or a computer. Miyo is my journal. Everything I've learned over the years is now in her and part of her. She carries my words so well.

"I wish I could say you must make her part of the Warriors—that without her you will face some battle where she is a critical component to your success, but I don't know that for certain. I haven't heard it spoken from the Spirit even though I believe it to be true. So it is your choice whether to grant my wish or not. Nonetheless, I will say she is true of heart and spirit, and I believe she would be a fine addition to your team.

"Who knows, you might even grow to trust her to the point where you'll have her read your journal back to you. I'm certain you haven't memorized everything between its pages. It is highly possible you've forgotten some of the things it contains, which you might need to be reminded of in the future and be of help in your time of need."

He thought of his journal, which Doug had found in Reece's backyard after Zennon's attack a year ago. He carried the journal with him everywhere now, even though he couldn't read it. Maybe Doug was right. Maybe he would let someone read it back to him someday. Not Brandon. Dana? Marcus? Possibly. Maybe even Miyo. He shook his head and focused on Doug's recording.

"You have given me life, Reece Roth. So much life, friend. So many adventures of the spirit and soul. And soon we will continue those adventures in ways that will make our time on earth seem shorter than the blink of an eye.

"Go forward in full strength, Reece. I know you think you need me. That you won't be able to face the coming battle with Zennon without me. This is not so. You have the Spirit. He will guide you in all things.

"One more thing. Forgiveness. And blame. I've heard those words over and over again these past few weeks. I don't know what it means, but by the time you read this letter, my imagination says you will.

"For you, I believe it will be years till we are joined together again, but for me, I imagine I will turn the moment I walk through the gate into heaven and see you coming through the door only an instant after me.

"As always, I am your friend. Now, through all time, and beyond time."

Reece sat in the silence and let the emotions of the moment wash over him. Forgiveness? Could he forgive Brandon? If Reece didn't it would leave a crack for the enemy to enter into. And if Doug and Miyo were right about the coming battle with Zennon and whoever else the demon brought to the arena, Reece needed to get that crack filled soon. He leaned forward and took his head in his hands. Forgive. He didn't know if he had the strength to do it.

Regarding allowing Miyo to join the Warriors, his emotions were a fifty-fifty mix of yes and no. It didn't feel right, but he couldn't tell if that was because of his pride at realizing she knew things he didn't or if she wasn't ready for it. So young. Yet did that matter? Maybe she was ready, but were they ready for her? He would think and pray about it. An image of Doug filled his mind. Reece already knew the answer to his mentor's request. Why hadn't he seen it? It was obvious.

Reece slogged across the wood floor and out the door. In minutes he found Miyo overlooking the river.

"No wonder Doug didn't tell me. I would have rejected the idea immediately." He smiled and shook his head. "You're the one, aren't you?" Reece cocked his head. "You certainly stepped before me with boldness."

The glow around Miyo brightened. Like a spiritual smile, only he was able to see.

"The one what?"

"The one of the new prophecy."

"Yes, Reece. I am."

TWENTY-ONE

BRANDON OPENED HIS LETTER DOWN BY THE RIVER. IT was written in longhand, and he stared at the pattern of the words for a long time before reading them. If Miyo was right, the letter would bring hope and despair. Hope he could use. But despair? He'd already seen that on the menu too often over the past month, and he'd eaten more than his fill. Did he have a choice? He could burn Doug's letter and pretend it didn't exist or toss it into the river and let it float away. Why not? He crumpled the letter into a ball and lifted his arm, ready to fling it into the undulating current.

He'd come to Well Spring like Doug and Reece had asked, and the result was disaster and his utter failure. Had his inaction killed Doug? No. But that didn't matter to Reece. And didn't matter any longer to Brandon. Any guilt he'd felt from that lie was gone, but it had been replaced with another conviction he knew was the truth. A poster appeared in his mind with the headline *Worthless*, and his picture was underneath.

He sighed, uncrumpled the paper, and read the letter. He owed Doug that much.

Dear Brandon,

I fear for you as I pen these words. Ever since your battle with the religious spirit, I've been seeing the same thing over and over again. It's an image of you surrounded by darkness. And the darkness is unbelief. Unbelief that you have the strength to do what must be done in the coming war. Unbelief that you are still the Song. And a deep conviction that your presence among the Warriors Riding matters little. That you have nothing to offer.

If this is true, I ache for you because you have believed the lie. Whatever pain you now carry, hold on to it no longer. I have told you this before, but allow me to say it one last time: You matter. You are the Song. It is your destiny. Night comes swiftly, but the day is not yet over. Do not lose heart. You will be restored to your former glory and beyond it. You will sing again, and when you do, great healing will come, far more than you can conceive of.

Seek the King now, Brandon, and the answers will come. Listen for his voice and he will speak to you. Great freedom will manifest if you are willing to have ears that hear.

Believe with me. With everything you hold dear, believe with me.

Your friend,

Doug

Restored? Hope surged inside Brandon, but before it could take root, he crumpled up the letter for a second time and tossed it into the river. Believe with Doug? Nope, sorry, he'd been ejected from the spiritual Super Bowl and didn't want to get back into the stadium. He wasn't the Song any longer. And a sentimental letter from Doug wouldn't change that.

✛ ✛ ✛

Dana sat on a small rise a quarter mile west of the main cabin that overlooked the ranch and fought an aversion to opening her letter. Did the others feel the same? Maybe, but probably not for the same reason she did. She didn't want to read Doug's words because she didn't think they would surprise her. And if she was right, her letter wouldn't contain much of the hope Miyo spoke of—only a liberal dose of foreboding. She turned the letter over again and again, trying to work up the nerve to read it. Finally she slid her finger under the flap of the brown envelope and tore it open.

Dearest Dana,

You have fought well and led with such strength. I am so proud of you. But as you might already realize, your ability to lead will soon be tested like it has never been before. I told you and the others, Brandon is the key to the coming war. But your role is no less critical than his. You each have your part to play, so take courage, dear heart, for the Spirit is indeed with you.

Also, you must open yourself to what lays inside the deepest part of your soul: your feelings for Brandon. I know you are scared. I know you fear that if you give him your heart again, he will treat it in a way that will not allow you to survive. But this is a risk I feel you must take. Not for me. Not for Brandon. But for you. Don't let your self-protection turn into a weapon for the enemy to use against you. Against the Warriors.

Rejoicing as I think of the day we will be together in eternity,

Doug

Great. Doug poking into her personal life from the grave. Or from the heavens. Risk her heart again? No. She knew him too well. Knew that even though he'd sacrificed himself for her during the battle with the religious spirit, in some ways the sacrifice was for himself. Because of his need and desire for her, it was highly possible there was a part of him that rescued her because he didn't want to lose what she gave him.

All through their courtship and engagement, she'd met all his expectations just like she'd done all her life in all her relationships. Dana Raine. The perfect girl, always straight As in high school, summa cum laude in college. The top salesperson when she sold radio, exceeding goals as a sales manager, exceeding them now as the station's general manager. Even as the Leader in the Warriors Riding, she'd done more than anyone had expected.

But what would happen if she gave her heart to Brandon and she failed to be perfect for him? Did he really love her for her, or for what she gave him? He was an amazing talent, charming, funny, charismatic, and kind, but there was still a significant part of him that was all about Brandon. Even his reason for breaking off their engagement was about himself. Crushing her heart because he was worried about her leaving since his mom had left when he was young. Didn't he ever think about the fact she had the same fears from being abandoned so often as a child?

She let out an aggravated sigh. Why did she let herself think like this? It wasn't helpful. But she couldn't stop it. Maybe if life were normal, she could take the time to figure out what she really wanted and how she really felt. But life wasn't normal.

Dana sighed again and rubbed her lips with the back of her hand. It was all so mixed up and confusing because part of her still needed him. What *did* she want? She didn't know. Didn't care. Or better said, she didn't want to take the time to care. Her mind was too caught up in what Doug's letter had said, because he was right.

She did sense her role would be bigger than she wanted it to be, and while Doug said she would be able to accomplish whatever it was she was supposed to do, she didn't share anything close to his level of faith.

The ache of Doug's absence struck Marcus again as he sat in front of the fireplace on the outside of the main cabin and held his letter. Too soon—far too soon—for him to have gone. Already he imagined the day coming when he and the rest of the Warriors would soar together with Doug through the heavens.

Dear Marcus,

Do you see it? The change inside? I do. You have chosen so well and are seeing the fruit of those choices in your life, in Kat's life, and the lives of your daughters. Without you the Wolf would not have been defeated back in June.

Now, as I sit writing these words to you nearly two weeks later, I continue to ponder what role you will have in the coming melee. It seems—if I am hearing correctly from the Spirit—that your friend Simon will play a significant role, which means you must play a role with Simon. I believe this involves bringing him to Well Spring. And bringing him to another place as well, I don't know where. Ask the Spirit, he will tell you. There is much more to Simon than you can imagine.

And you must pray, Professor. With great intensity. For your fellow Warriors. And especially Simon. For while I sense he will be your salvation once again, there is also darkness surrounding him.

Your friend across time,

Doug

Marcus folded Doug's letter and placed it back in the envelope. He would most certainly pray. And getting Simon to Well Spring? That would be a challenge given the last words the magician had spoken. But Marcus would find a way. There was no question in his mind that he had to.

TWENTY-TWO⊙

THEY GATHERED LATE ON SUNDAY EVENING AROUND THE kitchen table, and Reece got right to the point. "I assume each of you has read your letter and worked through what it contained."

Brandon and Marcus nodded, as did Dana. Were their letters as ominous as hers? She didn't really want to know.

"Good." Reece clapped his hands together. "You can share the contents if you wish—all, some, or nothing." He turned toward Miyo. "From mine I want to introduce an idea from Doug that I believe will bring strength to all of us. But a decision on this idea ultimately isn't mine. It is ours."

"And that idea is?" Dana said.

"That Miyo would join Warriors Riding and take her grandfather's place at our side."

"Wow," Brandon said and faced Miyo. "You want that?"

She didn't answer and turned her eyes to Reece.

Reece folded his arms. "Doug wanted it."

"Sorry. Not seeing it." Brandon glanced at Miyo, then back to Reece. "No offense, Miyo, but the prophecy says there are four Warriors. Not five. Four. So unless the prophecy changes, she can't—"

"Knock it off, Brandon, you sound ridiculous. Doug wasn't part of the prophecy either, but he certainly was one of us." Reece shifted toward Dana. "Thoughts?"

"I don't know." Dana folded her arms. "It seems a little premature."

Another woman in the Warriors? Yes, long overdue. It would be refreshing to have another female around. But Miyo? Something didn't feel right. Yes, there was strength in Doug's granddaughter. It almost rivaled Reece's. And it was clichéd to say Miyo was an old soul. But she was. She held wisdom in her that spoke of deep pain and exhilarating highs and multiple acts of courage. In other words, she met all the qualifications, but still, Dana's mind balked at the idea of Miyo joining them.

Lord?

An answer came from the Spirit so fast Dana blinked.

Yes, dear heart. It is right.

But I don't want—

Life isn't always about what you want, Dana Raine.

Heat rose to Dana's face as Reece clasped his hands behind his back. "All right. So far we have a yes vote from me, a no vote from Brandon, and an abstain from Dana who needs time to—"

"No."

"No, what? You're voting no?"

"I don't need time. I believe she should join us."

"What changed?"

"Just . . . I . . ." Dana shoved her hands under her thighs. "I think the Spirit is saying she should."

Reece nodded and turned to the professor. "Marcus? Thoughts about Miyo joining us?"

"I concur with Dana."

"Excellent," Reece said. "Brandon? Do you want to give us the real reason you don't want Miyo to—"

"You don't need my reasons now." Brandon sprawled back in his chair. "It doesn't matter what I think. Majority rules."

"No, unanimity rules." Reece leaned toward Brandon. "Your vote?"

"Sure, why not. I mean, it's good."

Reece frowned. "You're sure?"

"I'm sure."

Reece started to say something to Brandon but stopped, scowled, then turned to Miyo. "Welcome to Warriors Riding."

"I'm honored." Miyo glanced at each of them and held Brandon's gaze a fraction of a second longer than Marcus's. "Thank you."

Reece opened his watch and felt the face. "It's late. I suggest we all get some rest."

Dana stood and went to the restroom. When she finished and walked back into the living room, everyone had left except Brandon. He stared at the dying coals in the fireplace, his body wrapped in the thick quilt that always rested on the end of the couch.

"So everyone else left?"

Brandon nodded and continued to stare straight ahead.

"Aren't you going to bed too?"

"Nah." Brandon sat up and let the blanket fall to his sides. "I'm going for a hike."

"Now?"

"Yes. Now."

Dana looked at her watch. "It's quarter to twelve."

"Yeah, late." Brandon shrugged. "But it's a short ways to where I'm going. Just a half mile or so up the river. Or maybe down to the post. I need to hear from God. Doug said I would. I tried to shut the desire down, but who am I kidding? In Peter's words, where else would I go? But that's not saying I'm doing peachy. Either I hear from the Spirit tonight or I'm going home."

"How long will you be out there?" Dana frowned.

"You're worried about me, huh?" He gave a sad smile.

"Yes, I am." She didn't elaborate but returned his smile and guessed her eyes probably held more warmth for him than they had for a long time. Doug's letter had opened a door she wasn't sure she wanted to open any further, but she wasn't sure she wanted to shut it again either. "What do you hope to find?"

"An answer. I've tried to bury the question, but it keeps shoving its ugly head up into my face 'cause of that stupid letter from Doug."

"What's the question?"

"Same as it's been since we were last here five weeks back and I destroyed my voice." Brandon stood and folded the blanket. "What am I supposed to do with my life now? Do I have any purpose left in this group? Am I worth anything? And of course what role do I have in this supposed coming attack from Zennon?"

Brandon picked up his North Face jacket and slipped it over his T-shirt.

"It'll be cold out there. You might want more than that." Dana smiled and gave his hand a quick squeeze before she could stop herself.

He blinked, his face went soft, and he stared into her eyes like he did in the old days when they'd discovered their mutual love of old jazz records and drinking cream-laden coffee in Dana's back-yard gazebo as rain pounded down on the roof like thousands of miniature drummers.

Oh boy. One hand squeeze was all it took, huh?

"Can I ask you something?" Brandon said.

"Umm . . ."

"Is your thaw a result of Doug's letter?"

Dana put her head down for a moment, then raised it. "You should get going."

His countenance shifted and his eyes got hard again. Brandon ambled toward the sliding-glass door and opened it, then turned to her and didn't step through. "Can I ask you something else?"

Dana didn't answer.

"Why were you hesitant about Miyo taking Doug's place?"

"Why were you?" Dana asked.

"She's too young. We barely know her. And I like things the way they are. Add a new member to a group, and the dynamics of the band and the music they make turns out way different than it was before." Brandon slid the door open farther. "Your turn."

Cold wind sprinted inside and chilled Dana. "I don't know why."

"I do."

"No, you don't." Dana scowled at him.

Brandon gave her that smile she'd loved when they were dating. Part kindness, part mischievous, and a splash of being able to read her feelings like a billboard. The smile she'd loved back then. Not now.

"Yes. I do know. But I'm not going to say it."

"Why not?"

"I doubt you could handle it." Any hint of a smile was gone from Brandon's face.

"Try me." She yanked her arms across her chest.

Brandon eased one foot outside onto the patio and breathed deeply before answering. "You're worried about abdicating your position as the number one female on the team."

"What are you talking about?" Dana's face went hot.

"It's clear Miyo's got leadership oozing out all over her. You're worried she's going to lead better than the Leader."

"Shut up, Brandon." She hated him knowing her that well. "Have a nice hike. I hope you freeze."

✛ ✛ ✛

Brandon stood at the sliding-glass door as Dana disappeared down the hallway toward the cabin's main bedroom. He shouldn't have said it. But it was true. She didn't want Miyo taking the gold medal. So much of Dana's identity was wrapped up in performing for people. Being number one. Getting results no one else could. Her greatest strength was also her greatest weakness. Her greatest wound. Be everything people expected her to be. And Brandon had played into it. Called her the perfect woman when they dated. Praised her for it so many times.

Whenever he did, she'd tell him that she wasn't perfect. And now he finally understood why. What if she *wasn't* perfect? Would he still love her? That had to be her greatest fear and the foundation of the wall between them. And now it was too late to prove to her that she didn't have to be perfect. Impossible situation. If only he could stop loving her, life would be so much easier.

He slung the thoughts to the back of his mind, slid the door shut, and trudged up the trail along the river, carrying one of the ranch's green folding chairs with him. A quarter mile should do it. He just wanted to be sure he was far enough away not to worry about the others making an unlikely surprise appearance, which would be a shocker this time of night. But with the Warriors, and with Miyo now hanging around, anything could happen.

Dana's comment about the temperature was an understatement. Within minutes Brandon's feet and hands went numb, and his face felt like he wore a Frosty the Snowman helmet. He picked up his pace and it helped. Within a few minutes he found an open spot in the trees where he could see the river.

Brandon set up the chair, then sat and stared at the black water flowing past him thirty feet below. The chair was like ice and its cold seeped into his legs and back up his torso. But he ignored the cold, closed his eyes, and turned inward.

"I need to know, Lord. Will I sing again like I used to? Doug said I'd hear from you, so let's go."

No answer.

He looked up at the trees silhouetted against the stars, and the image of a tree house sitting between their trunks thirty feet in the air shot into his mind. He grunted out a laugh. Maybe that was the answer God was trying to give him: build a tree house somewhere on the acreage in his backyard, put in lights, heat, running water, and live in it like a hermit. Forget everything and everyone in his life. If only God would let him off that easy.

Brandon slumped forward and closed his eyes. "How can I be the Song if I can't sing in the spiritual realms when I need to, let alone the physical? And what are these songs I'm getting for other people? Yeah, I'm singing for a few minutes, but it's not even my voice!"

Brandon didn't need to look at his watch to know an hour had passed. Then two. Still nothing from the Spirit. At four o'clock he rose stiffly and picked up the chair. The Listening Post flashed into his mind. Everyone would be asleep by now. Why not go there and sit in the spot where miracles had happened in the past?

He settled down at the post with his back to the cabin and looked up and down the river. A sliver of the morning sun crept over the north ridge, and still there was no answer. But minutes later as the light edged down the sides of the mountains and across the stream, Brandon heard a sound like he'd never experienced. Music. A song. So faint he couldn't distinguish it from the chatter of the river. But it was there. A sensation of warmth surged inside, and he sniffed in a quick breath. The sound of it pierced his heart like a laser.

"Lord?"

Listen.

Brandon strained to hear the song. It floated toward him and it seemed to come from the mouth of the river. He turned his head and stared at the current as if it were the instrument that played the tune. Then the music encircled him and suddenly grew louder. It came from his right and left, above and below, as if he were hearing the song in 3-D surround sound.

He'd never heard anything like it. Each note was as pure and clear as if the music was from another realm. And the melody was far more than haunting. Shattering. Full of freedom and sorrow in equal measure. A lost song, a melody that could crush mountains and birth worlds. Its richness sliced through his spirit with soul-splitting pain and immense pleasure.

It only lasted a minute. Maybe less. But even if it had gone on for hours, it wouldn't have been close to long enough. As the tune vanished, Brandon felt like his life had been sucked out of him, then it rushed back in with so much force, he lurched forward, then it faded again. He gasped.

The song so powerful that its absence felt like death. All he wanted was to hear the song again. He sat for half an hour, waiting for its return, begging the Spirit to bring it back, but the song didn't come.

"Will I hear the song again, Lord?"

The answer was soft but immediate. *Yes.* And laughter seemed to be in the answer.

"When?"

And you will sing it.

The idea immersed him. "When?" he asked again.

The Spirit didn't respond this time, but he didn't have to. Knowing he would hear the song again was enough. The warmth-tinged rays of the early-morning sun fell on his face and brought hope. He hadn't felt like this for what seemed like ages.

"What is the song, Lord?"

It is a song of immense healing.

"For who?"

It is a song to be sung once. For one person only. And for that person, extraordinary restoration will come.

"Who is the song for?"

The one who needs it more than any other.

The words from Doug's letter flashed across Brandon's mind, and his body grew warm. *You will be restored to your former glory and beyond it. You will sing again, and when you do, great healing will come, far more than you can conceive of.*

Brandon sat stunned in the midst of the revelation. He would be healed. Not now. Not yet. But restoration would come for his voice. He would be the Song once more.

After another ten minutes, Brandon shuffled up the long stone path back to the main cabin but hesitated before going in. If any of the others were up, he wasn't ready to tell them what had happened. It was too raw. Too glorious. He glanced through the sliding door. The fireplace was cold and no lights were on. He was probably okay.

Brandon slid the door open and stepped inside. The sound of

the river faded as he closed the door behind him, and the silence inside the main room smothered him. He glanced at his watch. Five thirty. Too late to go to bed. Too early to start breakfast. Too tired to read, too wired to sleep. A light snapped on behind him and Brandon spun as adrenaline surged through him.

"This will help you see better. I don't need it, but you might."

TWENTY-THREE

"WOW! ARE YOU TRYING TO GIVE ME A HEART ATTACK?"

Reece sat in a back corner of the main room in a sweatshirt and jeans. His thick stockinged feet rested on the ottoman in front of him. Steam rose from his *Jefferson Airplane* coffee cup cradled in his hands. A leather book sat next to him. His journal? Brandon hadn't seen that in ages.

"Trying, yes. But not succeeding obviously." Reece pulled his legs off the ottoman and sat forward. "Coffee's brewed if you want some."

"Yeah, okay." Brandon rubbed his head and blinked against the lamplight that seemed to burrow into his brain. "What are you doing up?"

"I think that should be my line."

"I never went to bed."

"Hmm, that's a long night." Reece took a long sip of his coffee.

"I needed time to think."

"I understand."

"Do you, Reece?"

"More than you know." Reece let out a low whistle. "Do you want to talk?"

Brandon ambled into the kitchen, found hazelnut creamer, and poured himself a cup of coffee. He raised the cup to his nose and breathed in the aroma. Nothing like a cup of joe to wake a guy up after he'd been up for twenty-three hours straight. He gave Reece a furtive glance. Maybe if he ignored the big man he'd go away.

"As I already said, you're not in this alone, Song."

"And as I already said, don't call me that anymore." Brandon set his coffee on the kitchen counter and stared at Reece. Why couldn't the guy still be asleep? Brandon wasn't ready to talk to anyone—especially Reece—about what had just happened out by the river.

Reece didn't respond but continued to somehow stare at him through his scarred eyes.

"I'm not the Song, so do me a favor and let's stop talking about it."

"Is that what you heard out there?" Reece slowly rose and strolled over to the sliding-glass door and faced the river. "Or are you hiding your glory?"

"What's that supposed to mean?" *Here it comes.*

"You have the look about you of a man who heard something he desperately wants to hear again." Reece continued to face the river. "And my guess is what that man heard was music and the thought that he might one day become the Song again."

"You and your X-ray spiritual vision."

"Yep."

The room went silent.

What was the point in trying to keep what had happened from Reece? For some reason God told the man with unsettling frequency what had happened or what was going to happen in Brandon's life. It'd been that way since the Warriors began. But that didn't mean Brandon had to be happy about telling Reece anything.

"What if you're right? What if that man heard a song at dawn's breaking that went to the core of his heart?"

"I'd say the Spirit would be doing a powerful work in that man's soul and spirit."

"I don't know." Brandon slumped into a chair next to the cold hearth.

"You do know."

"I'm not up for an interrogation this morning." Brandon squeezed his coffee cup. "Have you forgotten you blame me for Doug's death?"

Reece shuffled into the kitchen and poured himself another cup of dark-roast coffee. "What did you hear out there? Am I right about it being music?"

"How do you know I heard anything?"

"Because I think you would still be making like a statue down at the Listening Post if the Spirit hadn't revealed something to you. A man who stays out all night isn't going to leave till he gets an answer."

"How did you know I was at the Listening Post?"

"Just because I don't have eyes doesn't mean I can't see."

Brandon had to smile. A man with spiritual eyes who could often see angels and demons all around them and could see some kind of outline of Brandon down at the Listening Post. "You're right. I did hear music."

"Tell me about it."

Brandon described the song he'd heard and what it had done inside his heart.

"Is this the first time you've heard a song like that?"

Brandon shook his head. "I've been hearing songs for the past four weeks. Sometimes visions as well."

He told Reece about what had happened with the couple in Edmonds, and Sandra, and the guy named Garen on the John Wayne Trail.

"'And they sang a new song before the throne and before the four living creatures and the elders; and no one could learn the song except the one hundred and forty-four thousand who had been purchased from the earth.'" A small smile crept onto Reece's face. "From the book of Revelation."

"What are you saying? That I'm hearing the songs the 144,000 hear?"

"Not possible. Those songs are for their ears only. But maybe you're hearing songs for *your* ears only. Ones only you can sing. Songs coming from heaven."

Reece spread his hands. "Think about it. What if everyone has songs written for them in heaven? Specific songs only for us? What if there are hundreds and thousands of songs for every soul who has ever lived and they're waiting to be sung to each of us throughout eternity? Songs of joy and sorrow and comfort and battle, freedom and glory?"

Reece's voice grew more animated. "'For the Lord your God is living among you. He is a mighty savior. He will take delight in you with gladness. With his love, he will calm all your fears. He will rejoice over you with joyful songs.'"

"Zephaniah 3:17," Brandon said.

"Yes. And whose songs do you think God is singing? And do you think it's possible that an infinite God has only a finite number of songs—and he sings the same ones for everybody? Or does the God who has names for all the stars and knows each hair on the heads of everyone who has walked this earth create intimate songs for each individual?"

Brandon sat stunned as Reece talked.

"What if God is teaching you a few of those songs?" Reece paused and opened his hands wide. "I'm seeing into the spiritual realm. I think you're hearing into the spiritual realm."

Brandon nodded. Reece was right, but his mind couldn't help but spin toward thinking about the song he'd heard by the river. If the ones he'd heard back in Seattle were the songs of heaven, then the new one was straight from the throne room.

"The one I heard out there was . . . so much more than the others." Brandon didn't know how else to describe it.

"Have you asked the Spirit what the song means?"

"Yes." Brandon allowed a thin smile to reach his lips.

"Healing is coming for you, isn't it?"

"Yeah. It is."

Reece leaned on the kitchen counter, still as granite. Brandon shifted and drew in a long, silent breath. Should he ask the question? Or let it lie dormant a little longer?

"What about healing between us? Forgiveness?"

The question hung thick in the air like dark smoke, and for a time Reece seemed to grow even stonier, if that was possible. Finally he took a breath of his own, blew it out in a slow stream, and started to speak. But before the first words escaped, the moment was stolen as the front door of the cabin swung open.

TWENTY-FOUR

DANA STROLLED INTO THE CABIN FOLLOWED BY MIYO. Dana studied Brandon's face. She knew the look. They'd just interrupted a conversation Brandon wanted to finish with Reece. But Brandon looked better. Much better. It was clear he'd gotten an answer he'd been hoping for during the night or early-morning hours. A few moments later, Marcus stumbled down the stairs from the loft, his brown hair a mess, the skin underneath his eyes puffy.

"Everyone seems to be up early today," Reece said. "Good."

"I wonder why." Marcus rubbed his head and glared at Reece and Brandon. "It couldn't have anything to do with the rather loud ponderings emanating from your vocal chords at an hour where silence is the socially acceptable and preferred behavior."

Brandon wiggled his forefinger at the professor. "You manage to talk like a vocabulary teacher even when you're still half asleep."

Reece ignored the comment. "Brandon and I had an interesting discussion just now about what the Spirit is doing in him. Healing is coming. And we will need it. We will need everyone to be healthy. Regarding our next gathering, I'm sensing we need to reconvene here at Well Spring sooner than later. To be more precise, I'd like us all back here by Thursday night."

He looked at Dana. "But I know some of you have work. Can you get the time off from the station?"

"Sure. I still have plenty of vacation time built up and things are running extremely well, so long weekends are doable." It would mean working more hours the days she was there, but that was fine. The station was close to beating projections by seven percent this month. With a concentrated effort she knew she could get it to eight.

"Marcus?"

"I teach only on Tuesdays and Wednesdays during summer quarter, so my schedule can accommodate that as well."

"Miyo?"

"I've taken a leave from my job. I have no commitments for the next two months." But the intensity in her dark-brown eyes said the coming four days wouldn't be simple.

Marcus must have noticed the look in Miyo's eyes. "What will your priorities be during the coming week?"

"You might have noticed there was one more letter in the box when I gave all of you yours." Miyo pulled an envelope from her back pocket and tapped the edge of it against her palm, then put it back in her pants. "And there's a bigger package that goes along with it."

"Who is it for?" Dana asked.

"I don't know."

"There's no name on it?" Brandon frowned. "No instructions from Doug?"

"Just a first name. And my grandfather did give me instructions. But they don't offer much help."

She opened what Dana presumed was Miyo's own letter and read from it.

"*You must deliver the letter to him as soon as you and your father discover the box that contains all the letters. I don't believe he will remember me as he's been through quite an ordeal. But he needs to remember. Just as you and all the Warriors are critical pieces in the coming battle, he is as well. I didn't realize it was him till recently. I'm not sure why I didn't figure it out till now.*

"*Funny how our lives are intertwined isn't it?*" Miyo smiled delicately as she continued to read. *"'Marcus would call it quantum entanglement, I believe, or string theory, or some such thing. I'll call it God's way of weaving a magnificent universe-spanning tapestry where we all are of the pattern he is weaving. Find him. Deliver the letter as soon as you can. My prayer is it will start his restoration and put him in a position to play his role well.'"*

Miyo looked up from her letter. "I have no idea how to find this man. My grandfather never spoke of him. I searched his computer files, journals, cell phone records . . . but there doesn't seem to be anyone out there he might know with this name.

"There is certainly the option of opening the envelope and reading the letter, but I'd rather not do that for two reasons. First, I doubt the contents would give me much clue, and second, my grandfather specifically said in his instructions that the contents of each letter were for the recipients' eyes only."

"What's the name?" Brandon said.

Miyo glanced at each of them before answering, her eyes questioning. Dana knew what it would be before the word was spoken and silently agreed with Doug that God certainly was weaving a fascinating tapestry.

"The name is Simon."

TWENTY-FIVE

"Are you in there, Simon? I am not an enemy."

Simon stared at the back of his front door. It was a woman's voice. Confident sounding. And young. Not yet out of her twenties, he guessed, and stressed and felt all messed. Not his enemy? Maybe not. But maybe she was. Maybe she was Zennon. Couldn't tell these days, couldn't tell these daze. He smiled at his own joke.

Yes, he could tell, yes, he could, yes he could. And he should. He was free. Except for the fact the humming in his head shot into his mind at least three times a day. No, not free. It felt like a rope was attached to his soul and the person holding it on the other end could yank him back anytime he wanted to.

"Simon, are you in there? I have something for you. From an old acquaintance of yours."

He padded over to his front door slowly enough that his feet didn't make any sound on his floor. He peered through the peephole. Intense brown eyes, they could be spies, full of lies. But he didn't think so. Something about her was true. Her eyes had the same thing in them that the professor's did. The Spirit's light, much delight. Showed that she'd traveled in the spiritual realms. That made her dangerous.

She stared at the peephole as if she knew he was looking at her. "I am a friend of Marcus Amber's."

Was she? No way to know for certain. But how could she have found him unless she was? Simon pounded his knuckles together. Should he speak? Why not? What could she do? Break down the door, fling him to the floor? No, no, no. He didn't have to open up for her.

"Who are you? What is your name?"

"My name is Miyo. A friend of mine apparently was also a friend of yours, and he said I must deliver these to you."

"Tell me about 'these' so my mind doesn't squeeze."

"A letter and a package, neither of which have been opened because they are only to be opened by you."

"Who is it from? Who is this acquaintance?"

"He asked me not to say."

"Don't play games. Tell me the name of the man who gave you this."

"I'm honoring his request."

Simon twisted the knob of his front door and pulled it open a crack. "Why should I let you in?"

"I already told you."

He opened the door wider. The woman didn't move. She held a business-sized envelope in one hand and a large manila envelope in the other. "Both of those things are for me?"

"Yes."

Simon opened the door all the way and still the woman didn't move. That he liked but his pulse still spiked. "What did you say your name was?"

"Miyo."

Simon shifted his weight from one leg to the other. "I used to do a trick with an unsealed envelope. I'd read the contents before anyone opened it, then a spectator would unseal the envelope and confirm I'd gotten every word right." Simon rubbed his fingers. "I could attempt that with this letter if you like."

"He said these are important." Miyo extended both envelopes to him. "That you needed to read them right away."

"This he of whom you speak . . . if I wanted to talk to him after I read what he wrote, would that be possible?"

"No."

Simon raised his eyebrows.

"He's dead, Simon."

"I see." He ran his tongue over his lips. "Any other plea?"

"He said he hoped you would remember him."

Simon's eyes widened. "No one knows me. No one. Only Marcus. I've been gone too long, no one still sings my song." He frowned. Song? A song for him? He didn't have a song.

"Good-bye, Simon."

The woman bowed and strode away. As she did the sun seemed to bounce off her shoulders in a strange pattern of light, and it raised a memory that faded too fast for him to hold on to it. A memory from the days when he . . . The reference point slipped from his mind and he couldn't locate it again.

Simon closed the door, walked over to his tiny kitchen, and set both envelopes in the center of his small table. Sunlight from the window high on the east wall of his apartment seemed to spin in circles as if a whirlpool were drawing him to the contents of the large envelope.

He stared at the envelopes for a few minutes, then settled into a chair and placed his hands on either side of them. The envelopes didn't move. They didn't mock him. They just sat there and stared back in his direction, daring him to rip them open.

✜ ✜ ✜

Simon reached Ravenna Park a mile and a half north of the University of Washington just before dusk. No one stood or sat or played on the grass or hit tennis balls back and forth on the courts. Good. He needed to be alone to examine the contents of the envelopes. Not in his apartment. Too confining. Not in a bar or restaurant or coffee shop—he didn't want prying eyes. He needed open spaces—a place where he and his mind would have no distractions.

He eased up to one of the picnic tables and frowned before sitting down. Why did it feel so ancient and familiar to do so? When was the last time he'd sat like this at a picnic table, unable to face a life that cut like a knife? He ran his finger along the envelope's seam twice before sliding it under the flap and tearing it open. He sighed, closed his eyes for a moment, then opened the letter and read.

Dear Simon,

You revolutionized my life. I deeply regret I was not given the chance to tell you why on this side of eternity. I would have enjoyed that and enjoyed meeting you in person.

I can't imagine what kind of reaction seeing your manuscript again after all this time will elicit in you—it might be powerful; it might be painful—but I believe the Spirit has told me to give it to you. From what I've been able to learn from Marcus, I believe a gift has been stolen from you—the most precious one you were ever given—and this might be the catalyst that brings it back.

When Marcus first told the Warriors about a street magician, I suspected it was you, but I always thought of you more as an illusionist. However, I came to realize that many illusionists perform close-up and parlor-style magic as well. It wasn't until the end that I knew for certain it was you who had been trapped in multiple realities and somehow made it back to this world.

Before I explain how I know you, let me say what you did for Marcus dealt a major blow against the enemy. Well done, Simon, well done.

Long ago—as you might recall—I held the title of publisher for a small imprint located just outside of New York. I vividly remember the day your query came across my desk. It was on a Thursday in late May—the 31st, if I recall. I was of course swamped with work as usual and had an anniversary happening later that evening to distract me, but a feeling told me to slow down and take my time with this one before sending out our standard rejection letter. I did slow down and it transformed the way I saw the physical and spiritual worlds. I've never been the same.

Simon set the letter down and swatted his head as if that could stop the humming sound that had grown louder. "Get out of my head!" But the noise continued. What was this man talking about? He'd never written anything down—not even a journal—let alone an entire manuscript. Revolutionized this man's life? He didn't need this stupid letter; it would only serve to fetter.

He slipped off the bench and stumbled down the slight hill in front of the picnic table and tried to ignore the feeling that he did very much need the letter—that the letter needed to be fully read, for souls were to be fed, nothing to dread. Simon ignored the humming and staggered back to the letter and snatched it up.

From the moment I finished the first page—if I recall correctly it was just after lunch—I did nothing but fill my teacup and use the restroom till I finished your book. The experiences you documented and backed up with Scripture stirred my heart and spirit in a way I could not explain. Two days later I read the entire manuscript again. You can't imagine how hard I searched for you when I never received a response to my letter offering publication! After I found your book in the mail, it was as if you simply vanished.

But not being able to find you did nothing to abate the allure of what you had written. I pressed into the deeper things as you suggested, but not alone as you also counseled. I gathered a small group of men around me, and we learned together about the greater things of the Spirit. Oh, the adventures your book sent us on! The worlds you opened and the depth of the Trinity we began to experience was astounding. It is fascinating to me that the circle has now completed its cycle.

Do you remember who you are, Simon? Are you willing to act out of that strength once again? And if you aren't, are you willing to find the answer to the question of who you once were?

Simon set the letter down a second time and tried to slow his heart. He didn't know why it pounded like a drum. Fragments of memory flitted through his mind. An image of him at a typewriter, an open Bible and stacks of open books, him addressing a thick envelope. No, that couldn't have happened, couldn't be him. Maybe in one of the alternate worlds he'd existed in, but not this one.

Simon refolded the letter and slid it back into its envelope and set it on the picnic table. The sun was close to slipping below the tree line. He should go. He loved parks when the sun shone and turned the grass brilliant shades of green—when parks grew dim, though, he didn't like being in them. But he had to at least look at what was inside the large manila envelope.

Simon lifted the package and jiggled it up and down. It was heavy. He set it down, stood, and circled the table. Why did it frighten him? Yes, this Doug Lundeen's cryptic description of the package was part of the reason, but something deep inside said it was far more than that. That he was attached to the contents in a way that would spin him down a corridor as dark as the ones Zennon had trapped him in for all these ages past.

He finally slid a thick bundle of papers out of the envelope and set them on the picnic table. The edges were yellowed and a few of the pages were cracked. On top was a title page.

Going Deeper and Deeper Still: A Manual for the Follower of the Ways of Christ Who Wants to Explore the Unexplored Spiritual Realms by Simon P. Donelson.

Simon's face grew warm. This had to be a joke. He'd never written anything. He pulled the rubber band off the stack and slid off the cover page. The next page was a table of contents.

- Soul Travel
- Traveling Like Philip
- Becoming Unseen
- Speaking to the Dry Bones
- Going Deeper into His Love Than Ever Before

- Fighting for Freedom
- Healing for Others
- Putting on the Armor of Light
- Swords and the Sword of the Spirit in Spiritual Realms
- Arrows of Power
- Wearing the Cloak of Strength

He leafed through the manuscript, still refusing to even consider that he was part of this. A few of the chapter titles had been lined out with a red pen and retitled. Notes were scribbled in the margins on almost every page. At first he thought the notes were editorial comments, but as he looked closer, Simon realized the person who made them—Doug presumably—was recording his own experiences after trying the things this manuscript contained. Just as this Doug said he'd done.

The last page was a letter with a sticky note on top of it. The sticky note read:

Simon, this is a copy of a letter I sent you after reading your manuscript. I assumed you never received it as I didn't hear back from you. Then again, maybe you did. In any event, I wanted you to have it.

September 2, 1962

Dear Mr. Donelson,

Allow me to forgo common pleasantries and say your manuscript has consumed me. The concepts are fascinating and have captivated my imagination. While I find myself vacillating between believing and not believing what you propose is possible, I without question feel the body of Christ needs to explore the ideas you are promoting.

There are numerous grammatical errors throughout the manuscript, and I would suggest giving your book a different title, as the one you have now is cumbersome, but these are small issues and easily remedied.

Please contact me at the phone number below at your earliest convenience.

Warm regards,

Doug Lundeen

Simon set the letter down and stared at the fading light. He needed to talk to the professor as soon as possible.

TWENTY-SIX

"YOU MUST HELP WITH THIS, FOR I AM AMISS." SIMON rubbed the bridge of his nose with both forefingers on Wednesday afternoon and paced in front of a cherry tree in the quad at the U-Dub. Marcus had never seen Simon this agitated. He suspected whatever Miyo had given the magician was the catalyst.

"I thought you were out of my life," Marcus said.

"No! Not anymore, must step through the door, tired of hiding, must talk about Warriors Riding."

"You want to discuss the letter Doug Lundeen wrote to you."

"Yes, of course, must get on that horse." Simon kicked at a leaf on the ground, then broke a small branch off the cherry tree and pointed it at Marcus. "Help me. Please."

Marcus gave a slow nod. "Tell me what the letter said."

Simon paced again. "He says I wrote a book and it makes me uneasy—"

"And quite queasy?"

Simon stopped pacing and glared at Marcus. "That is not funny. I don't want to rhyme. I can't help it."

"I'm only attempting to shock you out of this dither you've worked yourself into." Marcus patted the air with his palms. "Relax. It will be okay. Now, what did the letter say?"

His face devoid of color, Simon handed him a thick manila

envelope and stared at Marcus. He'd never seen that look on Simon—the look of a little boy who just heard his first ghost story. He leaned forward and Simon tapped the package. "Open it. Take it out and look at the name on the front."

Marcus slid the stack of papers out and stared at the top page. "Is that your last name?"

"It used to be. One of them, anyway. I can't remember exactly who I was here. At least not most days, and today is a most day."

"Did you read through this?" Marcus riffled through the pages, stopping occasionally to read a few sentences.

"I've read the whole thing. Twice. And it's not mine." Simon rubbed his forehead hard enough to leave a red mark. "I didn't write that, Marcus!"

"Then who did?"

"I don't know why this Doug person would send it to me." Simon paced again and pulled his silver coin out of his pocket. "It makes no sense, Doug is so dense." He stopped and drilled Marcus with his gaze. "I didn't. I didn't write it. I didn't."

"Then I fail to understand why you would be this upset."

"Because what if I did?" Simon's eyes widened. "It would change everything." He pointed at the manuscript. "Read the table of contents."

Marcus did and when he finished, his heart thumped double-time. Was it possible?

Simon pulled a wrinkled envelope out of his back pocket and handed it to Marcus. "Read it. My letter from Doug, made me want to crawl under the rug."

As Marcus read the letter, it stunned him. When they'd met at Reece's home back in mid-July, Doug had hinted at the person who had taught him all he knew. It was Simon? Unbelievable. And yet at the same time, it somehow made imperfectly perfect sense. It explained how Simon could be so instrumental and insightful in Marcus's life—and if Simon had written the manuscript, it explained the reason why Zennon would have been so intent on taking him out. And why Reece felt the magician was so important in the coming war. If Simon could remember who he was, the results could be staggering.

"Look at me, Simon."

The magician stopped rolling his silver coin and complied.

"You need to come to Well Spring with us. We're going there this weekend. No is not an option."

TWENTY-SEVEN

"Is Simon still coming?" Dana asked.

She sat with Reece, Miyo, Brandon, and Marcus around the fire pit at Well Spring early on Thursday evening after a quick dinner that had been filled mostly with small talk. Not usual for them, but it was a nice break from their usual intense conversation that was often good but could also be exhausting. It was refreshing to simply sit and talk about nothing in the place where God seemed to show up in great measure. And she allowed herself to enjoy being around Brandon without thinking one moment into the future about her and him and what might or might not come. Nice to just *be* for once.

Marcus tossed a piece of wood on the fire, which sent a stream of red sparks into the air. "He's given every indication he'll arrive sometime tomorrow evening."

"You think he'll show?" Brandon asked Marcus.

"Yes. Why wouldn't he?"

"From what you've described, he doesn't seem the overly social sort." Brandon tried to balance a small piece of kindling on his palm.

"You think he needs to be here, Professor?" Reece spoke over folded arms.

"You've indicated Brandon is critical to our success against whatever is coming our way. I feel the same about Simon. We need him. I more than feel it. I know it." Marcus picked up a long stick and poked the fire. "And he will need us."

"So be it." Reece stood. "I'm going to go for a hike. Clear my head. Try to hear from the Spirit what we're supposed to do if Simon shows and figure out exactly what this battle is. What are the rest of you planning?"

"Finishing up the paper I'm presenting at the university next week." Marcus stood and ambled toward the main cabin.

"I'm thinking of taking my camera up a ways into the mountains and getting some shots before the sun sets," Dana said.

"Veg out," Brandon said.

"You mean waste time?" Reece kicked at a rock near his boot.

"No. I mean relax."

"Yeah. Right."

Brandon stood, shook his head at Reece, and strode off along the river. Dana let the silence linger till Brandon was out of earshot.

"You have to stop blaming him, Reece. And stop blaming yourself."

Reece folded his arms and didn't answer.

"Reece?"

"You're right."

"And?"

"I'm working on it." He turned toward Miyo. "What are your plans?"

"I'm going in." Miyo stared across the river to the chalk cliffs north of the ranch, her eyes like stone.

Reece clasped his hands together and gazed at Miyo with his sightless eyes. "By going in, do you mean—?"

"I don't think you need to ask what I mean." Miyo laughed and the early-evening sun lit up her black hair like polished ebony. "You know exactly where I'm going."

"Into the spiritual realms."

"See?" She tilted her head down slightly. "Told you."

"Who's going with you?" Reece stood like a rock except for his mouth.

"No one." She lifted her head. "This is a solo run."

"It's extremely rare for one of us to go into any kind of spiritual realm by ourselves. Why do you think the Spirit is leading you to do this by yourself?"

"Rare for you, maybe," Miyo said. "Not rare for me."

"I'm not your mentor, Miyo, or your father or your grandfather. But I do have experience and lessons I've learned in the spiritual realms over the past thirty years that will save your life. And one of the fundamentals is the same as the old scuba-diving adage: Never dive alone. Always take a partner."

"I don't need a partner for this excursion."

"I disagree."

"I appreciate you offering your opinion."

Reece tilted his head back and took in a long, severe breath. "Where exactly is your excursion going to take you?"

"Into the hinterlands." She glanced down and rubbed her hands back and forth over her knees. The light from the sinking sun flashed off her purple nail polish, which matched her eye shadow. "Always interesting things to see when I do that."

"What are the hinterlands?" Reece cocked his head and put his hands on his hips.

"The classic definition is the land directly adjacent to and inland from a coast, or a region remote from urban areas, backcountry. It comes from the word *hinter* or *behind*, which comes from Middle High German, which developed from the Old High German word *hintar*."

"I see, but I'm thinking you're not using it in that way."

"True. I mean it more in the sense someone familiar with *World of Warcraft* would define it."

"*World of Warcraft*?"

"It's an addictive online role-playing game," Miyo said.

"And what is their definition?"

"The Hinterlands are both a center for the Wildhammer dwarves to the west at Aerie Peak and the forest trolls to the east. It is an ancient region with pine trees, troll ruins, and one of the few remaining high-elf settlements."

"So you're off to see dwarves and trolls and elves?"

"No. I never went in for those role-playing video games. I enjoy the real thing. And I would substitute the words *demons* for *trolls* and *angels* for *elves.*"

"So you're off to some unknown spiritual realm to engage in battle by yourself?"

"Not unknown. I've been there many times."

"For what reason?"

"The Spirit told me to." Miyo lifted her head. Her eyes were intense, and although her words and tone of voice could have been taken as lighthearted, her countenance said the opposite. She glanced at Dana. "Does he grill all of you like this?"

"Usually not. He must like you."

She turned back to Reece. "I'm twenty-three, not twelve."

"In the short time I've known you, I've decided I definitely want you to reach twenty-four."

"And you think I won't because . . . ?"

"I believe you're reckless." Reece spread his feet and folded his arms. "And cocky."

"Based on?"

"Everything you've shown me so far points to that conclusion." Reece turned his face into the sun. "You've never had any problems in a soul or any other spiritual realm?"

"I didn't say that. I said I don't need anyone tagging along."

"As I indicated, that's not wise."

"Where did you latch on to that view?"

"From your grandfather."

"Hmm." She clasped her arms behind her back. "Interesting."

"Not the same advice he gave you?"

"When I started out, yes. I never, ever went in alone. There were never any exceptions. But that changed."

Reece still stood like one of the Easter Island statues. "When you decided it should change?"

"Not a chance. I never even thought about breaking that rule till my grandfater said I was ready to go in by myself."

A breeze brought a strong aroma of pine to their noses, and it took Dana back to camping as a kid. But this wasn't camp. It was a confrontation she'd never seen before. Brandon, Marcus, and she had been so overwhelmed when Reece had first trained them, they'd never challenged or questioned him. Miyo was a very different animal. She wasn't mesmerized by Reece's knowledge and experience because it was clear by now hers likely exceeded his. Maybe by a wide margin. She respected him, but she wasn't going to give a millimeter simply to appease him.

"With age comes wisdom, Miyo." Reece tilted his head down slightly. "I'm offering some of mine."

"Maybe you're not ready to go in alone yet."

"You're joking, right?"

"I never backed out of the arena, Reece. From what I've been told, you did. Got off the field to build that photography business of yours. Maybe if you'd stayed in, you wouldn't be a few grades behind."

The silence that followed was like a snow-covered forest in the dead of winter. Reece stayed in the silence for at least thirty seconds. When he spoke again his voice was tinged with irritation. "As I said before, I am not your mentor but—"

Reece stopped, turned his head in Dana's direction, and rubbed his upper lip. She'd learned this was a clue he was seeing something in the Spirit with his new eyesight. She expected the resulting emotion on his face to be anger, but instead it was surprise. "Do me a favor. Take someone with you this time. Not that I'm saying you need to. Maybe he or she needs it."

"Agreed," Miyo said softly and turned to Dana. "Would you like to have a little adventure?"

No, she wouldn't. It would mean having to face the issues about Miyo that Brandon brought up the other night. Or at least shoving them down deep where they belonged. But at the same time, Miyo was someone she could learn from. "Sure, I'll go."

After they'd strolled away from the fire pit, Dana said, "Don't mind Reece. He's a little overprotective of you."

"Why?"

"I think it's because you remind him of someone," Dana said.

"Who?"

"His daughter."

"My grandfather told me Reece had a daughter and that she died young. But he didn't say much more than that."

"Zennon."

"The demon who killed my grandfather." Miyo's eyes darkened. "What about him?"

"Twenty-six years ago Reece took his wife and daughter into a soul with him and he made a mistake. They ended up in a different soul than Reece thought they were going into. Zennon murdered both of them there."

"Oh wow." Miyo sat back. "Zennon has certainly made his mark among the Warriors."

"Reece said his daughter—her name was Willow—didn't fear anything. Not in a bravado way, but she had strong confidence. A strength in the way some people would describe as an old soul in a young body. He was so proud of her and loved her so much. He was training her at a young age just as Doug trained you from a young age. She was bold. Confident. Ambitious."

"You mean often too driven for her own good and sometimes confident bordering on cocky?" Miyo pointed at herself.

"Maybe something like that."

"I am confident. But not cocky. Maybe early on. But not now." Miyo sighed. "Is there a good spot to go in from?"

"Everywhere on the ranch is good. Since Reece owns the place, there's never an interruption. But I say let's go in up the river a ways."

"He owns Well Spring?" Miyo frowned. "Really? My grandfather never told me that or much about Reece's working life."

Dana led them up a path directly in back of the cabins on the western edge of the property. It wound up a gentle slope for two yards and ended at a small clearing Brandon, Marcus, and she had created together six months ago.

"Photography was extremely good to him over the years. So when he sold his company eleven years back, it meant he never had to work again. He could probably buy twenty ranches this size and it still wouldn't dent his portfolio much."

"Photography?"

"He owned one of the most prestigious lines of galleries in the world."

"Reece is Roth Photography? You've got to be kidding me."

Dana burst out laughing.

"What's so funny?"

"That's exactly the reaction I had. I never put the pieces together till I saw his camera bag out here fifteen months or so ago."

"Couldn't be the just-off-the-street, classic-rock-T-shirt look Reece sports, could it?"

They both laughed. Dana looked at Miyo. "A bit of contrast to the way you dress. I'm guessing the fashion gurus get advice from you."

"I'm just being me. No agenda in it. I don't wear Emilio Pucci and Roberto Cavalli because they're trendy. I wear them because I like them. I hate the attention it brings."

"Really? Sorry to be blunt here, but I had to assume you dress like you do to get a reaction out of people."

"If I dressed down in order to stop the reaction of people, I'd be just as guilty as the people who dress up to get a reaction. In either case I'd be playing small. If everyone in the world was blind, I would still dress like this."

"Playing small?"

"Most people live in fear of what others will think, how they'll react, and it holds them back from being their true selves." Miyo stared deep into Dana's eyes. "Where do you play small, Dana?"

She almost gasped. The question went to her heart like an arrow. But it was the right question—one she needed to face. She played small at work. With the Warriors. At home. Basically everywhere. But there were times she didn't. Those moments didn't come often enough. "Is my jugular vein sticking out so far you just had to go for it?"

"Sorry. I've been told more than once my tongue is one of the bluntest instruments people have ever seen."

"I like it." She did. Miyo said what she thought. No typical female games. Refreshing. But it didn't mean Dana had to like Miyo becoming a star among the Warriors.

"Why did he sell his galleries?"

"He says he liked it too much. Not the photography, the business side of it. Creating an empire. Crushing the competition. The rush of growing something huge. Making lots of money for the sake of making lots of money. And probably more reasons. He rarely talks about it, and then only after I push him to."

They reached the clearing and peace came over Dana. Two chairs sat in the small clearing, and the view the spot gave of Well Spring always made her relax. They both sat and rested in the silence for a moment.

A few minutes later, Miyo held Dana's gaze and there was kindness in it. "You're sure you want to go with me on this ride?"

"Positive."

"Because the roller coasters I ride on don't come with seat belts."

Dana grabbed the sides of her chair and smiled. "Don't worry, I know how to hang on tight."

TWENTY-EIGHT

MIYO GRABBED THE CHAIR'S ARMRESTS, SPREAD HER FINgers over the edges, and squeezed. Then she laid her arms in her lap and slowly leaned her head back till it rested on the back of the chair and closed her eyes. "Ready?"

"Aren't you forgetting something?"

Miyo kept her head back, rolled it toward Dana, and opened one eye. "Not thinking so."

Dana held her hand out, but Miyo just stared at it. "What? You want me to hold your hand? I like you, but aren't we a little old for that?"

"We always hold hands when we go in."

"Really?" Miyo opened her other eye and laughed.

"Always. I thought it was something we had to—" Dana stopped herself.

"Fascinating." Miyo sat up and studied Dana. "You think it's like some connection point so you both go to the same spot? That if you weren't touching you'd spin off into different realms?"

Dana stared at her. It was exactly like that. It's what Reece had taught them. It's why they lost Marcus last year in a spiritual realm when the crevasse opened up and the professor couldn't reach them, and he'd nearly been sucked into one of Zennon's alternate realities. But obviously it wasn't an issue with Miyo. Had Doug taught her an advanced technique?

"You don't touch?"

"First, since I can't really remember the last time I went in with someone, there hasn't been the option to hold someone's hand. Second, I'm not sure what the purpose of doing it would be. Unless it strengthens the— No, you're right." Miyo looked up as if she was remembering. "We used to do that when I was in my early teens, but when I was about sixteen my grandfather said I'd grown beyond needing to do that." She frowned. "But if it makes you feel better, I don't mind doing it."

Yes, it would make her feel better. Dana felt like she was six years old talking to her babysitter, and here she was fourteen years older than Miyo. Dana's face grew hot and she hoped her embarrassment wasn't obvious to Miyo. If it was, Doug's granddaughter didn't act in any way like she'd noticed it.

"Yes. It would help."

"Then let's do it." Miyo grasped Dana's hand and Well Spring vanished.

Every time Dana had traveled into a soul or into another spiritual realm, there had been a sensation of movement, a changing, a sensation she was swimming. With Miyo, one moment they sat on the chairs hearing the sound of the river in the distance, the next they stood in a forest of thick alder trees. Lush moss and ferns carpeted the ground, and a smattering of sunlight filtered through the emerald leaves. Large, round boulders dotted the landscape.

"How did you get us here so fast? It was almost instantaneous."

"Not almost." Miyo tilted her head and stared at her. "This was unusual for you?"

"We've never traveled this fast."

"Then you've placed a limitation on yourselves. Time is a restraint embedded in the soul and body. Our spirits have no such limitations, and since our spirits are what travel into souls and spiritual realms, the journey from the physical world into the spiritual does not need to take any time unless we choose for it to."

"You sound like Marcus."

"I'm looking forward to the day Marcus realizes many of the theories in his books are not theories but realities."

"He's realized some of them."

"Far fewer than he knows." Miyo glanced around the forest, then turned back to Dana. "How many armies have you spoken into existence such as Ezekiel did?"

"I think Reece or Doug might have mentioned the possibility at some point."

"In other words, none."

"Are you always this direct?" Dana grinned.

"Too much?" Miyo narrowed her eyes. "There I go again. My apologies."

"Not needed. As I said earlier, I like it." Dana squeezed Miyo's hand. "I'm not really a play-the-game type girl."

"I knew that about you the second I met you."

For the first time since Dana had met her, Miyo gave an unrestrained smile where her eyes and smile were in perfect concert with each other.

"You're beautiful when you really smile."

"Really smile?"

"A smile with your guard down."

"I see a heightened sense of perception is one of your gifts." Miyo shook her head and smiled again.

"Sometimes. I lead a radio station in Seattle. Often success is more about knowing people than knowing numbers."

"I bet."

Dana studied the forest. The beauty of it captivated her, but something was out of place. Not out of place. Missing. Ah, that was it. There was no sound. No birds, no sound of water from a far-off stream, no buzzing of insects, no breeze through the leaves above them. The forest was still as if it were frozen.

"Why do I feel like we're the only things here that are alive?"

"We should be." Miyo stopped on the edge of the clearing and motioned Dana to do the same. "But I can't be certain. Let's be watchful."

They padded over the forest floor, both turning their heads back and forth. Five minutes later they reached a small clearing thirty or forty feet across. Long, wispy grass leaned to the left and covered the meadow, and with the sun now directly on them, the temperature of the realm seemed to rise five degrees.

The tree in the center of the clearing made a perfect half circle as if it grew out of two separate places in the ground and met seamlessly in the middle. The arch was ten or eleven feet wide at the base and seven or eight feet tall.

"An elegant tree," Dana said.

"That's more than a tree. It's a gateway. Do you want to go through?"

"A gateway to where? We can see right through it. There's nothing on the other side."

"You know how in the Field of Doors the doors appear to go nowhere? When in reality they take you into a person's soul?" Miyo moved her right hand under her left in a fluid motion.

Dana nodded. "Like Marcus when he went through the door of his memories. The inside was so much bigger than the outside."

"Marcus went through his memory's door?"

She nodded. "Changed his life."

"I bet. I've heard of those but have never seen one. I suppose the only time you would see one is if you're viewing your own." Miyo pointed at the tree. "It's the same thing here as with Marcus's door. This is a gateway or a door into another realm." Miyo motioned Dana forward. "Shall we?"

Miyo winked and held out her hand. Dana smiled and took it. As they approached the arched tree, a thin line of light appeared on either side of the trunk. After two more steps, the air in between the half circle of the tree began to shimmer.

"Ready?" Miyo asked.

"Sure." Her heart pounded but she had no fear of stepping through—only anticipation. Two more steps. One more.

Just before they stepped into the shimmering air, Miyo leaned back and yanked Dana's hand hard. Both of them stumbled backward and Dana fell to the ground.

Miyo kept her gaze riveted on the gateway as she helped Dana up. "Sorry."

"What was that for?" Dana brushed herself off and stared at Miyo.

"Are you okay?"

"Fine, but what—?"

"Something's not right." Miyo's gaze roamed all around the tree. "Can you feel it?"

"No."

"It's there. Believe me, whatever is on the other side of this gate is not our friend." Miyo glanced back at the archway. "We need to get geared up before we go through there."

"We're still going through?"

"Sure." Miyo smiled. "But first, are you still certain you want to be here? This is my mission, not yours. This trip has just turned from one of discovery into one of battle. We can leave right now."

Dana didn't want to go on. She wanted to be safe and warm and cozy and have a perfect little life of no struggles and no worries, where she had a man who truly loved her for who she was, not for what she did. But that wasn't reality and never would be. Life wasn't white chocolate and wedding invitations and happily ever afters. Not hers anyway.

"Absolutely."

"This is no time to posture, Dana. I can see it in your eyes and feel it pulsating off your spirit. You're scared."

"I'm terrified, yes. But I don't posture." Dana narrowed her eyes. "Ever."

"I believe you."

Dana glanced at the air in the archway. It had grown thicker during the time they'd talked. It looked like the frosted glass in the wall of her shower back home. Only this glass swirled like liquid.

"Is that going to continue getting thicker?"

"Yes, and it's easier to navigate the thinner it is. So we should go through in the next few minutes. I got stuck one time in something similar for seventeen hours. It wasn't fun." Miyo looked at Dana from under her eyebrows. "Still good to go?"

"Yes."

"Then let's get armored up. We'll be glad we did."

Miyo tilted her head back, closed her eyes, and held her slightly raised arms out to her sides. A soft yellow light appeared at Miyo's feet and moved up her legs as if it were water flowing the opposite direction gravity would take it. As the light moved past her knees and over her waist, it changed, growing thinner and brighter till Dana had to squint against its brilliance.

In seconds, Miyo was surrounded and she opened her eyes and turned in a slow circle, gazing at the landscape and then at the arched tree. "Much better. I think we'll be glad we put these—" She stopped and stared at Dana. "We don't have time to waste. When I said a few minutes I meant it. You know we're not supposed to spend too much time inside any kind of spiritual realm. Ever."

Dana gawked at the light swirling around Miyo. "How did you do that? And what is it?"

"You don't know?" Miyo laughed, and the light around her seemed to grow thicker. "It's light. Pure light of God. Didn't Reece ever show you how to do this?"

She shook her head. Dana had the distinct feeling Reece would be as startled as she was at Miyo's revelation.

"How do the four of you protect yourselves when you're inside?" Miyo frowned. "What things did he teach you?"

"He started with showing us how to send our spirits into a soul. Then teleportation. Then—"

"It was a rhetorical question. I'll get you started on your armor and you can finish it." Miyo raised her hands and held them wide and then six inches from Dana's body. Slowly, a paper-thin light formed and spread around her feet just as it had a moment ago on Miyo's. And the pressure was like a spa bodywrap but the feeling was far better.

Warmth and strength surged through her body, and part of her wanted to burst out in laughter. The light inched up her legs as it had done with Miyo. By the time it reached Dana's stomach, a powerful sense of peace filled her mind.

"What is this?" Dana didn't need to ask the question. She now knew exactly what it was—not because Miyo had told her, but because it had become a part of her—but she had to say something.

"It's armor, Dana."

"Armor? Made of light?" The question seemed silly once Dana asked it. Why couldn't armor be made of light? Maybe it was impossible in the physical world, but what would stop God from doing it here?

"Yes. Light. Made of his power and strength and invulnerability." Miyo seemed to examine the thickness of the light surrounding Dana with the precision of a surgeon. When she came to Dana's right shoulder, Miyo moved her hand in a circle a half inch above the light and it thickened. "I thought you read the Bible."

"Your point?" She glared at Miyo.

Miyo grinned in return. "'The night is nearly over; the day is almost here. So let us put aside the deeds of darkness and put on the armor of light.'"

"Romans," Dana said, feeling like she'd heard the verse for the first time.

"Ah, so you do read the Word." Miyo tapped her forehead.

"Don't mock me."

"I apologize."

"I never took that verse literally." Dana stared at the light cocooned around her and laughed with a joy she couldn't keep inside. Of course. That had to be another part of this. The joy of the Lord was strength.

"Sometimes the Bible is taken far too literally; sometimes it is not taken literally enough. As you can see, this is a case where the latter is the truer of the two statements."

"This is amazing. Why didn't I ever see that?"

"The Word of God is living—it's not a stagnant book. It's animated. Things will come alive to you that you have missed for years. Still others will take years more before you see them."

"But still—"

"Don't feel bad. I just discovered this armor two years ago." Miyo's eyes grew distant. "And believe me, it would have saved me a great deal of pain if I'd learned it earlier."

"I thought you were going to teach me how to do this for myself."

"I can't teach you. I can only show you—which I've done. Now it's time for you to practice the technique."

"How?"

"The only way any of this works," Miyo said. "Think about it. How have each of your battles been won so far?"

"Belief."

Miyo nodded. "If you had the faith of a mustard seed, Dana, you could toss mountains into the sea like they were pebbles. I showed you so you could believe it was possible. Now it's time for you to believe."

Dana stared as the light around her body faded. Slowly at first, then faster like it was being sucked into an invisible drain under her feet. In ten seconds it was gone. She felt vulnerable. "Where did it go?"

"I created it, which gave me the power to release it. Now you're going to create it and you'll have control over the armor."

"I'll try."

"There is no try."

"Yoda." She pointed at Miyo. "I thought you were a geek when you made that comment about *World of Warcraft*. This confirms it."

"You must be one, too, if you know the quote." She pushed back her black hair.

"Not me. Brandon. When we were—" Dana stopped. She didn't need to be spilling all her secrets to this woman. Besides, the subject of Brandon wasn't one she needed to be worried about right now.

"I suspected you two had a history together."

"No you didn't."

"It's pretty obvious." Miyo smiled.

"What is? I don't—"

"Don't what? Let your eyes always linger on him a fraction of a second longer than is normal?"

"What!" Dana scowled playfully and shook her head. "Don't you mean the way he lets his gaze stay on me?"

"Uh . . . no." The smile stayed on Miyo's face.

"That's it? Just 'no'?"

"Let's concentrate on you putting on your armor, okay?"

Dana shook herself as if that could get rid of thoughts of Brandon. Armor? Right. But she had no idea how she would make it happen, and Miyo didn't seem to be offering any coaching other than to believe. But that was fine. Dana had seen and experienced enough over the past year and a half to know leaping off a cliff with the flight plan already in place was the exception, not the rule.

She closed her eyes, pushed her doubt away, and pictured a cocoon of light surrounding her feet and moving up her legs. Instantly her feet felt surrounded in the same warmth she'd experienced a few minutes ago. She opened her eyes and stared at the liquid light swirling around her toes and arches and ankles. "Oh wow." But a moment later the light faded and seemed to soak into the wild grass at her feet.

"What happened?" She turned to Miyo.

"You lost concentration. You let your thought of astonishment crowd out your belief. With the thought of wonder came the thought something along the lines of, 'I can't believe I'm really doing this.' Am I right?"

She was exactly right.

"It will help if you let go of the idea that you're doing anything.

You're not. He is the one creating the armor. You're only tapping into the power that is already residing in you. You have all the power of the God of the universe at your disposal. We have been seated at the right hand of the Father in the heavenly places. Think about that. You don't have the power of Dana. She's dead—crucified with Christ. But the Dana that is now alive with Christ has incredible power. So creating a small armor of light around your body is nothing. Go again."

This time the light started at her feet and streaked up her legs and torso like wildfire. In seconds, her entire body was surrounded by light—thicker across her chest and over her head, thinner around her hands and fingers. It felt stronger than the earlier armor Miyo had created and Dana said so.

"Yes. The armor you create for yourself will always be more powerful than armor created by another. The only one who knows your weaknesses better than yourself is the Spirit. And since you are creating it in unison with him, the result is a protection perfect for your spirit, soul, and body."

"Amazing." Again came the thought of how incredible the light was, and the armor started to fade. But Dana torched the thought before it had time to take hold, and the light thickened again to the level it had been.

"Good. You're learning quickly." Miyo padded around her in a complete circle on the soft grass. "Well done."

"Can the enemy pierce this armor in battle? Will it hold up?"

Miyo stopped when she completed the circle and her face grew somber. "I'm going to give you a chance to find out."

"So we're going in."

"No."

"What? I thought—"

"Look at the opening."

It still swirled, but now at an eighth the speed it had earlier. It had turned to a dark gold reminiscent of honey and just as thick.

"We wouldn't be able to get through that, would we?"

"Getting through would be extremely easy. Getting back out would be the challenge. And what's inside is not our friend."

"Then why would you take me in there?"

"The Spirit told me to." Miyo paused. "I'm not an outlaw, contrary to what Reece might believe. I'm not doing these things on my own. This is not a playground. I only ever do what the Spirit tells me to do. The Spirit told me to invite you, and Reece mentioned it before I could. He saw it, too, and was true enough to admit it.

"You try going into spiritual realms without the Spirit's invitation and at best you'll get severely hurt. Worst case is you'll be headed into eternity earlier than the divine design called for. So I have to assume God wants you to learn something inside that realm."

"Then why did you make it seem like a suggestion for me to come? Like it was my choice and I could take it or leave it?"

"You can take it or leave it. That's the Spirit. He's never going to force you into anything. While I believe there is a specific destiny God has planned for each of us, I also believe we have free will. We have choice. If I presented my invitation in a way where you couldn't say no—'God told me you have to come in with me!'—then you'd either have to say God didn't tell me that and act against it, or disobey. Besides, sometimes I'm wrong. Sometimes I think the Spirit has told me something he hasn't. I figure if God is part of it, it'll work itself out."

"But doesn't that keep you from fighting hard for things he's told you to fight for?"

"No. When I say I hold decisions loosely, I mean other people's decisions. When it comes to my own actions and obedience, I'm fierce."

Dana stared at the archway as she mulled over Miyo's words. "So if you were supposed to take me in there, does that mean we can try again sometime?"

"Most certainly."

"When?"

"Tomorrow."

"Why does the look on your face concern me?"

Miyo stared at her, a little smile at the corners of her mouth. "If I'm hearing the Spirit right, what you will learn inside there will be really freeing for you, and really hard."

TWENTY-NINE

TRISTAN BARROW PACED ACROSS THE NARROW RIDGE, HIS
boots tearing into the loose shale at his feet and sending it falling
into the river canyon below him. His six-foot-six frame moved like
a lion, his thick blond hair and broad shoulders completing the picture of a world-class athlete.

Orson—to Tristan's left—shifted the weight of his chunky
body back and forth and stared straight ahead. Jotham stood on his
right, his short lean frame twitching as if ready to strike. To either
side of them were two more angels. In the distance, on the other
side of the canyon, Tristan saw a small cloud of dust rise from three
figures that moved toward them.

"I don't like it." Orson folded his arms and glared at the three
beings. "What's the point of having even a shred of discourse with
him?"

"Let not your heart be concerned. His goal for this encounter is
knowledge. To poke and prod at us. Not battle."

Of this, Tristan was certain. Both Orson, Jotham, and the two
others had been under his authority for seven centuries of human
time and were proven warriors who had joined him in more than
six thousand battles. If this encounter came to war, so be it. He had
not even a sliver of fear that he and his warriors wouldn't emerge

victorious. Their enemies knew it as well. Which was why swords would not be drawn. Today.

A jagged wind surged up from the canyon below and buffeted them like a sandstorm. A current of evil designed to instill doubt and fear. None of his warriors would succumb to the lie, but it was irritating nonetheless.

"I don't like this either." Jotham reached for the hilt of his sword and massaged the leather-wrapped hilt. "We should destroy them the moment they appear."

"Patience," Tristan said. "We are here to listen." He turned to his left. "Rantor, take a position twenty paces farther out." He turned to his right and issued the same order to the angel there.

When the three figures were two hundred or so yards away, they vanished. An instant later the ground shook with the strength of an earthquake, and the three figures stood across the canyon from them, thirty yards away.

The one in the middle took out a gold coin and flipped it in the air, caught it, and stared at the markings on its surface. He glanced up at Tristan, then back to the coin.

"I like the human's worship of this mineral." Zennon rolled it around his fingers. "It is quite beautiful. But its beauty is nothing like the garden before the earth was corrupted."

"Don't waste the moments I have given you." Tristan's voice was ice. "If you have words to speak, say them now."

"Quite right." Zennon grinned. "By the way, old friend, I'm sorry you didn't arrive in time to keep Brandon Scott's throat from being slashed open. How is he doing? Still dedicated to the cause? Rumor says not as fully as he once was."

Tristan still stood like granite, his hands at his sides, his fingers loose. "Why did you ask for this time, demon?"

"Demon?" Zennon stopped twirling the coin and looked at Tristan in mock amazement. "You're not seriously using that word, are you? Have you been truly humanized from walking around in those flesh suits too often?"

"Get to the reason you've come."

"You don't remember me, do you, Tristan?" Zennon frowned. "From the old days, I mean."

"Why did you call us here?"

"Come now. Think back. I was a lowly angel in those days. And you were the mighty Tristan, the great avenger. I asked to be in your battalion. I came to you and pledged my loyalty. You took your sword and offered me your strength. I asked for more. To have power equal to yours. To stand by your side for eternity. But you refused. You said I needed to do more to earn that kind of power."

Tristan didn't answer.

"Good. I see in your eyes you do remember. Do you also remember calling me your brother? Your friend? Is that why you were assigned to Reece and the other Warriors? Because of our history? I'm simply curious."

Again, Tristan didn't respond.

"We explored the universe together. Past the Milky Way to the outer reaches. We were like brothers, Tristan Barrow. I wanted to be like you. And then the renting came. And you seethed with anger at our leap into freedom. You even cried out in rage when you discovered I'd gone with the Morning Star. Do you remember?"

Tristan tensed. "Lucifer is only a depraved imitation of the true Morning Star."

"He hasn't lost any of his beauty, contrary to how man has painted him. Who would want to follow a monster? Remember when the battalion used to watch him go through his exercises? None could match him. His power. His speed. His strength.

"He still does them. And he will win. Why? Because the Master isn't relying on humans who have shown such weakness again and again over the centuries. He relies on us who have sworn loyalty to him till the end."

Zennon stepped up to the edge of the canyon so the front of his feet hung over the side. "Do you know why I turned? I asked him to give me what you would not. He answered by taking my shoulders and waiting till I lifted my eyes to his and held his gaze. Then he said, 'You shall have the power you crave and more. And I will not delay.'" Zennon tilted his head back. "It was a glorious moment. I believed him. I embraced the Morning Star in that moment and my heart was his.

"He asked that I bow to him and pledge my strength, and I did. He asked that I follow him to the depths of Sheol and the heights of heaven, and I swore I would. He asked me to pledge my life to him, and I agreed. And then he asked me to worship him, and I did. He raised me up and held me like a son, and in that embrace I felt power flow into me like I'd never known. A power you could have given me but refused."

Zennon paced along the edge of the cliff, and with each step the rocks under his boots shattered. He lifted his hand toward a massive column of rock to his right and it exploded in a shower of baseball-sized chunks. In the next instant, Zennon whirled and flung his hand toward the angel on Tristan's left. A boulder the size of a bus hurtled toward him like lightning.

Tristan spun to his right and threw a bolt of light like a javelin at the boulder. It pierced the stone in the center and reduced it to dust long before it reached Rantor.

"I see your reflexes are still in working order." Zennon stared at his palm. "But I'm not so sure about them." Zennon pointed at Jotham and Orson. "Or him." He jabbed a finger at the angel on Tristan's right. "Or him."

Zennon motioned to the soldiers on either side of him. "If you tried the same attack on my friends, they would not have needed me to come to the rescue. And when we next meet in battle, I assure you, you will have too much to occupy yourself to have time to come to the aid of your friends here, or the humans."

"Are you finished?" Tristan asked.

"Are your precious Warriors—these tents of flesh you've grown so fond of—truly ready for what you must sense is coming?" Zennon swept his hand over the horizon. "No. They are not. And because they are not, they will be destroyed.

"One more thing." Zennon steepled his fingers. "Do you wonder if I'm more powerful than you now? If I could defeat you in battle?" Zennon laughed. "I think you're worried I would dance in the pool of blood that poured out of your side if I had the chance to face you alone.

"But this isn't a war between you and me. The humans are irrevocably intertwined. And as I've said, they are not anywhere near ready. Give them to me now. Lift your protection of them. Hand them over to me and there will be no war between us."

"They have defeated you multiple times."

"Those were skirmishes. You know this. Yet you haven't told them. They think they've won great victories."

"They have." Tristan laid his hand on his sword. "And they will. They are complete."

"Oh, you think adding Miyo will make a difference?" Zennon shook his head. "Hardly. She's too young, too impetuous. Brash. Cocky. Splattered with pride. You're resting so much hope on her and she will fail. All of them are deluded about their skills and ability to stand against me, and you continue to let them believe the lie. You who say you are of the truth. We are not so different, my commander." Zennon spit on the ground and rubbed it into the dirt with the toe of his boot. "This will be you very soon."

Tristan again remained silent.

"Come now, old friend. There must be words of response waiting to explode against me. I know you. I feel it radiating off of you like the sun. You long to see how much stronger I am than you and if you have a chance of winning."

"This is over." Tristan's words rang out over the canyon and echoed back to them like a cannon shot. "Go, demon, in the power of the One!"

Zennon and the demons at his side vanished.

"What was that?" Jotham spat out the words. "How could you take that refuse from Zennon?" He lifted a hand and flicked it toward the spot where Zennon had stood. The ground exploded in a geyser of rocks, and when the dust cleared, that part of the cliff was demolished.

"Unnecessary anger does not befit a warrior."

"Righteous anger always befits a warrior."

Tristan stared at Jotham but didn't speak.

"Fine." Jotham jerked his neck back and forth.

"Your chance for retaliation will come, brother. Soon." Tristan paused and looked at the rest of his warriors. "That was time well spent."

"To have him insult you and the rest of us was time well spent?"

"We learned two critical elements about the coming war. First, that Zennon is worried about Miyo, so we must guard her well." Tristan's hand went to the hilt of his sword. "And second, that Zennon longs to meet me in single combat."

The angel smiled, bowed his head, and raised both palms. "If it be your desire, I will answer the call with all that I am."

THIRTY

THE NEXT DAY AFTER BREAKFAST, MIYO AND DANA AGAIN
stood in the clearing with the arched tree in the center. The forest
was just as still. The shimmering light in the archway was clear again.

"Still feeling good about this?" Miyo pointed at the gateway
they were about to step through.

"The adrenaline pumping through me right now is about to
burst out of my veins."

"Good. That means you're on high alert. You'll need that."

"Are you taking me into something I can't handle?"

"We won't know till we're back at Well Spring," Miyo said. "One
more time. Are you sure you want to do this?"

Dana stared at Miyo and then at the arched tree. She was far
from sure. Her nerves made her response come out in a squeak. "I'm
sure."

Miyo laughed. "That's not real convincing."

Dana glared at her. "Let's go."

"Yes, let's."

They both covered themselves in light-armor, and when she
finished, Miyo studied Dana's construction.

Miyo circled her. "Well done. You've learned faster than anyone
I've taught." Dana couldn't help but smile at the compliment.

"Now make it a bit thicker all around."

Dana closed her eyes and pictured the light around her as more substantial, and seconds later the warmth intensified and the pressure on her skin grew.

"Excellent." Miyo turned to the gateway. "I can't tell you much about what we'll find once we pass through. It changes every time. But I will remind you that the greatest battle is in your mind. Okay?"

An icy chill shot through Dana's body as she stepped through the shimmering air in the archway, but it vanished as their new surroundings came into focus. They stood on a tropical white sandy beach with medium-sized waves crashing onto the shoreline.

Both of them wore khaki shorts. Miyo had on a black tank top. Dana glanced down at the *Life is good* T-shirt she wore. True. Some of life was good. But not all. And she had little doubt what they were about to walk into was one of the not-all parts. Because something about the scene was extremely familiar, and the feeling it stirred in her was not good.

A few clouds dotted the sky and a breeze pushed at them from the front, carrying with it the scent of suntan lotion. The day was hot and the sun bright even though it was on its way toward setting. She guessed it was around four o'clock if there was time in this realm. The beach was empty where they stood, but she spotted adults, children, and teens playing in the water and sand fifty yards ahead of them. The brightness of the sun made Dana's armor almost imperceptible and she frowned.

"It's still there, Dana. Trust me. Trust yourself. Trust the Spirit. Even though you can't see the armor as well, can you still feel it?"

Dana nodded. "But not as strong." She gazed down the beach at children cavorting in the water, and the sand filled with women reading books under bright-red beach umbrellas or tossing Frisbees and baseballs with their kids.

Dana scowled. If the scene was designed to give her a false sense of tranquility and lightness, it wasn't working. A dark current of dread pricked at her as whatever this reminded her of tried to surface.

"Are you ready?" Miyo asked.

"Sure."

As they walked toward the people, Miyo said, "Remember, the enemy's greatest strength is deception. Illusion. Making what is true invisible and making visible that which is not true. If we react to those external and internal images, he will use those emotions against us, and in an instant we can make agreements about ourselves that aren't true. Let's lock this truth into our minds right now: emotions are not reality."

After a minute they approached a dark-red lifeguard tower. A small group of five or six people stood at its base. Most of them pointed at her, gave sad little smiles, and whispered to each other.

"Steady, Dana. Concentrate."

Dana's face grew hot. Why were they pointing at her? She had to let it go. It wasn't real. But she couldn't shake the feeling it was entirely real. She turned to Miyo to ask for an answer and gasped. Her friend wasn't there. Dana spun in a circle but Miyo had vanished.

"Miyo!"

"Problem, ma'am?" a male voice called. The lifeguard sitting at the top of the tower. Tall, dark haired, tan with a ripped six-pack. He stood and jammed his fists onto his hips.

The words sputtered out of Dana's mouth before she could stop them. "My friend just—"

"Friend? Oh, Dana, I'm so sorry to be the one to break it to you. You have no friends. Not true ones, anyway." The lifeguard grinned and swept his hand in a wide half circle. "Just like back in high school." He paused as if waiting for some kind of acknowledgment from her. "C'mon, Dana, you have to remember this scene we've created for you. No one can bury a memory that deep."

Seconds later the memory flooded her. Mid-July after her ninth-grade year. She and the rest of the girls from her youth group were gathered on this beach—no, not this beach, one *like* this beach— where they all watched the sun melt into the horizon.

Her youth leader, Sherri, stood as the girls sat crisscrossed in a semicircle around her. Nineteen years old—still young enough to understand high school girls but old enough to really be somebody—Sherri had started the youth group with just Dana.

"I think God brought us together, Dana. I see a uniqueness in you. Strength. He wants to build something special and you're the one I want to help me. And besides, I just like you."

She'd been chosen. Singled out. Loved for who she was. Sherri and Dana met every Wednesday for five weeks, getting to know each other, praying together, talking about who Dana could invite, discussing how the meetings would go. Sherri made her feel like her pappy did, but this was someone who wasn't supposed to love her but still did, and loved her deeply.

Dana started asking all of her friends to come to the group, and soon there were almost ten girls gathering at Sherri's apartment every week. Sherri seemed to praise her more for each new girl Dana invited. By the time she'd brought sixteen girls, they'd moved the meeting to Dana's house, and Sherri spent at least a couple evenings a week hanging out with Dana, goofing off, going to movies or talking on the phone. Mentor, friend, confidant, spiritual leader, big sister, all rolled into one.

But as the year went on and the number of girls coming grew, Sherri called less often—their dates were spread out further and further, and during their meetings, Sherri didn't ask how Dana felt about things much anymore. And the look she used to give Dana now went to Kendal and Morgan and Emma.

Sherri dug her feet into the sand. "All right, girls. I know it seems like school just got out, but September will be here in a flash, and that means I'm going to need some of you to be my key advisers as you head into your sophomore year. But it will take some time." She smiled and pointed to Kendal, Morgan, and Emma. "Will you three girls be willing to meet with me one extra day per week?"

All three shifted in the sand and cried, "Yes!"

Dana's stomach felt like lead.

"Great! I'll call all of you tomorrow." Sherri glanced around at the rest of them and pointed down the beach. "Okay, girls, let's get that campfire lit before the light fades!"

As the other girls shuffled off, Dana went up to Sherri. "Can I talk to you for a minute?"

"Sure."

"I'm not . . . I don't understand."

"What is it, Dana? You can tell me."

"I thought maybe I would be one of the council members, you know? 'Cause I've been here since the group began. I mean, we kinda started this thing together and—"

"Oh, Dana." Sherri laughed. "Don't think that you're not very, very important. You are."

"But I like hanging out and it doesn't seem like you have much—"

"Time for you lately?"

"Yes." Dana dropped her head and studied the sand. "And I'm feeling like the reason you don't is because I'm not . . . not doing enough for you." She dug her toes in the sand. "That that's the reason you . . . Like when I was inviting my friends to come to the group . . . you and I were doing a lot together. So I'm thinking maybe—"

"Oh, Dana, don't take it like that. You're awesome! It's just that . . . well, some people are feet and some people are elbows and some people are heads. We're all the same body but with different things to do, you know? And I just think these girls are best at brainstorming and leadership-type things, okay?"

"I think I can maybe be a leader. In school I've been on—"

"Tell you what." Sherri smiled. "You get some more girls to come to the group during the first half of the year, and we can talk about you maybe joining the other council girls and me after winter break, okay?"

Sherri patted Dana's arm and strolled off to where Emma, Kendal, and Morgan waited halfway to the campfire.

When the calendar reached November, Dana had brought ten more girls to the group, and Sherri started spending time with her again. Lunch dates, an occasional movie, and she was invited into the inner circle. By the time June appeared, Dana had introduced fifteen more regulars.

But in her junior year, Dana was buried in AP classes, track, the school paper, and she stopped inviting girls. And Sherri stopped calling. By December, Dana stopped going to the group. Sherri never called to ask why.

Dana snapped herself back to the present. "Those memories have no hold on me." She spun to glare at the lifeguard, but he was gone. The beach was empty except for a teenage girl around fourteen with shiny brown hair and sky-blue eyes.

"Hi, Dana." The girl smiled, crossed her legs, and patted the sand. "Sit down."

"I'll stand, thanks."

"You don't remember me, do you?"

Dana stared at her as flecks of recognition peppered her mind. "You look like—"

"Alene Richardson."

"Yes."

Alene laughed. "I am her, but we both know that's not really true. But God thought it would help you work through things if there was someone from those days who was in the group, who truly understood how painful it was."

"I see."

"Will you sit?" Alene patted the ground again. "It won't be easy, but it will be so good. You've now been taken back into the wound so we can get it healed."

Dana sat and as she did, Alene said, "To start, I think you're honest, Dana. Too honest to make statements like, 'That memory has no hold on me.'"

"Okay. That's true."

"I mean, even when you figured out that performing to get people to love you was a trap, you kept doing it. Because by that time it was a habit you just couldn't break. Since then you've always had to perform better than anyone else. I remember you in high school running the 1600 meters and being so driven to win. And then on the school paper so determined to get the editor position. Then in college in your photography classes having to get straight As.

"Same thing with your friendships, always being the one to come through for them. When you were a salesperson starting out in radio, your entire focus was to become the best. Same thing as a sales manager, and now as your station's general manager. Even with the Warriors—you are loved because you perform well."

"What?" A chill raced down Dana's back. "It's not just because—"

"No time for lies here. What would happen at the station if you stopped performing? Fired. What would happen to all your friends if you stopped coming through for them? Do you think Miyo would still like you if you stopped picking up her training so quickly? What about Reece and Marcus and Brandon? Ah yes, Brandon. Take a close look at him. You always met all his expectations, and even that wasn't good enough for him. Because you're not good enough. And certainly not good enough as the supposed Leader."

Dana stood and staggered back three steps. Alene stood and took a deliberate step toward her.

"I don't even have to tell you to take a close look at Miyo, because you already have. She leads like a lion. You've done a few good things in spiritual realms, but compared to Miyo you're a bunny rabbit. It would take years to become the leader she already is. And face it, when the Warriors truly see Miyo's skills, they're going to discard—"

"Stop it!"

"They'll leave. Just like Sherri left. Like your new, uh, *friend* Miyo just did. Not very nice to skip out like that. But I'm guessing she figured it was better to get rid of you now rather than drag out the process."

The Spirit's voice stirred deep inside. *Fight it, Dana.*

Fight it? With what? Her armor of light was gone from sight, and even though she still felt it, she also felt it getting thinner, as if Alene's gaze was melting it.

Know the truth.

Dana blinked and dug her feet into the sand. Yes, the incident on the beach had happened back in high school. Sherri wasn't a friend. But Reece, Doug, Marcus, Miyo, and even Brandon were her friends. But even if they weren't, it didn't matter. She was called friend by the King of kings. And he didn't love her because she was useful or executed well. He loved her for her. Nothing else.

"I don't have to perform. I don't have to be perfect."

Alene flicked her finger repeatedly toward Dana in cadence with her voice and walked in a slow circle. "Miyo is not your friend. She has her own agenda. So does Reece. You think he would be your friend if not for the prophecy? And for what you've done for his little band? He's using you."

Dana dug her feet farther into the sand and pushed the lies from her mind. "I bind you by the blood of the Messiah. I know who I am and I know what you are. Get away from me by the power of his rule." The pressure around her increased—her armor thickened.

As Alene circled again, her form shimmered and Dana blinked. Alene was gone and the lifeguard stood in front of her again. He grinned and wagged a finger toward her.

"Your days of performing in hopes of getting a man are over. No man wants you any longer, Dana. You're too old now. You're frustrated. Damaged goods. How many guys have dumped you since your first little romance with Johnny boy your freshman year?"

The guard drew closer as he continued to circle. "Brandon says he dumped you because of his own wounds. You don't truly believe that, do you? When are you going to wake up and understand that it's because he finally got to know the real you? And found out you'll never be able to come through for him, never be able to drop the walls really. Not enough for someone to want to marry you. And just like all the guys who have gotten to know the real you, Brandon vanished."

The words pounded against Dana's mind, and the thickness of her armor again shrank as the lifeguard's eyes grew darker.

"No, he's interested in me again."

195

The lifeguard burst into laughter. "The only reason he's showing a shred of interest is because he's even more damaged than you. Grasping at anything to make him feel better. Let him get close and you know how it will turn out. Dumped again. Brandon is for Brandon. You know this is true." The lifeguard was only a few feet from her now.

"I am not alone. And I'm not loved for exceeding people's expectations."

"Always have been. Always will be. We're coming for you, Dana. And we can't be stopped."

"Yes. You can." The words sputtered out of her mouth.

"Are you kidding?" The lifeguard's white teeth seemed to glow even in the bright sunshine. "And let me tell you a little secret. Even if you do get out of here, Miyo will leave you in the real world too. She will turn on you. Mark my words. She will abandon you in the moment of your greatest need."

Dana slashed at the thought and replaced it immediately. "A lie. Miyo is my friend. And I am his beloved and he is my shield and my strength. Go, in the name of Christ."

"Nice try."

"He will never leave me, never abandon me, even till the end of the age." She stabbed her finger toward the demon. "I am his workmanship. Fearfully and wonderfully made. I have the power of the risen Christ flowing through my body, soul, and spirit. And you cannot stand against that power. In the name of Jesus Christ, go and be judged by the Alpha and Omega!"

Darkness flashed over the lifeguard's face.

"Jesus. Lord. Lion of the tribe of Judah. He is my shield. My fortress. I am more than a conqueror. And I won't listen to your lies any longer." She took a step toward him. "King. Warrior. Savior. Jesus!"

Strength pulsed through her and the armor around her felt like steel. The lifeguard staggered back, his eyes flashing dark light. "When you are left utterly alone in the midst of the war, we will kill you. It is coming. We are nearly ready, and when we are, you will die."

Dana almost laughed. This time the words made no impact. They didn't raise any emotion of fear. She felt her side. The armor of light. Even thicker now.

"Go!" She pointed at the demon again. *"Now!"*

The lifeguard vanished, and the instant he disappeared, Miyo appeared beside her.

"Let's get out of here," Miyo said.

"Where did you go?"

"You know the answer."

She stared at Miyo as the realization washed over her. "You were there the whole time but blocked from speaking."

"Yes." Miyo smiled, her dark eyes lit up with joy. "You agreed with the lies. You gave them power. In order for your eyes to be opened, you had to break the agreement that you are only loved when you perform well and meet expectations. And by the way, believe me, I am your friend."

They both slipped back into their bodies and Dana let out a long sigh. "Wow. That was like nothing before. I expected the battle inside there to be one with swords and fireballs and—"

"As I've said before, the battleground is in our minds. That's where the war will be won or lost." Miyo stood and squeezed Dana's shoulder. "You were excellent in there. I had no doubt. Take some time to celebrate what you learned about the battle and about the strength you carry so well. I'm going to take a shower."

Dana sat by herself at the same spot above Well Spring where Miyo and she had gone in from yesterday. Not the lesson Dana expected, but most certainly the one she needed. She took her time meandering back to the cabin she and Miyo shared. When she reached it, she went inside and sat on the bed. Shower? No. But she did want to freshen up a little.

She tapped on the bathroom door. No answer, so she eased into the bathroom, assuming Miyo would still be behind the closed door that separated the shower from the rest of the bathroom. In the same moment Dana stepped inside, Miyo stepped through the shower room door into the main part of the bathroom. When Dana saw her, she couldn't help but gasp.

THIRTY-ONE

"You're building a what?" Marcus adjusted his glasses and stared at Brandon. He wasn't sure the musician was serious.

"Like I just said. A tree house."

"In your backyard?"

"Yes."

"A tree house akin to the ones kids construct using old two-by-fours and scrap lumber?" Marcus pulled his New England clam chowder out of the microwave, gave it a quick stir, then placed it back in for another minute.

"Not this one." Brandon grinned. "I'll have you over for a glass of wine when it's finished."

"Have me over?"

"Not just you. Kat, your girls . . . we'll have a little party."

"This sounds like a formidable structure."

"Two stories. Room for six on the first floor. Double-pane windows. Lights. Heated." Brandon slipped off his stool and gestured with his hands. "Spectacular structure."

"You're serious."

"Very. It should be done soon."

"Why are you building it?"

"Two reasons. First, I've always wanted to build one, but my stepmom wouldn't let me, so I'm fulfilling a lifelong dream."

"And the second reason?"

"Because of a hope I can't get rid of."

"And what is the nature of this hope?"

"That's a secret." Brandon twisted his forefinger and thumb in front of his mouth as if to lock his lips.

"It doesn't involve a member of the female species, does it?"

Brandon walked to the refrigerator. "Want to eat down at the Listening Post? I'll give you a few more details about the tree house."

"Negative. I'm going to my room. I need to finish a letter to Kat."

"Letter?"

"I've been writing to her every third day since I told her about what happened with Layne. The unmerited grace she extended set me free, and the letters are a way to thank her for it."

"Why don't you just e-mail her?"

"No, no." Marcus shook his finger. "These letters aren't for her to read—"

"That makes sense. Write her letters, then don't let her read them. Excellent. Love it. You're an insane romantic, Professor."

"They aren't for her to read yet." Marcus pulled his chowder out of the microwave and doused it with pepper. "They are simply thoughts about her, about us, my memories of Layne . . ." Tears tried to surface, but not tears of lament, tears of gratitude for the eight years he had with his son. "After I accumulate a year's worth of letters, I plan to bind them into a book and give them to her as an anniversary gift to commemorate one year of my new freedom from regret."

"Wow." Brandon nodded. "I take it back. I really do love it."

The musician pulled three hot dogs and a Dr Pepper out of the refrigerator.

"Fueling your body with health food today, I see." Marcus shook his head.

Brandon rubbed his flat stomach. "Gotta give the metabolism something to do."

"Enjoy." Marcus poured himself a glass of ice water. "Are you going to eat in here?"

"Nah, I'm going to look for Miyo. I want to see if our newest member can take a little good-natured challenge."

THIRTY-TWO

Miyo stood in the door frame of the shower room, a large towel wrapped around her chest, hips, and upper legs, but her back, shoulders, and arms were bare. Rough dark splotches covered her shoulders and biceps as if her skin had been burned. Thin jagged lines and half circles were spread across her back as if someone with a serrated blade had played a sick game of tic-tac-toe there.

"Don't you know how to knock?" Miyo spat out.

"Oh my gosh." Dana lifted her hand and covered her mouth. "Miyo, I . . ." What could she say?

"Seen enough?" Miyo spun back, fire in her eyes.

"I did knock, but there was no answer, so I—"

"Fine. Now leave."

"I'm sorry, I thought you'd still be in the shower." Heat rose to Dana's face. "How did you get—" She didn't finish the sentence. Dana knew exactly where she'd received the scars. And why Miyo had bristled at Reece treating her like a schoolgirl the day before with regard to entering spiritual realms. Miyo had paid dearly for her experience.

"Would you like to examine my legs too?"

"No, I—"

"Then what do you want?"

In that moment, Dana's triumph over the lifeguard took hold. She didn't care if Miyo was more skilled and more knowledgeable and better equipped to lead. It was still a struggle to keep the thoughts of needing to perform out of her head, and there was still a part of her that resented Miyo for coming into the Warriors like she had, but the victory had provided enough that Dana had to ask. She wanted to learn, to grow stronger, more accomplished.

"Will you train me? Like you did this morning but on a regular basis?"

"Train you?" Miyo yanked her towel tighter.

"Yes."

Miyo flicked her hand at Dana as if to shoo her out of the bathroom. "Now I have to . . ."

"Have to what?"

"Leave. I'll be out in five minutes."

Dana sat again on her bed and tried to think of what to say when Miyo came out, but all she could focus on was the idea of being trained by Doug's granddaughter. When Miyo emerged from the bathroom four minutes later, her anger had vanished. She sat next to Dana on the bed and clasped her hands on her lap.

"The new prophecy Reece and my grandfather spoke of was given to me. That I would join the Warriors. And that I would train one of you."

Dana stared at her. Of course Miyo was the one of the prophecy. It was obvious. Why hadn't they seen it immediately?

"Why haven't you told us?"

"About the training, or that I'm the one of the prophecy?"

"Both."

"In time I knew you'd figure it out. And because I didn't know which of you I would be training. My grandfather's letter said it would be the first of you who asked."

"But why didn't you go to Reece and tell him that you were supposed to—?"

"I know who I am, Dana. But the rest of you do not. I'm twenty-three. Headstrong in many ways. Blunt to a fault. I couldn't train any of you till I'd earned your respect. Maybe I haven't earned Brandon's or Marcus's yet, but I believe I have yours. And now that you've asked, your formal training can begin."

"I can get the others to agree to train with you as well. Even Reece."

"Yes, I believe you could." Miyo smiled. "You are the Leader. But this is not the time. The prophecy says I'm to train one. Only one. You are the one. Not the others."

"Why?"

Miyo rose from the bed and ran her fingers through her wet hair. "I can be ready in fifteen minutes."

"To start training?"

"No." Miyo patted her stomach and went to the tiny kitchenette in their room and opened the small cupboard. "To start lunch. I'm starving."

✠ ✠ ✠

As they sat at the Listening Post and ate their lentil soup, the sound of the sliding door opening floated toward them. A few seconds later Brandon glided down the path with three hot dogs, a bag of Doritos, and a Dr Pepper in his hands. How he stayed trim eating as much garbage as he did had always confounded Dana.

When he reached them, he sat in a chair next to Dana and across from Miyo. "Mind if I join you?"

Dana shook her head as did Miyo.

"Good." Brandon took a large bite of his hot dog and talked with his mouth full. "Saw you two out here and decided it's time to learn from the Mighty Miyo."

"Is that right?" Miyo took another spoonful of soup and glanced at Dana. She didn't think Miyo would take easily to Brandon's mocking tone.

"What in the world would you ever have to learn from me?"

"Hey, if Doug said you should be in, and Reece says the same, then you must be a superstar warrior." He rubbed the side of his dirty-blond hair and grinned. "I'm sorry, I'm just teasing. And I want to apologize for last night. It wasn't right. I am truly glad you're part of us. So I'm hoping this can be a new start."

"But even though you have fully accepted me, you're still skeptical of what I can bring."

"Yep." Brandon took a swig of his Dr Pepper. "You would be too, wouldn't you? I mean, you're young. Not that much life experience."

"Yes. Very possible I would have the same doubt you have." Miyo nodded and set her soup to the side. "I suppose we'll simply have to look for opportunities where you can learn more about me."

"Why wait? Why don't you tell me about a few of your experiences?"

Dana sensed Miyo's body tighten as she leaned forward and zeroed in on Brandon with her gaze.

She waved her hand in front of Brandon. "Try to ignore him. It's been a tough couple of months, and it makes him provoke people."

Miyo sat up straight and looked at Brandon as if he were a child. "I know you believe you have fought great battles in the spiritual realms, and in one sense you have. I would never seek to diminish what you have accomplished and the freedom you have given others. But the resistance you have faced is minor compared to what I sense is coming. And you're not anywhere close to ready."

"Really." Brandon laughed. "I don't think you know anything about the battles we've faced over the past year and a half. I think you're the one who has been taught a trick or two but hasn't figured out much more than that."

Miyo turned and looked toward the chalk cliffs across the river. "You don't know my story."

"Maybe not. But I know her story." Brandon motioned toward Dana. "I know Reece's. And I know mine and Marcus's. I know the experiences and training it took to get the Warriors to where we are today."

"I imagine you've learned a few skills, and it's clear you have passion, but you have much to learn, Brandon. If we were to spar with one another, the outcome would be certain."

Miyo's eyes flashed with intensity and Dana knew where this conversation was headed. Brandon wouldn't back down from a challenge like that.

"Yes, I believe it would," he said. "But I am loath to humiliate a girl."

"But perhaps you would be open to humiliating a woman." Miyo stood and stared at Brandon for at least ten seconds. "Let's do this."

"What are you looking for? A fight? A duel?"

She nodded, a thin smile on her face. "Absolutely."

"Don't do it, Brandon." Dana waved her palms back and forth, one on top of the other. "You have no idea what you're up against."

He ignored her. "What are you thinking? Are we going to do pistols at high noon?"

"No. That would be far too clichéd for my tastes, and for yours, if I'm reading you right. I suggest something in the spiritual realm since that's what your doubt centers around."

Should she warn him again? Nah, this would be a good lesson.

"Fine. Let's go." Brandon turned to Dana. "Are you going in to see this?"

She nodded and smiled. "Wouldn't miss it for all the tea in Colorado."

Thirty seconds later the three of them stood on what looked like high-desert country under a reddening sky. Miyo didn't waste any time and circled Brandon in a wide arc with slow, rhythmic steps. Her eyes were like coal.

Brandon glanced at his right hand, then his left. A fireball materialized in each. "We can stop this at any time." He tossed them in the air. "But if you're feeling like being the catcher, I'm happy to step onto the mound."

"I don't think it's a good idea for me to hurt you even in showing you how mistaken you are." Miyo dropped her gaze. "We shouldn't have come here."

"I'm touched by your kindness. But let's go ahead and play ball. Let me just toss a few and see how you like my heat. I think I can bring a bit of warmth into your life."

"That is an unacceptable proposition." The hint of a smile showed on Miyo's face. "As well as an impossible one."

"Really. Is this where you make a speech about me never even getting close enough to scratch you? How my skills pale in comparison to such a seasoned warrior as yourself? How you will engage me in battle to the fullest extent I care to go but will at the same time keep me from harm?"

"Thank you." Miyo bowed as she extended her hand to Brandon with a flourish. "Now that you've made the speech for me, we can begin without further delay."

"You're sure you want to continue?"

"Positive. Throw them, Brandon."

"I can't do that." Brandon dropped his hands, but the fireballs still burned bright. "Now it's time for me to apologize for doing this. What say we go?"

"Throw them."

"Do you understand what I can do with these things?"

"I know what I'm dealing with, and you could no more hurt me than hurt the sun."

Whether she'd provoked Brandon into action or he was tired of talking, he reared back and slung both fireballs toward Miyo. The angle looked like they'd strike near Miyo's feet. Dana knew there was no way he'd throw them anywhere near her body. He'd grown so adept at controlling the size, shape, and velocity of the fireballs, she had no doubt they would tear into the ground exactly where he wanted them to without any danger to Miyo.

This way he probably imagined he could show Miyo what he was capable of without coming close to hurting her. But Dana guessed he was about to realize his imagination was severely uninformed.

As the fireballs streaked toward her, Miyo moved so fast Dana couldn't follow her. An instant later she stood four feet closer to Brandon, holding one of his fireballs in each of her hands. She'd caught them? How?

Miyo squeezed her hands and the fireballs vanished. An instant later she planted one leg in front of the other, flicked her fingertips toward Brandon, and he was covered by . . . What was it? Liquid? Light? It was a dome of translucent . . . She couldn't describe it, but it encircled Brandon for five yards on every side.

Before it stopped moving, he conjured a fireball and flung it into the base of the dome. It didn't even shudder.

Brandon stared at Miyo for ten seconds before uttering just one word. "Wow."

"Have you seen enough?"

He nodded and a second later Dana watched the scene fade from sight.

+ + +

After Brandon slid back into his body at the Listening Post, he sat on the chair for a few seconds with his eyes closed. What an idiot. He'd made a fool of himself and his life was still a joke. Couldn't sing. Couldn't perform any longer. Couldn't come through when Doug's life depended on him. And he'd just gotten his butt kicked by a twenty-three-year-old hotshot.

Sure, he was supposedly hearing the songs of heaven and heard the song of his coming healing and restoration, but how long till that scene would play out? Months? Years? What was that Proverb? "Hope deferred makes the heart sick"? Yep, and some days it felt like he was lying in the proverbial hospital bed. Yes, God was going to give him his voice back, but why did he have to take it away in the first place?

He rubbed his face, sighed, and then opened his eyes. Miyo stared directly at him but said nothing. Her eyes didn't gloat. She didn't say, "I told you so." And the look on her face was not one of satisfaction but one of concern for him.

"You have skill, Brandon."

"No. Sorry. Not going to let you do it. I didn't give you a ticket to the patronizing party, so I can't let you in the door."

"I've been training intensely since I was ten years old. You've been training for less than a year and a half. The skill you've gained in that time is considerable. You are already a strong warrior. In time you will be a great one."

Brandon started to respond but was interrupted by Reece's voice booming down at them from the main cabin.

"Come on up and settle in. It's time for us to have what I believe will be an intriguing meeting. Arriving in less than twenty minutes at Well Spring Ranch will be the one and only Simon the magician."

THIRTY-THREE

FROM THE MOMENT MARCUS PICKED UP SIMON AT THE
Colorado Springs airport in Reece's old Chevy pickup, the magician had talked nonstop about why he shouldn't have come to Well
Spring. How it wouldn't be good for him, for them, for the future, for
the past. How Zennon was coming after all of them. Only a smattering of it made sense, and for the past half hour, Marcus had tuned
out the conversation. He believed the magician needed to come,
and nothing Simon could say would change that.

His feeling was confirmed when they stood looking down on
the main cabin of Well Spring and Marcus sensed a thin, translucent mist coming off Simon. His imagination? Marcus didn't think
so. He couldn't see the haze, but he had little doubt it was there. All
doubt vanished when he felt something cold bump up against his
chest. Immediately he called on the power of the Spirit to banish
anything of the enemy from grabbing hold of him. The mist vanished, but Marcus took an uncertain step to his left.

"Are you all right this night?" Simon peered at him through
half-closed eyes.

"Sure. Yes. I'm fine. Are you?"

"Yes."

But the magician's voice betrayed him. Something had just
come over Simon or emerged from within him. Marcus couldn't

tell. But whatever it was made him uneasy. Marcus firmly believed the Warriors needed Simon, but it was now abundantly clear Simon needed them just as much.

When they reached the main cabin, Marcus opened the door and motioned Simon in. They eased down the short hallway together to the edge of the great room. The other Warriors were already gathered—Brandon sat in front of the fireplace leafing through what looked like a coffee table book filled with pictures of the Oregon coast. Dana was on her laptop, probably editing her photos, Reece was in the kitchen somehow peeling a slew of potatoes, and Miyo stood in a corner of the room with her arms folded as if not willing to do anything until Simon and he arrived.

Simon stopped and motioned Marcus to do the same. His gaze darted from the floor to the ceiling to the walls. "Just promise me we're still in the real reality," he whispered. "Because those two giant warlords standing in the corner over there are really, really, freaking me out."

"You see two warlords?" Marcus glanced at the corner, saw nothing, and then looked back to Simon.

"No, of course not. What? You think I really am crazy?" Simon rubbed his hands on his pants and whispered a touch louder, "Sorry, just nervous meeting the big-time spiritual warriors, you know?"

"There's nothing to be—"

"Afraid of? Maybe not, but this Well Spring nation is filled with intimidation."

"You're going to be fine." Marcus gave Simon what he hoped was a comforting smile, then turned and raised his voice. "Fellow Warriors, it is with great pride that I introduce you to the man you've heard much about and the one who not only kept me from entering into a great darkness but gave me the knowledge to make a choice that has given me much freedom. My friend and brother, the magician, Simon."

After a smattering of applause, Marcus introduced everyone, and Simon gave a slight nod to each of the Warriors.

"It is a great honor to be here." Simon grimaced and Marcus could tell he was fighting the urge to rhyme.

"We are the ones who are honored." Reece strolled from the edge of the kitchen to the center of the room. "I won't need to finish prepping for dinner for another three hours, so why don't we gather at our favorite Well Spring spot and get to know each other a bit."

☩ ☩ ☩

Fifteen minutes later, the six of them sat around the fire pit watching the crackling logs and watching Simon. The small talk about travel and a brief description of Well Spring by Reece had ebbed and Dana guessed the conversation was about to turn serious.

"I've described in detail to the other Warriors what you saved me from, but if you'd acquiesce to making any additional observations, I know they would welcome it." Marcus pushed his glasses up on his nose.

Simon nodded as he reached into the front pocket of his black jeans and pulled out a silver coin and laid it on the fingers of his right hand.

Marcus had talked about Simon's silver coin, so it shouldn't have surprised Dana to see the magician pull it out and roll it around his fingers. But he did it the exact same way Zennon did, and she couldn't stop the revulsion that stirred inside her at the sight.

When the silence grew awkward, Marcus seemed to read her mind with his next question. "Why do you carry a coin like Zennon has? Why imitate him with the coin roll?"

A bitter laugh escaped from Simon. "I'm not imitating him. He's imitating me. I taught him the roll. So I carry the coin as a reminder of Zennon." He stared at the coin. "Of what he stole from me. Of what he did to me. Of where I've been and where he took me. Of where I will not go ever again. Where I do not belong—a reminder to stay strong."

"When did you first meet him?" Brandon asked.

Simon held the coin between the tips of his thumb and forefinger, tossed it into the air, and it vanished. The man certainly had skill in sleight of hand.

"Just like that, I was gone. For a long, long time. I paid in full for my supposed crime."

"What happened?" Dana said. "How did you end up in the alternate realities?"

Simon leaned forward, knees on elbows, and stared at Marcus. "Did I ever tell you I sat on that same ledge you sat on overlooking a lush green valley? You must have imagined I did."

"No, I haven't."

Brandon tossed another small log on the fire, but that was the only movement around the fire pit.

"And I made the choice to live in one of the realities. And for days I was happy. But it didn't last. I longed for the past when happy did last. But I couldn't go back. So I chose another reality and another, deeper and deeper into the pit. Couldn't escape. Not even Houdini could have escaped. I should have asked him about it, but of course at that age I didn't know I'd need it later on."

"What?" Brandon gave a flick of his head. "Did you say you should have asked Houdini?"

"Houdini was a fascinating man."

"Uh, are you saying you knew him?" Brandon stirred the fire and glanced at the rest of them with a Simon-is-crazy look.

"I did." Simon stared into the fire. "He made a lasting impact on me even though I was young."

"You mean you know of him through others?" Marcus leaned forward as if to offer protection to his friend. "You've studied his life."

"No." Simon winked at Brandon, then turned to Marcus. "I met him. Spoke with him."

Marcus frowned. "Your age would preclude you from knowing him except through the knowledge of others, since he died in 1926."

Simon's eyes lit up. "I'm impressed. Everyone knows who Houdini was, but few these days know the year he passed. Do you know the day?"

Marcus shook his head.

"October 31," Brandon said.

"Well done!" Simon grinned at Brandon and rubbed his hands together. "Now for all the money and the grand prize of substantial size, tell me how he died."

"Everyone thinks he died performing the Water Torture Cell thanks to that lame Tony Curtis movie," Brandon said. "But that was Hollywood. The truth is much more boring. He died from a punch. Some kids came backstage and asked if he could take a hard blow to his stomach. Houdini absentmindedly said yes, so the kid punched Houdini in the stomach three times, and it ended up rupturing his appendix."

Simon grinned and glanced back and forth between Brandon and the others. "Again, well done, that was indeed fun. Brandon, did you do magic when you were young?"

Brandon smiled slightly and a dreamy look came over his face. It was the same look Dana used to see when he played songs for her when they dated. It surprised her. She'd never heard him talk about doing magic when he was a kid, but it was obvious he'd enjoyed it.

A natural connection point between Simon and him, and she could see from the movement of the magician's shoulders that it relaxed him to be with someone else who understood—even in a small way—the world that was so much a part of his life.

"I did. I got an Adams magic kit for Christmas one year, probably around eight years old."

"And did you learn any of the tricks?"

"Yeah, quite a few of them. I was into it all the way through seventh grade. I got really good at the cups and balls, actually. It was my favorite trick. The kit had a set of three plastic cups. After I showed it to my grandma, she got so frustrated she slammed those cups so hard, thinking that was the secret, that she cracked one of them." Brandon laughed. "I should have kept up with it."

"Why didn't you?"

"It turned out the girls seemed to think magicians were geeks and the musicians were cool. So I switched."

"Ah yes, 'tis true, I'm afraid, the right decision was likely made."

"Might we revisit the Houdini comment?" Marcus interjected. "About your knowing him? He died a significant number of decades ago."

Simon held out his hands and tapped three of his fingers together. "Yes, quite a few."

"You're looking good for someone ninety-plus years old, Simon."

"Thank you, Brandon Scott. I appreciate that."

"When were you born, Simon?"

"Before any of you, of course." Simon pointed at Reece. "And that includes him."

"What are you telling us?" Dana asked.

"No time to explain it all. Makes me thin and makes me tall." Simon waved his hands. "Something now that must be seen, while lessons and knowledge can still be gleaned."

"It might be painful to speak of, Simon, but I believe there is healing in explaining more fully what happened to you." Reece stood and folded his arms.

Simon shifted in his chair like a little boy who had been kept inside from recess. "Time manipulation. You haven't studied that?" He stared at Reece. "Inside alternate realities time shuts down, and the body doesn't age. Spiritual cryogenics. He kept me on ice, wasn't very nice. To keep me from whatever it was I was supposed to do."

"You're saying—" Marcus began.

"Yes, yes! I'm saying it. Already said it. Aren't you listening? I was in the spiritual realms. Outside of time."

"So when you went in, you were in your early fifties and still that age when you escaped fifty-one years later?"

"Faugh!" The magician let out an exasperated sigh. "Think, Professor. Didn't you notice that when you slipped in and out of your alternate realities? That no time had passed when you returned?"

Simon flicked his hands toward the fire. "Can we move on now? There's something I must show you."

Simon snatched up a long, flat piece of kindling leaning against the gray concrete of the fire pit and stuck it into the center of the fire with his right hand. When he pulled it out, a tiny burning ember was balanced on the end of the stick. He held it up to his face and blew on the ember till it glowed bright red.

"We'll get back to my new little friend in a moment, but for right now keep a steady eye on my left hand. That's the spot where you're going to wish you'd watched with greater intensity." Simon opened his palm and spread his fingers wide. Then he slowly turned his hand over and showed the back, then leveled his palm, then brought his fingers together to form a loose fist.

"Ready? Drum roll please. Don't miss this. Don't look away, not tomorrow and not today." Simon brought the stick with the burning ember over the top of his hand and dropped the bright coal into the small opening between his fist and his fingers. His face contorted in pain, but he kept his hand closed tight.

He dropped the piece of kindling and grabbed his left wrist with his right hand. It was the moment of distraction, but Dana wasn't fooled. She kept her gaze riveted on Simon's left hand. It had to be painful, but the magician didn't cry out.

A moment later, Simon released his wrist and waved his right hand twice over his fist. Then he opened it and pointed at its center. The ember had vanished. There was no burn, no red mark, not even a hint of soot on his palm. Then he showed his right hand was empty as well.

"No curtains, mirrors, trap doors, or even smoke. Well, I guess there's a little smoke. Or should have been when I stuffed that hot coal into the folds of my skin." He showed both hands front and back completely empty.

"What? That's impossible," Dana said.

"No, it's very possible." Simon grinned. "You just witnessed it."

"Let me see your hand again."

Simon extended his hand and Dana stared at it, but even inches from her eyes there was nothing to indicate the coal had touched any part of his skin.

"That trick's a keeper; it had to tweak your peepers." Simon slapped out a quick drum beat on his legs.

"That's incomprehensible." Marcus stared at Simon's hands. "How did you accomplish that?"

"Quite well, that one I performed quite well." Simon glanced around the circle at the stunned faces and laughed. "This stuff isn't real. It's an illusion. It's deception. You are missing something that is right in front of you. You think you're seeing one thing, but you're really seeing another."

"How many years did it take to learn that trick?" Dana said.

"Not years. In fact, less than days is how this one plays. If you had three bucks and the willingness to practice for a couple of hours, you too could have this miraculous power."

He glanced at Brandon, then back to her. "I wouldn't be surprised if Brandon was given the tools to perform that trick in his kiddie magic set." Simon winked at the musician. "You probably even know how it was done."

Brandon winked back. "That I do."

"Really?" Dana turned to him and Brandon nodded.

"And what is the lesson you're teaching us?" Marcus said.

Simon's voice grew quiet, and it seemed he was listening to the words he spoke as if he was hearing them for the first time.

"You were given the ability to perceive what the natural man cannot. The deception with the ember was right there in front of you the whole time, and you never knew it. The curtain hung in front of you and you couldn't figure out how to bring it down. But if you are to be victorious against him, the curtain must be pulled away."

Both Reece and Miyo had remained silent the whole time, and it didn't surprise Dana. Reece was undoubtedly seeing things about Simon in the spiritual realm none of the rest of them could. And Miyo was likely tuning into the Spirit and trying to figure out exactly who Simon was. She hadn't heard the story of what the magician had done for the professor, so she wasn't biased to like him. It would be fascinating to see Simon's story unfold over the next few days.

THIRTY-FOUR

HE NEEDED TO HEAR GOD'S VOICE. NEEDED TO. HAD TO.
Simon sat at the Listening Post after dinner leaning forward with
his elbows on his knees. It was a good place to be alone. God was
here. He sensed it. So why wouldn't God speak?

Simon turned over the deck of cards in his hands, opened the
flap, and pulled out the Queen of Hearts. He wasn't ready for the
King. Didn't deserve the King. Wouldn't deserve the King ever
again. He'd bowed to the wrong throne. The scrape of shoes along
the stone pathway startled him. Simon turned to find Marcus standing ten feet away.

"Good evening, Simon."

"Good? It is? I hadn't noticed." He took the Queen and launched
it fifty feet out over the river and watched it float down and land in
the center of the current.

"That's an impressive throw." Marcus slid into the chair across
from him. "Care to share your assessment of Well Spring so far?"

"Full of life with little strife."

"I agree. For me it's a fortress of solitude."

"Like Superman's place?"

"Something like that." Marcus smiled. "I'm curious about one
of your mannerisms. Might I inquire as to why you speak in rhyme
so often?"

"You may question like a dancer, but I might not always answer."

"I think I know why." Marcus picked up the hatchet next to the fire pit and a small log and split it into kindling. "I think it's a way to keep your mind occupied against the constant pummeling from yourself and from the enemy about what happened to you. But I also think it's part of his continued influence over you. That you can't stop from rhyming sometimes."

"What are you saying, Professor?"

"You assisted me greatly in making a choice that brought me great freedom. Motivated to a significant degree by your desire to prevent another person from entering into the choice you made and the subsequent consequences."

"No doubt you could tell me what you're saying in a way less roundabout."

"How do you deal with the fact that you made a choice you regret with such vehemence?"

Simon went silent.

"What was your choice, Simon? The one that took you out?"

He shook his head. No. No. What was Marcus thinking? That question wasn't allowed. Didn't the professor know? It wasn't part of the show. It couldn't ever be asked because there was no door to that memory that could ever be laid hold of. It was locked shut and tucked away in a place no one could ever find, no matter how long they searched. Gone forever!

Simon gave a soft whimper and wished that was true and the memory wasn't pounding on the door almost every second of every day, screaming to get out and bury him again. He scraped the card in his hand against his forehead as if that could brush the memory to the ground.

"What was your choice?" This time the professor's voice came from galaxies away because the door had already opened and Simon had already fallen through the doorway and was hurtling into the darkness of the choice he'd made fifty-one years ago.

✠ ✠ ✠

Simon's eyes had been closed on that ancient rainy Monday evening in early March, but the lamp to the left of his old leather, overstuffed chair cast enough light through his eyelids to keep him from falling asleep. Or was he asleep? His brain wouldn't answer. A series of dull thuds echoed in his muddled brain. Was he dreaming? Could be. Didn't know. Didn't care. His arm twitched as the thudding in his brain continued.

No, he was awake. Might as well admit it. He squeezed the wine glass in his hand and opened his eyes. Was it day two since the accident? If he made it to day three, he might make it to the funeral. He might be able to pour out all his grief on those who came to offer him their pity and condolences. Sure. And he might learn to build human-sized butterfly wings and soar away from all this in the next thirty seconds.

Stay strong in my strength. I am with you.

No. He didn't want to be strong. Only fifty-two years old and his life was over. All he wanted to do in this moment was pour more red wine into his glass, then lift it to his mouth and feel it trickle down the back of his throat where it would do magic on his mind. The pounding increased and Simon realized the sound didn't come from his head but from the front door.

Stay in me.

Why couldn't God leave him alone? Just for an hour. Let him drown in his sorrow.

"Simon!" The voice was oddly familiar but he couldn't place it. Thoughts of high school and college peppered his mind. A classmate from eons ago? Grade school? No, it was a time far back, yes, but from days more recent than high school. College? It didn't matter. He wasn't going to open the door for anyone ever again.

"Simon, let me help you." The voice was softer this time but no less insistent. "Let me in. Please."

Should he? Whoever it was would probably tell him it would be okay, that his wife was in heaven now waiting for him to arrive so they could skip together in fields full of poppies or some such inane platitude he would have to nod and agree with. From a person who had probably never experienced this type of ripping of the soul.

"Leave me alone!" Simon screamed as he sat forward in his chair. The wine in his glass sloshed over the rim and splashed onto the armrest and then onto his tan carpet. He stared at the wine as it soaked into the carpet fibers. How could it look like anything but blood? He wouldn't clean it up. He'd leave it there forever as a reminder of what God had done to his life. Done? Allowed to happen? Either way was stark evidence of God's betrayal of him.

The crash was an accident? Impossible. If every hair of every head was numbered? All the stars of the universe were known by name? If that was true, then accidents could not exist. They were planned. And God was the planner.

A lie. Do not go down that path.

He knew the Spirit was right. The thought was poison. And wrong. Knew it better than most. He had an enemy that would target everything in his world for destruction, including his wife. He'd written about it extensively in his manuscript that would never be read by anyone. He'd lived it for years now—fighting the spiritual forces and principalities in high places, exploring unbelievable spiritual realms, doing the things in the Bible he thought were impossible in the modern age. But how did that fact change *anything*? It didn't. It made it worse.

Was there something he could have done to keep the enemy from taking her life? Was it his fault? He didn't know. Didn't even start to care. He was done listening to the Spirit. At least for a decade or two. Quench the Spirit? Yes, he was about to show himself how. His mind continued to spiral as he lifted the wine glass to his lips.

The Spirit spoke once more, but Simon ignored it and the words faded into whispers that didn't reach his heart or mind. But the rapid knocks on his door and the voice behind it were more difficult to brush off.

"Simon." The voice was soft now. He blinked and looked up at his front door. This guy wanted in. Clearly wasn't going away. Why not grant him entrance? Nothing mattered anymore.

"Come in. It's open."

The door opened only a few inches, then stopped as if the person behind it was either respectful of Simon's condition or fearful of entering.

"I said come in." Simon raised his glass as the door swung wide. "All the way."

The man stepped through the doorway. Dim light from the lamp at Simon's side cast just enough light on the figure to make out the man's features. Could it be him? The lines on his face and the graying of his hair spoke of the years that had passed, but it had to be him. Simon sat stunned, a mixture of wonder and long-forgotten memories swirling through his mind.

"Aaron?"

"Hello, Simon."

"It's really you."

Aaron nodded. "Why did we ever lose touch with each other?"

Aaron. The one who rescued him that day a million years ago after his dad almost destroyed his heart. The one who brought him to the magic club and who had taught him all those tricks for all those years. The one who had been the big brother and dad he'd always wanted.

"I can't believe you're standing here. I've followed your show in Vegas off and on for years. It seems they love you down there."

"Yes, the town has been good to me."

"It's been so long."

"Far, far too long since we've seen each other. I read about your wife's passing in the newspaper. Which is why I'm here. I have no words to say. I wouldn't know where to begin except to say my heart is torn for you." Aaron eased forward and pointed at the couch next to Simon's chair. "Do you mind if I sit?"

"Yes, yes, of course." Simon stared at his friend in amazement as he settled onto the couch. "You've aged well."

"Don't humor an old man. I haven't. And if you don't want to see it in more detail, keep these lights low." Aaron's eyes darkened and he pointed at Simon's glass of wine. "How much have you had so far?"

"Half a glass at most, but it will be much more in the coming days and months, I suspect."

"You don't want to do that. It's not the answer. You know this."

"Do I?" Simon swirled the wine. "What happens if I get rip-roaring drunk every day for the rest of my life? Will God send me to hell for it?"

"No, but this is not you, friend." Aaron stood and stepped close to Simon's chair. "This is not a choice the true you would make and one I will not allow you to continue making. As I just said, it is not the solution."

"You don't know my pain."

"No, I don't, but I know where giving in to this kind of pain leads." Aaron extended his hand. "Just for this moment, let me have the glass, and I'll tell you of a better way to ease the pain."

"Tell me."

Aaron smiled. "What is the best part of being a magician, Simon?"

"Knowing how the trick is done."

"And what is the worst?"

"Knowing how the trick is done."

"Yes." Aaron stepped next to Simon's end table and picked up the bottle and waggled his fingers toward Simon's glass. "Please?"

Simon handed Aaron his glass, and his old friend set both the glass and the bottle of wine on the floor in front of the couch and sat again. As he did so, something inside Simon lurched as if he'd been grabbed by two hands, but he shoved the feeling aside.

"And why is the worst part knowing how the trick is done?"

"It steals the wonder."

"Exactly!" Aaron poked the air. "We are no longer astonished. We've met the man behind the curtain and we marvel no longer. We cease to be children and the world becomes dull and plain."

"Yes."

"But from time to time we capture our wonder once again. How, Simon?"

"When another magician fools us and takes us back to the moment where we believe—if only for an instant—that the magic is real."

Aaron nodded, a tiny smile at the corners of his mouth, and Simon knew the escape his friend was offering. A chance to go to a place where he could be a child again. "You're still meeting with the old group, aren't you?"

"Yes. I fly up once a month to be with them." Aaron's smile grew. "I won't pretend to understand the depth of your anguish, Simon. But come do a little sleight of hand like in the old days. The meeting starts in forty-five minutes. Come with me. Escape into that world of wonder. Take your mind off the devastation that wants to consume you. You don't have to remember any longer. You can forget. I can show you how."

"Still my friend after all these years."

"It's even better than that."

"How so?"

"You're sure you want to ruin the surprise?"

Simon nodded.

"I'm growing old. I can't do the show much longer. I had no sons to pass it on to, so I need to find a successor."

Simon shook his head.

"Yes, you, Simon." Aaron sat forward. "I want to teach you all my illusions. My most closely held secrets. I want you to headline my show in Vegas when I retire."

"You're not serious."

"Deadly. But we can talk more about that later. For now simply come away for a few hours and let the pain lie in a corner of the mind where we will shut the door without using wine."

Aaron was true to his word. Right after his wife's service, Simon spent three weeks in Las Vegas and worked four hours every day perfecting Aaron's illusions. He spent another week performing alongside Aaron onstage, and at the end of a month, Aaron said the time had come to turn over the show.

"I'm not ready. It takes years to perfect a Las Vegas show." Simon sat in what would soon be his dressing room in the Sahara Hotel on the Las Vegas strip.

"You *are* ready." Aaron winked. "Almost. There's one more illusion I'd like to show you before I fade into the back row of the audience."

Aaron led him through the hotel to the theater where Simon had labored for the past four weeks. In the center of the stage was a thin black box—barely wider than a man—that rose at least fifteen feet high from the floor. When they reached it, Aaron opened a hidden panel and motioned toward the box.

"Let's go inside."

Simon stared at the small enclosure. It would barely fit him, let alone both of them. He looked back at Aaron in question.

"Don't worry. We will both fit, and after you've gone through, you will be astonished like you never have been before. I promise you that." Aaron smiled. "I've been waiting to show you this for an extremely long time."

Simon's heart pounded, although he didn't know why.

"Are you ready?" Aaron motioned toward the box. Simon gave a slight nod and stepped inside.

THIRTY-FIVE

THE INSTANT SIMON STEPPED INTO THE BLACK TOWER, all light vanished and then exploded back on him so bright, he shielded his eyes from whatever the source of the light was. After his eyes adjusted, he found himself standing on a cliff overlooking a large valley that flowed with lush green trees and a river set in the center of the land. The scent of lilacs played on the wind. A palpable sense of peace settled on him.

"Do you like it?" Aaron's voice sounded behind him.

Simon turned. "What is this?"

"A gift." Aaron opened his arms toward the valley. "The greatest gift that can be given to any man or woman."

"I don't understand."

"You will." Aaron pulled a gold coin from his pocket and laid it on his palm. "Watch the coin with all your concentration, old friend."

Aaron adjusted his gold coin till it sat in the exact center of his hand. As Simon stared at the coin, it began to fade, then seemed to melt into Aaron's palm. A moment later it simply wasn't there.

"Impossible." Simon didn't feel the astonishment of a child. He felt fear. Because this was not a trick, not an illusion. "I don't—"

"I've brought you to a place where the magic is real, Simon."

"What is this place?"

"Like I said. A gift." Aaron eased to the edge of the cliff and gazed down on the valley. "Let me ask you a very important question."

"What?"

"Do you feel the pain? Of your wife's death?"

Simon searched his feelings and frowned. It was gone. He felt at peace about her death. Impossible. The past month of working nonstop with Aaron on the show had buried his sorrow deep, but every morning and every night it ripped into his mind like a giant serrated blade that felt like it would slay him. He knew learning the show was itself an illusion—a momentary covering of the pain, but it was his only way to cope with the sorrow.

Aaron stepped closer. "This is a place where the illusion remains. Where it is real. The valley is a gift from God that removes the pain but not the memory. The only part that remains is the joy of knowing you will see her again."

"How can it remove the pain?"

"When I say remove, I don't mean the pain is gone. It is still there."

An image shot into Simon's mind of his wife sitting on their back deck in north Seattle, a glass in her hand toasting him, her laughter filling the summer evening. Sorrow seared his mind and Simon started to sob. But Aaron waved his hand and a few seconds later the overwhelming grief vanished.

"I'm sorry to do that to you. But I want you to be assured that you will lose nothing of your love for her or your memories of her." Aaron smiled. "But the pain will vanish forever."

"Are you saying I can stay here?"

"Yes. Where every part of your life is the same as it is now. Your show, your friends, everything."

"What's the catch?"

Aaron nodded as if he'd anticipated the question. "You're right to ask. Although this place is a free gift of God, there are consequences to all our choices, and this choice is no different."

"Tell me."

"As you can see and feel, this place is one of joy and hope." Aaron pursed his lips. "But you can only come here once. If you choose to leave for any reason and go back to the real world, you can never return here. And that means you need to choose now if you're going to stay."

"What about my affairs? My house, my things?"

"You will have them all here."

"But won't the people back . . . ?" Simon spun in a slow circle, expecting to find the door to the black tower that would lead them back onto the stage in Las Vegas, but there was no door. "Won't they—?"

"They will not see you again. You will live out the rest of your days here if you choose to. Happy. At peace."

"But I wouldn't have a chance to say good-bye."

"Good-bye to whom, Simon? First, you'll still have them all here. Second, is there anyone that must hear from you, do you think? My old, and your new, assistants?" Aaron shook his head. "They are not your friends. It's not show friendship; it's show business. They were acquaintances. Your uncle lies in a nursing home and doesn't know your name. Your parents are gone. You have no children. No brothers or sisters."

"The friends from my church."

"Yes. They were true friends. Were. But how long has it been since you've seen them? Will you miss them? No. You'll have them here. Will they truly miss you?"

"What happens to my body?"

"It will remain where it is, in the physical world."

"So I'm not really here?"

"Your spirit is here. But not your body. While you are here your body will not age. It will remain with me till such time as you want to return."

"But what happens if you . . . ?"

"I think you've realized I'm not ever going to die, Simon."

229

Aaron's body grew taller and thicker, and light seemed to radiate off of him like the mirrors of a lighthouse. "I think you've suspected it since the day we first met."

Simon nodded and the words came out of his mouth before he could stop them. "I will stay."

The sensation of fog descended on Simon's mind, but it was a sweet mist, a mist of forgetfulness, and he breathed it in deeply.

Simon jerked his mind back to the present and locked his gaze onto Marcus's. "I can't be in that memory. A place I can't go, too much of the show. Don't ask about that ever again if you claim you're my friend."

✜ ✜ ✜

"My apologies." Marcus studied Simon's face. Fear was mixed with sorrow and deep regret, but terror was by far the greater of the two emotions. "I didn't mean to cause you pain."

"It's okay." Simon squeezed the sides of the card in his palm and it leapt to his other hand with a perfect flip. "So many parts of my mind are ones I can no longer find."

"I won't ever ask about the alternate realities. I promise."

"But you want to ask me something else. I can see it in your eyes."

"I can't help it." Marcus smiled wide. "I'm a physics professor."

"What?"

"Where was your body kept for all those years?"

"You want the history of that mystery, eh?" Simon shook his head. "Wasn't in an exotic or high-tech location as you might suspect. Zennon, of course, wanted to keep an eye on me, so he stored me in the back of his huge Las Vegas warehouse filled with all his other full-stage illusions. I was lured into one of Zennon's boxes and I stayed in that box till the day I left."

"Escaped."

"I didn't escape, Professor. I went to sleep one night and woke up in the morning in that black-colored box."

"Why would he let you go? Why keep you all those years? Why didn't he just kill you?"

The magician pressed his temples. "I'm part of his plan."

"What plan?"

"I don't know." Simon continued to massage his head. "But there's the tiniest piece of me that suspects at one time, long ago, I might have walked strong with the Spirit. That I really did write the manuscript Doug Lundeen says I did." Simon's voice was more stable and coherent sounding than Marcus had ever heard it. "Does that sound crazy to you, Professor?"

"Not at all. I believe it's true. I've believed it all along. But it doesn't matter what I believe. You must remember who you are."

Simon dropped his King of Hearts and shuddered as he picked it up off the stones at his feet. He flipped the card back and forth between his hands again.

"Look at me." Marcus waited till Simon stopped looking at the card and held his gaze. "Restoration is coming."

"How can you know that? How can you say that when you don't know for certain about the veil and about the curtain?"

"I do know. I believe the Spirit has told me restoration will come for you. I choose to believe this. And I invite you to join me in my belief."

Simon turned back to his card and spun it on his fingertip like a basketball. "How do I know you're not Zennon again? And this whole place"—Simon waved his hand toward the river and the white chalk cliffs and the cabins of Well Spring—"isn't designed by him to steal my soul once more?"

"You were in devastating pain when he attacked you and offered a solution to that sorrow. You were vulnerable and open to suggestion. He exploited your weakened accessibility."

The magician didn't answer. "Even so, the choice was still made . . . for which I have paid dearly. I accepted Zennon's solution."

"Let me repeat, restoration is coming." Marcus waited till Simon met his gaze. "Just as it came for me, it will come for you."

"When? When will it come? When I die and to heavens I fly?"

"Oh no." Marcus smiled. "Many ages before that."

Simon stared at him for a long time before speaking, and when he did, his eyes were full of tears. "Do you promise me that?"

"With every molecule that makes up my being." Marcus took the King out of Simon's hand and grasped both the magician's palms. "You will be restored."

"Thank you, Professor Marcus Amber." Simon's head bobbed up and down. "So what happens now?"

"I think you already know."

Simon swallowed and rubbed his hands. "I suspect that tomorrow, you and the rest of the Warriors are going to ask if you can enter into my soul."

THIRTY-SIX

"WHAT DO YOU THINK OF SIMON?"

Reece sat alone with Miyo at the Listening Post on Saturday midmorning and let the warmth of the tenth day of August soak into him. Doug was right. She was wise far beyond her years, and he wanted to get her take on the magician separate from the others.

"You first." Miyo seemed to shrink back in her chair. "What did you see last night?"

"I saw the outline of his coin. It left a trail of light like phosphorescence in the ocean. As if his hand is wrapped in a million tiny stars."

"Evil?"

"I don't think so. It feels neutral, but I'm not one to say anything is neutral in the heavens or on the earth." Reece leaned forward, elbows on his knees. "But Simon is not of the enemy. I'm not worried so much about Simon as I am about what cloaks his soul."

"I agree, he is for us. And he is a son of God. But there is also much darkness and confusion that swirls around him. He speaks of a curtain? Simon has a curtain around himself so thick, I can't start to see past it."

"As might we all if we'd lived in over four hundred different realities." Reece rubbed his hands. "All I could see was the faintest outline of light around his body. Whatever he carries, it weighs on him like a coat made of concrete. He fights it, but without much success."

"Have you considered asking him if we can go into his soul?"

"Yes."

"And?"

"I asked him early this morning, and he's agreed."

"You're kidding."

Reece shook his head. "From talking to the professor a little bit ago, it seems Simon wants restoration more than he wants to avoid the memories from his past."

The shuffle of feet coming down the white stone path filled the air a few minutes later, and soon all the Warriors sat with Simon in a circle, ready to enter the magician's soul.

✚ ✚ ✚

"Simon?" Brandon called out the magician's name for the third time since they'd arrived inside Simon's soul, but again, there wasn't a response. "Where is he?"

Dana didn't answer and neither did any of the others. The question was rhetorical. She spun in a slow circle trying to take in the kaleidoscope of images that surrounded them. They stood on the top of a building at least forty stories high. Spread out for miles in every direction were other buildings almost as tall. Every one of them was lit up like a multicolored lighthouse.

The streets below were filled with people laughing and milling about as they entered and exited the buildings.

"I'm getting why Magic Man would go Las Vegas inside his soul, but isn't this a little over the top?" Brandon said.

"Where do we go from here?" Dana asked.

"Down," Reece said. "Let's see if we can talk to any of the people on the street."

By the time they'd exited the building's lobby and reached the street, all the people in each direction had vanished.

"Nice disappearing act," Brandon said. "Any other ideas?"

"You know him the best, Professor," Dana said. "Where do we go?"

"No idea." Marcus pointed at a door across the street bordered by three sets of neon lights: bright yellow, bright red, bright orange. "And since I have little indication of where to go, why not start here?"

They reached the door and Marcus turned the handle. But the instant he did, the door and building vanished.

"It makes sense," Reece muttered.

"What makes sense?" Brandon asked.

Reece pointed up and down the street. "Try all the doors up and down the entire block."

The Warriors spread out. In five minutes all the buildings were gone in every direction. Nothing remained. They now stood on a desolate field of loose gravel and sand. It was hot. Not unbearable, but uncomfortable compared to the coolness they'd felt when they first arrived.

"All of it, an illusion."

"There has to be something here." Brandon gazed in each direction. "His soul can't be entirely empty."

"There." Miyo pointed toward a slight rise along the horizon. "Can you see it? Ten, maybe fifteen miles away."

Dana stared in the direction Miyo pointed and saw nothing. Brandon voiced what she was about to say.

"I don't see a thing. Talk to us."

"It's a small cabin. One light on in the window. A few evergreen trees." She turned to her left. "Reece?"

"I see it. That's where he is."

Marcus turned toward Miyo. "I would surmise based on your earlier demonstration that you can get us there instantly."

She smiled and nodded. "Let's go."

As soon as they landed outside the dark log cabin, Dana saw Simon through the window. He sat on an ottoman and tossed playing cards at something beyond her sight.

Reece knocked and Simon opened the door a few seconds later.

"This is very strange." The magician took time to lock gazes with each of them.

"Why is that?" Reece asked.

"Because I know what you're doing. You're all inside my soul, aren't you?" Confusion passed over his face. "And somehow I have no doubt I used to do this kind of travel, still a mystery to unravel." He ushered them in but stayed standing. "Does that strike you as odd?"

"Not at all." Reece took a slow spin around the cabin, and his gaze landed on a large stack of posters sitting on an oak table. "What are these?"

"My collection. Priceless. Houdini's King of Cards poster. An original of Carter's most famous. Thurston. All the greats. I guard them. Protect them. And look, look here." He lifted up the corners of the first four posters and pulled them off the stack. "Do you see this?"

It was a poster of Simon. He stood on a lavish stage with his arms raised as if lifting by magic a woman five feet over his head. He was dressed in a tuxedo and a wide smile split his face. It was evident from the dress of the crowd looking up with astonished faces that the poster was from the late sixties or early seventies.

Reece glanced at Miyo who nodded at him. The big man did the same with Marcus and Brandon. When Dana had nodded her assent as well, Reece widened his feet and instantly a sword appeared in his hands. He raised it above his head. "Here we go."

Simon's face went white. "What are you doing?"

Reece brought his sword down hard on the posters. They exploded, and as they did, the cabin vanished in a flash of light. Where the table had stood was now a small fountain made from a series of granite stones. A soft green moss surrounded the fountain that still sat on the small hill the cabin had sat on. Below the rise, jade grass swept out in every direction and ended miles away at the base of snow-covered mountain peaks.

Brandon gazed at the surroundings, then back to the fountain and grinned. "Living water, I'm guessing."

Next to the fountain sat a flat stone roughly the size of the table the posters had sat on. On the stone rested what looked like a yellowed manuscript, and on the manuscript sat a pen made of wood.

Simon stared at each of them as if he were Rip van Winkle waking from a hundred-year sleep. Which probably wasn't far from the truth. He turned to the stone table, picked up the manuscript, and ran his thumb down the edges of the pages. "I didn't think I'd ever see this again. I didn't remember . . ." He hesitated, then gripped it tightly with both hands. "I wrote this, didn't I? Every sentence. Every word. There is power here. And here." He pointed to his heart. "Unfathomable power. Because of who lives there." He looked at each of them for a long time before speaking again. "This manuscript can change the world. And with the power of the Spirit, it will."

✛ ✛ ✛

The moment Reece's spirit slipped back into his body, he sat forward. "Well done, all of you. Simon, how do you feel?"

"Are you kidding? New. I feel new." A grin split his face. "Reborn. Every adjective you can think of. I don't know how to thank all of you."

They chatted about what had happened in the magician's soul for another four or five minutes, but eventually everyone headed for their cabins. Only Miyo remained.

"Reece, might I speak with you for a few minutes?"

"Of course." Reece waited until the sound of the others' footsteps faded away. "What would you like to talk about?"

"Even after what just happened, I still feel Simon is tied to Zennon. There was great victory just now, but I feel that whatever role Simon has in this play has not been fully acted out. Put another way, what Simon just experienced is a start, but there is more healing needed. And in the meantime, I think Zennon is still pulling some of the strings inside his soul."

"In other words it was too easy."

"Yes. I can't shake the sense Zennon is still going to use the magician against us somehow."

"I trust him, Miyo."

"I do too. No question. I'm simply saying we must be careful." She stopped and brushed back her dark hair.

"Of course. But I'm more open to Simon than I was before. Being in another's soul and understanding more of his story tends to make that happen."

"I think it's clear the magician has a good heart, but Zennon's attack is still coming. And he won't stop till every one of the Warriors is dead or he's sent to the pit. We must stay vigilant in every way. Alert. Strong."

"I agree."

"So while it's good that Simon is getting healthy in the midst of the approaching war . . ." Miyo grew quiet and closed her eyes.

"Don't stop now, friend."

Miyo opened her eyes and leaned forward, and when she spoke, her voice was close to a whisper. "I believe the Spirit wants me to say something to you, but my intent is not to pry."

"Say it."

"If you hold on to the blame you've carried toward Brandon, and more accurately carried toward yourself, it will grow inside your soul. And this is not the time to allow that kind of growth."

She was right. Why couldn't he let it go? His grip tightened on the stick of kindling in his hand. Brandon wasn't to blame. Reece himself was. He'd hesitated. He'd stayed back when Doug had waved him off, even though Reece knew he should have ignored his mentor's request. Doug's death was senseless. He should be sitting here right now, the three of them strategizing together, trying to hear from the Spirit on how to get ready for Zennon's attack.

Why could he forgive himself for causing Willow's and Olivia's deaths but couldn't forgive Brandon or himself? He didn't know. Yes, he did. He needed time to process the loss of his dearest friend. The one who had stuck with him during the years he'd been absent from the arena and the one who had drawn him back in with strength and truth and mercy. Doug had helped him find life again, and Reece had imagined many more years together embracing that life. The Warriors were not the Warriors without Doug. He just wasn't ready to move on. But that didn't change the fact he had to.

"You're right, Miyo. I will let it go. I will forgive. It must happen." But he couldn't. Not in this moment. It had taken almost twenty-seven years to forgive himself for the deaths of his wife and daughter. It wouldn't take that long this time. But it would take time.

"It's good to hear that. You are the Temple, and as your health goes, to a great degree goes the health of the Warriors."

A thin, light-green mist passed over the fire pit, then swirled past them. It smelled . . . sweet, and Reece rubbed his chest right over his heart as the cloud vanished. His chest was tender but a good kind of tenderness. Strange.

"Are you all right?" Miyo asked.

"Did you see that?"

"What?"

"In the Spirit. I just saw a mist sweep past us."

"I didn't." Miyo stared at his chest. "But if I'm seeing in the Spirit now, the left side of your chest looks sunburned."

"It's fine. It's nothing."

"You're sure?"

"Positive."

☩ ☩ ☩

That night Brandon sat on the small deck off the building where they trained new students. It was late, but Brandon wasn't tired. He turned to study a waxing moon that seemed ready to settle down on the ridgeline of the mountains across the river.

The clomp of feet coming up the small set of stairs to the deck pulled his attention away from the view. It was Dana. Why? She'd avoided any chance of the two of them being alone. She slipped into the wooden chair next to him without looking his direction and pulled her arms across her chest.

"Hi." Brandon looked at her, but she only nodded and continued to stare straight ahead. But something about her body language betrayed her secret. This wasn't a chance meeting. She was here with a specific purpose in mind. And her wall was down.

"Nice of you to stop by for a visit."

"Thanks."

"Is there a reason you came by?"

Dana shifted in her seat. "What do you think of Simon now that you've seen him up close?"

No problem. A warm-up of small talk was fine. "He's different than I expected. Definitely twitchy and affected by something unknown going on inside his brain. But I like him." Brandon wiggled his fingers like he was about to make the kindling at his feet rise into the air. "Makes me want to take up doing sleight of hand again."

"Really?"

"Yeah. He inspired me with the hot coal trick. And since I won't be wasting my time going out on dates, I figure I need to find something else to fill the evening hours."

"Nice segue into the awkwardness that always lingers just below the surface between us, Song."

"How many times do I have to repeat, I'm not the Song."

"You'll always be the Song."

"You sound like Doug and Reece."

"Look at what the Spirit has been doing in you."

Brandon stared at her till she turned and looked at him. "Now remind me why you came over here?"

Dana pulled her eyes away and pressed her lips together. She waited so long to speak he almost asked her a second time.

"You say you know me, right?"

"Yes."

"And I know you." The volume of her voice dropped in half and the tone of it grew soft. This was going to be really good or really bad.

"Okay."

"I'm going to tell you something, but you have to promise me you won't say anything about it."

"I promise."

"I love you. I think I always will."

Brandon's body went hot with a good kind of heat but in the next moment it turned to ice.

"But I can't chance it."

Brandon waited. Everything in him wanted to ask her what she couldn't chance. But asking would break the moment and her wall would go back up.

"If we know each other, then you understand why I can't risk giving you my heart again, even if I do have feelings for you buried so incredibly deep. Because if I let those feelings surface, you won't be able to handle it."

"What do you mean?"

Dana glanced at him long enough for him to see tears in her eyes. "You don't need me to answer that question, do you? Really?"

She turned again and her eyes pleaded for him to say no. And he did, because she was right. He didn't need her to verbalize that Brandon Scott was still not worthy of her. Not till he could let go of needing to be worth something. No, that wasn't the right language. He was worth everything because of the love of the Trinity. But that knowledge wasn't enough to keep him from trying to find the answer outside of the Father, Son, and Holy Spirit. He'd died to so much of himself, but if he faced the mirror with eyes wide open, he'd see a man who was still focused on what he'd lost, and what he wanted to become again, and what she could do for him, and not enough on what he could bring and give and lavish on her.

A smoldering anger rose up inside. He was angry at her, angry at himself, angry at God. Restoration was coming, it was coming, it was coming. He was tired of hearing it over and over again, always off in some future he couldn't grasp. He needed restoration to come now.

Dana didn't speak and neither did he as she rose from her chair, shuffled down the stairs, and faded into the night. As she did, a thin, green haze appeared between Brandon and the moon. The smell of vanilla, similar to the scent from his backyard *fothergilla gardenii* shrub, filled the air. He frowned as the haze shimmered and then vanished along with the smell as quickly as they had come.

THIRTY-SEVEN

"I BELIEVE OUR LIVES ARE ABOUT TO CHANGE."

Reece paced in front of the fireplace late Sunday morning, more animated than Dana had ever seen him. As if a megadose of caffeine had been injected directly into his veins and the high was at its peak.

"I've figured it out." He took off his dark-tan Stetson and tossed it onto the hearth. "I wondered why the Spirit asked us to come here to Well Spring for these days together. Certainly meeting Simon and assisting in his healing was part of it"—he nodded toward the magician—"but there had to be more. Now I believe I know what it is and what the Spirit has been trying to tell us. I woke up at four thirty this morning and it rolled out like a scroll." Reece clasped and unclasped his fingers in rapid succession. "Also, I believe I know where, when, and why Zennon will attack us."

Reece stopped moving and put his hands behind his back. "After lunch—let's say around two—I'll lay out the map that will take us where the Spirit wants us to go. And if you grasp it with a tenth of the passion I feel inside, we are going to turn the world upside down, and nothing Zennon does will be able to stop us."

✠ ✠ ✠

"Mexican food is the perfect meal," Reece announced as they all sat down to lunch.

Perfect? Marcus didn't agree. Sautéed mushrooms and shrimp with pesto sauce over angel hair pasta was the perfect meal. But Mexican did come close, especially the way Reece made it. Even Kat, Abbie, and Jayla now ate Mexican after Marcus had started using Reece's recipes at home.

"Could you pass the salsa?" Miyo said.

"Which one?" Marcus asked.

"The hot one, of course."

"I'll take some after you," Simon said.

Miyo glared at the magician as she scooped out a spoonful of salsa and dropped it on her plate. She slammed the jar down on the table and didn't pass it on. She'd seemed agitated all morning, but this was the first sign of outright hostility.

Marcus continued to study her eyes. She now looked at Simon with both confusion and anger as if the magician had done something horrible to her. As she continued to gaze at him, the look intensified.

"Are you feeling okay, Miyo?" Marcus said.

Miyo nodded but placed her hands in her lap and just stared at her food. Marcus started to ask what she'd felt, but before he could get the words out, Brandon grinned at Miyo. "Gearing up to send that fire into your mouth, Warrior Girl? Yeah, you better. This is Reece's specially concocted hot sauce. Spread it on the side of a house and it will peel the paint off faster than the most powerful pressure washer on the planet."

Miyo glanced at Brandon, Reece, and then drilled Marcus with her gaze as if trying to tell him something. Then, without a word, she shoved herself back from the table. She stood quickly and the motion flung her chair backward. It slammed against the wall and she half strode, half jogged from the room.

"Wow!" Brandon leaned back, his hands locked behind his

head. "It's that powerful, Reece? Just looking at your fire sauce drives people insane with fear."

Marcus pointed at Miyo's plate. "I would propose it wasn't the fear of the sauce but something else that caused Miyo to propel herself from our presence. Something strange has been happening. In the air. I've been meaning to talk to you about it. Like a spiritual mist—"

Brandon snorted. "Most of the time you're a certifiable genius, Prof, but every now and then you say something so obvious and bonehead simple it makes me think I can keep hanging around you a little longer." The musician grabbed the sauce, spun off the lid, and stared into the jar. "I feel no fear. You're right. Miyo's reaction has gotta be coming from something else."

"My suspicion is it's tied into this haze I—"

"I'll talk to her." Reece put both hands on the table and made to stand up.

"No, let me." Dana pushed her plate to the center of the table, stood, and walked to the door. "I have an idea what this is about, and it's definitely a woman-to-woman thing."

After Dana left, Marcus again tried to tell them about the mist he'd felt on the night Simon arrived, but neither Reece, Brandon, or Simon paid him any attention.

THIRTY-EIGHT

AT TWO O'CLOCK THAT AFTERNOON, REECE LED THE FIVE of them up to the lookout spot on the hill where Miyo and Dana had gone in from the week before. But this time Miyo was missing. No matter. Her absence wouldn't dampen the mood. Something stirred inside Dana as if the energy and excitement Reece had been throwing off since his morning announcement had been transferred to her. Whatever their mentor was about to announce, it would be big.

"Look down." Reece pointed down the hill. "Look at Well Spring Ranch spread out before us. It has launched a worldwide ministry. Changed hundreds and thousands of lives. But what we've done so far is only the beginning."

A light wind rolled up the ledge as if on cue, and the smell of pine spoke to Dana of adventure. The scuffle of boots drew her gaze to the path below them and she frowned. It was Miyo. Dana had tried to locate Miyo after she bolted from the main cabin during lunch and couldn't find her anywhere.

Their eyes locked and Dana gave her a questioning look. Miyo looked down and stopped five yards away from the rest of them and acted like she was a cat among a gathering of rabid hounds. But the look on her face wasn't one of fear but of anger. She folded her arms and glanced from person to person as if expecting one of them was about to attack.

"Hey." Dana waved at Miyo. "You okay?"

Miyo nodded. "I'm fine. But right now I need some space. Don't bother asking why. I won't explain it."

Brandon lifted his forefinger and middle finger together. "Scout's honor, Miyo. I promise I'll get Marcus to take a shower tomorrow."

Miyo didn't laugh. Didn't smile. "I appreciate that."

"Why don't you join us?" Reece motioned her up next to him. "This is important."

"I'll listen from here."

Reece continued to face her for at least thirty seconds. Probably trying to see what was going on with her with his spiritual eyes. Dana certainly wasn't getting anything. But if he got something he didn't speak it aloud.

"Okay then, let's start." Reece turned his back to the ranch and smiled. "Here's how we're going to change the world. I've always said the Warriors were supposed to stay small. And we were. But that was a season, and like any other season, it's coming to an end. A new one is about to be born.

"Dana, being in the position you are at the radio station, leading teams in the corporate world will help you understand where the Spirit is taking us better than anyone. The days of playing small are over. We need goals. We need clear objectives. We need an effective strategy for this ministry. Up till now we've operated on a wing and a prayer. It's worked well. But we're entering into a new phase of the ministry, and we will be buried if we don't know where we're headed a month from now, a year from now, five years from now. And none of us will be able to lead that charge as well as you. You are the Leader. You are exceptional. We need you now more than ever."

As Reece spoke, something cool seemed to surround Dana's chest. It felt like a mister she'd walked through at a restaurant in Arizona a few years ago. Whatever it was smelled almost sweet. But was it good or evil, or even neutral? No time to think about that now. She ignored the sensation and concentrated on Reece's words.

Yes, this felt good. She would have a chance to lead the Warriors like never before. She would develop teams. Inspire them. Guide them.

This was her glory, her strength, and it was nice to have Reece recognize it once again in front of all the other Warriors. But a moment later Dana felt odd. Part of her was thrilled at Reece's words, but another pulled at her like taffy, which said this was completely wrong. No, it was the enemy, trying to steal this away from her. She would not give in.

Reece turned to Brandon. "You understand this too. You were a god in the music industry. We need to tap into your experience and use it to take Warriors Riding further than any of us have imagined we can go. You know how large events work. How to promote. How to create a following."

He turned to Marcus. "You have at least a feel for how a major business like the University of Washington runs. And can teach people better than anyone. You will teach our teams how to function on a massive scale."

"And, Miyo, I don't know if you've had any life experience in building a business, but nonetheless I am looking for your wisdom as we map out our future."

Miyo stared at Reece but didn't answer.

Reece's voice grew in excitement. "I had a strategic plan for my photography business. It's what allowed it to grow into one of the largest chains of high-end photography galleries in the world—and certainly the most profitable. It's far past time we tried to accomplish the same with Warriors Riding. Let's get down to specifics." Reece pointed at Marcus. "Professor, have you talked to Carson Tanner lately?"

"Yes, I have."

"Did you talk numbers? How many people he's reaching these days with his show?"

"He did volunteer that his audience has increased twelve percent since he changed the focus of his broadcast, blog, and e-zine to a message of freedom."

"Outstanding." Reece smiled and rocked back and forth on his boots. "And how often is he promoting our ministry?"

Marcus frowned. "He's not. He offered to, but I explained that's not what we do. That we are not about getting big and never—"

"Never say never. As I said, that's all about to change, and Carson's help will be critical."

Marcus's brow furrowed more. "That's not what I've been sensing from the Spirit—"

Reece ignored him and raised his voice a notch louder. "We need Carson to start pumping the training weeks and our CDs and DVDs as often as possible." He turned to Dana. "What is it you always say about advertising, Dana?"

"Frequency sells."

Reece turned back to Marcus. "We need frequency on Carson's show. If we're going to grow this ministry like God has just told us to, we need continual exposure.

"Dana, I want you to work with Carson to develop a marketing plan using his outlets and influence. Develop a series of radio spots, get us testimonials from our followers, get us going on some promotions and cross promotions with other ministries, get a fully functioning website going, everything."

"Love to. And with my radio contacts, I can get some serious exposure for us on a significant number of stations, networks, and podcasts all across the country to go along with Carson's show."

The feeling of disharmony in Dana seeped away as she pictured how she would orchestrate all the elements they would need. Reece wanted leadership? Watch out.

"Sounds like you've come up with a serious no-wings cliff jump." Brandon grinned. "I love it. It's about time."

"I agree. And in some ways it involves you more than anyone else, Brandon. You've been down lately. We all understand why. But this project won't allow you any time to dwell on what has been, only what is to come."

"I almost believe you." Brandon leaned forward. "Lay it on us."

"This ministry is ready to explode, and we're going to light the fuse with an event that will be seen by millions. We are going to rent Safeco Field in downtown Seattle. We are going to ask our friends who have been through our training and taken our message of freedom throughout Puget Sound to fill that stadium and join us in a celebration of what God has done and what he will continue to do. We are going to broadcast this event to our allies around the world. It will be shown in homes, churches, arenas, and on the Internet around the globe."

Reece was almost dancing now. "It will be a time of rejoicing and a time to lay out the next phase of our ministry and what God is calling every one of our partners across the world to engage in. We will take our rightful place at the head of the charge the Spirit is leading against the forces of darkness."

Reece spun and looked out over Well Spring. "This no-wing cliff jump, as Brandon puts it, is to reach twenty-five million people with this message."

Brandon shifted his weight. "And my role in this—?"

"Don't you know?" Reece spun back and laughed. "You haven't figured it out yet? You are going to sing."

"Come again?"

"You heard me."

"Do I get to lip-synch?"

"You are the Song. What heaven gave you the other day down at the river is the song you will sing on that stage in front of millions. It will be your moment of restoration and usher in great healing in your soul and the millions of souls you'll sing to. You will be healed in front of the world."

Brandon smiled and nodded. "If only—"

"No." Reece stepped toward him. "We will give no quarter to doubt. Think of what Doug wrote to you, what God himself confirmed. This is your moment. Our moment. Where we become known to the world."

"If that could happen . . ." Brandon rubbed his face and glanced at each of them. "We have to do this. Have to."

Dana stared at Reece and struggled not to break out in joyful laughter. He was right. This gathering would be epic. She looked at Marcus. He looked more like he was a taster at a lemon factory than a warrior ready to enter into a grand, new arena. "Professor?"

Marcus glanced at her and then turned toward Reece with combative eyes. "If we go ahead with this, where would we get the money to rent Safeco Field?"

"No ifs, Professor. As you know, I have money. I stockpiled more than I know what to do with from my photography galleries. And I still bring in tens of thousands of dollars a month from my sales and licensing agreements. I don't care about the money. I care about reaching the nations."

Marcus's countenance grew hard. "We *are* attaining great reach into the nations. We don't need this. It's wrong. Our method has always been—"

"How many times do I have to repeat myself? That's changed. Last night and this morning everything changed." Reece put his arms behind his back and paused for a moment. "We've been on the enemy's radar for a long time, but this move will expand our ministry even more exponentially than it has already and deal our adversary a crushing blow."

Reece turned to Miyo. "And one of the reasons we'll be better equipped for what will certainly come against us is because of you, Miyo. You will war for us in the spiritual realm, because the prophecy that was spoken over you is clear to me now. The attack Zennon is going to bring will attempt to shut down the gathering before it starts. And then he will attack again during the event itself. You must head up our resistance."

Miyo's only response was a sigh and an almost undetectable nod.

"There is a time for everything. We've had our season of being small. That is no longer our time. Believers who have only heard smatterings about us will get a chance to fully understand our message."

Dana studied Miyo as Reece continued to speak. The earlier look of anger had been augmented by a fierce determination. And yet Dana didn't have the sense the topic of their conversation was what bothered Miyo. It was deeper. Something they'd done earlier that day? Yesterday? Nothing came to mind.

"Thoughts on this, Miyo?" Reece asked.

"None." She tilted her head back and pulled her hood over the top of her head.

"No opinion? I'm supposed to believe that?" Reece laughed.

"You can believe whatever you want to believe."

"Do you want to be here right now?"

"No." Miyo folded her arms and fixed her gaze on the ground. "I don't."

"Then why are you here?"

"Because this is where I'm supposed to be. This is where the battle lies and where I am needed."

"Whatever the battle is at this moment, it lies inside you." Reece stepped toward Miyo and she stiffened. "We need to break whatever is coming against you. Right now."

"No." Her gaze darted to each of them. "You don't."

"I believe the Spirit is saying we have to."

"Then you would be mistaken." The scrape of Miyo's black boots on the path seemed to fill the sky as she stepped back two paces. "It's time for me to go."

"Miyo, stop." Dana stood and took a few steps toward her friend. "Tell us. We can help. What is going on? This isn't like you."

"I'm fine." Miyo turned. "Like I already said, I need some space and some time." She half walked, half jogged down the path.

"Do you want me to go after her?" Dana asked.

"No. Let her go," Reece said.

"Wow," Brandon said. "I know we're from the land of strange

at times, but it looks like Miyo has a cabin there bigger than any of ours. What's the deal with her?"

"What did you see when you looked at her, Reece?" Dana said.

"Not as much as I'd like to." Reece rubbed his hand over his eye sockets. "My special kind of seeing has been dimmed today. No doubt an attack of the enemy. But from what I *could* see, there was nothing around her that would give a hint as to what she is wrestling with. The only thought that struck me is that although everything we've seen from Miyo has been strong and full of truth, it's also true we've only known her for seven days.

"Yes, she is Doug's granddaughter. Yes, she is in some ways far more experienced than any of us in the spiritual realms. But at the same time, she is young and susceptible in some ways that those with more life experiences are not."

"Nice speech," Brandon said. "Why don't you just say what we're all already thinking in a language a bit less eloquent?"

"Because it's not what you're thinking." Reece paused as if not wanting to say too much but not wanting to say too little. He faced the path Miyo had walked down. "But I will say this. Stay alert. Be cautious. Be wise."

"What does that mean?"

"As you well know, God has his plans, but the enemy has plans as well. So for the time being, we must not let Miyo catch us off guard."

Great. Easy for the men to say. They didn't have to go to sleep with Miyo lying in a bed three feet away.

THIRTY-NINE

"WHERE ARE YOU GOING?"

After bursting into their cabin late on Sunday night, Miyo stuffed a few pieces of clothing into a workout bag, grabbed a blanket and a coat, and snatched a pillow off her bed. Dana hadn't seen her since she walked off the side of the hill hours earlier.

"Out."

"You're not sleeping here tonight?" Dana snapped on the light next to her bed, pulled off her covers, set her feet on the floor, and started to walk toward Miyo.

"Stop." Miyo pointed to the corner of the room behind Dana. "Stand over there."

"What is wrong with you?" Dana took another step toward her friend.

"Stop!"

The strength of Miyo's voice halted Dana and she stared at Doug's granddaughter in complete confusion. "Talk to me. Why are you acting like this? Why did you act like we were all lepers earlier today? Don't you understand what the Spirit is leading us all to do?"

"I'll be fine. But tonight I'm going to sleep by myself."

"Where?"

"I'll be back in the morning, I promise." Miyo's eyes were dark and commanding. "Now please, stand in the corner for just a moment."

"All right." Dana backed into the corner and watched Miyo shuffle along the back wall till she reached the front door of their cabin. "I realize my actions must appear very strange to you. But don't worry. I'll explain everything to you tomorrow."

• • •

On Monday morning, Dana was ripped from her sleep by the sound of her door slamming into the wall of her room. She pried open her eyes to find Miyo silhouetted in the doorway against a graying dawn, hands on her hips, her legs spread a little more than shoulder-width apart. The air that swirled in from outside was cold and smelled foul.

"What stinks?" Dana rolled over and pulled her blankets over her head.

"You have to come with me. Now."

"What are you . . . What time is—?"

"No time. That's the time." Miyo's voice grew in intensity. "We have to move." The clomp of her boots across the wood floor echoed through the room. "I told you I'd explain my behavior from last night. Now I'm going to."

Dana opened her eyes a little wider and looked at the clock on her bed stand. Four thirty. "Can you explain it to me in the morning?"

"Now, Dana. We have to go."

"How long have you been up?"

"I never went to sleep. Something has been stabbing at my brain like an ice pick since Simon arrived at Well Spring, and I've finally figured out what's wrong. And you are a key to fixing the problem before it grows beyond my abilities. Get dressed. We're going in."

"You didn't go to bed all night? Then why did you take a pillow last night when you left?" It was a stupid question, but more of Dana was back in her dream floating down a slow-moving river in the heart of summer than was awake. Couldn't Miyo turn off her rampaging energy at least till seven?

"Sixty seconds and we're going in whether you're wearing what you want to or not."

Dana swung her legs over the side of her bed and plopped her feet on the floor. Wow. Cold. It helped wake her up a little, but it was far from enough. "I suppose a quick cup of coffee is out of the question."

"You'd be supposing correctly." Miyo grabbed Dana's Seattle Space Needle sweatshirt off the dresser and flung it at her, then fished her hiking boots out of the corner of the cabin with her toe and kicked them over to Dana.

"You could have handed those to me."

"Thirty seconds."

"Why the countdown?"

"I'm serious."

Dana pulled off her pajama bottoms, pulled on her jeans, and struggled into her sweatshirt and socks and hiking boots. "Are you going to explain to me what is going on? Why this is so urgent?"

"Not yet. It would take too long. I will when there's time." Miyo strode through the door and looked back over her shoulder. "Ready?"

Dana nodded as she zipped up her sweatshirt and trudged toward the front door. For the next three minutes, Miyo led Dana at a rapid pace past Well Spring's softball field, the ropes course, and the outer cabins they used to house the students during training weeks. Once they reached the edge of the property, Miyo's pace increased till they were moving close to a slow jog.

"Where are we going?"

"Someplace safe."

"Safe for what?"

"Safe to go in from."

"Anywhere on the ranch is safe, I told you that."

"We're almost there. Seven more minutes at the most."

While they hiked on, Dana tried to make conversation about Reece's plan to grow the Warriors and how powerful it would be, but Miyo didn't comment, so they trudged along in silence. Six minutes later they arrived at a thick grove of aspen trees. Miyo pushed through them to the other side. A small clearing appeared that wasn't visible from the path.

"No one would spot this from the trail."

"Exactly." Miyo motioned toward a large boulder to Dana's right. "Why don't you lean up against that rock." Miyo pointed to the left. "I'll use this one."

"Why do we have to go in?" Dana sat back against the boulder and the coldness of the rock seeped through her sweatshirt. "Is there a reason we have to do this so early, and outside?"

Miyo settled back and stared at Dana. "If you have ever trusted me, you need to trust me more now."

A sensation grew inside Dana like wildfire that what they were about to do was a very bad idea.

"Do you trust me?"

"Yes, but I don't like this. It doesn't feel right."

"Do you trust me?" Miyo asked again. Her voice was softer but it lost none of its fervor.

"I don't like this." The spark of apprehension inside Dana burst into a small brush fire.

"I know." Miyo clenched her fists and shook them lightly. "I understand why. And I'm sorry. But I don't have time to explain it to you right now."

"Will you explain it to me once we go inside?"

"Yes. Fully. I will answer all your questions that the Spirit will allow me to." Miyo raised her voice. "Ready?"

Dana nodded even though everything inside her was saying no. Just before their spirits shot out of their bodies, a scream ripped through Dana's soul that said she had made a decision that would lead to her death. She tried to stop from going, and for a second she thought she'd succeeded, but it was too late. Something grabbed her and yanked her on.

Every time she'd gone in with Miyo, the trip had been instantaneous. Not this time. At first it felt like she was being pulled through molasses and every second the syrup grew thicker. Then like she was being pulled in every direction at once. Pain shot down her back, legs, and arms and seemed to grow exponentially. But just before she got to the point where it was too much, the pain vanished and she found herself standing on solid ground, breathing heavily.

She stood surrounded by a series of tall, evenly spaced boulders that formed a circle twenty-five or thirty yards across. It would be tough to squeeze through any of the gaps between them. The sand at her feet was fine and the color of honey. A gray sky hung low overhead.

Miyo stood facing her twenty yards away, her eyes like ice.

"Why did it feel like it was tug-of-war back in grade school and they chose me to be the rope?"

"Because there is part of you that desperately does not want to be here. Because everything inside you was screaming not to go and now you're scared. Because the enemy doesn't want you to be here. But like I said, Dana, you can trust me. This is where you are supposed to be. Where you need to be."

"You still haven't told me why you brought me here." Dana widened her stance.

"I'm about to explain it." Miyo began to circle Dana as if they were in one of their training sessions and ready to spar. Instantly it made sense. This was part of her instruction. Woken up and forced into battle without time to fully wake up. Without warning. Without explanation. And put in an arena where she couldn't run.

"So this is a training exercise. I get it. Why couldn't you tell me that? I would have gone without hesitation."

"You wouldn't have come if I'd told you that." Miyo continued to circle—her feet gliding across the thin layer of sand, ready to pounce—and perspiration broke out on Dana's forehead. The look in Miyo's eyes was chilling. "You would have found an excuse not to come. In fact, I'm surprised you came this easily."

"Why?" Dana backed away. This might be a training exercise, but everything in her shouted it was much more. She instinctively called on the Spirit to provide a sword. It appeared in her clutches an instant later, and she grasped it with sweaty hands. "Answer me. Are we here for training? Or something else?"

"You know we are not here for training." Miyo gripped her own sword that had appeared right after Dana's.

"Then what is it?"

The lifeguard's words came back to Dana in a rush. *Let me tell you a little secret. Even if you do get out of here, Miyo will leave you in the real world too. She will turn on you. Mark my words.*

"It is what is necessary." Miyo continued to circle and Dana continued to back away toward the towering boulders behind her.

"Why are you doing this?"

"I'm sorry." Miyo drew her sword and pointed it at Dana's heart. "This won't be easy for me. But I have no other choice. I promise you would do the same were our roles reversed. It must be done."

"Miyo, think about what you're doing!" Dana stared at her friend in disbelief.

Miyo dropped her gaze. "I thought about it all night." When her gaze met Dana's again, all compassion and friendship was gone. She looked at the sky, raised her sword, and dug her feet into the soft sand under them as if a gun were about to fire at the start of a one-hundred-meter dash. Her jaw tightened and her lips parted slightly, revealing clenched teeth. Miyo's breathing grew rapid as a strong wind came out of nowhere and whipped through her hair, pushing it behind her like a dark stream.

Miyo crouched down, her knees bent, her eyes on fire. She rocked back slightly, then pushed off and sprinted toward Dana. Her feet threw up little curtains of sand, and a fierce battle cry erupted from her mouth.

Dana snapped herself out of the daze of bewilderment and disbelief that surrounded her and raised her sword. But what would that do? Miyo was quicker and knew far more moves than Dana had even heard about. She tried to raise light-armor around her, but the disconnect of seeing the one who had taught her the technique streaking toward her with death in her eyes destroyed her concentration. She had to somehow avoid Miyo's attack long enough to think. Find some plan of battle that didn't involve sword-to-sword combat.

Jesus!

A quarter second more and Miyo's blade would sweep toward Dana's torso. Had to move. Faster than she ever had before. Because if she didn't, she would die.

FORTY

Zennon burst through the door of the council chamber and scanned for Caustin in the ill-lit room. Where was he? The table was full. All twenty seats were filled so he had to be here. There, his back turned, near the middle of the table.

In two strides, Zennon reached his rival, spun him around in his chair, and backhanded him hard across the face. Blood seeped from Caustin's eyes and nose. "You told me to report again when I felt I had made significant progress, so I am here. Are things progressing to your satisfaction now?"

Caustin's eyes didn't leave Zennon as he stood and faced him.

"Well, fool? Have you no words?" Zennon leaned in and brought his face within inches of his adversary's as he ran his finger along the edge of his sword. "Or would you like to express yourself with your blade, and me with mine?"

Caustin clutched the hilt of his sword but didn't pull it from its sheath. "I'd like nothing more."

"Answer Zennon's question." Their Master's guttural voice rumbled from the end of the table.

Caustin's eyes burned with rage. "Progress has been made."

"As if I needed your approval at this point." Zennon stepped away, turned toward his Master, and bowed. An asinine gesture and beneath him, but required. "My lord, the mission you sent me on has almost been accomplished. May I kill Caustin now?"

His Master gazed long at both Caustin and him before speaking. "You have done well. And your zeal is warranted. But we will wait for the outcome before I will allow either of you to act."

Zennon bowed lower. "My lord, allow me to exact my vengeance now. As you know from my last report, Doug Lundeen is dead. Reece Roth and Brandon Scott have been subdued by the warfare and the demonic strongholds launched against them. Marcus Amber has resisted, but I have foreseen him being of no consequence this time. Simon is still fully immersed in my deception, and Lundeen's granddaughter is about to—"

"Silence."

Although the word was spoken just above a whisper, it reverberated around the room as if shouted.

"Do not anger me, Zennon." The Master stared at Zennon till he dropped his gaze. "We will wait."

"Yes, my lord." Zennon bowed again, then turned to leave.

"Stop."

"Yes, Master."

"Report again in six days."

"Yes, my Master." Zennon bowed again, strode for the chamber door, and turned when he reached it.

Caustin pointed a gnarled finger at Zennon. "If you are not victorious, you are mine."

Zennon stood in the stone doorway of the council room and fixed his gaze on Caustin. "It will be with immense satisfaction when I grind you to your knees as you weep with pain, and then listen to you plead for your life as your lifeblood flows from your veins like water."

FORTY-ONE

EVEN THOUGH MIYO WOULD PROBABLY BE EXPECTING THE move, Dana had no choice. It was the only one she could execute perfectly without thinking about it—and at this moment she needed all her mental strength to find a way out of this nightmare.

She thrust her sword at a forty-five degree angle to block Miyo's strike while at the same time started a roll forward, inches to the left of her opponent's upper-right leg.

As she dove into the roll, Dana pulled her sword down low and aligned it with her body. If the roll worked well, she would avoid Miyo's attack, complete the somersault, and be back on her feet while Miyo's momentum carried her at least four feet in the opposite direction. If the roll worked perfectly, Dana's blade would reach its target and inflict at least minor damage to Miyo's left leg.

It worked perfectly. Dana completed the somersault and spun to face her attacker. Miyo turned on one leg and glanced at the other. The fabric of her pants was sliced open and the flesh of her leg was exposed. Blood seeped out of a long gash on her thigh. Miyo glanced at the cut but gave no indication she felt any pain.

"Well done." There was surprise and respect in her eyes. She glanced again at the wound and dabbed at it with the sleeve covering her wrist. "A move executed with perfection and the only one that could have saved you. And you made it into more than a defense and drew first blood. This shows mental strength and shows your synapses are capable of firing as fast as your reflexes even under severe stress."

Relief flooded Dana. It might only mean she would live a few minutes longer. But Miyo wouldn't attack again without a healthy dose of caution. And those few minutes might give her time to devise an escape. The answer flashed into her mind. Of course! Well Spring. She would send her spirit back to Well Spring where she might be able to get to the cabin and Reece and the others before Miyo could catch her. And who knows? Maybe Miyo's warrior skills weren't as developed on earth as they were in the spiritual realm. It was her only shot, and the look in Miyo's eyes said Dana didn't have time to consider any other option.

Dana focused inward and her spirit started to leave the realm, but a second later she felt like she'd hit a wall of three-feet-thick glass and was tossed back like a sack of concrete.

"It won't work, Dana. I've blocked you and it is impossible for you to return without my permission. I brought you here and the only way you're going to leave is with me."

"Let me go."

"I can't do that."

"Tell me why you're doing this. We can talk, figure this out. The enemy has a stranglehold on you. This is not you!"

"It is the true me. Truer than I've ever been."

"Is this about Doug? I'm not the reason your grandfather died."

Miyo's answer was a steady advance. Her eyes were full of rage, but also of ice, as if killing Dana would be executed without a hint of remorse. Maybe because of Dana's minor success. Maybe because Dana had brought up Doug. Didn't matter. Rage meant lack of control. And lack of control meant the stroke of her sword during the next attack would have less precision to it. Dana would use that lack of accuracy not to defend herself, but attack—a strategy Miyo wouldn't expect.

Dana shoved down the panic that pressed up from her stomach

like a geyser. If this didn't work, she would be dead. But if she didn't try it, the result would be the same. In a moment she would know if Miyo was as good a teacher as she claimed to be.

She waited till Miyo had moved to within three feet—well within reach of her sword. Again, Dana's move was perfect and hope surged in her. But this time the teacher didn't underestimate the student. Miyo's defense was faultless. It was as if she'd expected Dana's attack. And her countermove followed so fast, Dana stood no chance.

Miyo slid her sword down Dana's forearm and sliced hard on the back of Dana's wrist. She cried out and dropped her sword and instinctively clutched her wrist. *Foolish! Never drop your sword.*

Miyo kicked Dana's sword fifteen feet to the left and held the tip of her own blade at Dana's throat. "I would ask you not to resist, friend, but I know you can't do that. But out of respect for our friendship, I will ask anyway. If you place your hands behind your back and close your eyes, you will make this easier for both of us."

No. She refused to die like this. Dana spat into the sand at Miyo's feet, then dropped to her knees with her head down as if to submit to Miyo. A second later Dana swung her leg out like a whip and cut Miyo's legs out from under her.

Again she caught her opponent off guard, but this time it didn't buy Dana any extra time. Before Miyo hit the ground, she was rolling forward and lifted her leg straight up. Then brought it down on Dana's shoulder like a falling redwood and followed up with a blow to her ribs that felt like it crushed three of them.

Dana tried to strike out, but Miyo was behind her, pinning Dana's arms to her sides. Dana struggled with everything inside, but Miyo's grip was like iron.

"Fight it, Miyo! Don't let it control you! Talk to me!"

Miyo didn't answer.

Jesus, I need you! Come!

But there was no sense of the Spirit's presence. No tinge of hope for victory or survival. Dana struggled again to no avail. She looked back and stared into Miyo's eyes. "Before you kill me, don't you have anything to say?"

Miyo answered quickly and in a voice just above a whisper. "Do you want to be free?"

"What?"

"Do you?"

"Of course. But what you're doing is not—"

A gust of wind whipped sand into Dana's eyes and she slammed them shut. An instant later something hard smashed into Dana's skull and darkness swallowed her.

F·ORTY-TW·O

DESCRIBING THE PAIN AS AN EXPLOSION IN HER HEAD wouldn't come close to accurately describing what Dana felt. Because the pain wasn't just in her head. It extended down her neck into her torso, arms, legs . . . How could her legs feel like they were on fire while at the same time acutely aware that the little toe on her right foot felt like the nail was in the process of being ripped off?

Then a thought struck her. She was alive. If she was dead she wouldn't be feeling this pain. Right? Or was she in a spiritual prison like one of Simon's alternate realities?

Miyo. A demon? Based on her actions, yes, maybe. No. The thought was ludicrous. But Dana couldn't comprehend what she'd done. Twenty-four hours earlier she would have sworn Miyo was the epitome of the warrior Dana wanted to be. But now? If she wasn't a demon, what was she? A tool of the enemy who infiltrated their ranks to destroy them? It seemed just as impossible. Yet with what Miyo had done to her, Dana had no other explanation.

Something hard pressed down on her feet and she tried to open her eyes. Were they open? She couldn't tell. If they were, all that was visible was darkness. After a few minutes, images of microscopic green strands circled through her imagination as they rose from her body. She was inside her body and outside it at the same time. Thin translucent fingers reached inside her body, took hold of one of the strands, and pulled it out like the unraveling of a tapestry, where one strand was connected to all the other strands.

A lilting melody played in her head—or was it outside her?—from an ancient sounding flute. Then a far-off drumbeat joined in. Time seemed to slow and seconds took minutes to pass. And still the ethereal hands worked to pull the strands out of her body. Each time one of the green strands left, it felt like another piece of her flesh was being ripped out. The process lasted for hours—maybe days—and still the microscopic organisms seemed to fill every part of her.

Finally the last fiber was gone and Dana breathed a sigh of complete exhaustion even though she'd done nothing. For the first time since she and Miyo had left Well Spring and entered into this realm, she felt peace.

Jesus?

I am here.

Am I alive?

Yes, dear child.

A voice broke into her conversation with the Spirit. "Rest, Dana. It is what you need more than anything else right now. There will be time to talk later. You are not alone."

"Miyo?" It sounded like her, but how could it be? "Is that you?"

The owner of the voice didn't answer and Dana slipped back under. When she came to the second time, Dana heard a brook to her left, and the air smelled like it was early morning with the hint of a flower she felt like she should know from childhood.

She opened her eyes for a moment and caught a glimpse of Miyo before a sting of pain shot through her head and forced her to close them again. Her worst migraine was nothing compared to this. This couldn't be heaven, so Miyo must not have killed her.

"Good morning."

"Miyo." Dana risked opening her eyes again and paid for it with another twinge that shot through her head like a grenade going off inside her skull.

"Don't talk till you're able to without pain. And keep your eyes closed if you can. You've been through quite an ordeal."

"I'm alive."

"Very much so." Miyo stroked Dana's forehead. "Although keeping you that way took a toll on both of us, I'm afraid."

What was she wearing? Whatever it was felt heavy, like the lead-lined jacket she wore when she was ten and had to get X-rays on her wrist. And it was hot. Her forehead felt wet with sweat.

"Sleep if you can."

"But you have to tell me—"

"I will, all of it, just like I promised. But not yet. You need more rest first. It will help you heal faster." Miyo prayed a short blessing over Dana, and before the prayer was finished, Dana slipped back under.

When she woke for the third time, her headache had vanished. She opened her eyes and kept them open. Above her was an archway of red stone. It reminded her of a trip to Sedona she'd taken after her junior year of college. That would explain the heat. Next to them was a wide brook that flowed swiftly with crystal-clear water.

"What happened to me? Where are we? Why aren't we back at Well Spring?"

"You were deeply infected." Miyo pulled a damp white cloth across Dana's forehead. "I'm sorry. What I did to you had to inflict a great deal of pain. But I'm proud of you. You fought well and embraced the freedom that was offered. And you have advanced a great distance in your training."

Miyo grinned and rubbed her arm where Dana had landed more than one blow. "Far better than I could have hoped for. You have become a strong warrior. Or better said, you always were a strong warrior and the warrior has been more fully released, far more quickly than expected. My grandfather was right about you."

Dana lifted herself up on her elbows, but Miyo eased her back down and Dana didn't resist.

"Rest a little longer. It's okay. We must go soon, yes." Miyo paused and glanced around. "But there is time. The Spirit has given the stones of this place healing properties. Extracting the virus out of you has no doubt taken its toll. Lie on the stone for a while longer and let it soak into your body and bring relief."

Dana sank back into the stone. It didn't make sense. It didn't feel hard. In fact, no bed had ever felt this soft, and whether it was her imagination or real, heat seemed to seep out of the stone into her back and then down her legs in waves. And with each pass she felt stronger.

She stared into Miyo's dark-brown almond-shaped eyes. They were more tender than she'd ever seen them and they spoke of more compassion than her words could have. "I thought you were going to kill me."

Miyo smiled, dipped the cloth into the stream again, and squeezed out the water. "No, I like you far too much to do something like that. And I love you even more."

"What was inside me? You used the word *virus*."

"In human terms it is best described as a virus. A spiritual virus." She pressed the cloth onto the back of Dana's wrist where Miyo's sword had sliced it open. It stung for a moment but then seemed to pull away the pain and stiffness.

"Human terms?"

"You were infected."

"And in spiritual terms?"

"You let in a significant amount of warfare from the enemy."

"Are you saying—?"

"Yes. Warriors Riding has been attacked. Infiltrated because our guard was down."

"Guard down?"

"You've become adept at seeing the attacks coming at you from the outside but were vulnerable to an assault from the inside."

"You're saying one of us—"

Miyo shook her head and knelt closer. "Not one of the Warriors."

"Simon?"

Miyo nodded, dipped her cloth in the water, and brought it back to Dana's wrist.

"That can't be. He's not evil. He saved Marcus, which saved us during our battle against the spirit of religion. I can't believe he—"

"I doubt Simon has any idea of the warfare he carries. It would devastate him if he knew. I'm certain Zennon offered the warfare to Simon before or during his time in the alternate realities in a way that seemed to be right and an answer to his pain, and he took it in. I imagine it has lain dormant for many, many years. But now it has been set loose on us. And you took the bait, friend."

Dana gave her head a tiny shake. "Bait? I didn't take any—"

"Ask the Spirit, Dana."

She squeezed her eyes together in an effort to push beyond the pounding headache now assailing her. "I . . . I don't see—" But she did see. The lure was her chance to shine as the Leader of Reece's new version of the Warriors Riding. To be the A student once again. To be lauded for her skills and leadership prowess. To perform well and be loved for it.

Miyo took the cloth from Dana's forehead and dipped it once more in the stream, and this time placed it on her forehead.

Dana closed her eyes. "What about you?"

"I resisted and narrowly thwarted the attack. I've learned to guard myself at all times with the armor of God I taught you to build. I always keep a thin layer of it around me. That gave some protection. Even so, it took everything I had to fight off the warfare. It weakened me. If it came at me a second time, I don't know if I could do it again so soon."

"It was sweet and cool and promised me . . ."

"Yes."

"How did it get in? What did I do wrong?"

Miyo hesitated. "It's time for us to leave here."

Dana grabbed Miyo's wrist. "Tell me."

"I'm not your judge."

"But you know something."

"I know the only way the warfare can get in is through an opening. A crack in our souls. Those cracks come from sin. Things we are holding on to. I don't know what it is in you. Hardness of heart? Having to prove yourself? Needing to perform? Those are only guesses. But whatever it is, it allowed the enemy to more easily get past your defenses. You offered him a seam, and he was able to worm his way through and plant thoughts and images and promises and suggestions and warfare inside you."

Dana closed her eyes again. Of course she had cracks. Everyone did. Her two biggest? Miyo nailed one of them. Needing to succeed. Perform. She thought she'd finally defeated it on that beach inside the spiritual realm she'd gone to with Miyo. Obviously not. The second crack was Brandon. To all outside appearances she'd forgiven him completely. Given up every shred of bitterness. Let go of all her woundedness over his breaking of her heart. But it wasn't true. There were still shards left she hadn't fully acknowledged till this moment.

"I need to give up being the Leader."

"Our greatest strengths are so often our greatest weaknesses."

"And I have to forgive him completely."

"The Song?" Miyo said.

"Yes."

Miyo squeezed her hand. "We need to go."

"Back to Well Spring."

"No, it's not safe there."

"But we have to warn the professor. Warn Brandon and Reece—"

"Do you know the moment the warfare came on you?"

She blinked. "It . . . it was when we stood on the hillside, listening to Ree—" Dana blinked. "You're not saying Reece is already infected, are you?"

"What do you think?" Miyo stood and folded her arms. "He does a complete 180 on the direction and focus of Warriors Riding right around the time the warfare was unleashed?"

"It's hard to believe Reece couldn't resist, as strong as he is in the Spirit."

"I agree, which is why I want to go to a place where we can know for certain if he's been infected."

"Where?"

"To a spiritual realm I hear you've already been to."

Dana raised her eyebrows.

"The Field of Doors," Miyo said.

"The gateways of all souls."

"Yes. We need to see Reece's door."

FORTY-THREE

Moments later, they stood above the Field of Doors on the dais where the other Warriors and Dana had gathered when they were here the first time. The air temperature was just above cold. A hint of jasmine tickled her senses, and the brightness of the sun and the blue of the sky made the place feel like early spring.

"Does it look different from the last time you were here?" Miyo asked.

Dana studied the field. In the distance to the right were the same green cliffs, thousands of feet high. Waterfalls still divided the mountains in sporadic sections. As before, an arid plain spotted with massive red-rock bridges and formations sat to her left. And in front of them were the doors—thousands of them stretched out as far as she could see. But there were slight differences.

"The colors aren't as bright in certain places and the air isn't quite as clear."

A man approached them from fifty yards to their right. His robes covered his feet, adding to the illusion that he floated over the surface of the huge dark-wood platform.

"I still can't believe that's what they wear in heaven." Dana pointed at his robe. "Seems a little clichéd if you ask me. Something out of a bad Sunday school painting."

When he reached them twenty seconds later, he stopped and gave a slight bow. "First, this isn't heaven. Second, would you prefer I wear jeans and a T-shirt?"

Dana felt her face flush.

He laughed and his eyes radiated kindness and joy. "There is no shame and are no secrets here, Dana Raine. So don't allow the world of men to creep into your mind in this place."

"You remember me." She blinked and frowned.

"Of course." He turned and winked at Miyo. Even without them speaking, Dana could tell the two were friends. "Few humans visit us, so those who do are remembered. But even if I'd met millions of other spirits, I would remember you. You are the Leader."

"Yes . . ." Dana looked away and tried to compose herself.

"I see you are still struggling by comparing yourself to your friend." The man smiled. "We don't recommend that. It is a trap that must be released."

"I've been learning that lately." Dana pointed at her head. "I know it here."

"But not yet so well there." The man pointed at her heart.

"Yes."

"There is a difference between seeing a path on a map and walking it with your feet touching its surface." He didn't wait for a response. "If I understand correctly, you had an encounter recently in the heavens with a number of demons, yes?"

She nodded.

"You refused to give in to Zennon when he pretended to be the Christ in Revelation. You were the one among the Warriors Riding who remained strong and led Brandon and Reece back into the truth."

"I suppose that's true." Dana gazed over the Field of Doors as a feeling of confidence grew inside.

"Every evidence in front of you said you were in the presence of the Christ. Your fellow Warriors said the same. And yet you refused to bow. To give in. And you pressed into truth despite the resistance. What would have happened to Reece and Brandon if you hadn't led well? Where would they be? In the same place Simon was for so many years? Or simply destroyed?"

She smiled at him in thanks, but he wasn't done.

"Are you still allowing the enemy to put doubt in your mind as to the strength of your gifting?" He folded his arms, glanced at Miyo, then looked back at Dana. "Allowing him to taint it by tempting you to compare yourself to another daughter of Eve?"

He shook his head. "You cannot play Miyo's role and would not like it if you stepped into it. Just as she was not born to lead in the same way as you and could not wear your yoke."

Dana only nodded again.

"But there is a deeper truth you are beginning to know and need to know fully."

"The beach scene before my sophomore year. Expectations."

"Listen to me with ears that will hear." The man stared at her and she seemed to lose herself in his flashing green eyes. "He is not disappointed in you and never will be disappointed. There is no performance he requires. No expectations you need to meet. You are his daughter and loved without reservation."

Something snapped inside Dana and tears flooded out of her. After what felt like hours, she rose and stared into the man's radiant eyes once again.

"Now that we have broken the hold of this sin, you need to repent of it to complete your healing."

"What?" Did she hear him right? "Sin? Repent?"

"Yes." The man smiled. "If you consciously allow yourself to continue to allow a thought to stay in your mind you know not to be true, a thought that keeps you from living fully in your glory, yes, I would call that sin. And to repent means to turn from one way of thinking and embrace another. I suggest you turn for good from thoughts that are lies and believe fully that you are loved simply because of who you are."

Without thinking—without knowing if it was all right—Dana grabbed the man in a hug. It must have been okay, as the man hugged her back, and warmth and acceptance radiated into her. When they released, Miyo took her by the arm.

"We can't take too much time here." She turned to the man. "I'm sorry, we can't stay longer."

"I understand. May the Spirit go with you in power and in love."

"And also with you."

Miyo asked Dana to close her eyes, and the instant she did, she felt a rush of wind from behind. She was lifted into the air, but seconds later felt solid ground under her feet again. She opened her eyes to find herself surrounded by doors in the same astounding variety she'd seen the last time she was here.

Massive doors. Small ones. Thick and thin doors. Ancient-looking ones and ones that looked brand-new. Some of stone, some of wood. Some that appeared made entirely of various types of vegetation and some of crystal. But the one directly in front of her and Miyo caught Dana's attention more than any of the others. Something pulled at her as if it wanted her to come closer.

This door was taller and wider than most. Thick redwood logs cut into a circle served as a platform. Rough-hewn stairs were cut into the platform and led up to the door itself, which was made out of rich brown boards in a variety of light and dark shades. Not straight up and down, but woven together in a fascinating pattern.

"I feel drawn to it. It makes me feel safe and apprehensive at the same time. As if danger and glory and life and hope and risk are all wrapped up in a package. And I feel like I know the person whose door this is."

"Yes, it is the door of someone you've grown close to."

She voiced what she already knew. "It's Reece's."

Miyo nodded.

"It's just like him. Strong and full of mystery and hope and the unknown."

"But it's not just like him."

"I think it's stunning." Dana reluctantly pulled her gaze away from Reece's door and looked at Miyo.

"It's all the things you've said, but it isn't right." Miyo glanced around the field at the other doors near them. "Many of these are wrong now. It is spreading."

"What do you mean 'wrong'? What do you mean 'it's spreading'?"

Miyo didn't answer. She circled Reece's door like a lioness sneaking up on its prey, her feet barely making indents into the thick grass that circled Reece's door.

"Look at the grass closely."

Dana bent over and studied the blades. Some of them were lighter than the others, and some were thinner and light brown as if dead. "The grass is dying."

"Yes." Miyo studied Reece's door and spoke without turning. "We need to see what Reece's door looked like a week ago—before Simon came."

"How would you hope to do that? Some sort of spiritual-realm photo album?"

"Did my grandfather teach you anything about time manipulation?"

"Doug and Marcus talked about it when we were all at Reece's house a month ago. The conversation lasted maybe thirty seconds. I thought he might be kidding."

"Kidding? We have the Spirit of the God of the universe in us. The God who created the earth. The God who moved time backward as recorded in Isaiah thirty-eight. The God who says we can move mountains with the faith of a mustard seed. The God who—"

"I get it. So are we going?"

"Yes." Miyo looked at Dana from under her eyebrows. "This might feel a little strange."

Without warning Dana's mind felt like it was pulled out of her skull, down through her torso, down through her legs as if split in two and each half emerged from her feet. Then the rest of her body followed her mind, collapsing on itself until it formed again as if she stood on her head. She felt like she was about to throw up.

But the feeling dissipated as quickly as it had come. Her eyes came back into focus, and she blinked as Miyo took her by the shoulders. "Are you all right?"

"That wasn't fun."

"No." Miyo gave a thin smile. "I'm sorry to say it never gets any easier." Miyo slumped forward, knees bent, and rested her hands on her kneecaps. She looked for a moment like she was going to welcome her lunch back to the land of light. "At least I haven't figured out how yet and if GPD knew, he never taught me."

"GPD?" Dana dabbed at her mouth as if that could wipe away the nauseous feeling.

A sad smile surfaced on Miyo's face. "Grandpa Doug. My pet name for him."

She gave her head a quick shake, and Miyo's countenance shifted back to the granite Dana had come to know. Miyo motioned toward Reece's door.

"Take a look at it now."

Dana stared at the door in astonishment. What had been solid in the present was vastly different in the past. The rich light and dark browns were no longer solid but liquid. They moved up and down the door like small individual rivers undulating and pressing against each other, widening and narrowing as they formed an intricate dance against, around, above, and below each other. It was beautiful. Free and full of life.

She stared at Miyo. "It's alive?"

"Yes. Of course." Miyo glanced at Dana, then turned her gaze back to Reece's door. "Every door is alive. They are the gateways to our souls. So they live just as a soul lives—because the gates are a part of the soul they allow access to."

"And Reece's is hardening." Dana sighed. "He's carrying the warfare."

"Yes. Carrying it and spreading it." Miyo's face grew worried.

"And getting ready to unknowingly unleash it, along with a horde of demons on thousands of susceptible believers."

Realization struck Dana like a tsunami. Of course. The gathering. Which Brandon had clearly bought into. And Marcus was clearly resistant to.

"Brandon?"

"Infected, I fear."

"The professor?"

"I don't think so," Miyo said. "But I'm not sure. And we need to be."

"I agree." Dana paced. "We need to hear from the Spirit, figure out where we go from here."

"I'll tell you one thing I know for certain." Miyo bit her lower lip. "We're not going to tell Reece, but we have to go to his gathering."

"Are you mad? Why would we go and put ourselves in the center of this virus or warfare or whatever it is?"

"We might be the only ones who can stop it."

"Just the two of us?"

"Oh no, we'll have three others with us of such staggering power, the enemy will not be able to stand."

Dana knew she meant the Trinity. "I was thinking more along the lines of people."

"I know." Miyo smiled. "Don't worry. We have eight weeks to prepare. We might not be ready to face the warfare now, but by then we will be. Trust me." Her eyes grew soft and her gaze dropped to Dana's arm. "I'm sorry about your wrist."

Dana smiled and pointed toward Miyo's leg. "And I'm sorry—"

"They are wounds for the King. Do not be sorry."

Dana ran her finger next to the gash on the back of her wrist. *Yes, for him.*

Miyo took Dana's hands. "We need to get back to Well Spring."

"I thought you said—"

Miyo shook her head. "No choice. Our spirits are here. Our bodies are not." Miyo's face darkened. "Let's just pray Reece and the others haven't found them yet."

They slid back into their bodies and Dana glanced at her watch. Still early. Maybe the others weren't up yet. A moment later the crunch of boots coming through the underbrush answered her question. In another ten seconds, Reece and Brandon came into view.

Miyo leapt to her feet. "Stay away from us."

"What?" Brandon opened his arms. "You have an early-morning party and don't invite us?"

Reece wasn't as flippant. "What have you two been doing?"

"What is necessary."

Brandon pointed at them. "I'm thinking something strange is going on given the gash on the back of your wrist, Dana, and the chunk of skin someone took out of your thigh, Miyo."

"We're fine."

Reece took a step toward them and Miyo grabbed Dana's arm. "Stay away from both of us." Miyo's voice grew hard.

Brandon scoffed. "Are you going to tell us where you got your ticket for the Loony Wagon or do we have to guess?"

"No closer, Reece, or we're gone."

"Not without the power of the Spirit, you're not."

"I believe he will lend us his power if your boots come an inch closer."

Reece seemed to grow taller. "I don't know what has you secure in its talons, Miyo, but it is time to break free of it. It's time to stop trying to brainwash Dana into whatever skewed way of thinking you've allowed yourself to get sucked into."

Miyo jabbed a finger toward Reece. "Where is Marcus? And Simon?"

"The professor had to return to Seattle. A minor emergency with Kat and the girls. And Simon became agitated with the idea of being here without Marcus. So we gave them our blessing and allowed them to go."

Dana stared at Reece. *Gave our blessing? Allowed them to go?* Not his language. The comments sent a shiver down her spine.

"Whatever is bothering the two of you, we can work through it.

But for the moment we need to put it aside and focus our energies on the gathering."

Dana dug her feet into the ground. "We're not taking part in the gathering, Reece."

Frustration passed over his face. "There are four of the prophecy, Dana. Without you, the Warriors are incomplete. Do not let the enemy plant lies in your soul. Do not accept them."

"You've been infected, Reece. So have you, Brandon. With warfare orchestrated by Zennon that is taking you both down a path of deception."

Reece didn't answer. He turned to Miyo as his face darkened. "I didn't see this coming. Not from you. So gifted in the things of the Spirit. And a legacy from your grandfather to be envied. And yet you have fallen. You've been deceived. Come back to the light, Miyo." Reece reached out his hand. "Let go of your ego and youth and the deception you have accepted as from the Spirit. I see the light around you trying to overcome the darkness. Allow it to happen. Allow the Spirit to take control and return you to the truth."

Suddenly Reece strode toward them, his long legs chewing up the distance between them like he was running. Just before he reached them, Dana felt Miyo's arm on her shoulder, and the woods vanished.

FORTY-FOUR

ON TUESDAY EVENING, SIMON WALKED INTO LUCID ON the Ave and headed for the back of the lounge to try to make sense of the past few days. He'd been set free. Without question he had thrown off many of the cloaks of deception he'd worn for decades. And yet he still felt like he was standing on a stage with seven illusions to perform but the memory for only two.

Even knowing two was wonderful. After living backstage for more years than he wanted to count, knowing even one trick would feel like Eden. And he would learn the routines once more, and ride again in the spiritual realms.

The clink of glasses and the smell of beer filled his senses, and he tried to relax. He slid into a booth near the corner, ordered a pale ale, and studied the room as he waited for his waitress to return with his drink. Two young men and one woman—students it looked like—huddled at one of the tables over their laptops and talked rapid fire about something. Another table held four women who looked to be in their midtwenties and giggled like it was their first time in a bar.

The rest of the place was empty except for three musicians pumping out a nice assortment of acoustic jazz. Good. He needed a place to gather his thoughts. Some people needed silence. Simon needed noise. Something to compete with all questions pinging around his brain, asking how he'd allowed Zennon to deceive him for so long. Asking what Simon was supposed to do now that he had an idea of who and what he'd been. And why Marcus thought he was important to Warriors Riding. Before he'd left Well Spring, Reece invited him to the gathering, but Simon wasn't sure if he'd go. More than anything he wanted to have time alone to process everything he'd been through.

He pulled out a pad of lined paper and started to jot down his impressions from Well Spring. Get them organized. Record what he remembered from the old days that had inspired him to write the manuscript. Jot down what the Spirit was saying now.

So good to have you back, Simon. I've missed you.

Simon smiled at the clear voice of the Spirit. It would take time, but the professor was right. Restoration had come. He pressed his pen to the paper, but before he could start to write, a familiar voice sliced into Simon's soul.

"Simon."

His chest tightened and his gaze stayed fixed on his paper. He didn't have to turn to know whose voice it was. He prayed for clarity and closed his eyes. He felt the being slide into a seat two tables down.

"Hello, old friend. It's been such a long, long, long, long time."

Simon continued to stare at his paper and prayed again.

"Are you going to pretend you didn't hear me?"

Simon turned and bit into his upper lip. Zennon sat in a corner of the room ten feet from him, looking exactly the same as he had when he'd introduced himself as Aaron to a brokenhearted twelve-year-old boy. Hair just as dark. Eyes just as penetrating.

"Leave me alone."

"Of course. My apologies." The demon rose from his seat, sauntered toward Simon, and stepped past his table. But a second later Zennon spun back, his dark eyes blazing, and slid into the seat across from Simon. "But I cannot. It's so good to see you again. I can't leave without catching up. I'm sorry I didn't come visit you when you were . . . um . . . in the other place. How long were you in your last reality?"

"You know exactly how long." Simon gripped the edge of the table and tried to keep his hands from shaking.

"True. But do you? And how do you know this isn't just another reality I've created for you?"

"I escaped from those realms forever. I'm never going back." Sweat covered Simon's forehead and palms. "And the Warriors went into my soul. Set me free. I know who I am again. Your illusion is finished."

"Yes, you have to feel grand about that." Zennon leaned back and spread his arms along the seat back of the booth they sat in. "Do you remember all the magic we used to do together? Sessions that would last until the dark hours of the night?"

Zennon took out his gold coin and placed it in his left hand, then closed both hands into fists. A second later he opened them and the coin had vanished from his left and appeared in his right. "That was one of the first vanishes and reproductions I taught you. Do you remember?" Zennon extended his hand. "Do you want to hold my coin?"

"Your coin?" Simon narrowed his eyes. "I have the power of the Spirit inside me and he is greater than you, and what you can do, with a power—"

Zennon laughed. "You're no threat to me. You must know that." Zennon pointed at Simon's shaking hands. "Relax. You're of no consequence now that you've served my purpose. Although I must give you credit. You played that part so well."

"What purpose?" Simon's stomach tightened.

"Why, old friend, you have to have suspected." Zennon leaned forward and smiled. "You already know you didn't escape. There was no heroic breach of the alternate-reality wall. So you have to ask yourself, why did I let you go?"

"I . . ." Simon's mind went blank for a moment. "It doesn't matter. I helped the Warriors gain a victory over you. And then I taught them at Well Spring the nature of deception and how to look past the illusion and—"

"Oh my, you're not serious." Mock astonishment splashed across the demon's face and laughter spilled out of his mouth. "You really think you were at Well Spring for God's purposes? How interesting. I love that. It makes everything so much sweeter."

"What are you saying?"

"Before I tell you, be honest with me." Zennon leaned forward and clasped his hands in the center of the table. "You really don't know?"

Simon started to answer, but Zennon cut him off.

"You're the key to my plan. This gathering your precious Warriors are planning? That's not of God. Not at all. That's my event." Zennon rapped the edge of his clasped hands on the table. "You see, I planted warfare in you long ago. I offered it to you on the ledge that day, and you took it and cherished it and it embedded itself deep in your soul.

"And then I let you go. And you got involved in Marcus Amber's life. And gained his trust, which allowed you access to Well Spring and the other Warriors. There you passed the warfare to Reece and Brandon. Marcus unfortunately isn't offering much of a crack to sneak through these days. And Miyo is a little too paranoid to fool. Then she yanked Dana back from the abyss—which I will probably kill her for doing."

Zennon leaned in till his head was inches from Simon's. "No matter. Reece and Brandon are the ones I need. Reece's bitterness toward Brandon for not saving Doug, and Brandon's lack of ability to think of anyone's restoration but his own have served me perfectly. Think back to your last day at Well Spring. Even with your brain full of fog, you had to think it strange the way Reece suddenly decided to revamp his ministry, and you had to wonder why they went after the missing Dana and Miyo like they were hunting game. Why they 'allowed' you and Marcus to leave like they owned you. Why all the way back to Seattle, Marcus talked in riddles about his concern for the rest of the Warriors. And then when you pinned him down for an answer, Marcus told you he feared greatly for his friends. That they had been attacked by some kind of mist that burrowed into their souls with demonic warfare."

Simon stared at the demon and tried to breathe. It felt like all the air had been sucked out of his body and a massive foot stood on his chest.

"You did it, old friend. It was you!" Zennon smiled and flipped his gold coin into the air, where it vanished. "You know how most decks of cards come with an extra card that shows the rules of poker or offers a discount on your next pack? Those are the cards people throw away. That is you, Simon. Your chance came and went back in the sixties before you chose to sleep your life away in other realities. All you're good for now is as a pawn in great wars far beyond your comprehension."

Zennon cupped his palms together, and when he lifted them a red deck of cards rested in his hands. He flipped the top card over and pointed at it. "At best you're the joker. Wild, unpredictable, and rarely needed in card games. If the jokers are lost, no one really notices, just as no one noticed when you were gone for decades."

Zennon gave an exaggerated shake of his head. "You are a forgotten, utterly useless being. You wrote a manuscript. As of late you remember doing it. So what? You're not living what is written in it and probably never will come close to living it ever again."

"Get out."

"I could take you away, you know. To someplace you wouldn't remember. And you could be a king again." Zennon showed the front and back of his hand. Empty. A second later a King of Spades appeared at his fingertips. "I would do that for you. You have to admit, there were times when you liked living there."

"Get out. Leave me."

"By what—?"

"By Jesus Christ. The Son of the Living God. And his Spirit who lives in me."

Zennon shoved himself back from the table hard, stood, and his eyes turned black. "There is no place for you in this world, Simon. Maybe in the next, but not this one. Give it up before you destroy anyone else. You say these pretend Warriors are your friends? Then stay away from the gathering before you ruin someone else's life like you've ruined theirs."

Shame and self-loathing washed over Simon. Was it true? Had he brought warfare on the Warriors? Simon shook his head like a dog after a bath. If it was true, there was no question—he had to stay away. Had to. Had to. Had to. Heat filled him. As much as he wanted to believe Zennon's accusations were a lie, he knew they were true. Yes, he knew who he was: the joker. And he needed to get as far away from the deck as possible.

FORTY-FIVE

"Report."

Zennon bowed before the Master, then glanced at the only other one at the council table. Caustin.

"All things are in place, my lord. The musician is poised, ready to sing the song of heaven for himself. Simon is buried even deeper in deception because I allowed him to discover a slice of who he is again—but now he sees his depravity—which will prevent him from searching for who he is fully. More important, he knows the attack against the Warriors came from him, burying him in guilt and shame, and he will go nowhere near the gathering.

"Miyo has some skill, but her understudy, Dana Raine, is far from ready to face my full wrath. If they choose to show themselves during the gathering, they are only two and cannot hope to stand against me. Reece Roth is now being steered like a ship and I am the rudder. He will unleash my army and its warfare on more than fifty thousand people who come to the gathering, and that will in turn affect hundreds of thousands more across the world. It is not possible at this point for my legions and me to be stopped." Zennon bowed lower.

"Yet I sense it in you. You want something from me."

"Yes, my Master, you are right. I request more power and more resources to build an impenetrable shield against the enemy."

"Against who?"

"Tristan Barrow and those under his command."

For the first time in centuries, the hint of a smile appeared on the Master's cratered face. "Is it possible your old friend has you worried? This surprises me."

"No, my Mas—"

"Scared he's going to come to the rescue like last time, eh?" Caustin pulled his ragged fingernails across the table. "And this time take you out? Admit it. You're terrified."

Zennon pressed his thumb hard into his sword blade. Calm. The moment was almost upon him. He felt it. "I am not frightened of Tristan Barrow. I long to meet him in battle with such intensity that the tang of blood from his soon-to-be-slaughtered body is already on my lips. But there is a far greater purpose here than—"

"Wah, wah, wah. You looooong to meet him in battle." Caustin laughed. "You sound like a freak the way you talk, Zennon. Just admit it. You're petrified of him. You're—"

The Master lifted a finger to silence Caustin and leaned back. "Why do you feel you need this?"

"Because those who are overconfident in their abilities and positions of power are often undermined by that arrogance." Zennon resisted the urge to look at Caustin.

"It would require a considerable amount of resources to hold back the angel and those with him."

"Enough strength was provided to hold back Michael for twenty-one days in centuries past. I don't require anywhere near that kind of force. I only need three hours."

"A well-spoken answer. You will have what you need."

"Thank you, my lord."

"Is there anything else?"

"I have no desire to overstep my position, Master, but I do have a final request."

The Master smiled again at Zennon, glanced at Caustin, then back to Zennon and nodded.

Zennon's first stroke sliced off Caustin's left arm. His second tore off half his rival's leg. Caustin's knife bit into Zennon's upper left arm, but he barely noticed it because he was busy severing Caustin's head from his body.

⛨ ⛨ ⛨

"Talk to me." Tristan stalked the thick, green mountain ridgeline in long strides as Jotham and Orson half jogged to keep up with him. "Something feels very wrong. I've been blocked from getting any kind of read on Zennon for the past three days."

"We as well." Jotham almost growled his answer.

"This is not good." Tristan spun to look at his second in command. This had never happened before. Zennon was skilled. Formidable. Cunning. An enemy to be taken very seriously. And Tristan and his team always had. But this sudden cloud of silence meant they had to take Zennon more seriously than ever before.

"Tell me of the Warriors Riding."

"Marcus Amber is strong," Jotham said. "As are Dana and Miyo."

"How bad are Reece and Brandon?"

"Not good. Both."

"And Simon?"

"The Warrior's journey inside his soul was a start."

"But he has far to go."

Jotham nodded.

Tristan turned and strode up the mountain. This was disconcerting. He needed to take time to go see Dana and Miyo. Speak to them. Offer them hope. They would need all the faith and courage they possessed, plus a great deal more.

FORTY-SIX

"You haven't heard anything from Dana or Miyo?" Kat slid her plate to the side of their kitchen table and leaned forward on her elbows toward Marcus.

"Nothing." Marcus swirled his plate still half full of spaghetti. His stomach was far from amenable to food at the moment. It hadn't been even slightly receptive since returning from Well Spring.

"You've called—"

"Called, e-mailed, stopped by Dana's house. Nothing. They disappeared from Well Spring and maybe from this realm as well without any explanation of where they've gone or why they went there."

Kat grabbed his hand and stopped him from swirling the noodles around his fork. "It's only been a week."

"Only? With what's going on with Reece and Brandon, that is seven days too many."

"I still don't understand—"

"The Temple and the Song are out of equilibrium. Imbalanced. It's all discombobulated. Every last nanobyte. They're both fixated on this gathering. It's all they talk about. Every moment is dedicated to developing the program, getting sponsors, negotiating the contract with Safeco Field, talking to lighting people, sound people, film crews, people who will help stream the event around the globe. They keep saying they want to bring freedom to the masses."

Marcus slammed his fist down on the table harder than he intended. "I can't put my finger on it, but there's something wrong with this idea of taking the Warriors big. There's something wrong with Reece and Brandon, and there's something wrong with the fact I am now the only member of Warriors Riding who seems to be thinking straight."

"Then it seems the only option is to—"

Three sharp raps on the front door stopped Kat from finishing her sentence.

She raised her eyebrows. "You want to get that?"

Marcus answered by rising from the table and marching toward the door. He swung it open and blinked twice. "Dana? Miyo?"

"As you might recall, we've met before." Miyo motioned past him. "Can we come in?"

"Yes. Of course." Marcus stood aside and they walked by him into the entryway.

A few minutes later, Dana, Miyo, Kat, and he were settled on the back deck in a tight circle of chairs.

"So you're here to enlighten us as to what you feel is transpiring in the heavens and on earth?"

"Precisely," Miyo said. "But it might be easier if you simply ask your questions, and we'll try to answer them as succinctly as possible."

"Why haven't you been in touch?"

"Dana and I needed concentrated time of uninterrupted solitude to hear from the Spirit on what we're supposed to do next."

"Does that include me?"

"It does now." Miyo scooted her chair closer.

"Why now and not earlier?"

"We had to be one hundred percent certain you hadn't taken on the warfare Simon was carrying."

"Simon? Warfare?" Marcus fiddled with his glasses. "I don't understand."

"You're about to." Miyo raised her palms and stared at Kat and him for a good five seconds. "Simon infected Brandon and Reece."

"Infected them. What do you mean?" But as he thought about it, Marcus knew exactly what she meant. It was the mist he'd felt the first night when he and Simon stood outside the main cabin.

"In simplistic terms, the warfare and demonic oppression Simon is carrying has been transferred to the Temple and the Song. We trusted Simon, we allowed him to get close to us because of what he did for you, and we let our guard down. It's like a cold or a computer virus. We didn't have our defenses up. We weren't cautious enough, and his warfare shifted onto us."

Marcus gave a tiny shake of his head and glanced at Kat. "I can't believe this. Simon would never—"

"It's not his fault. I doubt he has any idea what he was carrying."

Kat frowned. "What has it done to Reece and Brandon?"

"We believe it's stolen their identities."

"Stolen?"

"Masked them. Clouded them. They took the bait and they're not living out their true selves. They're living out of the flesh."

"How do you know Reece and Brandon are . . . ?" Marcus didn't need to finish his thought. Miyo's raised eyebrows confirmed what he knew to be true. It explained everything. Why Reece was now obsessed with growing Warriors Riding into a monolith. Why Brandon had become fixated on relaunching his singing career and becoming a star once again.

"Explain why I wasn't . . . to use your term, *infected* at Well Spring."

"To continue the analogy, your immune system is extremely strong right now." Dana offered a gentle smile as she looked between Kat and him. "You know your identity. What you went through recently alone and with Kat has made your spiritual defenses strong. The demonic needs a crack to enter through. It needs permission. An agreement. Some dark longing inside that will entice a person to embrace the lie the enemy is offering."

"Such as?"

Dana held out her hand and counted on her fingers. "Bitterness. Unforgiveness. Entitlement. The need for adoration. The need for control. Fear. A hundred different things. And the enemy always offers a compelling solution."

"And what is the result if the warfare is let in?"

"The same effect it had on Simon for so many years."

"As you just said, the loss of identity." Marcus blew out a low breath.

"Yes. The magician forgot who he was, as has Reece, as has Brandon."

"Reece has slipped back into the businessman who created a photography empire. In control of everything and gaining his identity from how large he could grow it." Marcus laced and unlaced his fingers.

Dana nodded.

"And Brandon has become the musician once again acquiring all his self-worth from the adoration of others."

"Precisely."

Marcus adjusted his glasses again. "Neither of you were affected."

Dana glanced at Miyo. "I was. But the newest member of Warriors Riding rescued me."

"Rescued how?"

"She took me into a spiritual realm, subdued me, and prayed the warfare off of me. Fought it off. Pulled it from my soul piece by piece." Dana bowed her head. "My sin was subtle but potent. I believed I was only worth loving if I was perfect. Achieved great things. Led well. Exceeded expectations. On top of that, I vowed to never give my heart to Brandon ever again. A vow can be a dangerous thing."

"Pride," Miyo whispered.

"Your sin?" Kat asked.

Miyo nodded. "I have a friend who owns a home on the Oregon coast who says acquiring great wealth or renowned abilities at an early age is often a detriment to one's soul, and I agree. Pride has been a struggle for me. I was strong enough to resist the attack. But just barely. I knew the warfare on Dana was the weakest of the three, so she was the one I chose to rescue. If I'd gone after Brandon or Reece, I likely would not have succeeded. The warfare is growing stronger in them. It is not wise for me to be around them for any length of time till this is over."

Doug's granddaughter smacked the armrests of her chair. "We have to fight this. Stop the gathering from happening or be there to stop the warfare from spreading."

Kat frowned. "How will it spread? I'm not sure I understand."

Marcus took his wife's hands. "We opened ourselves to Simon, let our guard down because we trust him. Fifty thousand people will be in the stands and even more across the world, trusting Reece and Brandon. They will open themselves to what they have to say. And if there are any cracks in their souls, if they are in a state of weakness . . . if they are open in any way to the sweet lie of the enemy, the oppression will invade them as well."

Kat's face went white as she realized the scope of damage the gathering could inflict on hundreds of thousands of believers.

Miyo clapped her hands. "Now it is time to make our plans. Any thoughts, Professor?"

"Two." Marcus opened his notebook and pawed toward the back few pages. "As I've been praying over the past three days, the following things have become abundantly clear: First, I didn't know why, but I've felt the need to develop a small team of allies who would pray for whatever was going on in the Warriors. Now I know what it is. They must pray for us from this point on up through the night of the event. Second, I have to make sure Simon gets to Safeco Field the night of Reece's gathering."

"I'm not thinking having Simon there is going to help our side of the equation."

"Trust me, Miyo. It is critical."

"Can you explain why?" Dana glanced between Marcus and Kat.

Marcus looked at her over the top of his glasses. "The short answer is Doug's letter told me I needed to, and as I mentioned a moment ago, I feel like the Spirit has confirmed that."

"And the long answer?"

"There isn't one." The idea of Simon not being there gave Marcus an image of the Pacific Ocean going dry. "There is no doubt in my mind. Simon must be there."

After twenty more minutes of discussion, Dana and Miyo stood to leave. They had decided Marcus would continue to meet with Brandon and Reece regarding the gathering, and Marcus said he would attempt to explain the warfare that was on them. The women said it was a waste of time, but he had insisted.

As Kat and he walked them to the front door, Miyo reached into her tote bag and handed him a book wrapped in a light brown cloth.

"What is this?"

"Open it."

It was a leather-bound notebook. Marcus ran his fingers over the worn cover. "Is this—?"

"Yes. Reece's journal. I was compelled to grab it the morning we left Well Spring. Who knows, maybe this is why. Maybe you'll find something inspirational in it to tell your prayer team."

"When do we meet next?" Marcus said.

"I think until the gathering we need to meet every other day. We're only seven weeks out. Thoughts?"

"Agreed. And be praying for me. I'm meeting with Reece and Brandon tomorrow."

"You won't convince them."

"I have to try."

FORTY-SEVEN

MARCUS GRITTED HIS TEETH IN UTTER FRUSTRATION.
Dana and Miyo were right. This was pointless.

"Let me repeat, implementing the gathering is not the right
decision for the Warriors. Did you hear me? You've both been
infected by Simon. Don't you comprehend what I've told you? The
decisions you're making are a result of warfare and demonic oppression you've let in because of your sin. Don't you see? You took the
bait. You have forgotten who you are!"

Marcus spoke to Reece and Brandon as the three of them sat
on the back deck of Reece's wooded home northeast of Seattle, but
his words would have made more of an impact on two marble statues. They'd been arguing for twenty-five minutes, and not a shred
of progress had been made.

"Enough, Professor." Reece stomped his boot on his dark
stained deck. "Wake up. I don't need the enemy playing with your
head like he's done with Dana and Miyo. The Spirit has told us to do
this, so we're doing it. I know who I am."

"You've lost your spiritual sight, haven't you?" Marcus jabbed
a finger at Reece. "It's gone cloudy or vanished altogether. Why do
you think that has hap—?"

"Be quiet. It's an attack of the enemy. Nothing more."

Marcus spun toward Brandon. "You have to fight this, Song.

You're caught. Deceived. Think about what you're feeling! You want to be the rock star again. Revive your career. But that's not the true you. You are a leader of *worship*, Brandon, to point to the One. Not to yourself."

"You don't understand, Marcus. This is my path. My destiny."

Reece jumped in. "Brandon knows what the Spirit has spoken to him of his restoration. It was confirmed by Doug. There is no doubt. We have continued to pray for Dana and Miyo, but their silence confirms they are still mired in deception. We have tried multiple times to reach them and they have not responded. At this point I'm assuming they won't. We haven't given up on them being there, but it's clear the enemy has them in a stranglehold at the moment.

"Back to you, Marcus. The gathering is happening in less than seven weeks and you need to be sharp. You're going to make sure Carson is pumping this thing for all he's worth, especially during the last three weeks, correct?"

Marcus lied and nodded. He'd spoken to the talk-show host after speaking with Dana and Miyo and had explained why all promotional materials and ads for the gathering had to be pulled.

"Speaking of the other members of the Warriors, do you know where Miyo and Dana are?" Brandon leaned forward and stared at Marcus with intense eyes.

"Yes."

"Where?"

"As I've already said three times this evening, I intend to honor their request for that information to remain unknown."

"They need to be at the gathering."

"That is their choice."

"Are they coming?"

"I will not answer for them."

"Friends," Reece said, "we're not making progress at the moment, so let's stop while we are still being civil to each other. Is there anything else before we break?"

Marcus grabbed his satchel. "Yes, I want to read you something."

"From what?"

"From your journal."

Reece stiffened but didn't ask how Marcus had come to have possession of it. "Fine."

Marcus cleared his throat and read without looking up.

The most potent attack of the enemy will always come against our identity. He does not want us to know who we are. He does not want us to know our talent, our true heart's desire, our destiny, our path. For if we know these things and live out of them with passion, we become extremely dangerous to him. If we live in our true, free, Spirit-infused identity, he will do everything possible to thwart our realization of that knowledge.

Once we discover our glory, our gifting, our calling, the evil one will seek to cloud it like a dark fog, to taint it, spin it, twist it to such a degree that we forget who we are and become only a shadow of what the Lord has made us to be. He will lead us back into captivity, back into who we were before we stepped into the freedom and power of our true self.

He will tempt us to question who we are. To doubt what God has spoken of. It is the attack he used against the Son during his time of fasting in the desert. "*If* you are the Son of God, tell these stones to become bread" . . . Then the devil took him to the holy city and had him stand on the highest point of the temple. "*If* you are the Son of God," he said, "throw yourself down."

If you are Reece Roth of the prophecy. *If* you are loved unconditionally, irrevocably, by the great I Am. *If* you are the mentor of Warriors Riding. *If* you have the power and strength and courage to carry out your destiny.

Lies. Because there is no "if" in the kingdom of the One. Know who you are. Know who you are. You must know who you are, Reece!

Marcus shut the journal and glanced up. Neither Brandon nor Reece looked like they'd heard any of the words he'd just read. Both were back to being marble statues. Finally Reece spoke.

"Give me what is mine, Marcus." He held out his arm ramrod straight.

"Know who you are, Temple. What you have become is not the true Reece. You are not a man who must control his world. You are not a man who needs to fill his emptiness with a vast empire of success to prove his worth. You are not a man—"

"Hand me my journal now, Professor."

Marcus set Reece's journal on the coffee table between them and slid it to the center. He stood and walked out of the room without anyone saying another word.

FORTY-EIGHT

DURING THE NEXT SIX WEEKS—AS LATE AUGUST SLIPPED into September, then into the first days of October—Miyo stayed at Dana's home in Seattle. They trained together, prayed together, and tried to rest in the knowledge that God was God and he would prepare them for Reece and Brandon's gathering.

Dana worked most days at the station even though her mind was barely in it, and Miyo did business for her dad's publishing company as well as she could remotely. They also continued to meet every other day with Marcus and Kat.

At first the days moved slowly, but the final three passed by in what felt like seconds. Two nights before the gathering, Miyo appeared in the door frame of Dana's family room and smiled. "I want to take you to one more place."

"Now?"

Miyo nodded, shuffled over to the couch, and sat next to Dana.

"I thought we were going to rest up."

Her friend smiled. "Exactly."

A few minutes later they sat on the end of a small cape that jutted out into an almost wave-free, light-blue ocean. They didn't speak. Didn't move. Simply soaked up the peace that floated through the air like dandelion spores.

Dana glanced down two hundred or so feet below them to a

trail that meandered back and forth from the water up the side of the cape to where they sat. Was that a man? She turned to Miyo. "I thought you said no other soul knew about this place."

"That's right."

"Then who is that?" Dana pointed to the man who jogged up the trail toward them.

"Don't be concerned. It's a friend."

"A friend of yours or mine?"

"Both."

"Who? I don't think I have any friends who travel these parts."

"You'll see." Miyo rose and brushed off her shorts.

The man seemed to cover the distance between them in giant strides, and while he was still a hundred yards away, Dana realized Miyo was right. It was a friend. And a warrior. A few seconds later the massive form of Tristan Barrow stood before them.

She smiled and pointed between Tristan and Miyo. "You know each other?"

"Yes, Dana. We know each other well." The angel fixed his gaze on Miyo. "How is she progressing?"

"Beyond my expectations." Miyo spoke in a low voice without emotion. "She is ready."

"Good. She needs to be."

"And you?"

"I'm fine." The angel spoke the words with firmness, but there was also hesitation in his tone.

"You are fighting well, Miyo." Tristan rubbed his blond hair and glanced at Dana, then back to Miyo. "You set a critical captive free at significant personal risk."

"Thank you." Miyo's tone didn't match the words.

"You're angry with me." The angel cocked his head.

"Why won't you help us?"

"Help you?"

"Fight this war for us. Come in and take out Zennon once and for all. Take down—"

"You need this explained to you?" Tristan frowned.

"Yes."

"It is not the way the Spirit works. The Spirit gave Ezekiel the power to speak life into dry bones, but God was not the one who spoke. God gave Moses the power to split the sea, but the Lord was not the one who raised his arms. In more circumstances than you know, we war for you. But in this battle we are called to war *with* you. It is with great rarity that I understand the Spirit's ways, but it is with great frequency that I trust him. I suggest you do the same."

Miyo frowned. "But you will be there to war with us."

"We hope to be, yes." Tristan turned to go.

"Hope to be?"

"Yes, hope." Frustration passed over Tristan's face. "Zennon has been given power far above his normal authority."

"What does that mean?"

Tristan didn't answer for more than twenty seconds. "That our every intent is to be there to fight with you."

"That's not filling me with a great deal of comfort," Miyo said, concern etched into her face.

Tristan gazed at the darkening horizon. "So much responsibility has been placed in the hands of humans. It has been this way throughout the ages. The Creator gives you great respect with his invitation to play a significant role in the larger story. The accomplishment of his will could not happen without you."

"You have to explain that to us."

"It means I suspect an opportunity to fight in the coming battle is not up to us. It is up to you and the other Warriors. The key to unlock that door is in your hands."

FORTY-NINE

BE READY. THIS WILL BE THE MOST SEVERE BATTLE YOU HAVE ever faced.

The words from the Spirit stopped Dana cold as she pulled into the parking lot of Safeco Field on Sunday evening. Since joining the others of the prophecy, she'd often debated if she heard God's voice when the Spirit spoke, or if she was making words up in her mind. Not this time. She held no doubt these words were from the Spirit. They shook her to the core. Because she'd felt this night was coming from the moment she started training with Miyo.

It shouldn't be a surprise. Of course there was a purpose to what she had been learning. Armor of light. Greater skill with a sword. Calling down the fire of heaven. Creating a shielded dome of light. And she knew facing Zennon again was part of Miyo's prophecy, and now Dana was part of that prophecy. But somehow she'd convinced herself it would be in a distant future when she would use her new skills. Now the future had landed with a crash into the present, and she felt far from ready.

Dana gripped her steering wheel as if it could keep her from falling into the chasm that seemed to have opened up beneath her. "Will I die?"

You will have to fight with everything you are, everything you have been, and everything you ever will be. There is no one else.

She asked again, "Will I die?"

Again no answer.

"Lord, speak to me."

I am with you, to the end of this age and beyond. With me, death no longer remains.

Dana stepped from her car and stared at the people already meandering toward Safeco Field. She wanted to stand on the roof of her car and scream at them, that they were walking into a trap, into an arena where the lions were prowling and ready to strike. That it was a stadium of war.

She shut her door and stared at her car. Funny. She didn't lock it, as if it didn't matter because she probably wouldn't be seeing it again. No, not true. God was in this. With her. With Miyo. With Marcus. Dana tried to convince herself the victory was theirs but had no success. Miyo, the professor, and her against the world. More than the world. Against Reece and Brandon. And if that wasn't plenty of kindling and logs for the bonfire, they were about to face Zennon and whatever forces he'd brought with him as well.

You are the Leader.

The Spirit didn't speak the words to comfort her but to state the reality of the prophecy that had become her life for the past year and a half. Maybe had always been her life. Maybe her entire life had led to this moment. Predestination? She didn't know. Dwelling on it wouldn't change anything. Did she have a choice to get back in her car and pretend the war about to break loose didn't exist?

A part of her wanted to. A part of her could easily pretend none of the past eighteen months had happened, that it was all in her mind, that both prophecies were figments of a man's creative imagination. That everything that had happened to her and Warriors Riding was a series of dreams and hallucinations. If she was offered the choice Simon had been given, would she have chosen to stay in this war-ravaged world?

Dana shook the thoughts from her mind. She couldn't start down that road because she would never get off. She needed to find Miyo. Get some time together before the gathering started.

Surround themselves with the thickest armor of light possible and pray like they'd never prayed before.

✠ ✠ ✠

Your time is nearly here, friend.

The voice in his mind was so soft, Simon wasn't sure he'd heard it. He rose from his couch, slipped on a light Windbreaker, and paced across his tiny apartment, his gaze fixed on the worn tan carpet. The smell of his earlier meal of chicken still hung in the air, and Bing Crosby filled the room with the sound of "Just One More Chance." The image of a battle flashed into his mind so fast he couldn't make out any of the details.

Yes, it is almost here, Simon.

The voice of the Spirit still speaking to him all these years later. "Lord."

A knock at the door snapped Simon's head up. Had to be the professor. Simon glanced at the tiny cuckoo clock on the wall. Time to go. Join Marcus and Dana and Miyo at the stadium. The professor had tracked him down, convinced him the warfare was not his fault, somehow convinced Simon he had to come to the gathering. He shook his head. It seemed right—he trusted Marcus—but the shame and guilt he carried were still so heavy.

He didn't want to be there, might be another snare, but Marcus had insisted. They had argued with great intensity, but in the end Simon had agreed.

Go. The peace of the Spirit wrapped itself around him and he walked to the door.

✠ ✠ ✠

After they got into Marcus's car and headed for Safeco Field, Simon rolled his silver coin around his fingers and turned toward his friend. "A battle is coming tonight, Professor."

"Yes. We will fight." Marcus nodded. "And I believe there will be something for you tonight at the gathering, Simon. Specifically for you."

Simon's mind spun. Pictures of lightning bolts raining down on a barren field were mixed with images of thirty-foot waves smashing into a blood-red brick wall that shuddered and moaned. Then scenes of him on the mountain ledge with Zennon once again and slipping out of this reality into the ones he'd been trapped in for decades.

"I can't do this. I shouldn't be there."

"Stay strong. 'We are more than conquerors.'" Marcus reached over and took Simon's forearm. "He is more than with us. He is inside us. You know this. You wrote it down in detail. Remember who you are and resist the lies."

"It's not easy to throw off a fifty-one year enchantment in eight weeks."

"What do you want, Simon?"

"I want to be free."

"So be it, and may it be so."

✠ ✠ ✠

Dana and Miyo met at the back of the stadium at six o'clock.

"Why couldn't we come here together?" Dana asked.

"I already told you. I needed time alone."

"You could have been alone at my house."

Miyo stared at her. "Do you really want to have this debate right now?"

They stood 150 yards from a security entrance and stared at two guards who lounged near the door they had hoped to enter the stadium through.

Miyo glanced at Dana, then back to the guards. "Lord, make seeing eyes blind."

"Here we go again," Dana muttered.

Miyo smiled. "Reece told me you studied Luke together and that the Spirit made seeing eyes blind for Marcus in that church when he confronted the demon ushers."

"You think—"

"The Spirit is going to do the same for us now?" Miyo pursed her lips. "I'm counting on it. Let's go."

Ten minutes later they were through the door and huddled in a supply room deep in the stadium.

"We'll stay here till show time," Miyo said. "Once it starts we'll work our way backstage and follow the Spirit's lead."

"Like I've said for weeks now, that's quite a plan."

"Yes, it is. And is the only one that has the minutest chance of working."

FIFTY

At 7:35, Dana watched Reece stride to the front of the stage at Safeco Field to deafening applause. The stage lights bounced off the sunglasses hiding his eyes, but nothing hid his megawatt smile. He waited till the roars of the crowd subsided, then stepped closer to the microphone.

"Welcome, Seattle! Welcome to the rest of you around the world! Welcome to *freedom*!"

The crowd exploded again.

"I wish you could see what I see tonight. I see revolution. Great change. Great power. Great battles that will be waged and won, not only tonight, but for months and years and decades to come! Warriors Riding has played small for too long. *You* have played small for too long! It's time to make a plan. Make things happen. Set the path and the vision for our lives and take control!"

Reece spoke on for another twenty minutes about how every man and woman in the stadium and every man and woman watching and listening around the globe would be taking the message of freedom, restoration, and healing to every corner of their world. Most of it sounded right, but mixed in were frequent references to growth, success, achievement, and structure. And money. Reece had never spoken of money, but now it seemed to be one of the centerpieces of his message. He couldn't speak for more than a few minutes without the crowd shouting its approval. Finally he stopped till the stadium grew silent.

Reece rubbed his hands together, then balled them into fists and held them in front of his chest. "We are all warriors together in this battle. We are all brothers and sisters together in the kingdom. So will you now join me in a symbolic gesture of unity by taking the hand of the person next to you and joining me in surrendering the remainder of this evening to our God. Open yourself to the Spirit's message. Open yourself to freedom. Open yourself to what he wants to do inside you."

As Reece prayed Miyo's face paled and she whispered to Dana, "This is bad. I should have anticipated this."

"Why?" But an instant later Dana knew why. Reece was directly asking the people to open themselves up. Exactly what they'd done with Simon back at Well Spring. "There's nothing we can do?"

"We will do everything we can. Take heart. And look." Miyo smiled and pointed toward the back of the stage across from them. Marcus and Simon stood less than fifteen yards away, almost hidden by the thick, black curtain that provided the backdrop for the stage. "We are not alone." Miyo tugged on Dana's arm. "The moment has come. I need to show you something else."

"What moment?"

"This won't be easy to see. But you have to in order to understand what we need to do next." Miyo prayed. "Open her eyes, Spirit of the Living God." She pointed out over the stadium. "Look along the rows. In among the seats. Up in the stands and all around the stadium." Miyo prayed again. "Allow Dana to see the enemy before us."

Dana gazed over the crowd and into the stands. At first she saw nothing. Then, as if a switch had been flipped, she saw a green mist swirling through the stands, and then thousands of dark figures moving along every aisle handing the crowd something. It looked like small crackers. Some refused the wafers, but the majority of the crowd took them and ate.

"Reece's words have opened the people to this. They believe in him so much they'll embrace almost anything he says. And right now he's speaking truth laced with lies, and the people are swallowing the lies both figuratively and literally."

Dana's body numbed. "Just as I must have swallowed them back at Well Spring."

Miyo nodded. "They're letting the warfare in. And soon they'll forget who they are."

As she watched, whole sections were turned to granite. She blinked, and the same people who were stones in the spirit, moved and nodded and shouted their approval with their physical bodies.

An invisible fist grabbed Dana's chest and her breaths grew short. "It's just like Marcus saw that one day in church where the demons gave the crowd stones of duty and guilt."

"Yes, he told me about that."

"But this is far worse." Dana's hands trembled. "Can't anyone else see this? We can't be the only ones who are seeing this."

"I don't know. I believe some in the crowd can and understand what is truly going on. May the Spirit urge them to pray."

"We have to stop it."

Stop it?

The voice echoed in Dana's head, then turned to laughter, then spoke again.

You can't stop this, dear Dana.

A figure at the back of the stadium at least eight feet tall strolled down the middle aisle toward them. Long dark hair flowed over his thickly muscled shoulders. He wore no shirt and his skin was bronzed and rippled with muscles. His face was flawless and strikingly handsome. Several demons with drawn swords joined him as he marched down the aisle. Just before he reached the front of the stage, he stopped and pulled a gold coin out of his pocket. He spun it around his fingers, then flicked it high into the air. It landed on the stage not more than twenty feet from Dana and Miyo.

"Hello, Dana," he called and gave a mock bow. "And Miyo as well."

Dana's heart hammered. Zennon. His evil gaze raked her body.

He waved one finger back and forth like a teacher scolding a grade-schooler. "You need to back off, Miyo. The consequences will be most regrettable if you don't." He turned his liquid-black eyes on Dana.

"Taking Reece's eyes and Brandon's voice was child's play. This is real. You need to leave now, Dana. I've always liked you and given you more space than most humans. But you've exhausted my compassion. This is my meeting, and if you do anything from this moment on to get in the way, I will end your life immediately."

Zennon walked up the steps onto the stage. The seven or eight demons with him filled in behind him. "This stadium is mine."

Miyo didn't budge. "All the earth is the Lord's."

"I was given an invitation to come, so don't make this difficult. As I said, I don't desire to destroy either of you. But if you force me to, I will."

He motioned out over the crowd. "You can't stop this. It's already been done. Simon has done his work and Reece is doing his right now. The warfare has spread. Its infection is complete and the people have embraced it. And I do not think the two of you would fare well against my most select warriors." He motioned behind him. "These are not like the ones you've faced before, Dana. These are the elite who have been under my command for millennia.

"And in case you decide to fight anyway, be aware there will be no safety net to save you this time. Tristan and his friends will not ride in on a glorious wave to rescue you. They have been, shall we say, contained."

It didn't make sense. Why weren't Zennon and his soldiers attacking them? The demon had no compassion. Why the long, drawn-out speech? Then two things hit her. Zennon's greatest weapon was deception. Fear. Illusion, Simon would call it. The ability to make things seem far worse than they were. Second, Marcus wasn't here just to watch. He and the team he'd rallied were undoubtedly praying hard and interceding for them in a way that was holding

Zennon back. They couldn't break through the prayer covering. At least not yet.

At the same time, why should he attack? There was no reason. Zennon was getting exactly what he wanted. Dana turned to Miyo. The look in her friend's eyes scared her.

FIFTY-ONE

"IT'S TIME." MIYO EXTENDED HER HAND AND PULLED Dana back, away from Zennon until they stood at the far corner of the stage—directly opposite Zennon and his demons. Dana still felt exposed. Naked. She couldn't help staring at Zennon's elite warriors, their swords drawn and evil pulsating from their eyes. Palpable fear radiated off them and seemed to sweep over her in waves.

"Time?"

"To go to war. Our moment has come."

"Against them?"

Miyo nodded.

Was she serious? Did Miyo mean the two of them were about to go up against Zennon's ninjas? Didn't she hear what the demon had just said? She stared at Miyo. Her friend's face was stone but her eyes blazed with light and fire

"Yes. Against them. I can't find anyone else to attack. Can you? And we're not here to knit."

"Just the two of us."

"'He trains my hands for battle; my arms can bend a bow of bronze. You give me your shield of victory, and your right hand

315

sustains me; you stoop down to make me great.' Let us be great in this moment, Dana Raine."

"We can't hope to—"

"We are not alone." Utter resolve filled Miyo's eyes. "'You will tread down the wicked, they will be ashes under the soles of your feet.'"

Dana's heart thundered in her chest and the fear pouring off the demons wrapped itself around her soul. "I can't do that. I'm not ready. Reece, Brandon, and I barely survived the last battle with Zennon. And this is not his throwaway army. I would be dead if not for Brandon. We all would have perished if Tristan, Jotham, and Orson hadn't shown up. It's not possible for me to—"

"You are not the same woman you were then. You are far stronger now, mightier than you can imagine." Miyo turned and took her by both hands. "It is time to lead like you've never done before. You must find that strength inside you don't believe you have. Not because you'll be loved for it, but because it is who you are. Step into your glory."

Adrenaline coursed through Dana's body and her legs bounced. "I don't know how, Miyo! Yes, we could attack. But my sword will do nothing against that army."

"Did I say swords?"

"Then what? You want me to create a light-shield that will be strong enough to withstand the strength of Zennon and his demons? I'm not ready for—"

"You're letting the enemy in right now. Letting Zennon play with your mind. You're believing the lies." Miyo's face was hard as iron.

"I'm believing in reality."

"'In the presence of the God in whom he believed, who gives life to the dead and calls into existence the things that do not exist.'" Miyo squeezed her hands tight. "And *calls into existence things that do not exist!*"

Miyo released Dana's sweat-soaked hands, took three steps

toward the demons, then turned to face her and stretched out her hand. Miyo's face of stone hadn't softened, but it was now also infused with a sense of triumph and great faith.

"Believe with me, friend. Believe that you sit with Christ in the heavens. That you have been given all power and all authority of Jesus because you have taken your rightful place as a child of the Creator of the universe and the heavens and the earth. Come. Join me in this battle."

Dana forced her shaking legs to move. One step, then two, then three until she stood next to Miyo.

"The darkness cannot overcome the light. Let us speak of the light." Miyo raised her right hand toward Zennon and spoke just above a whisper. "I bring the Kingdom against the powers of evil before us. A wall of light. A wall of power between us and them. I speak it into existence by the power of the crucifixion, the power of the resurrection, and the power of the ascension of the Messiah."

As Miyo spoke, the air between them and Zennon and his army shimmered and thickened like a giant pane of glass. It rose two stories above them, then spread out to their right and left.

Suddenly words poured from Dana's mouth that were hers, but not hers. "More power, Lord. Thicker. Stronger. Able to hold back—able to contain—the forces of evil."

The wall of light grew higher. It was now three-stories tall and fifty-yards wide. The sides bent down and formed a dome of light that descended on Zennon and his demons. In less than twenty seconds they were surrounded.

Zennon shook his head at them and grinned. He lifted his hand and waved it once across his body as if the edge of his hand was a blade. Instantly the dome shattered, fell to the stage, and vanished. "You think you can do anything against me? Don't you realize by now I used every minor victory you won to bring this moment to fruition? Do you not understand the culmination of everything you think you've done for your ludicrous kingdom of God has produced this night where I will infect millions of souls with my truth?"

Zennon threw his head back and a thick, guttural laugh spewed from his mouth. "No, dear Dana. There has been no lasting victory inflicted on me by your pitiful band. All that has come out of your feeble attempts to fight me is destruction. The loss of Reece's eyes. The loss of Brandon's voice. Doug Lundeen's death. And now the spread of the virus."

Shallow breaths puffed out of Dana's mouth. Was that true? Had they achieved anything? Had they?

Miyo's whisper sounded beside Dana. "Do not agree. He's speaking nothing but lies. If you agree, he'll use your agreement against you and throw a new lie on top of the old one while you struggle to fight through the first one."

Zennon spoke again. "Now, let's watch together as Brandon Scott puts the finishing touch on this evening."

Reece held his hands high to quiet the crowd and stepped closer to the microphone. "It's my privilege now to introduce you to a man many of you already know extremely well. He's sold over eighteen million albums and has created some of the most loved worship songs over the past ten years. Join me in welcoming back to the stage after an absence that has stretched out for far too long, Grammy Award–winning singer and songwriter, Brandon Scott!"

Miyo pulled Dana close. "Now the true battle begins. We must war for Brandon with all our strength. His moment is upon him."

FIFTY-TWO

BRANDON STRODE ACROSS THE STAGE MORE NERVOUS than he'd ever been in any concert. He glanced to his left at the giant screens broadcasting his image to the crowd in the stadium. Just like the old days. But broadcasting to hundreds of thousands of people around the rest of the world wasn't like the old days. And having no clue what kind of voice would come out of his throat when he opened his mouth to sing wasn't anything like the old days.

The spotlights that poured into his eyes seemed brighter than any he'd ever stood in front of. But this was his moment, and no amount of lights or nerves or anything else would stop him. The return of Brandon Scott. His rebirth. Once again he would rule the world of Christian music.

When he reached center stage, he stopped and held his hand up to the crowd and yelled into the microphone, "Welcome, Seattle, and everyone else watching around the world! I have a new song I'd like to sing for you."

His voice shouted back at him through the monitors. It sounded raspy, but if the crowd noticed or cared, it wasn't apparent. Their roar of approval was like a tsunami. Brandon pointed one finger over the stadium. "I love you!"

And they loved him back and it filled him and lit him up like the sun. Their thundering applause and shouts grew louder. He instinctually looked around for his band and laughed at himself for the mistake. Not tonight. There were no drums. No bass. No keyboards. Just his guitar, his shattered voice, and the glory God was about to launch him back into.

He bowed his head and the shouts of the crowd faded to a murmur and then into silence. And then there was no crowd. No giant image of himself on the stadium screen. No millions watching him across the globe. Only the Trinity and him. An audience of One. Waves of peace washed over him, each more powerful than the last until he stood in utter trust and faith in the One who had brought him to this place.

He would sing the song, and it would bring him the healing he longed for more than any other gift the Spirit could give him. He would be restored in front of millions, and seeing his restoration would infuse them with the faith that would fuel their own restoration and healing.

He was born for this moment. Destined for it from before time began by the grace and power of the Father. Brandon opened his mouth to sing for himself the healing the Spirit had promised, in utter faith that his voice would be the same one that had poured forth when he had sung the songs of heaven.

It is your choice.

Heat filled him. *What?*

The choice is yours.

What choice, Lord?

Who you will sing the song for.

Brandon frowned. What was the Spirit saying? *The song is for me. For my healing!*

No. This song is meant for another.

What? You said—

I did not. That is what you chose to believe.

A quiet rage grew inside Brandon and he stepped back from the mic. No. This was his moment. Doug had told him in the letter. The Spirit had confirmed it. Reece had confirmed it!

Sing for the magician.

He's here?

Yes.

Brandon turned and somehow spotted Simon standing next to Marcus behind the curtains to the left. This couldn't be happening. It had to be the enemy trying to steal his moment of glory. His moment of becoming whole. To wrest from him all he was meant to be once again. He would not give in.

No, Lord. It's a lie. I'm to sing for myself, not Simon.

The Spirit was silent in stark contrast to the crowd who started to murmur. Reece opened his palms in question of what Brandon was waiting for.

✚ ✚ ✚

"Why isn't he singing?" Dana said.

Miyo leaned in until their cheeks almost touched. "I don't know."

"But you have a theory."

"I have a feeling he's trying to decide whether to sing the song for himself or not." Miyo hesitated before she spoke again. "I believe if Brandon sings the song for himself, as his intent has been, it will bring him a kind of healing—his voice will be restored—but it will not set him free. It will release a spirit of self-glory over this arena, and we have plenty to deal with already."

"A spirit of what?" Dana turned to face Miyo.

"He who seeks to save his life will lose it. There is a part in all of us that wants to preserve what we have. We hold on to it in a desperate grip to maintain control of our lives. And we clutch for those things we've lost like a drowning man. But it's an illusion. We must let our lives go if we want to live."

Miyo took a slow breath. "If Brandon sings the song to save himself, there will be a subtle but great temptation for many others watching the gathering to do the same. He will celebrate his healing and it will provide yet another opening for the enemy to penetrate, where his thoughts of deception will resonate in the minds of the people and they will embrace the lie."

Dana's voice dropped to a whisper. "And a life focused on self takes us back to the garden."

"Yes, where we attempt to be gods, the message of true freedom is distorted, and we forget who we are."

"He has to die to self." Dana said it out loud but it was for her ears only.

Dana's words were what Miyo had just insinuated, but her friend didn't know the depth of what she'd spoken because in that moment, Dana realized why she couldn't open her heart to Brandon again. She didn't entirely trust him. And she didn't entirely trust him because life had always been about Brandon. His albums, his music, his fans, his label, his concerts—she'd never known if he could love her unselfishly. If he could put himself away and love her with his whole heart the way she had loved him. And suddenly the evening became about everything in her life, outside of her and inside, the epic and the minute, and the very, very personal.

✚ ✚ ✚

Sing for the magician.

Brandon clenched his jaw. *This is my moment. My restoration. I won't let the enemy steal it from me.*

Why are you trying to hold on to something that no longer remains?
What?
I took it away so you might have life.
I don't understand, Lord. You mean my career?
As much as you've sacrificed, as much as you've given, there is a part

of you that places your idol higher than me. And as long as you hold on to it, it will be your master.

Brandon knew the idol. His voice.

I've never loved you for your voice, or your songs, or what you've brought millions of people. I love you for you, Brandon. Now you have a choice to love me for me. But it is your decision.

Brandon stumbled back another step as all became clear. His worth was not about what he did, what others said, the albums, the songs he could point to being sung in churches across the country, the sacrifice he'd made for Dana, or even what he'd done for Sandra and Garen. His worth came from the fact God had offered his own Son so Brandon could become a son of heaven as well; that God's Son would be shredded on the most horrific killing machine ever conceived by man so Brandon could have life.

Yes, Lord, I love you for you. Nothing else matters. I will let it go.

Deep called to deep, and a freedom Brandon had never known before, buried him. He stepped back to the microphone, took one more glance at Simon, and began to sing. He expected an overwhelming joy to spread through him, but it didn't happen. The instant he sang, his body felt like it had been wrapped in thick foam rubber. And the rubber started to squeeze.

FIFTY-THREE

As Brandon began the second verse, a flash of colors streaked across Reece's spiritual vision. Strange. He hadn't seen in colors since Simon came to Well Spring. An instant later the faint images in front of him were once again only black and white. But the momentary return of his spiritual sight to the way it used to be gave him hope. He hadn't expected there to be healing in Brandon's song for his sight or any other part of him, but if the Spirit wanted to give it to him, Recce's hands were wide open.

More hope came an instant later. For the first time since they'd started building toward this event, he saw outlines around the objects and bodies in front of him. In silver. Not in gold as he had grown used to. And the silver outlines were dim and sputtered as if there wasn't enough power inside his eyes to keep them fully visible. But the outlines were there. He could "see" again.

But something was wrong. Heat rose in Reece's chest. Not a physical heat, an emotional one. Of anger. Toward Brandon, because Reece shouldn't be standing here watching the Song alone. Doug should be beside him, savoring this moment with him. Reece's anger grew beyond reason, but why? He'd forgiven Brandon. It was over. But a part of him hadn't. A part still blamed the musician for the loss of Reece's closest friend.

Enough.

The voice of the Spirit spoke in Reece's head like thunder.

"Lord?"

A moment later words from his journal that Marcus had read weeks earlier flashed into his mind:

The most potent attack of the enemy will always come against our identity . . . If we live in our true, free, Spirit-infused identity, he will do everything possible to thwart our realization of that knowledge . . . The evil one will seek to cloud it like a dark fog, to taint it, spin it, twist it to such a degree that we forget who we are and become only a shadow of what the Lord has made us to be. He will lead us back into captivity, back into who we were before we stepped into the freedom and power of our true self . . . Know who you are. Know who you are. You must know who you are, Reece!

Reece staggered back as if slugged in the stomach. "Lord . . ."

Watch the Song.

Brandon's voice rang out strong, more captivating than Reece had ever heard it, and as the melody seeped into his head, a vision swept across his mind. He saw a lump of dough the size of a football that sat on a gray stone cutting board. A pair of tan hands kneaded the dough and as they did, another hand, slender and stark white, hovered over the bread and sprinkled a small handful of light-red powder on top of the dough. The other hands continued their work and the powder disappeared into the dough.

The scene shifted and the hands pulled a perfectly shaped golden loaf of bread out of an oven. But within seconds, thin dark lines, like tainted blood vessels, streaked over the surface of the bread. Then the loaf turned jet black with only hints underneath of the golden loaf it had just been.

"What are the blood vessels, Lord?"

Not blood vessels. Roots.

Heat washed over Reece again. This time, from waves of remorse. "Roots of bitterness . . . which can defile many."

Yes.

Conviction pressed in on him and Reece didn't have to ask the Spirit what the vision meant. It was obvious. "A little yeast spreads through the entire loaf. My yeast. The sliver of bitterness toward Brandon I allowed to remain. And the enemy used it to enchant me." Horror flooded him. What had he done?

The Spirit didn't confirm his words. He didn't need to. Reece stared at Brandon and whispered the words he so obviously needed to speak, and even more obviously, speak from his heart. "Forgive me for my bitterness toward you, Song. For blaming you. I was wrong."

Instantly Reece's spiritual sight returned in full force and color, and what he now saw made him stagger back a step. Demons were scattered throughout the stands, surrounding the people in the stadium. He turned. Behind him, ten yards away, stood Zennon, a grin spread across his face.

"Forgive me, Lord, for what I've done."

You are forgiven.

"And give us strength and wisdom to fight this battle."

Peace soaked into him. He glanced around the stage and spotted the golden outlines of Miyo and Dana. Had they been there the whole time? He looked to his left and saw the outline of a figure so faint, he couldn't tell if it was human or demon, male or female. The outline was made of a gray light that dimmed and grew brighter and then dimmed again. But as he watched, the bright moments grew longer and the gray tinge to the light faded until there was only dazzling whiteness surrounding the figure. The white light lasted only a few seconds before it turned golden and grew from the width of string to the thickness of rope.

Now Reece could make out muted features. The figure was male. Average height and weight. Human. Hunched over slightly. As the brilliance of the light grew, the slouching man slowly stood straight, and as he did, he seemed to grow two inches taller. A moment later the golden light had grown so thick and brilliant that Reece knew exactly who it was: the magician. Simon Donelson. Reece was undoubtedly watching Simon's escape from dark corridors he'd traveled for so many ages.

Reece turned back to Brandon and saw images of gold and white-hot light swirling around him that shot out over the crowd like fireworks. But he also saw ink-black shapes advance toward the Song, and a moment later, Brandon staggered as if a massive weight had been dropped on his shoulders.

FIFTY-FOUR

"DANA! SNAP OUT OF IT."

She spun toward Miyo. Brandon's song had captured her so completely, everything else—Zennon, his demons, the crowd, Miyo, her own fears—had slipped into a well of insignificance. Nothing mattered except the song. It mesmerized her like nothing she'd ever heard. Brandon's voice was so clear, so pure, so strong it seemed to fill every molecule in existence. And the melody buried her in hope and triumph and healing and freedom.

"What's wrong?"

"Aren't you seeing this?" Miyo pointed at Zennon's demons and then at Brandon. "We must fight for him now. He has to finish the song before he's destroyed."

What was Miyo talking about? Yes, Brandon stood slightly stooped, but other than that he seemed calm and confident. The song continued to pour out of him as if it was effortless, and the tune continued to build in volume and power. His hands moved over his guitar as smoothly as a flowing river, and if the crowd's reaction was any indication of the impact the song was having, Brandon was breaking thousands of chains in the heavens and on earth, pushing back the warfare and demonic attack Zennon was trying to pour out over the crowd.

"Destroyed? What are you talking about? He's doing great. I don't get—"

"See with your spiritual eyes, Dana. Accept that world as more real than this one."

Something inside Dana snapped into place. Instantly the image of Brandon shifted. She blinked, trying to comprehend what she now saw. The difference wrenched her heart and she sucked in a stifled breath.

Brandon no longer stood still and confident. A thick, black cloud sat on his shoulders. His torso was contorted and his body shook from the impact of tiny flaming darts zinging at him from Zennon's demons on her right. Something still held them back from advancing. Marcus and his prayer team still? Yes. It had to be. Thank God.

But it didn't keep the darts from getting through. A thin layer of light covered Brandon's body, but it was like a patchwork with multiple openings that rendered the armor almost useless.

The darts drove themselves into his shoulders and legs and body. Where they struck they burnt small holes in his clothing and red welts appeared almost instantly. With each impact, he staggered and fought harder to keep standing.

At his feet, a thick green stalk circled around him and got closer with every second. Thin green vines grew out of it and crawled up his body. They wrapped themselves around his left arm and yanked it down in rapid jerks in an effort to pull his grip from the neck of his guitar. He didn't let go and didn't stop playing, but his voice sputtered and the words began to come out in bits and pieces.

Open my eyes more, Lord.

A thin, translucent demon faded into view right behind Brandon. The demons weren't being held back. At least not this one. He stood behind Brandon with his hands around the musician's throat. Its jagged fingernails tore into Brandon's skin, and tiny threads of blood appeared and snaked their way down to his shoulders.

The song from Brandon's lips grew softer and his breathing more labored, but he continued to choke out the words. Dana glanced at the audience. Some had confused looks on their faces.

Could they see part of what was happening? Others grimaced at her as if to ask what in the world she was doing flailing around on stage next to Brandon, but most acted like they couldn't see her and still heard the song being sung with power.

They were oblivious to what was going on in the spirit and maybe even in the physical. She doubted any of them could see the full extent of the enemy's onslaught. But a few, a remnant, stared at her with a mix of shock and fiery resolve. Somehow time slowed and her gaze was drawn to the lips of a woman and a man only ten yards from the stage who both mouthed the words *we will pray.*

Still, Brandon sang on, although Dana didn't know how. The words were now garbled and a second later his hand dropped from his guitar and he reached for his throat. He pulled at it with his fingers and thumb in jerking movements. The demon laughed and squeezed tighter.

He must finish the song, dear one.

Dana didn't consider what she would do. She simply jumped off the cliff and rushed toward Brandon, knowing the Spirit would give her wings before she hit the ground. Almost there, but when she was ten feet from him, two demons instantly appeared in front of her, grins on their faces, black swords in their hands. One waved his forefinger back and forth as a sickening voice came out of him. "Sorry, only one performance at a time. Please go back to your seat now."

The other demon laughed. The sound of it shot ice down Dana's back.

"Miyo!" Dana shouted over her shoulder and glanced at her friend, but Miyo didn't answer. For good reason. Doug's granddaughter was surrounded by demons. She spun faster than Dana had ever seen, and her blade flashed in the glare of the spotlights, blocking the swords of demon after demon. But there were too many.

More of Zennon's elite warriors had joined the battle, and it was clear even someone with Miyo's skill would not survive. Two of the demons leapt into the air while the others surrounding her slashed at her body. Dana was about to watch her friend perish.

But just before two demons took off Miyo's head, a sword out of nowhere was thrust into the fray and deflected the blades from Miyo's throat. Reece! He glanced at her only for an instant and turned back to the battle. But that instant was enough. His face had changed. She saw in his countenance that the power of the virus had been broken. Yes!

Dana spun back to the demons facing her. No time to see if Miyo and Reece could help. No time to hesitate. This was her battle. She called on the Spirit and her sword appeared in her hand. She swung it in a wide arc in front of her and let the momentum carry her into the roll Miyo had helped her perfect.

Before the demons could move, she was past them, on her feet again, and slicing her sword through their backs. They thudded to the stage and Dana spun toward Brandon. Her sword held high, she leaped at the demon that held Brandon's throat in a stranglehold.

Her next stroke was true and sliced a quarter of the way through the demon's torso. He released his hold on Brandon's throat and staggered back, his eyes now seething with rage and leveled on Dana. "You will die for that."

The demon leapt at Dana, his fingernails now razor-sharp blades streaking toward her heart. But before he could strike, Miyo's sword flashed down from her side and severed the demon's head from his body. The demon crumpled to the ground and began to fade from sight, but Dana had no time to finish watching him disappear. Brandon's face had turned stark white and the look of death filled his eyes. Still he sang.

"He's dying!" Dana spun toward Miyo, and as she did, her hope of victory shattered. A circle of demons closed in on them slowly, swords drawn, eyes full of dark fire.

"Where is Reece?"

"He'll be fine."

"What do you mean 'fine'?" Dana backed up one step at a time.

"No time to—"

"Tell me!"

"His right shoulder is cut open . . . left leg isn't doing so well. Marcus dragged him off. He'll be fine!"

Miyo stopped and spread her feet and shouted, "Now let's rock!" She unleashed a withering attack on the demons in front of her, then called back over her shoulder, "I'll hold them off but you have to shield him!"

"How?"

Dark balls of fire streaked toward them, and Miyo somehow extinguished them before they exploded on their bodies. "Can't explain!"

Dana understood. There was no time for instruction or coaching from Miyo. Again, Dana had to do this on her own. She had to be the Leader. Lead herself. Faith. Believe. Not her. Not her strength. Not her wisdom or power, but hers combined with the Spirit who lived inside her.

She raised her hands and cried out as loud as she could, "Shield him now, Lord. Your power. Your light. Your might rain down on him from above and rise up from below. Christ on his left and his right, above and below, in front and behind. Now." Then louder. "*Now!*"

A thin circle of light rose off the stage and surrounded Brandon. It was working and hope surged inside Dana. The light reached the height of his ankles, then his knees and continued to grow. But as it reached his beltline, a low voice coursed through Dana's mind.

Do you finally realize now what a failure you are? Miyo leads, not you. If you were truly the Leader of the prophecy, you would have seen this coming. You would have led the Warriors against the virus. You would have seen it instead of being ensnared by it yourself. Miyo is the Leader, not you. There is so much darkness in you. If you were of the Light, you would have protected Brandon. But now, because of your utter failure, Brandon is about to die.

Hideous laughter filled her head and Dana gasped as if she'd been slugged in the stomach. The shield of light encircling Brandon shuddered, collapsed, and vanished into the stage floor. Brandon's image shifted back into one of him standing tall and strong and singing with confidence. Her mind clouded over and a sickly sweet sense of peace came over her.

Yes, relax. Embrace my peace. You've fought well, Dana, but there is nothing more you can do. Let go.

Dana hunched forward. A crushing grip grabbed her lungs and squeezed and her vision grew dim, but she refused to give in.

No, I am the Leader. Your power is nothing next to his.

The darkness continued to rush in on her, but in the next instant a sliver of light appeared a long way off. Not in the arena. Not in the sky, but inside her in the deepest part of her soul. Inside her spirit. The light grew and laughter poured out of the light, not the insidious laughter she'd just heard, but the laughter of victory and strength and unquenchable joy. So bizarre to hear the laughter of the Spirit in the midst of the horrific battle, yet at the same time it made perfect sense. Joy was strength. His strength, spilling out of her spirit into her soul and into her body.

Dana stood straight, balled her hands into fists, squeezed her fingers so hard her nails dug into her skin, and raised them to the sky. "Far greater is the One who lives inside me than anything the one who lives in the world can try to throw against me. The power of love has destroyed the power of death. I stand on the truth and the power and the glory of the One who has ransomed my life from the kingdom of darkness and has made me royalty in the kingdom of light!"

She opened her hands, stretched her fingers as straight as she could, then grabbed . . . She didn't know what. But she believed something would be there. And it was. She dug her fingers into what felt like solid and liquid at the same time and pulled with all her strength.

At first nothing happened. But she continued to strain every muscle and ligament to its breaking point. *Your power, Lord!* A moment later something broke and it felt like the heavens opened with a flood of water. But it wasn't water.

Fire fell like rain in a circle and surrounded Brandon, Miyo, and her. The demons all around them were buffeted as if smacked by gale-force winds. They staggered back, faces contorted with rage. One lurched forward. He swung his sword toward the curtain of fire and sliced. The blade hit the curtain and the black steel of the sword melted like water, and the demon's skin was instantly scorched.

"Well . . . done." Miyo's labored breathing sounded like a steam engine as her shoulders sank and she dropped her sword on the stage. Her forehead was drenched in sweat and her face smeared with blood. Her clothes were torn and her hair looked like dark tangled twine. Blood seeped from a gash on her right arm.

Dana's face must have been filled with shock because Miyo gave her a weak smile. "No, don't worry. I'm sure I look much worse than I am. Cuts and maybe a sprain here or there, but I'm okay and there is still more fight in me than they can imagine. You?"

"I'm fine." She turned to examine Brandon. The darts now struck the curtain of fire and disintegrated. His clothes were in tatters and blood covered his body, but he continued to sing.

FIFTY-FIVE

BRANDON WAS CLOSE TO COLLAPSE. NOT CLOSE, ON THE razor's edge and leaning toward the abyss. Seconds from defeat. Keep singing? Impossible. But he had to.

Every moment of your existence has led to this time. And the choice you make now will shape you for eternity. Will you sing the final verse?

A realization swept over Brandon. If he finished the song, it would kill him.

You must choose.

The words of the prophecy echoed in his head. *"And one will die before the appointed time."* And then a verse from Hebrews appeared in his mind. *"Through Jesus, therefore, let us continually offer to God a sacrifice of praise—the fruit of lips that openly profess his name."* The sacrifice of praise. Sacrifice. His life. A living sacrifice. Sacrificing all he was in this moment and all he would be. Death was not death. Not now. Not ever again. It had no hold on him. And he was in the middle of the Pacific Ocean, but the waves were no longer water but ecstasy and he was swimming in it.

Brandon closed his eyes and let his arms fall from his guitar as he collapsed onto his knees. He barely noticed the pain that shot up his legs from the impact. All that mattered was the song, and he continued to sing. Finish the verse. There was no other choice.

One more note he had to hold with the minuscule drop of life still left inside him. He sat back on his ankles, his arms out to his sides, and pulled in the deepest breath of his life. As he did, a voice shot into his mind.

Stop the song now. You will live. Let it go, my son. You've done enough.

The voice of the enemy.

Liar.

No, it is I. Let it go. It is not too late for you to live.

It was too late. Brandon had chosen. And if the Lord willed it, he would live. If not, he would enter into glory. Brandon opened his mouth and the last note of the song erupted out of his mouth in a torrent of worship. As it rose over the arena, he opened his eyes and saw light fall like rain over the entire stadium. Then the darkness stole over him and his body sprawled lifeless onto the stage.

☩ ☩ ☩

Dana gasped as light exploded like a star going nova and lit up the stadium in unfettered brilliance. All shadows vanished, and as the last note of the song faded, Zennon and his army were blown back as if they were brittle autumn leaves slammed by a hurricane.

The demons lay on the northwest side of the stadium, most of them not moving. Even Zennon was on one knee, his face twisted in pain.

She turned to Miyo. "Have we won?"

"For the moment. The power of the Song and the power of the song were too much for them."

"Then why are they still here?"

"Look at the people." Miyo pointed over the crowd, and Dana stared in surprise at the thousands of rigid bodies in front of them. "They haven't changed. I thought the song would heal them of the virus. Burn it out of them. But it didn't. Which means Zennon still has his claws embedded in their souls. Which gives him the right to remain. This is not good. He will recover quickly, along with his army. And I'm guessing he's going to bring in reinforcements that won't be as easily defeated."

"Easy? You call what just happened easy?"

Dana glanced down. "Brandon!" For a moment she'd forgotten about the Song. She dropped to her knees beside his still body. Reece, battered and bloody, already knelt at his side. A moment later Marcus was there too.

✚ ✚ ✚

Strong arms lifted Brandon and a voice spoke from a thousand miles away. The Spirit's voice? No. This was human and Brandon knew the voice well. Reece.

"Wake up, sleeper. Arise from the dead."

"I'm not gone?" Pain radiated from every inch of his skin and it hurt simply to breathe.

"No, but I'm guessing you danced on the edge of death just now."

Then Miyo knelt beside him and Dana as well. He stared deep into her eyes.

"I didn't sing it for me." He smiled inside. She wouldn't have any idea what that meant. It didn't matter. He needed her to hear. "I've finally died."

"I know. More than you know, I know."

And then, whatever had hidden Dana's true eyes from him for the past year and a half was gone. He held out a weak hand and she took it in both of hers and kissed it.

"The spell has been broken," Reece said. "The light has returned. And once more the Warriors Riding are riding together." He smiled but the smile was grim.

"What's wrong?"

"Forgive me, Brandon. For hardening myself toward you. For forgiving you in my mind but not in my heart. For allowing bitterness to take root. And for leading you down a path of destruction these past two months."

"Forgiven." Brandon ignored the pain in his arm and reached out and squeezed Reece's knee with his other hand. "I finished the song?"

"Oh yes." Reece smiled and cradled the back of Brandon's head. "I suspect this moment will be celebrated in the heavens throughout eternity."

"The song wasn't mine." Brandon struggled to sit up. "It was Simon's."

Reece glanced over the top of Brandon's head. "In a moment I think he's going to tell you what it did for him."

Brandon sucked in a deep breath and slumped back. "So we won. It's over."

"No." Reece's face hardened. "If I'm right, I'm afraid it's about to get much worse."

FIFTY-SIX

DANA BLINKED AND STARED AT THE FIGURE THAT STRODE toward them from the left side of the stage. Simon? Yes. But so vastly different she almost couldn't be sure it was the same man. His back was straight instead of being slightly stooped over. The constant twitching in the magician was gone, and he looked fifteen years younger.

It was like staring into a mirror where the mirror image was clearer and stronger than the image it reflected. He held himself like an athlete in the prime of life or a king surveying his kingdom, ready to challenge all comers to whatever throne he'd ascended to. But the biggest difference was his eyes. Brilliant. Clear. And they held a depth that had never been there before. Dana saw a wisdom. A confidence. An authority that had been missing.

If the eyes were the window to the soul, Simon had just experienced a major remodel on the inside. He walked toward the four of them as if he were taking a stroll along the Seattle waterfront on a lazy Sunday afternoon.

Joy radiated from his face like a spotlight as he knelt next to them and fixed his gaze on Brandon. "I remember." The magician glanced at Reece, Miyo, and then Dana, repeating the words each time. "Not some of it as I did after you entered my soul. Now

I remember it all. Who I was in ages past." He raised his head and laughter poured out. "I remember it all!"

He squeezed his arms, his head, his torso as if feeling them for the first time. "My mind, I . . ." He stared at Brandon. "You don't understand what you've done, do you? You have no idea, Song. You have set me free. You have healed and restored me beyond what you can know. What was lost has been sought out and found."

Another peal of laughter poured from his mouth and it seemed to shake the stage. "But you have done so much more because I know what I am supposed to do right now."

Simon gazed at every section of the stadium—up high, across the field in front of them, to his left and right—as if seeing it for the first time. His countenance grew sober and by the time he finished, his eyes had turned to fire. He stood and stared down at them. "Get ready. We don't have much time. Zennon will regather his army quickly."

Simon stepped to the microphone, lifted his hands, and didn't move until the murmurs floating across the stadium faded into silence.

"Good evening. My name is Simon, and I greet you, friends, in the power and authority of Jesus Christ, the slain Son of God who destroyed the power of death and wrested from Satan the keys of hell, then rose and granted immortality to all who would prostrate their souls before him. The Giver of eternity and life beyond life, to him we surrender our bodies, souls, and spirits."

Simon's voice rang out so true, so clear, so strong, it seemed he didn't need a microphone. "Many of you have been living in a dream world. I understand this better than any of you will ever know. You have been deceived, infected with a kind of spiritual virus that would drain the life out of your soul, steal your identity, and replace it with self-focused ambition and self-love.

"That is not going to happen. I'm going to show you the truth, pull back the curtain—no, *destroy* the curtain of lies that has been draped over our souls. There are no works we can do to please God because we have already pleased him through his Son, Jesus the Christ.

"He is love. And love is patient. And kind. Believes all things. Eendures all things. The word *disappointed* is not in that list. The word *inadequate* is not there. The words *not enough* are not in there. You are his beloved. Now receive his healing."

Simon lifted his hands and prayed against the virus with such force and power, Dana could only marvel. As he continued to pray, tendrils of fire spread out all over the stadium and shot into every man, woman, and child. As the fire and light surged through them, they turned from the statues of stone she had seen in the spirit earlier, to bodies of life and light. In minutes it was finished and Dana knew the virus had been destroyed. But she also could tell from Simon's movements the night was not over.

"Now I need to show all of you something. For some this will be difficult. But you need to see it." Simon's gaze went to the northwest corner of the stadium where Zennon and his demons were rising to their feet.

"We have given permission for unwanted guests to be here tonight. We have invited them with our fear and grasping for life where there is no life, and by our lack of resistance. We have agreed with them and swallowed the illusions about our lives that they told us were real. They want to destroy us. Want us to believe the illusion that they do not exist." Simon paused. "Those days of deception are over. And now you will see them. Do not be afraid."

As Simon finished speaking, Zennon appeared on the far side of the stage and struggled as if to break through an invisible barrier.

He stabbed his finger at Simon. "You can't win, Joker. You are nothing. In seconds we will break through your pitiful defenses and destroy you. And then destroy all who stand here tonight."

Simon's eyes narrowed. "You are the great illusionist, Zennon. You trapped me for longer than I could have imagined possible. But you have claim on me no longer. Nor on any of these." Simon spread his hands over the crowd.

"You think being able to see again after all these years of darkness means anything?" Zennon seethed. "You are nothing."

"You have spoken truth, demon. I am nothing. I'm less than nothing because I am no longer alive." Simon unsheathed a sword at his side and swung it in tight arcs around his body. "I am a dead man. Crucified. Buried. But I have been reborn into a glorious, powerful, and dangerous new being. All things have passed away and all things are new.

"He who is faithful and true is beyond the stars with power." Simon balled his hand into a fist and slammed it against his chest. "And this is where he lives. And you are terrified of what I'm going to show these people right now."

Simon stepped toward the demon. "I'm going to show them a world you don't want them to see. I'm going to show them a reality that will send terror screaming down your spine like acid in your blood. Because when they see the truth, you are the one who will be destroyed by the Alpha and Omega who lives inside each one of them."

Again Zennon thrashed against the invisible wall that held him back.

Simon spoke out over the crowd. "Truth in this place. Open blind eyes. Open deaf ears. Let our vision see beyond what we have seen." He raised his right hand and spread his fingers wide, then drew it down like a man pulling down a great curtain. Loud gasps broke out all over the stadium as people's eyes were opened.

"Friends. Friends!" Simon held his hands up again for quiet. "Your eyes have been opened. I implore you to keep them open in the days and weeks to come. To keep seeing with spiritual eyes and hearing with spiritual ears. But now you must grant me a favor. It is time for you to go. But as you leave, stay in prayer for us. We need your strength as we face our enemy."

Simon glanced at Zennon and his demons encased behind the wall, then back to the crowd. A third of the people shuffled toward the exits. Another third looked too stunned to move. And the final third stood in quiet defiance. It was obvious to Dana that these people knew exactly what was going on and had not been taken in at any point during the evening.

"Please, it is time to go. A war is about to begin and it is not make-believe." Simon motioned with his hands as though he could push the crowd toward the exits. "If you feel you must stay, then stay, but move to the upper seats in the stadium and war for us from there."

Dana was amazed at how quickly the stadium emptied. In less than five minutes, only a quarter of the people remained. She pulled her gaze from the crowd and looked at the demons gathered together far to their right. Miyo was right about the reinforcements. Or maybe her eyes had simply been opened wider by Simon.

Regardless, Zennon's army of demons was no longer just the ones he'd called his elite. A massive horde now strode toward them from the northwest corner of the stadium, and they were not of average height and weight. They were huge, almost as tall and broad as Zennon. She wished she had Simon's belief. Because these demons striding up to join Zennon onstage looked severely dangerous.

FIFTY-SEVEN

Brandon stared at Zennon, transfixed. Reece was right about it getting worse. The warlord had now been joined on stage by at least ten demons on each side of him who slashed at the invisible wall. And the wall was weakening.

As Brandon struggled to his feet with the help of Dana, Miyo, and Reece, Simon spun, strode over to him, and knelt. "Song, you are needed."

"What?" Brandon almost laughed. "I can't do anyth—"

"Yes, you can." Simon took Brandon's face in his hands. "Sing it again, Song."

Even Simon's voice had changed. A bit deeper. A tone that spoke of great love and epic battles at the same time, and none of his words were wasted. Somehow Brandon knew it would be rare for Simon to ever utter another rhyme.

"Singing the song almost killed me."

"Yes. That is true. But it didn't, did it?" Simon dropped his hands to Brandon's shoulders. "And it won't this time either." Simon's hands grew unnaturally heavy and heat radiated off them. "Receive his healing."

The warmth from Simon's hands shot into Brandon and brought a strength beyond what he'd ever felt. It raced through him

344

and pushed hard against the inside of his legs, arms, head, body, and feet. And extreme joy pulsed through him. If he hadn't seen his feet resting on the stage, he would swear he now floated two feet off the ground. "What . . . what was that?"

"Healing. Restoration of that which once was." The magician smiled. "Which you brought to me and I now have given to you." Simon's eyes blazed. "Sing it again, Brandon." He drew his face to within inches of Brandon's. "Be the Song like you've never been before. You can't imagine what will come when you do."

Brandon glanced over Simon's shoulder. The twenty or so demons pounding away at the wall holding them back had been joined by at least another twenty of the same size. "What I see is an army of sizable demons about to break through whatever you threw up and wanting to slaughter us. Which means there's no time—"

"Which is why you must sing now." Simon released him, stepped toward the front of the stage, and pointed west toward Puget Sound. "Hold nothing back, son. Give it everything inside you. Everything you've ever been. Every dream you've carried. Every sorrow, every joy. It has all led you here. The balance of the universe has been given to you; you hold it in the palm of your hand. It is a gift from him, so take it now and live in the fullness of his glory."

"The song was to be sung only once."

"No. Only sung once for healing. And the healing has come." Simon glanced behind him at the demons. "Sung twice for battle. But you must decide now. There is little time left. They will break through my wall in less than two minutes at most and reach us in seconds after that. From that moment on I can offer no hope of victory for any of us."

"We're about to die."

"Oh no, that is not true." Simon's laugh echoed across the stage. "We have already died. There is only life for us now. But I would still encourage you to sing."

Brandon closed his eyes and began the song for the second time. His voice rang out clear and true, and the opposite sensation happened this time. Instead of strength leaving, power and hope flowed into him. He let everything around him fall away and he sang as Simon had said to, with utter abandon.

Thirty seconds into the song, the Spirit spoke in a whisper. *Open your eyes.*

A gigantic, jet-black wall hung in the sky far out over the stadium and moved slowly toward them. It was half a mile wide and almost as tall.

He stopped singing in wonder and the wall slowed. Could it be? He clutched the microphone with both hands and turned to look at Simon. The magician's arms were raised to the sky, his eyes closed, his mouth moving in worship, which stood in stark contrast to the swarming demons leveling their assault on the unseen shield less than forty feet to his right.

Simon opened his eyes and gazed at Brandon. He nodded twice as a smile grew on his face that said, "Yes, it is you doing it, Song. You are the catalyst. Now you see another glimpse into the indescribable power of worship."

Unbelievable. The song, through his voice, had drawn the wall here. Brandon drew a deep breath and pushed into the next verse. Immediately the giant wall surged forward. As he continued to sing, the darkness of the wall shifted from black to gray. Then swirls of pure white began to sweep over the surface of the wall in patterns that reminded Brandon of the most exquisite marble he'd ever seen.

As he continued to sing, a faint sound started above him and seemed to sink down until it surrounded him. Was it . . . ? Yes, music. In perfect harmony with the song pouring from his mouth. In seconds the music became loud enough for him to hear all the instruments. Part of him wanted to stop. Their skill was too far beyond his. He was too human to take part in something this full of rapture.

Not true.

The voice of the Spirit tore through him and filled him with fire. An invisible orchestra played along with him, every note containing the power to destroy or build a kingdom. He spun in a slow circle even though he knew he would see nothing. But in the next moment he did see. A gathering of luminescent beings. Male? Female? They didn't seem to be either, or maybe they were both. They held . . . what? Instruments? But they weren't instruments—the objects seemed to wrap around their bodies and seemed to be a part of the beings. The instruments were alive.

They moved as the beings played them. Shifted. Changed as the sound filled the stadium like a thousand waterfalls. And the wall continued to move closer.

The music shifted into an epic, pounding rhythm, and Brandon's confusion turned to laughter as a new verse to the song flooded his mind and he raised the mic to his lips.

You have need of that no longer.

The microphone? How could he possibly be heard over the music without the microphone and speakers?

Put it away. You will see.

Did he hear laughter in the Spirit's voice? Brandon set the microphone back into the stand, stepped away, and sang. He expected his voice to carry no farther than the first few rows of the stadium. But the opposite happened. It was now far louder than it had been through the speakers. Clearer. Stronger. The sound of his voice reverberated back to him from every point in the stadium.

Was it his voice? Of course. But it was different. There was no way to describe it other than to say it was more him than he'd ever been. More his true self. The one he'd known and felt in the deepest parts of him. And the part of him that would go on living forever.

The wall moved toward them faster now, but something was wrong. The top of the wall shuddered as if it had been struck. The shaking moved down the wall as if giant battering rams were pounding to get through. Thin cracks appeared at the top and slowly moved down the wall. Their speed increased exponentially and streaked down in jagged patterns.

Brandon whipped his head around and stared at Zennon. Fury grew on his face as he stared at the wall and he and his demons ramped up their intensity. They would be through the shield and launch an assault on the Warriors and Simon in seconds.

Tiny clouds of gray dust escaped from the cracks and floated down the face of the wall. The fissures grew wider and razor-thin light poured of out them. No wonder Zennon was furious. Whatever was behind the wall appeared to hold the light of heaven.

Massive sheets of the marble wall pulled loose and fell toward the floor at the far end of the stadium but stopped halfway to the ground as if waiting for the rest of the wall to join them.

Brandon continued to sing, but it wasn't him singing. He was intertwined with the Spirit, and he felt as though the Brandon he'd always been didn't exist anymore—had never existed. His body was gone. His soul and mind were gone as well and all that remained was his spirit.

The rest of the wall had now fallen, and the chunks had all merged with each other into a vast, swirling cloud of whites and grays and now golds and silvers. The cloud morphed into something solid and lay out in front of them like a flat building or a road or . . . What . . . was it? Then it dawned on him. The wall was forming into a massive bridge, so bright Brandon shielded his eyes. A bridge of light, a bridge from heaven, brought into the natural world by a song.

The bridge surged forward and rolled out like a massive wave. Light exploded off of it. Reds. Greens. Blues. Yellows. It slammed down and the noise from the impact was ear shattering. Then a swirling mass of white clouds, miles away at the back of the bridge, streaked toward them. It rolled on like an avalanche, each cloud at the top spilling down the slope of white till it was buried by the next wave above it.

Moments later they were no longer clouds but horses—great thundering beasts—and on the horses were thousands of warriors, dressed in brilliant blues and greens and reds. At the front of the charge rode a being at least twice as large as the rest.

"Oh. My."

Brandon spun at the voice. Dana now stood beside him and took his hand in hers. "Do you see him?"

Laughter came from his right. Reece. Next to him stood Simon, and to his left on the other side of Dana stood Marcus and Miyo. "He comes," she said.

Could it be him? Yes. It was him. Tristan Barrow. On his right and left, Jotham and Orson rode, but they too were changed. So much larger than how he knew them, with a frightening intensity in their eyes. Brandon turned once more to look at Zennon and his army and his heart lurched. They had broken through and were sprinting toward the Warriors.

FIFTY-EIGHT

JUST BEFORE THE DEMONS REACHED BRANDON, DANA, Miyo, and Reece, Simon spun toward the onslaught and raised his arms. "This battle is no longer ours. Sprit of the Living God, take us."

Instantly they vanished and reappeared a moment later in the stands above the stage. Brandon smiled at the small clusters of people who had stayed that dotted the stands around them. Excellent seats for the scene about to unfold.

Brilliant flashes of light exploded from behind Tristan, Jotham, Orson, and the rest of the angel warriors as they pulled silver arrows from the quivers on their backs. Each of them held the arrows up close to their mouths and spoke as if giving the arrows instructions while the whole time they galloped like a tempest toward Zennon and his host of demons.

"What are they doing?" Dana said.

"Don't you see it, Dana?" A look of wonder came over Miyo's face and her eyes brightened. "This is Habakkuk chapter three come to life." She pointed at the angels and her smile lit up her face. "'His brightness was like the light; He had rays flashing from His hand, and there His power was hidden . . . You rode on Your horses . . . Your bow was made quite ready; oaths were sworn over Your arrows.' Those arrows are carrying the One's power."

The moment the last horse and rider crossed the midpoint of

350

the bridge, Tristan shouted, "Ready!" And as if one, all of the angels nocked their arrows at the same time, pulled them back, and leveled them at the swarm of demons.

Brandon expected their pace to slow as they took dead aim at Zennon's army, but their raised bows seemed to spur the horses to even greater speed and their velocity increased. Foam seeped from the horses' mouths and roars of battle erupted out of the mouths of the angel army.

"Now!" Tristan's voice shook them—a cry full of rage and triumph at the same time. The arrows left every angel's bow in perfect unison, and in less than a second they'd nocked another arrow on their strings, waiting for Tristan's next command to fire.

Most of the first waves of arrows struck the shields of the demon front line and exploded into light, but at least forty got through and slayed those the arrows hit. One of the arrows sank into the chest of a demon that had fought alongside Zennon to break Simon's wall. He stumbled back, but if he felt pain, he didn't show it.

The demon reached up and yanked hard on the arrow to pull it free, but it didn't budge. He pulled with more force with the same result. The arrow grew brighter and then it turned into a golden liquid that puddled over the demon's chest, spread like water over his body to his feet, and up his neck, over his face and head. A puff of sound followed and the demon vanished.

In another blink of the eye, the liquid had reformed as the arrow. A demon to the right stooped and grabbed the arrow, then reared back writhing in pain, his hand no longer attached to his body.

Zennon stood twenty paces behind the front line, his face contorted with rage as Tristan, Jotham, Orson, and the other riders in the front row spilled off the bridge onto the stadium field.

"Again!" Tristan roared.

The second wall of arrows rained down on the demons, but this time they were ready and held their shields more closely together.

"Attack!" The war cry spewed out of Zennon's mouth, and before the sound of it faded, his army, swords at the ready, sprinted toward the coming riders. For the next few minutes, chaos reigned and it was difficult to follow the battle. The clash of swords and fire and smoke filled the field as angel met demon in open battle.

But in less than ten minutes, a scant few of Zennon's army remained alive. He pulled his army back and stood in front of them, watching Tristan. The angel army had suffered losses as well, but far fewer than the demon's.

Zennon pointed to the center of the field and Tristan nodded. They each strode to the middle of the field and stood five yards apart. They spoke to each other but far too faintly for Brandon to hear. Their conversation didn't last more than thirty seconds, and then they returned to their respective armies.

"What was that?" Brandon said.

"My guess is they came to an agreement," Reece said.

"A truce? That doesn't sound like Tristan."

"No," Reece said.

Simon nodded. "Reece is right. Not a truce. But a way to end this, just between the two of them."

Miyo folded her arms. "One-on-one combat to the death."

FIFTY-NINE

AFTER A BRIEF WORD TO HIS ARMY, TRISTAN STRODE BACK to the middle of the field. Zennon was already there. They circled each other, studying, anticipating, preparing to strike.

With a screech, Zennon sprang toward Tristan and launched his sword at the angel's neck, but Tristan ducked under the blow and slashed at Zennon's leg and drew first blood. After that came two or three minutes where they matched each other blow for blow.

As they battled, their bodies grew—one in glory and one in horror—till the brilliance pouring off of Tristan was like a river of blinding light, and the shadows swirling around Zennon were so dark Brandon couldn't make out any of the demon's features. The darkness seemed to suck the light from Tristan into itself as if Zennon were a black hole, but as it was captured more quickly, the brilliance of the light encircling Tristan continued to grow till Brandon had to squint against the light.

Once again their swords clashed against each other. The collision sent an explosion of colors screaming across the sky and the sound shook the earth. The impact threw the two warriors back and they staggered as they regained their balance.

The moment they did, they rushed toward each other again. Both angel and demon moved almost too fast to follow. Their swords rang out again and again. Another massive crash against each other and again they fell apart—both breathing heavily. Both drenched in sweat. Both with blood dripping from their swords.

They engaged once more. An attack, a parry, a slice across arm or leg or chest that drew more blood, neither gaining a sure advantage.

Brandon turned to Simon and Reece. "Will he defeat Zennon?"

Neither man answered, both their faces grim.

Zennon's body continued to grow larger and the darkness that poured from it leapt at Tristan. The blackness wrapped itself around the angel's body like a legion of snakes—so fast the angel had no time to raise his sword. Tristan's face twisted in agony and a scream tore from his lips. The darkness continued to twist its way around him until it covered Tristan entirely and he vanished from sight.

Laughter spewed from Zennon and a rancid smile stayed on his face as he stared up at all of them and shouted, "It is over. He won't be there to rescue you ever again. And I am coming for you."

No. It wasn't possible. Brandon glanced at the shock on the others' faces. Reece looked ill, and Dana and Miyo looked ready to throw up. Simon's was the only face among them that showed no emotion. He turned and looked at Brandon. "It's not finished."

"Why?"

Simon didn't answer and continued to stare down at the field.

"Why, Simon?" Brandon asked again.

"Because darkness cannot ever overcome the light."

Brandon turned back to the field as a shudder coursed through the giant cocoon Zennon had created. Another shudder and then a deep-throated shriek of pain erupted from the demon's mouth. Then another. The globe of darkness he had smothered Tristan with began to glow, and every second it grew brighter as if a star-powered light had been turned on inside. A second later the globe exploded in a kaleidoscope of colors, and Zennan was flung to the ground. Tendrils of fire shot into the sky like a twisted fireworks display, and then a final screech ripped through the air as Tristan stood next to Zennon's writhing body. Tristan took a deep breath, then plunged his sword into Zennon's heart.

The remaining darkness that had enveloped Zennon faded and his features could be seen again. But as soon as they were visible, they changed. Brandon had always assumed the true appearance of a demon would be unspeakably hideous.

Brandon didn't know what he had expected. Maybe a tortured countenance or a demonic face out of a horror movie. Or a visage of evil rampant with scars and grotesquely twisted eyes and ears and mouth. But nothing was there. Not even the hint of a face. Just a dark gray nothingness devoid of feature or form, color or nuance, joy or sorrow.

Reece, Simon, Miyo, Dana, and Brandon stood without speaking. Brandon's gaze swept back and forth over the field of battle. A group of angels, including Jotham and Orson, gathered around Tristan. They grabbed his shoulders and arms, wide grins on their faces. The remnant of Zennon's army that was still alive had vanished. The small crowd still in the stands stood in silence, apparently stunned at what they'd just witnessed.

As Brandon's gaze focused again on Zennon, the demon's remains slowly faded into oblivion. But something remained. A shiny object so small Brandon squinted to see what it was. Could it be . . . ?

"Yes." Simon smiled and held out his hand. In it rested the magician's silver coin. But as Brandon and the others watched, the coin slowly changed from silver to gold. He glanced back to where the shiny object had been on the floor of the stadium. It was gone. It was now in Simon's hand.

"Are you kidding? That's not Zennon's—"

"No, it is not. It's mine. It has always been mine." The smile on Simon's face grew and the magician laughed. "I remember. Zennon stole it long ago." He laughed again. "How could I have forgotten? But what was lost has been found. What was stolen has been returned. Thank you, Abba."

Simon frowned as if trying to recall the rest of the memory. His face cleared and he held up the coin. "A gift from my grandfather many years ago." He looked at Miyo. "Grandfathers give extraordinary gifts, wouldn't you agree?"

Miyo nodded, her eyes full of light. Simon closed his fist tight around the coin and gazed down on the field. Tristan looked up at them, nodded once, then he and his army faded from sight.

"So it ends." Reece adjusted his Stetson.

"No, Reece." Simon took a step forward, his eyes fixed on the star-strewn sky above. "Not for me. For me it is only the first day of a glorious new beginning."

Reece squeezed Simon's shoulder. "May it be so for each of us."

SIXTY

Dana pulled into Brandon's driveway late on Wednesday afternoon and shut off her engine, but didn't get out of her car. She checked her hair in the rearview mirror, reapplied her coral lipstick, and smoothed her blouse.

Get out, Dana. It's just Brandon.

But she stayed in her car a few minutes longer. Time enough to remind herself of what he had done for Simon, instead of for himself. What he had done for all of them. The Song had unequivocally died before the appointed time. Died to himself so he might live to Christ. And it had set him free. And melted her heart. But even so, the tiniest part of her was still afraid. The only thing still protecting her might be a papier-mâché fence, but she wasn't quite ready for him to break through it.

When she reached his front door, she fixed her hair for the fiftieth time and rang the bell. He opened the door and smiled, his eyes brighter than she'd seen them in . . . years.

"I brought you a present." She pulled a bag of sunflower seeds out from behind her back.

Brandon laughed, took them, offered thanks, and squinted at her with his head cocked to the side. "I'm not exactly sure how you do it, but you have this amazing ability of getting more beautiful every time I see you."

"Wow. I don't think I've heard a line like that since college."

"Is it still considered a line if it's sincere? And true?" Brandon stepped aside and motioned her inside.

"Yes."

"The really important question is, did it work?"

"The evening is just begining. I'll let you figure out the answer as the night progresses."

"Then let's get started." Brandon bowed and the smile that lit up his face was so free she almost gasped. The bitterness, the frustration, the sorrow he'd carried since his voice disappeared was gone, along with the worthlessness he'd carried since the battle with the religious spirit.

For the first time in ages, she noticed lines etched into his face that squiggled out from the corners of his eyes, and it made him even more handsome. More joyful. More . . . free, as if the trueness of God's love and wild abandon had been chiseled into his face. Aging would be kind to Brandon Scott, she suspected.

He offered his hand to her and she took it and squeezed but didn't hold on. She wasn't ready for that. Yes, she was. No, she wasn't. Yes, she was. *Arrgh!* Was it possible to be absolutely sure and not sure at all, both at the same time? They walked together down his hallway into the living room. Strange being back in his house after four and a half years away. Dana glanced around the room. It hadn't changed much. A picture of the two of them standing on the edge of Hurricane Ridge caught her attention, the wind whipping her hair back, the sun lighting up their faces.

"Oh my." It was the day he'd asked her to marry him. The day she'd said yes and given him her heart. "When did you put that back up?"

Brandon put his hands on his hips and smiled as he gazed at the picture, then turned to her. "That's my favorite photo of us. Did you know that? I can still remember how nervous I was before I asked."

"Are you going to answer me? When did you put that back up?"

He gazed at the photo for a long time before answering. "I never took it down."

Warmth and joy surged up from inside. Did she really want to be here? Yes, she did.

Brandon turned toward the sliding-glass door that led to his back deck. "I want to show you a project I've been working on."

"What?"

"I did something with the backyard." He reached the door and slid it open. "I think you'll like it."

He led her onto the back deck and stopped at the top of the stairs leading down to his lawn. "What do you think?"

She gazed around the yard but nothing stood out as being different.

"It's been a long time since I've been here, so maybe there's something new and I'm just not seeing it."

"Look up." Brandon smiled like a little boy.

Dana saw it immediately. Thirty, maybe forty feet in the air, nestled between two massive Douglas firs, was a tree house. It appeared to be made out of cedar, and the wood was stained a rich redwood color.

A winding staircase wrapped around one of the firs up to a front door with a stained-glass window made in the shape of a guitar. Of course it would be. Thick six-by-six beams created the foundation for the tree house and the walls shot up from there. The structure seemed to be more windows than wood.

"Am I seeing things, or is it two stories tall?"

"Your eyes are fine." Brandon grinned. "It has a loft up above for sleeping and then a love seat and a few chairs on the first floor for hanging out, reading, singing, whatever. It's wired so there's heat and light."

"No kitchen? No big-screen TV? No hot tub?"

"I know. Shocking. They even refused to put in a racquetball court." He offered his hand again and this time she locked hers around his and held on. She almost stumbled. What was wrong with her? She wasn't some flighty junior high girl. She blew out a quick breath. Funny how a simple touch could send such strong emotions streaming through her.

"Want to see inside?" Brandon led her down the stairs onto the grass and to the base of the tree.

They climbed up the winding staircase, and just before they reached the tree house, Brandon turned. "But my favorite place isn't even inside. It's on the little deck out front."

They settled into the two chairs on the tiny deck and gazed at the view of trees and neighbors' yards and the thick greenbelt that ran from the edge of Brandon's backyard into the distance.

"So when you said you've been working on something, this is what it was?"

"Yep, in all her glory."

"Don't tell me you name tree houses after women like you do with ships."

"You're only allowed to name your tree house after a woman if you call it Dana."

"You didn't." She turned to see if he was serious.

"No, of course not. I chose a Hebrew word." He pointed to the top of the door. She had to squint to see the symbols: הנד

"Which means what when translated into English?"

"Dana."

She couldn't help but smile. "It's stunning, Brandon. You didn't do this yourself, did you?"

"Hardly. I hired Nelson Tree House and Supply right here on the eastside to help me. They're just eight miles from here but build tree houses all over the world. Plus, they have a spread just outside of Preston they call TreeHouse Point with six tree houses they rent out like hotel rooms."

"And you saw what they do and were inspired."

"Very."

"How'd you discover them?"

"About five years ago I went looking for something special to do for the woman I was going to marry. I thought staying there for the weekend after we got back from our honeymoon would be a wonderful way to extend it for a few days."

Dana allowed herself to imagine what that would have been like. Then she went further and allowed the idea to seep into her heart. She took his hand. "I want you to sit up here by yourself on a summer evening when the heat of the day still hangs in the air, and the sun is just dropping below the horizon out over the Olympic Mountains, and do something for me."

"Anything."

"Something you can't do on your own, that you can't make happen or control."

"Then how can I do it for you?"

"I have a feeling you'll get your chance."

"Tell me."

"I want you to listen very closely and hear something very specific." Brandon ran his finger along the back of her hand. "And that is?"

"I want you to hear my song." She put her other hand around their joined fingers and leaned closer and didn't even try to stop the tears that welled up in her eyes.

"And then what?"

She didn't need to answer. Brandon knew.

"Sing it for you."

"Yes." The word came out in a whisper.

"To be able to do that would be my favorite performance ever."

"Better than the one for Simon?"

"Not even close." Brandon leaned toward her until his lips were next to her ear. "I'm not in love with Simon."

There it was. They'd danced around it since the moment she'd arrived at his home, and now he'd said it. What should she say? That she felt the same and was ready to confess it?

Brandon pulled back and smiled. "So, you want me to be up here and have the Spirit open my ears to hear your song?"

Dana nodded.

"I'm sitting here now."

"You need to be alone."

"I see." Brandon nestled his face into her hair.

"Will you do that for me?" Dana pulled away to look into his eyes. "Will you ask the Spirit?"

"What if he's already answered?"

Dana sat up and leaned back in her chair. "What are you saying?"

He grinned and gave a slight nod. It couldn't be. Had he already heard something? She shook her head. "Are you serious?"

"Last night I was up here with my guitar, thinking of what all of us have gone through over the past three and a half months and how God came through in the end. For Simon, for Miyo, Reece, and Marcus. For you, for the ones who have embraced the message of Warriors Riding, and for me.

"The final hints of light were seeping into the west and the stars looked like they did on my bedroom ceiling when I was a kid. As I sat there, a song lifted off the ground and drifted up into the trees. It sounded like it was played on a piccolo. And then came the vision, clearer than any of the others. I was stunned by what I saw." He leaned back and rubbed her neck, closed his eyes, and dropped into a silence that extended well past a minute.

"What are you doing?" She shoved him. "Tell me!"

He laughed and opened his eyes. "You're sure you want to hear this? You realize the vision was of you, right?"

"Would you like me to push you off this tree house? We have to be at least forty feet up."

"Forty-five." Brandon stood, went into the tree house, and came out with one of his guitars. He played a chord on his guitar and it sounded like falling water in her ears.

"In the vision, you stood on Hurricane Ridge in the exact spot as we did in the picture in my living room, but the wind wasn't blowing this time. You were in profile, and I could tell you were staring at something intently. A soft smile grew on your face and then you walked toward whatever you saw. A moment later the perspective drew back and it was me. You embraced me and didn't let go for a long time. And even though I was watching it from the outside, it almost felt as if your arms were physically holding me. And then a kiss came that was even longer than the hug. The vision shifted and the song poured into me instantly."

She lifted Brandon's guitar out of his hands and placed it gently on the deck.

"Don't you want me to play your song?" he said.

"Yes. Someday soon."

She knew the day. Maybe he did too. If he didn't, he'd have to figure it out on his own. Dana took his face in both her hands, leaned in until the tips of their noses touched, and whispered, "How long did this visionary kiss last?"

"At least thirty seconds."

She leaned in, and just before her lips met his, she said, "Let's make the real one at least double that."

"Triple."

Dana smiled. "Deal."

When they finally pulled apart, she snuggled into his chest and rested her hand on his shoulder. "I'd really like to go on a little trip with you tomorrow."

"Hurricane Ridge."

She pressed deeper into him. "I can't wait."

SIXTY·ONE

THE SMELL OF A BARBECUE DRIFTED THROUGH THE AIR around Brandon as he ambled toward the backyard of Reece's home—as well as great peals of laughter from the members of Warriors Riding who had already arrived. This was an afternoon he would savor. An October sun still warm enough for them to eat outside. The leaves on Reece's massive maple trees on fire with reds and golds. And the chance to celebrate what they had all come through together and dream about what the future might hold.

He turned the corner and smiled. Miyo, Dana, and Marcus sat on the back deck while Reece stood at the barbecue, bathed in a thick smoke that poured out of it. Next to Reece stood Simon, talking with a significant amount of animation.

Brandon clipped up the steps of the deck, walked over to Dana, and gave her a quick kiss.

"Whoa!" Miyo grinned. "Hold the press. Is there something you two would like to share with the rest of us?"

Brandon spun and grinned back at Miyo. "I think we just did."

"Congratulations," she said.

"It's about time," Marcus added.

"Here, here," called Reece.

Brandon offered a mock bow to all of them. "Thank you, thank you."

He settled into the wicker sofa next to Dana as Reece closed the lid of the barbecue and took a seat across from them. "Should be ready to eat in under ten minutes."

When they sat down to eat, they feasted on salmon and chicken, baked potatoes, and asparagus. A Caesar salad rounded out the meal, and Reece produced Moose Tracks and Cookies and Cream ice cream for dessert, served on top of freshly baked brownies.

For the next three hours they spoke of their past year and a half together. What they had learned, how they had grown, their greatest joys and sorrows. How Simon had been part of them long before they existed, and how the circle was greater than they could have imagined, and the way it had come to a close. By the time the shadows grew long, their conversation waned, but that simply made the time together richer. To sit in silence with those he loved more than any others was food for Brandon's soul.

He and Marcus built a fire in Reece's pit that sat a hundred yards behind the house while Reece, Miyo, Simon, and Dana finished cleaning up from dinner. Soon Dana slid into the wooden chair beside him and took his hand, raised it to her lips, and kissed it.

When they'd all settled in and the fire blazed bright, Reece cleared his throat and turned his head slowly around the circle. "We've had an amazing run together."

"You say that like it's past tense," Brandon said.

Reece nodded and let out a soft sigh. "I think it might be. Both of the prophecies have been fulfilled and unless there's another one no one's mentioned . . . Plus, I'm sensing the Spirit saying he has other things in store for each of us now."

Brandon's heart sank a little. But only a little. He'd sensed the same thing, and Dana and he had talked about it. They both felt God was inspiring the two of them to do something together, and it didn't necessarily include the rest of the Warriors.

Reece turned to Marcus. "Any idea what you'll do with your Warriors Riding time?"

"Yes. More time with Kat and the girls, and I feel I need to do a serious revision to my book on alternate realities. I believe there are at least two new books in me that need to be written. "

"Simon?" Reece asked.

"The professor and I will be adventuring down similar paths." He glanced at Miyo. "It's not every day you discover you're the author of what a few might call one of the most powerful treatises on the spiritual realms ever written, which you neglected for more than five decades."

Miyo nodded and smiled at Simon. "And I'm thinking that author might need a publisher to work with who believes passionately in the book, so it can reach a few more people than it has so far."

She glanced at all of them and grinned. "And from what this author tells me, apparently the first book only contains two-thirds of what this author knows. I can't wait to learn the rest of his secrets. I think if I help him get published, he might take me on as a student. I cherish the idea that the teacher of my teacher would now teach me."

Simon looked at Miyo. "Are we still on for next Wednesday morning?"

"Without question." Miyo pointed at him and grinned. "We are going to rock the world, friend."

Reece leaned back and pulled up something wrapped in a light-brown cloth from behind the bench he sat on. "If that's the case, then let me make a contribution to the research part of the project. You might find a few things in here worth including in your tome." He pulled off the cloth and tossed the object toward Miyo like a Frisbee. Before it reached her, a smile broke out on her face. She caught it in one hand and lifted it high for all of them to see.

"Reece's journal," Brandon said.

"A treasure," Simon said.

"What about you, Reece?" Brandon asked. "What are your plans?"

"I don't know and I'm allowing myself not to know. I'll continue to run the training school at Well Spring, but I'm going to cut back to only three classes per year." He pointed at each of them and his voice grew stern. "You're still committed to teaching at least twice a year, right? That includes you, Simon."

They all laughed and agreed that they would.

Silence fell over the six. They all let it linger until the wood in the fire pit became a bed of dark-red coals and a sweet sadness seemed to emanate off the remnants of the fire. Finally, when the night sky had finished turning from blue to a star-studded black, Reece spoke once more.

"It's okay, you know." He smiled. "This season might be over, but we'll never be able to get rid of each other. In fact, next month I'd like us all to get together again. I want to go to a place that might even surprise you, Miyo."

She looked up and a smile broke out on her face.

"Where?" Dana asked.

"Let's just say it's not on earth." Reece tilted his head back slightly and grinned. "And once we get there, I promise you'll want to stay forever."

AUTHOR'S NOTE

Dear Readers,

I hope you've enjoyed reading *Soul's Gate, Memory's Door,* and *Spirit Bridge.* I hope you were wildly entertained. Most of all, I hope the Well Spring series caused you to think harder, made you feel deeper, and helped your passion grow for the King and Lord of all worlds, Jesus Christ.

I've loved writing this series and will miss Reece, Dana, Marcus, and Brandon. So much of me is in them, and now much of them is in me. I'll miss Simon and Miyo as well. But I think those two might crash one of my story parties before long, and I'll get the chance to catch up on their further adventures.

With *Spirit Bridge,* I tried to create an epic conclusion to the series because that's what I believe our lives can be: an epic part of the larger story God is weaving in every second of our lives. The small moments that are in truth never small, and the grand moments that will echo throughout eternity.

If you'd like to find out the latest on what's going on with me and my writing, you can sign up for my newsletter at www.jameslrubart .com. And don't hesitate if you feel like shooting me a note. I'd love to hear from you: james@jameslrubart.com.

Press on, dear friends, in the depth and breadth and height of his unquenchable love,

James L. Rubart
September 2013
www.jameslrubart.com

READING GROUP GUIDE

1. What themes did you see in *Spirit Bridge*?
2. Which character did you relate to the most? Why do you think that is?
3. Miyo, a new character to the Well Spring series, was introduced in *Spirit Bridge*. Did you like her? If yes, what did you like about her? Are there qualities she has that you'd like to have? If you didn't like her, why didn't you?
4. Simon was introduced in *Memory's Door*, but his role was expanded greatly in *Spirit Bridge*. Was he an intriguing character to you? Did you see his full-circle role at the end of the book coming, or was it a surprise?
5. The enemy had blinded Simon's eyes from seeing who he truly was. He'd forgotten his identity. Do you feel like that has ever happened to you?
6. The theme of spiritual warfare runs through the Well Spring series. Do you think this kind of spiritual warfare exists? What is your experience with spiritual warfare?
7. Throughout the Well Spring series, there were ideas that aren't at the forefront of most Christian's minds, such as teleportation, being unseen by others, building armor made out

of light . . . What do you think about those kinds of things? Are they possible?

8. The spiritual virus set in motion by Zennon, blinded Brandon and Reece and they reverted back to acting out of their false selves instead of their true selves. Have you had seasons in your life where you've been walking strong, and then felt like you forgot who you were? Where you forgot your true destiny and calling?

9. The biggest themes in the Well Spring series are freedom and restoration. Do you see freedom coming in your life? Do you see restoration coming? In what ways?

10. A number of people have experienced freedom and restoration not *after* reading one of the Well Spring novels, but *during* the time of their reading. If that happened to you, are you willing to talk about it? What happened?

ACKNOWLEDGMENTS

THIS NOVEL WAS THE MOST COLLABORATIVE SINCE MY first story, *Rooms*. I had brilliant input from a number of people. Here they are, in no particular order:

- Five of the MMs (Susie Warren, Randy Ingermanson, Tracy Higley, Mary DeMuth, and Thomas Umstattd) who allowed me to sit in the hot seat during our Austin retreat and brainstormed myriad ideas with me to work from.
- My friends Sarah VanDiest and Ruth Voetmann.
- My agent, Lee Hough, who is now exploring the type of glorious worlds I imagined in the Well Spring series.
- My brother from another mother, Allen Arnold.
- My editors, Amanda Bostic and Julee Schwarzburg.
- My best friend and love of my life, Darci.

If you enjoyed *The Spirit Bridge*, please thank them. If you didn't, blame me. As my friend Bob Lord is fond of saying, it's all in the execution.

And finally to Jesus, for giving me Life, and for gifting my mind to work this way.

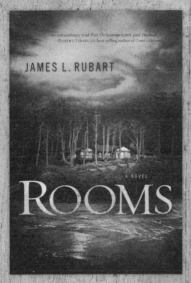

CONNECT WITH
JAMES RUBART

WWW.JIMRUBART.COM

 James L. Rubart

 @jimrubart

ABOUT THE AUTHOR

Christophoto, Bothell, WA

JAMES L. RUBART IS A PROFESSIONAL MARKETER AND speaker. He is the author of the best-selling novel *Rooms* as well as *Book of Days, The Chair, Soul's Gate,* and *Memory's Door.* He lives with his wife and sons in the Pacific Northwest.